# So we beat on

## By Alina Graça

Copyright © 2021 Alina Graça
All rights reserved.

ISBN: 9798788281933

# Prologue

*Death?*

I do not fear it. I have died before. I take solace in the inevitable fact that my final countdown of this lifetime is approaching its end. Unlike my prior departures, I am now ready to go, ready to move on, ready to see what path I take when I am born again. I know that this is not the end, it never was, and I don't think it ever will be. I see this moment as a cliff-hanger, an exciting climax to a whirlwind adventure that had come to its conclusion but on the verge of an inception of a new experience waiting on the other side.

I watch the slightly hunched figure walk slowly away from my bedside towards the dark mahogany door, and then hesitantly pause to look back at my frail bedridden shadow barely resembling my own self as the heavy door pries open letting more light into the room.

*It's alright.* I want to assure the visibly upset doctor, who had been by my side since he delivered the initial diagnosis only a year ago. At that initial appointment in his impressive white marble and glass office encompassed in floor to ceiling windows located in Lower Manhattan, he was able to expertly pinpoint that the cause for my recurring blinding headaches was a sizeable growing tumour lodged in my brain, that was impossible to be removed due to some very complicated reasons riddled with medical terminology that I never bothered to delve into or understand. That was then.

"There is not much time left, Mrs. Anderson. All we can do at this point is ensure that you have enough medication to subside any pain that you may experience. I am very sorry", was what he had just said, when he made the latest house call to visit me in my peril state.

"I do not like to give timelines, but I would highly encourage you to have your assistant make proper arrangements for your family to fly in to see you before the month's end."

I slightly nodded to show my comprehension of the latest update on the fast-approaching finale, as I felt his firm hand reassuringly squeeze my own before he got up to leave.

It won't be long now. I feel no fear or anger, I mostly feel relief that this would soon be over. I stare at the doctor as he looks back at me before exiting the room, his furrowed bushy eyebrows signifying a puzzled look as he tilts his head in confusion. I quickly catch myself, knowing that I am smiling back at him, a genuine smile filled with unbridled reprieve.

*I'm fine*, I nod again to him and watch him finally leave the room haltingly shutting the door behind him.

I reach for the pen and leather-bound notepad resting on my nightstand and switch on the intricate table lamp, I take comfort in being able to maintain my confident grasp and sound mind to still be able to write. My children would sigh at the sight of me with a pen in my hand, instead of the many complicated gadgets they tend to gift me every year that "would undoubtedly make my life easier". In their mind a pen is equivalent to a quill, and they never stop teasing me about it.

I stare at the blank pages before me, wondering for a moment on the best choice of the first words to write down and then start hastily scribbling, filling page after page with messy but legible text.

I don't have long, but I want to share my story, my fate with you - my reader. I know you will think that the tumour had affected my sense of reality and you will most likely dismiss this testament as a creative writing piece of a mad woman. But, please know, that everything you read next is a true and factual declaration of my life, lives, my existence.

Chapter One

*Lifetime I*
*December 25, 1984*
*Birth*

    The memories of my original birth elude me, unlike all my subsequent rebirths. The fact is, my first emergence into this universe was no different than any of the other births in the hospital that day. There was absolutely nothing remarkable about my entry into the world during my first chance at life, but it remains to be the one path outside of my own choosing in my ever-changing lifetimes.

    The one anomaly of that day was that there had been a disturbing lack of snow during that seemingly typical winter prior to the Christmas morning. It was peculiar for the residents of Georgetown, seeing how the blizzards would typically envelop the state of Delaware from November onwards with periodic storms and occasional ice pellets. It was an unfortunate travesty for the locals, since the town was heavily dependent on the passing out-of-state visitors driving through towards New York for the festive activities.

    It is eternally ironic, how a human mind works, when a person can complain about tedious hours spent on snow shovelling, treacherous roads after a squall, or slipping on ice resulting in a bruised wrist, and then forget all about it a year later and endlessly moan about the absence of the frost on the ground. This was the case in the sleepy Georgetown that year, the residents incessantly grumbled about the snowless streets and the local radio show hosts were only able to talk about the prospects of the ruined Christmas if the destitute of skift continued.

    To the townspeople's avail, the residents woke up on Christmas Day to a wondrous blanket of snow covering their yards and driveways. The trees were enveloped in the feathery white clouds, while the roofs were draped by a blanket of untouched snow with only the darkness of the chimneys protruding through the froth resembling a lone cinnamon stick in a cappuccino mug.

That charming peaceful morning, my mother woke up abruptly from a stabbing pain in her stomach, immediately realizing that I was ready to climb out of the comfort of her womb and enjoy the wonders of life, slighter earlier than expected. Having done enough reading in preparation for the big day, she knew not to rush getting up and resisted waking up my father from his deep sleep, while she stayed in the warm bed waiting for the pain to subside. As the agony diminished, she slowly eased herself out of the cozy bed and walked over to the wide bay window to look outside, while cradling her bulging stomach with both arms. She observed the jovial liveliness on the street as some of the neighbours surfaced with their trusty snow shovels and hustled to clear their interred driveways, taking a break to wish a Merry Christmas to a passing neighbour who was dragging a snow gliding sled with his four-year-old son enthralled by the winter wonderland around him. The chimneys on the roofs exhausted the puffs of hazy smoke as the residents lit up the fireplaces to warm up their homes, where families gathered around their dazzling Christmas trees for the most anticipated event of the day as they busied themselves in unwrapping the many gifts.

"Well, little one, you chose a beautiful day to join us."

My mother softly whispered to her sizable stomach as she caressed it, which seemed to ease the growing anticipation. A rustling of the bed sheets, as my father shifted in bed, prompted my mother to turn her gaze from the jolly excitement outdoors to the comfort of her own tastefully decorated bedroom.

"Susan, what are you doing up? It's cold, get back in bed", my father mumbled, gradually emerging from his sleep. "You'll catch a cold; the draft by the window must be absolutely freezing."

As my father opened his eyes, he saw the snowflakes flowing downward in an undisciplined cascade outside their large window which captured my mother's attention earlier. Regretfully recognizing that he needed to leave the warmth of the bed to dig out the snow shovel from the depths of the unkept garage before spending an hour clearing the driveway out in the cold, he pulled the comforter over the lower part of his face to warm up the tip of his nose.

"We need to turn up the heat in this house, hope the boiler does not give up on us this winter. I will call Sam late in the week to come by and tune it up, to make sure it survives another year. Susan?" My dad raised himself from the bed, and propped his back against the wooden headboard, that he crafted himself out of old barn wood that they found on their weekend drive through the farmlands a few months back. "Everything ok?"

My mother turned her slender neck towards her husband and simpered with coy.

"We can call Sam later in the week. Also, don't panic because I know how anxious you can get."

She walked over from the brightly lit window illuminated by the radiant whiteness from the outdoors and sat down on the bed taking my dad's hand in her comforting grasp.

"No rush but we need to pack up the essentials and have some breakfast because I don't expect much from the hospital food." She saw the look of panic flash in my father's eyes and clasped his hand tighter. "Jack, there is nothing to worry about, I know our baby is anxious to get out, that's why he or she is trying to make their entrance a bit earlier than the anticipated due date. It is all good, nothing to worry about."

Dad was always a bit of a "worry bug", so he immediately shot up from the comfort of their bed and lunged across the room towards their closet to pull out the half-packed overnight bag that my mom started wisely preparing a few days earlier. He yanked it out of the closet, while also managing to knock over a floor lamp and topple over a pile of sweaters from the top shelf. Albeit his panicked rush and bumpy movements, while he quickly paced around the room, my mother heard his repetitive murmuring "I've got this... pack, breakfast, go.".

Amid the scurried commotion, my father paused for a moment when he heard a squeal from the bed and looked up at mom wincing in pain. "Oh darling, are you ok? Do you need anything?" He threw his body across the bed to be by my mother's side, while she clenched her fists to ride out the pain of another contraction, just as one of her birthing books had suggested. After a few minutes, my mother exhaled and stammered through her gritting teeth to my dad "Pack, breakfast, hospital".

"I got this!"

Dad proclaimed and stormed off to make his signature dish, which consisted of a slightly runny western omelette and mildly burnt toast, my mother's favourite.

"We've got this." My mother mumbled, trying to mirror her husband's determination, unsure if she was persuading herself that they could make it through the morning or that they were fully prepared to embark on the new challenging chapter in their lives. She had always been a strong-willed woman but the feelings of inevitable change, and realization of the magnitude of the moment engulfed her while she sat in the bed and observed the scattered mess on the floor left behind due to her husband's attempt at packing the bag. My mom knew that their carefree life would never be the same again, they will never be alone in this house enjoying their serene Saturday romantic dinners; they will never sleep in until noon in their comfy new bed or any of the other marvels of the childfree life.

Just as her anxiety level began to rise, she caught a glimpse of the ridiculous looking stuffed pig toy perched on top of the rustic dresser, the first baby toy her recently departed grandmother gave her as a gift when Susan shared the news of their growing family. The plush animal had the ability to blink its ocean blue eyes when titled upwards, and as Susan observed the goofy smile on the stuffed pig's face, she pictured her unborn child spending hours playing with the toy, willing it to wink anytime it was lifted high up in the air.

"We've got this." She whispered soothingly with increased confidence, resting her hand on her stomach.

Two hours later, my parents finally made it to the hospital after a few accidental *trips* and *falls* by my awkward father, who hastily tripped over his own feet when he ran up and down the stairs fetching items to put in the overnight bag with what he considered to be essentials. My mother remained seated on the bed, calmly filtering through the packed contents, pulling out the television remote control, the skinny jeans, and twenty pairs of underwear that dad had so keenly packed in his own helpful way. However, when they both finally got into their beat-up Dodge, which my mom inherited from her grandmother, my dad managed to collect himself and drove with heightened caution through the snow-covered streets to ensure the safety of the precious cargo.

The registration and check-in at the hospital upon arrival were completed without any delays, and they were quickly escorted into the spacious room in the maternity ward on the second floor that housed two separate hospital beds. By the time my mother settled in the crisp sheets of the hospital bed positioned closer to the door, my father had managed to mellow down after having adequate time to process the situation on their drive and additional assistance of his sly wife who sneaked in some valerian root powder in his morning coffee to reduce his anxiety. It was a trick she had to succumb to on a rare but necessary occasion, when there was an absolute need for my dad to calm down, and this was undoubtedly one of those times.

Once settled in their room, with my mother comfortable in the hospital bed and my father silently fidgeting in the incommodious chair by her side, an elderly doctor came to check on my fatigued mother to evaluate the progress of her contractions. Pleased with his observation, he advised my parents that they still had a few hours until I was ready to come out, and then retreated leaving my anxious mom and dad to figure out how to cope with their anticipation.

To reduce their angst, my father decided to pull out his indestructible travel chess set that he had owned since he was a child, and that he thoughtfully packed in the suitcase first. It was less than an essential item and my mother disapproved of it being packed, but to my father's reprieve she eventually determined that the chess set was a perfect distraction to their otherwise nerve-wrecking circumstances.

When they finally set their chess pieces up, halting whenever my mother had to endure another painful jolt, the door to their room unceremoniously opened and another patient was wheeled in towards the vacant bed in the room, arms length away from Susan. In the wheelchair sat a young girl with a dark mess of curly hair framing her pretty face, her youthful appearance revealed that she could be no older than eighteen years old, only a few years younger than my mother. The new roommate boasted a very thin frame which made her bulging bump appear even bigger than it was. My parents curiously observed the new arrival, waiting for the accompanying parents or partner to follow along but no one else entered the room through the agape door. The friendly nurse rolled the wheelchair towards the empty bed at the back of the room while trying to strike up a conversation with the new patient, who only responded with an occasional grunt, then she helped the pregnant girl settle in, and made a few notes in the chart before leaving the room promising to be back to check on the patients shortly.

Unaware of any proper birthing roommate etiquette, as this integral element was not included in any of the books my mother read in preparation for the big day, she struggled between introducing herself and leaving the new roommate alone. Eventually, the innate politeness and the belief that in her more senior age of twenty-one, she should be the one to introduce themselves, my mother raised her arm and waved to the young woman in greeting and exclaimed.

"Hi, guess we're roommates! I'm Susan and this is Jack", she gestured to my dad, who was busy considering his first move on the chessboard. "What's your name?"

"I'm Alison." The girl responded boldly.

"Do you know who you're having, Alison?" My mom continued the conversation casually while my father puffed and rolled his eyes in annoyance caused by the unexpected diversion from the game.

"No, I do not. Don't think it's important if you ask me", the new roommate snapped back, and then as if catching herself alerted by my mother's slightly offended look, she continued. "As long as they are healthy, I guess. What about you, boy or girl?"

"We chose not to find out, just like you. I'd be happy with either one, but I think Jack over here would prefer a boy." She joked, nudging her husband for a reaction. My father diverted his attention from the chess board after a strategically played move and defended himself against my mother's unfounded assumption.

"Nonsense. Sure, if it is a boy then we can work in my workshop and craft some furniture pieces, and then play hockey at the local ice rink. But I would be just as happy with a girl too, a proper daddy's girl." He vocalized his thoughts that he had pondered over the previous months in preparation for the day. My mother, being more in tune with people's reactions, sensed an immediate change in Alison's mood, as the roommate raised herself in the bed, squinted her dark eyes while furrowing her unkempt eyebrows.

"A mother can do all those things too, a kid doesn't need to have a father to build a shelf, you know." Alison raised her voice in an unarguable defiance, challenging my father to respond.

Jack straightened his back sitting up in high alert, aware that he had wronged their roommate in some way but unable to pinpoint the source of the problem. My mother quickly jumped in to diffuse the situation explaining to Alison that my father had no ill intentions and was just too excited about their baby to think clearly today. The audacious neighbour shrugged her shoulders and settled back in her bed, silently making my parents aware that the conversation was now over.

"Well, let us know if you need anything. Jack can get you some ice chips from the reception area if you like."

Mom jabbed my dad in his rib cage with the knight that she grabbed from the chessboard and expressively mouthed to him "She is alone, you can try to help".

"Aye" dad yelped from the jab "Yes of course, just let me know", dad replied, noticing a shrug of Alison's slender right shoulder to signify that she heard him.

My parents exchanged quizzical looks wondering what to do or say next, then dad shook his head juddering his messy dark hair that he forgot to comb in the morning, to show my mom that she should stop prying for a dialogue and diverted his eyes back to the chessboard. My mom put down the knight back on the board and after some hesitation made her calculated move, then nodded her chin at my dad prompting him to make his next play. Dad was gratefully pleased that the distractions had ceased, although after a few moves my mom declined to proceed due to another series of contraction aches seizing her body, so he continued to play both sides of the board. Periodically his attention was redirected to help his struggling wife through the increasing pain and to speak to the attentive medical staff when they came in to check on my parents and their still obscure roommate.

As the contractions grew stronger and more frequent, the attending grey haired doctor came to check on my mother and declared that she was finally ready to be taken to the delivery room. He left to get the nurse, so that his patient could be transported from the hospital room.

"It's time, Jack. I am so scared." My mother looked at my dad in fear.

"I will be right there with you. You are the bravest person I know, darling, and you will do great." Responded my dad assertively, while the nurse brought a wheelchair into the room and helped my mother ascend into it.

"Good luck, Susan." They heard a faint voice from the other bed in the room, as Alison gazed at them leaving.

Dad bravely followed behind the nurse without any visible hesitation, as he has been preparing for this moment for the last few months through a lot of coaching from my mother and their obstetrician. My mother insisted that he would need to be present in the room with her when it was time to support her and help her through the ordeal, but I believe that she did not want her husband pacing around the hospital in anxiety and panic when she was not around to help him through it. Maybe it was still the lasting effects of the calming valerian root, or my dad being fully prepared for the occasion, he stuck though the entire trial of my birth. He was holding on to my mom's hand even when she painfully clenched on to his as the agony got unbearable; he talked to her through the anguish; he stayed away from the doctors' and nurses' paths fully aware that he had to stay by his wife's side. Mom was confident that she could not have done this without dad, and she could be right, as I was finally born into this world surrounded by the eternal love of the most adoring parents.

"We've got her!" Announced the doctor excitedly after the final push. "It's a girl, a healthy-looking girl". The loud piercing scream bounced off the walls, alerting the world of my arrival, while the doctor placed the tiny body in the nurse's hands. Her strong arms cradled my body in their trained grasp and took me off to the side for a quick check up and clean up, and then carried back to the exhausted mother to finally settle me down on her heaving chest.

"Jack, she's absolutely beautiful." My mother finally looked up at her husband after longingly staring at my squirming body in disbelief, while gently supporting my tiny frame on her chest. As she looked up at her husband, she was shocked to see him inaudibly weeping. She had never seen him cry before, not even when her grandmother that he grew to love as his own, passed away just a few months ago. These were happy tears, tears of joy. Jack was smiling through his silent tears and could not take his adoring eyes away from his new baby.

After some time, he finally regained his speech and agreed.

"She is absolutely perfect.".

After some time, when the new mother and her newborn baby were taken back to the maternity ward to rest and to bond, my overwhelmed father excused himself to go outside and get some much-needed fresh air. My mother was too preoccupied with looking at me to object to him, so he was able to sneak out almost unnoticed. When he stepped outside the hospital through the wide sliding doors into the frosty outdoors, he was instantaneously hit by the searing crisp air that entered his lungs with brute force.

As he took a deep breath to replenish his energy and fill his lungs with the sobering coldness to dispel any of his previous fears of fatherhood, he admired the beautiful powdery snow on the cars and even the trodden yellow roads from the through traffic into the hospital. He took his time appreciating the immediate surroundings remaining in one spot, trying to memorize every detail of the very eventful Christmas Day. Jack took a couple more deep breaths before heading back into the warm hospital to join his family.

"Susan, I think I have the perfect name" My dad said as he entered the room where my mom was resting, while also keeping her uninterrupted gaze on me.

"Oh yea? Do tell." My mother glanced briefly at my dad, before diverting her gaze back to the hospital crib.

"Noelle. She is a Christmas Baby after all." He stated through his wide grin, his face glowing with delight.

My mother craned her neck gawping at me with wonder, pursed her lips and wiggled them back and forth for a second, which is what she typically tended to do when she was genuinely considering something important.

"What do you think, baby girl? Are you a Noelle?" She asked me a rhetorical question, while she assessed the proposal.

Then a smile lightened up her tired face, in her childlike manner, and nodded "I like that. It is ideal, she looks just like a Noelle".

At that moment, the door to the room opened and the girl they met earlier was wheeled in by their attending nurse, followed by her colleague rolling another baby forward in a hospital cradle. Alison seemed distracted while she was helped back in her bed, looking at her baby with unhindered curiosity, and a slight hint of sorrow. The nurses being used to the variety of reactions from the new mothers, calmly assured her that they would be back to check on her and to answer any questions that she may have. They then walked over to my mother and I, looked over the chart and took our vitals, then left the suddenly crowded room assured that everything was in order.

"Alison, congratulations!" My mom looked in her roommate's direction beaming with excitement.

"Thank you, you too." She mumbled in response, still enthralled by the bundle resting peacefully in the miniature bed next to her.

My dad walked over to Alison's side of the room and peeked into the cradle, where he observed a beautiful baby girl with a head full of dark curls sound asleep, completely unaware of the world around her that she still had to face. "She's wonderful, Alison. Did you come up with a name, yet?", my dad asked.

"I thought Roxie might be a good name, but I'm not sure if i..." Alison responded hesitantly, but my father's overpowering enthusiasm interrupted her.

"Roxie is a great name, it suits her." He exclaimed and then gestured to my cradle. "This is our Noelle, our beautiful Noelle".

Alison leered in my direction with growing interest and extended her neck to get a better look; then told my parents that she liked the name and found it very fitting for a Christmas birth. My parents were itching to bring up the topic of whether anyone was coming to visit their roommate, but they were too polite to intrude into the stranger's private life. Instead, my dad self-proclaimed himself the sole caretaker of the room and took up the general duties and responsibilities of ensuring the comfort of its residents and volunteered to help in every regard.

At first Alison was taken aback by my dad's persistence and constant questions and resisted my dad's offers to hold her daughter, when the baby moaned around in her cradle. However, as the day went on and Alison was succumbing to a well needed sleep, she relented and said that she would appreciate if dad could look after Roxie while she was sleeping.

Dad forgot all about his earlier anxieties and the stress of the day while he looked after the newborns with his watchful eagle eye, while their mothers were asleep. The chess board remained untouched as his undivided attention was devoted to the girls, he talked to the nurses when they came in to check on the patients and caressed the girl's heads when they made sounds which seemed to ease any of their nonverbal demands. He was in his new element, and he chuckled at the thought of him stumbling on the stairs when he anxiously ran around packing the overnight bag back at the house, none of that mattered anymore.

This was his new life, his whole new world.

## Chapter Two

*February 14, 1990*
*Age 5*

"Mom! Where's Winkie?"

I screamed on top of my lungs, as I was struggling to put on a pair of a new pair of snow pants my mother bought me. There was clearly something wrong with the pants, they were refusing to be pulled up and my feet were continuously being caught on some invisible obstruction. My mother was busy with the last-minute packing, carefully organizing the contents of the embroidered travel bag, preparing for my parents' long-awaited romantic weekend getaway. At the same time, I was anxiously looking forward to spending two full days playing with my best friend at her house. Mom had already packed up a sizable bag for me, that seemed to be larger in size than her own, with my toys and enough clothes to last a week.

We had never had a sleepover at that point, and while we spent countless hours on our playdates, we were never able to spend more than a couple of hours together. While I anxiously tried to put on my clothes, the anticipation of the weekend ahead was overwhelming. This was the most excited I had been, looking forward to all the plays that Roxie would make us act out, and the books Auntie Alison would read to us.

All I was missing was Winkie, my irreplaceable and the most huggable stuffed pig. My mom was the one who originally called it Winkie because when she gave it to me as a baby, it winked at me when it rolled over in my crib with its long eyelashes revealing the bluest eyes that matched my own. However, over time with the many starring roles in my games, the eyelashes have fallen out and both eyelids have stuck in their sockets leaving one eye perpetually open and one eye closed shut.

This did not concern me, as now it looked like Winkie was playfully winking at the world permanently, which was so like him since he was the friendliest and most loving pig in the world.

My mother walked into my room, summoned by my yelling, looking a bit tattered and tired from all the packing. She glanced under the bed and then lifted the pile of other toys from the floor to look for Winkie, but she could not find it.

"Do you remember where you saw him the last time?" My mom asked patiently, as she sat on the edge of the bed next to me and pulled off the defying pair of pants. She turned them inside out and gave me an encouraging smile, demonstrating that the smooth fleece had to be on the inside and not on the outside, which made no sense since the fleece material was bright orange and I wanted everyone to see it.

I rolled my eyes and said "Yes, he was with me all day. We had breakfast together. Oh mom, I told you that Winkie does not like the yucky oatmeal so please stop making it."

"Winkie is getting pickier and pickier", she sighed, knowing that all of Winkie's fussy dietary preferences were copied by me. "I'm sorry, honey, but we have to run. We will look for him when we get back. Your dad is already outside waiting for us in the car and Roxie is waiting for you. You do not want to make her wait. Do you? I promise you Winkie will be here when we are back, ok?"

I considered crying for a brief second demanding that we extend our search efforts, but then thought of Roxie looking out her window anxiously waiting for me to come, and gave in to my mother's plan. I finally pulled the dreaded snow pants up with the orange colour hidden from sight, resisting mom's attempts to help me, and skipped down the stairs. My eager Dad honked the horn in the car, which made us rush even faster as we put on our rubber soled boots and chill resistant winter parkas to prepare for the freezing cold. Mom opened the front door immediately letting in the bitter cold air into the narrow hallway and placed the packed bags outside so that my dad could come up to the porch and pick them up.

She bent down on one knee and lowered her body to adjust my hat and scarf, then gave me a tight hug.

"I can't believe you won't be spending the night with us. We have never been away from you for this long yet. You sure you will be ok, baby?

"Mom," I said, trying to sound like a grown up "I'm not a baby, I'm five and two months."

"That's right, she is." I heard my dad chuckle by the door, as he lifted the heavy luggage, "She will not even notice that we are gone." He started cautiously descending the porch steps and turned back to us. "Be careful as you walk down, it's very slippery outside".

"I don't care if you're fifty-five or five, you're still my baby." My mom said to me and extended her slender arm. "Ok, take my hand, and don't rush down the steps or you will fall." My mom reached for my palm, which I grabbed without a pause, as I always loved the comfort of my mother's soft hands.

We walked out into the icy morning and locked the front door behind us. My dad was busy arranging the bags in the trunk of the car, while we slowly paced ourselves down the slick porch steps holding on to the railings. The treacherous steps almost made me fall but my mother's grasp kept me upright. I could see that my dad made the effort of putting salt on the surface to prevent any unfortunate accidents but there had not been enough time to let it set. Mom and I sidestepped cautiously on our way down and managed to get to the car unharmed. I climbed into the spacious backseat of our Dodge and was adjusting my bulky clothed frame to get comfortable, as dad walked over to help me.

"You know, I found a friend of yours hiding in my coat sleeve today." He said, while buckling me in, then reached under my seat and pulled out the runaway winking pig. That was when I remembered that Winkie wanted to play hide and seek after breakfast in the morning, but I got distracted with all the hasty preparation and forgot about our game.

"Winkie!!! You found him!" My mom and I exclaimed at the same time.

Dad slammed the back door of the car shut and walked over to the driver's seat. "So, we're good to go now?" he asked, settling into his seat.

"Let's go!" Winkie and I yelled, both of us winking at my dad as he looked at us in the rear-view mirror and winked back, then he pulled out of the driveway onto the cul-de-sac and turned right to merge into the speeding traffic.

That was pretty much the last happy memory I have of my blissful childhood with my amazing parents during the first lifetime, and the rest of the events following our departure from the house only flash in fleeting moments. I remember playing with Winkie in an oblivious childhood happiness in the backseat of the car without a worry in my little head. I remember the annoying but ever so popular Simply Irresistible song blaring through the speakers and my parents singing along loudly while my dad laughed at my mother's attempts at dancing in her seat.

The terrorizing moments after that haunt me until this day. I remember my mother's shrilling scream, chilling, horrific scream that still penetrates my nightmares. Then my last memory is of my dad's eyes in the rear-view mirror looking back at me, full of despair of the inevitable as our car ploughed into the big pileup of other pounded vehicles in front of us followed by an even more impactful crash from behind. Then the flashing memories end, as the damning darkness followed, scary and lonely blackness, the darkness that shadowed me for the rest of my eternity.

The next foggy memory I have, after the obscurity around me began to slowly dissipate, was of two people speaking in low voices, one of them who seemed vaguely familiar, but my troubled consciousness was not yet fully alert to comprehend who was around me.

"The severity of the accident was immense, as you very well know fifteen people lost their lives in that tragic pile up when the semi-truck skidded into the cars. Absolute tragedy! I am shocked that our little survivor only has a few broken bones, but they should heal nicely within a month. The only concern I have right now is the brain injury from the swelling, which is why we must keep her sedated. Does she have any other relatives? Grandparents? Aunts, uncles? She has been here for two weeks, and you are the first person to visit her." Asked the deep unfamiliar voice.

"No, that's what I've been telling you guys, there is no one else. She is all alone. The poor child." The second person responded sounding a bit agitated, then the tone became more accusatory when the voice continued in a much louder pitch "To be fair, I would have come sooner but your tyrant receptionists wouldn't let me, hospital policy they said, only family is allowed to visit. Bullshit! This kid is on her own. All alone! No family at all."

*No family at all...that is very sad*, I thought as I wondered who this unfortunate child may be without her mommy and daddy, thankful that my parents were always by my side. Then the darkness swallowed me up again in its encompassing depth and I drifted off to sleep.

Over the next two months, the murkiness around me was my only constant companion as I drifted in and out of consciousness. There were only occasional hazy moments where the gloom lightened briefly allowing me to hear voices around me, to see flashes of white sterile walls and ceiling, to be vaguely annoyed by the monotonous beeping from the machines beside my ear and sense the feeling of someone holding my hand. These were not my mother's hands; they lacked the recognizable softness that always gave me comfort as I fell asleep, while they caressed me or held me tight when I cried from all the insignificant problems endured being a careless child. The callouses on the hands that were holding me now felt rough on my skin, the dry skin could not compare to the smoothness of my mother's palms but even the coarseness of the unidentified hands was soothing, as I longed to be comforted through the frightening lonely darkness.

The moment the dismal shadows finally lifted, happened just as suddenly as they had initially consumed me, and it was one of the scariest instances in my memory. It was my first vivid recollection of feeling ultimately helpless and fearful of the unrecognizable surroundings, as I finally became fully aware of the hospital room where I was laying, and the strangers dressed in white robes standing by my side.

As any child, even prior to the awakening, I had been terrified of doctors who had only made a negative impression on my life when my mother took me to see them for painful shots and sour medication. So seeing the strangers in the white robes when I finally opened my eyes, was not the most pleasing moment and contributed to the overall sinister atmosphere of the occasion, as I immediately recognized the uniform. I suppose my facial expression mirrored the turmoil that was going on in my head, as the smooth faced doctor smiled and said.

"Hi Noelle, it's so nice of you to join us. I'm Doctor Hernandez, but you can call me Doctor H. How are you feeling?"

"I…." My hoarse voice was barely audible, while I struggled to speak which made the moment even more terrifying, as I looked alarmed back at the doctor.

"Not to worry, just take it slowly." Dr. H continued to smile, which helped to slightly reduce my panicked state. "It has been a while since you were last awake, so it may take some time for you to regain all your senses. Can you move your toes and fingers for me?"

*What an odd question,* I thought, *but then all doctors are just odd people.* It was especially strange when the doctor and his colleague seemed to loudly cheer when I successfully wiggled my toes and fingers. To make them even happier, I decided to raise my leg one at a time. As I performed the simple movements, I felt the stiffness of my muscles and reluctance of my body to respond quickly to the simple instructions.

"You're a champ, Noelle. But do not rush it, as I said, just take it slowly." The doctor said, as he neared my bed and took out an instrument that resembled a miniature hammer from his coat pocket. He then tapped it around a few spots on my upper and lower body prompting my hands and feet to jerk, which made me giggle at my own unexpected responses.

"Good, your reflexes are great considering everything and it looks like your vocal cords are doing just fine too." He said while feeling my throat with his cold hands. "Do you remember what my name is?" He looked at me questioningly.

"D..Doctor H." I was taken aback by the scratchiness of my throat and the dryness in my mouth.

Doctor H. smiled at me and then turned to his colleague behind him.

"Looks like her short-term memory is intact too. This girl is a warrior, to go through what she did." He shook his head in disbelief, as his spectacles struggled to remain in place.

I blushed by the strange compliment, still puzzled as to why the doctor seemed so amazed by what I always thought were such simple activities. Then suddenly a sound of squealing brakes from the outside invaded the serene space of the room, prompting a momentary flash of my mother screaming and the loud crash zoom in front of my eyes, and I croaked to the doctor in almost a whisper.

"Mommy?" I looked to him for an answer, while trying to raise myself upward to look around the room. I could not imagine my mother leaving me here to fend for myself, she would never let me see the doctor on my own, so she must have been here somewhere.

The doctor's smile disappeared for a quick second as did the joyful look in his eyes, and then he seemed to catch himself as he showcased another grin that seemed much less genuine. I also noticed that the silent colleague quickly lowered his eyes and turned around to leave the room.

"Don't you worry about that for now. How about you take a nap and then we will come back to check on you." Dr. H replied with haste, while walking around the bed over to the drip attached to my arm. "Sleep, Noelle and everything will be alright. You are such a trooper."

My eyelids started to feel heavy, and I rubbed my eyes with the one free hand that was not hooked up to the machine, to try and stay awake, but the dreaded darkness draped my awareness once again.

I woke up the next day to a rustling sound in my room, *must be mommy and daddy*, I thought with joy, and hurriedly opened my eyes. Instead, as I woke, I saw a lone bright pink balloon bopping by the bed and then noticed a woman facing the window with only her back visible.

I instantly recognized the familiar sea of dark curls wildly sticking out in all directions, an oversized sweater in every colours of the rainbow with the typical 80's shoulder pads and the neon violet leggings to complement the look of a figure I did not expect to see.

"Auntie Alison." I heard myself croak with my still raspy voice.

"Oh, you're awake! You're finally awake!"

She quickly turned around and flung her slender body across mine in a big hug. Then being aware of all the wires and tubes connected to my body, she pulled back in frustration.

"Those doctors, I tell you! All they know is how to drug someone. They have been keeping you all drugged up for months now. Charlatans with deep pockets."

She stopped herself from going on about the failures of the health system, while she observed my small body in a huge hospital bed, and then I noticed tears gathering in the corners of her darkened eyes. I looked at her puzzled at her emotions, as I had never seen Auntie Alison be sad before. I have seen her make people cry more than once, but never herself.

I still remember when my parents and I went to the public pool in the neighborhood with Auntie Alison and Roxie, where Roxie and I were learning how to swim. We were paddling around and splashing each other when a group of rowdy teenaged boys decided to dive in the pool creating a mighty ripple effect. The wave made Roxie and I lose our footing and we were having trouble staying afloat, Roxie managed to yelp in desperation and my father jumped in at once to carry us out to safety. Not a minute passed by before Auntie Alison jumped in the pool and dragged two of the teenagers out of the water by their ears, with them screaming for help to anyone that would listen. Auntie Alison was not much older than the teenagers then, but her presence and determination always made her a force to be reckoned with, so no one interfered in her disciplining the teenagers. I have never seen older boys cry before, but these grown teens were bawling their eyes out whether it was from pain or embarrassment.

That is why I was taken aback by the sadness in Auntie Alison's face, this was not like her at all. Then I shrugged it off and asked the only question that had been bugging me since I first opened my eyes and that the doctor left unanswered.

"Auntie Alison, where is mommy and daddy?" I whispered, still unable to fully vocalise my thoughts.

The tears were now running down her face and just as she realized that she quickly got up from my side and ran over to the chair to get a Kleenex out of the depths of her woven purse. I saw her shoulders shudder, as she was exhaling and inhaling deeply to stabilize her breathing and collect her thoughts. It was a technique I have seen her use before when she was talking to her landlord complaining about a burst pipe when I came to play with Roxie last time.

As I was looking over at Aunt Alison in the far corner of the room, I heard the door open and turned to see Doctor H. walk in with another unfamiliar man who looked much older than his colleague, but he was also dressed in a white coat.

"How's my favourite patient today?" Doctor H. asked me entering the room, then noticed Auntie Alison in the corner of the room. "Oh, Alison, I didn't realize you were here." Then he noticed the red puffy eyes on her face and the tissue clenched in her fist.

"You didn't say anything, did you?" He asked with a note of concern, and Auntie Alison shook her head. Dr. H directed his attention back to me, gesturing to the man with him "This is Dr. Thompson, he is a children psychologist here at the hospital and I thought it would be best if he was the one to …" Dr. H stopped talking as if not knowing how to continue.

"Hi Noelle, so nice to meet you. I've heard so much about you." Upon approach, as he walked closer to the bed, the new doctor was indeed much older than Dr. H with a head full of gray hair and a pair of thick framed glasses on his kind face covered in wrinkles. "I was hoping we could have a chat. Do you mind if I prop your bed up, so you could sit up?"

I nodded cautiously, and felt my bed turn into a comfortable lounge chair.

"How are you feeling, Noelle?"

"Ok, I guess. I just really want to see my parents." I said in a lower voice, as I strained to speak.

"That's what I'm here to talk to you about. Do you remember what happened before you woke up here?"

"We were all driving to Auntie Alison and Roxie's house and then there was a loud bang."

"That is right, Noelle. You were in an accident; a lot of people were in an accident that day because of the ice on the road. You are one brave and strong little girl though, aren't you?"

The older doctor paused for a moment waiting for an answer that never came. I was tired of everyone telling me how great I was. I pursed my lips trying to recall the accident, but I did not remember much more than I already said, so instead I looked at the venerable doctor straight in the eyes and asked:

"What about my mommy and daddy?"

"Noelle, you're a strong girl so I can tell you the truth, because I know that you can handle it." He paused before taking a deep breath and then continued. "Unfortunately, your parents died in the accident. Do you understand what that means?"

The words that came out of the doctor's mouth swallowed me whole, as I struggled to breath in disbelief of this revelation. I knew what death was, my parents talked me through it when our friendly neighbour Nancy passed away a year earlier. It meant my loving and happy parents would no longer tuck me in at night before bed, my dad would never read me a bedtime story, we would never walk around the neighbourhood park as I hold both of their hands lost in the happiness of my own thoughts. It meant that my mother and father would not come into this huge room that just seemed to get even larger now and comfort me. I was now on my own.

I struggled to say anything, while the worrying thoughts twirled in my head spinning faster and faster with increasing speed, making me feel nauseous. My eyes paced around the room from one face to another, looking for a crack of a smile hoping that this was a very bad joke, and the old doctor was mistaken.

"I understand that this is very sad news. I know that you love your parents and they loved you very much too. It is ok to be sad, and if you want to cry then do not hold it in. You may feel alone...", the doctor continued in his calm and calculated tone that sounded like a well-prepared script.

"Oh, these stupid swindlers, I swear on my mother's grave!", exclaimed Auntie Alison, as she glared at Doctor Thompson and rushed to my side to grab my hand.

Her touch seemed to jolt me back to my senses, and I squeezed back recalling the roughness of the hands, that helped me through the darkness. It was her calloused palm that held on to me as my awareness drifted in and out of this cruel reality.

"A child needs comfort, not all your useless words. Look at her, she is scared witless. The poor girl!".

Auntie Alison was right, the brutal truth that the doctor spilled out was earth shattering to me and my body began to tremble refusing to accept the hard facts.

"Noelle, honey, *this doctor*" she winced at the term, "is right in one thing. Your mom and dad did die, but you are in no way alone. You have me and obviously Roxie. We have been with you in this room while you were zonked out on all the drugs these people gave you." She glared at Dr.H and Dr. Thompson, and continued, "Roxie is at daycare now, but she will come to visit you later today and then when you are all better, then you can come and stay with us. How does that sound?"

"Alison, I need to stop you right there." Said Dr. H. interrupting Auntie Alison's speech "Can I see you outside for a second?".

Auntie Alison hesitated but stood up and followed the doctor out of the room, leaving me with Dr. Thompson, as he continued with his professional and clinically approved talk. I could not focus on what the older doctor was saying and instead tried to listen to the voices behind the door that remained slightly ajar, as I knew that all the important talks always happened behind closed doors. I learned that much from eavesdropping on my parent's conversations about money and my dad's unsuccessful attempts at finding a better job. At first, I could not hear the doctor and angry Auntie Alison at all, as they both kept their voices very low, almost to an indistinguishable murmur but then their voice tones drastically increased allowing me to hear everything they were saying.

"I completely disagree", yelled the female voice.

"You know you can't promise something like that to her yet. Social services must be consulted; courts have to be involved. Obviously over the last few months, I have seen you spend hours with Noelle and most definitely heard all your concerns, so I know you genuinely wish the best for our little patient. Regardless, I don't think you should promise to be her caretaker, if you can't keep to it. Noelle is fragile enough as it is right now."

"Oh yea? Watch me, I will be taking this girl home in no time. Straight to my house, the only household where she will be safe and sound. Watch me!"

My attention switched back to the droning voice of Dr. Thompson, and I realized that there was a silent pause as he looked directly at me waiting for me to respond with a gentle reassuring look in his eyes, sensing that the most appropriate response from me could be a positive acknowledgement of what was asked of me. I nodded in response, which seemed to satisfy the doctor.

"If you need to talk to me, just tell the nurses to get in touch with me, but I'll come and check up on you now and then." Then he paused looking at the door where the loud debate between the doctor and Aunt Alison continued, and then turned to me and leaned in closer as if to tell me a secret, "But, to be honest, I don't think you will be here much longer if your Aunt Alison has anything to do with it."

Dr. Thompson was right. Aunt Alison was able to get the judge to issue a temporary order for me to be allowed to stay with her, while the paperwork was being approved for her to be my legal guardian. A week later, I was being checked out of the hospital with all the tests showing significant improvement and no lasting consequences from the crash. Only I knew that the painful hollowness in my chest would be a permanent impediment that I would carry throughout my lifetime.

# Chapter Three

*September 2001*
*Age 18*

"They are all losers, trust me. Think about it, they go off to college and spend all that money and time, so that they can work at a desk job for the rest of their lives making enough money to just pay their bills. We can skip the college part and start living our lives now, making real cash."

Roxie was sitting on the dirty counter with her long legs dangling off the edge, looking down and admiring her new pair of Converse sneakers that we found on our latest trip to Goodwill. I could tell she was listening to me because she was intensely chewing her gum and nodding as she was processing the information. This has been a subject of our many discussions this summer, as we looked at our friends preparing for their moves to different state universities. We celebrated their successes but insisted that college life was not for us, when they asked us about our plans.

There was a farewell party almost every day that August, whether it was at someone's house or by the beach just outside the town. So many happy faces leaving their childhood behind, as they were ready to face the world and leave the nest. Roxie and I always showed our solidarity with everyone's happiness, but when we got home to our shared bedroom, we couldn't help but wonder if this was something we should have pursued. Not that our grades would allow us to get into any of the good schools, nor did we have the money but there was a gnawing feeling of missing out that we began to resent. The resentment overtime developed to judgment of our many friends for leaving, and we began to consider alternatives for us.

So here we were hanging out at Fat Joe's Gas Station and Diner, our dreadful place of employment that reeked of a whole mix of atrocious smells, that I was certain followed us everywhere. The aroma of the nauseating grease from the kitchen in the back of the diner, where Roxie was tirelessly flipping burgers and making fries attracted all the stray dogs in the area to us when we walked home every night. Regardless, I would have had gladly traded her burger scent over the headache inducing gas smells from the pumps and the body odour from the atrocious truckers who stopped by always trying to grope me on their way in or out of the store.

I spent most of the time behind the counter, cashing out the customers or stocking the shelves inside the store with the overpriced snacks, resenting my life. We had been working at Fat Hoe's for almost two years, after Alison sat us down one day and said that if we want anything more than bread and water for dinner going forward then we need to start making our own money. She had recently been downsized at the local factory where she worked for as long as we've been alive and was only able to find occasional part time work, which was merely enough to pay most bills.

"Ray said that he could help us get modeling gigs in New York. He's well connected, you know?" I continued with my spiel, cautiously approaching the subject of my boyfriend.

Roxie did not like Ray, at all, not from the first day we met at one of the farewell parties in early August. Ray was like nobody I had ever met at that point, he stood out in the crowd with his tall muscular frame and luscious locks of dark hair, that he always brushed his fingers through.

The night we met Ray, Roxie and I were late leaving work because Fat Joe made us do inventory at the store. We did not have time to run home to change out of our uniforms and rinse off the odours of grease and gas, so we used some Wet Naps, which I always stashed under the counter, to cleanse ourselves and put baby powder in our hair to give it some volume. A few magic touches of the mascara wand and the black eyeliner, that Roxie had in her purse, and we were ready to go.

When we arrived at the beach, we saw our friends chatting away by the bonfire, so we joined them and sat on the blankets that were spread out on the warm white sand. As I sat down and looked at the burning fire, finally ready to let loose and have some fun, my eyes met the eyes of a stranger across the sizzling flames I had not seen before. I diverted my eyes from the intense gaze to look back at my friend Adam and asked who that was. Adam indicated that it was a guy he recently met at another party, he was in town from New York and that he had the best weed that we simply must try. Roxie winced at the proposition as she had been opposed to any forms of drugs, and she was never shy to tell you to not use the paraphernalia either. She and Alison would get into fights regularly if she ever caught her mother smoking pot, which Alison always somehow managed to acquire, even during hard financial struggles.

"Hi, would you like some?"

I felt a tap on my shoulder and looked behind me. There stood the Greek god as I would imagine one to look, with the glimmer of the flames illuminating his body.

"No, we wouldn't. Thank you very much." Roxie jumped in immediately, as I stretched out my hand and took the joint being offered.

I laughed and said. "Pardon my amazing but utterly prudish sister. This is Roxie." I nodded in my sister's direction. "And, I'm Noelle." I introduced myself, while taking a deep puff of the strongest weed I had tried to that date.

"Nice to meet you, ladies. I'm Ray. Must say that you don't look like sisters."

Roxie and I looked at each other and shook our heads in dismay, because over the years we have heard the same comment anytime someone heard us call each other a sister. While we knew we were not related by blood, we could not see each other as anything but sisters. We have shared everything from the age of five when I came to live with Alison and Roxie, the small but cozy room, the clothes, the toys, the makeup. We were a unit, there was no me without Roxie and no Roxie without me. We fought each other's battles and cried over each other's misfortunes. This was beyond a mundane friendship; Roxie was my sister by all accounts.

Ray sat down on our blanket and remained seated next to me for the remainder of the night, telling us about New York. We had never heard much about the Big Apple, other than what we had seen in a few television shows or movies, but who could ever believe those to be factual. We revelled in his vivid descriptions and colourful stories of the skyscrapers, exclusive clubs, wild parties, it seemed like a whole different universe to us. As the night drew to the end and the fire had burnt out, Roxie got up to help clean up the area and pack up the blankets, and Ray used the opportunity to sit closer to me with his bare thigh grazing my leg. An instant shiver shook my body, when I felt his touch, sending an array of tiny bumps all over my body. That was when he leaned in to kiss me. This was a proper good kiss, not like any of the slobbery make out sessions I had shared behind the bleachers at high school with Bud from the football team. A new whirl of emotions overtook me as his tongue explored the elasticity of my own tongue and the depths of my mouth.

"Noelle, we need to head home."

I heard Roxie's voice through the thunderous whirlwind, reverting me back to reality. I leaned back separating from Ray's tight embrace, exhaled sharply and bit my puffy lip to stop me from yelling back at Roxie.

"I should go too." Ray said. "I will be here until mid September though staying with some distant family. How about I see you tomorrow and everyday until then?"

"I think we can arrange that."

I responded in awe of the moment, as he got up to join our mutual friend Adam to leave, waved me goodbye and walked away.

The next day I stood behind the counter at work, reliving the most romantic moment of my semi-adult life, with real life around me being nothing more than a hazy nuisance. Fat Joe yelled at me to get my butt moving a few times, as I was at my ultimate slowest checking out the customers at the till. I had hardly slept that night too, as I bugged Roxie with play by play of the events that led to the passionate kiss and my cloying feelings until she fell asleep. I stayed awake just thinking about the handsome man that entered my mundane life. So, in my slow haze at work, as I was stocking the shelves with Twinkies after another yell from Fat Joe, I felt a light tap on my shoulder. Thinking it was another trucker ready to grope me, I turned around in disgust but was met with the deep brown eyes of the man of my dreams from the night before.

"Oh, hi Ray! How did you know to find me here?"

I asked in surprise, blushing with joy from seeing him again.

"You know everyone knows everyone here, so it wasn't hard to find out. Wanted to see you today." He smirked at me, forming the most adorable dimple on his right cheek.

We had been inseparable since that day, except for when I had to work, a total of the most amazing thirty-five days. My longest relationship with anyone at that point, and I was not ready to give it up, even though it was time for Ray to go back to New York. I was completely and utterly head over heels obsessed with Ray and not ready to let go. I had never had anyone tell me how beautiful and sexy I was without trying to immediately grope my ass with their greasy hands, but

Ray made me feel glorious just by looking at me. Ray told me that if I wanted to, then I could easily make it as a model in New York, and so could Roxie.

The idea of being a model was not foreign to me, as I believe every little girl admires the pictures in the magazines and dreams to look equally stunning as the ladies on the cover. Roxie and I were pretty in our own unique ways. We both had slender figures, probably from being on our feet all day long at work and not overindulging in the fast food since being surrounded by the grease and smell of it everyday was more than we could handle.

Roxie's wild jet-black curls were by far the most stunning thing about her and turned heads on the street. She did not have to blow dry or put any hair product in her untamed mane as it was absolutely perfect on its own. Her delicate features vaguely reminded me of Halle Berry, but I always thought that Roxie was a lot prettier than the Hollywood actress.

My looks were more of a "Nordic princess", as my $8^{th}$ grade English teacher used to say, the only class I actually enjoyed at school. The blonde straight hair that only got lighter in the summer, was my favourite feature as I always kept it long, refusing any shorter cuts when we were growing up. The curviness of my slim body is what Ray found to be his favourite attribute, when I questioned him on what he liked best about me as we were lying naked in the car after another tender love making session.

After a few days of thinking about the career in modeling in New York, I found no reason why Roxie and I could not make it big in the City, and I would get to be with Ray indefinitely.

So, as the summer came to its logical conclusion and Ray was about to leave Georgetown, I decided that Roxie and I needed to move too. All I needed to do was convince my stubborn sister.

"What do we have to lose, Rox? Worst thing that could happen is we would come back and work in this godforsaken joint again."

I raised my arms in frustration, and demonstrated the grease-stained walls around us, while I continued with my well-prepared speech. Roxie lifted her gaze from the Converse sneakers and stared me directly in the eyes.

"Are you doing this for us or for Ray?"

She looked inquiringly, asking the question that had seemingly been troubling her since I brought up the idea of our move to New York.

"Because if you want to move for Ray then I am not going, nor should you. This guy is trouble. I know you never believe me when I tell you that I do not trust Ray, but I know it. I just know it in here." Roxie pointed her long index finger at her flat stomach.

I faltered for a second, which Roxie undoubtedly noticed.

"For me and you, obviously. I want to move, so we can have a better future. Ray is just a perk."

I smirked and looked back at her with confidence pleading for her to agree, just as I had done when we were kids, when I asked her to let me copy her homework or cover for me when I messed up at school. Roxie jumped off the counter with an elegance of a gazelle, looked around the spans of the grimy store and in the direction of the dreaded grill at the back.

"Fine, I will do it just so I can get away from this place for a bit. But you have to promise me, if this doesn't work out in a year then we come back. And you have to stop smoking weed so much. Ray has you on this stuff everyday now. That can't be good for you."

I loudly yelped at the news and jumped up from my stool, then instantly circled around the counter to embrace the surrendered Roxie in the strongest squeeze.

"I love you, so much! It's me and you forever!" I yelled boisterously in her ear.

We jumped around the store madly elated, forgetting all about the clients at the gas pumps, who stared at us through the blemished windows, smiling at our youthful and careless joy. After the exhausting impromptu celebration, we collected ourselves and started formulating a plan of attack on how to tell Alison about the move, since it was the one task neither one of us wanted to take on.

Alison made it a point to raise us to be independent strong women, so we figured that she would be happy that our upbringing had prepared us to make the ultimately difficult choice to leave home. On the flip side, we had never been apart from Alison, so did not know if she would be fine without us by her side when she needed help. Roxie did not want to be the one to tell her mother we would be leaving, sensibly neither did I. So, after a lot of deliberation and a few "rock paper scissors" rounds aiding us to pick the one to do the deed, it came down to me to have the heart-to-heart chat with Alison.

"Well, if I'm going to tell Alison then you're in charge of telling Fat Joe that we are quitting." I said in defeat, as the wheels in my head were turning on how best to approach Alison about the subject.

"Fine by me, it will be my *pleasure*." Roxie responded in a sarcastic voice, accentuating the last word.

"Don't think the boss would give a rat's arse about us leaving, he'll find other dimwits to work this greasy joint."

"Ok, so today is Sunday and Ray said that he needs to leave for New York on Friday. That gives us five days for everything."

I glanced at the calendar adorned with half naked Playboy bunnies that Fat Joe proudly put up every year on the wall behind the counter.

"We'll tell mom and Joe on Thursday, leave it to the last minute. Gives them less time to argue with us. Deal?"

"Deal!" I responded gleefully, already fantasizing about our glamorous life in New York.

The rest of the day flew by with me picturing Roxie and I weighed down by a variety of sizable shopping bags as we walk down the busy Fifth avenue, dining at all the bougie restaurants that Ray told us about and the myriad of cameras clicking away as we pose for the exclusive photographers for the glitzy magazines. There was no doubt in my gullible small-town mind that we would be happy living in New York, it was a city of dreams popularized by so many songs that I grew up listening to on our ancient stereo in the bedroom. If the Big Apple was advertised as a melting pot of the misfits, then we would blend in just fine and make it our home. We will conquer the city, we will take it by storm, New York won't know what hit it.

The next day, Roxie and I woke up for our early morning shifts at the rise of dawn. The diner at Fat Joe's opened at six in the morning for the breakfast crowd, so Roxie had to start up the griddle and set up the tables before the regulars started to trickle in looking for their oversized portions of bacon fried eggs and endless free refills of the lukewarm coffee. I also had to open the store at the same time and replenish the shelves with the new stock of candy and chips that was being delivered that morning. The thought of getting out of the comfortable bed to walk for a couple of miles to the gas station was always appalling but there was never an alternative, and for the last two years Roxie and I forced ourselves out of our beds on the weekends and holidays to start our regular shifts at Fat Joe's. This particular morning though, as I woke up dreading getting out of bed, the thought that flashed through my mind was that this is one of the last few shifts we had left until we left the forsaken town.

"Four more days, Roxie." I said out loud, still laying down, as I saw her wobbling out of her own narrow bed towards the hallway bathroom.

"Good morning to you too."

She growled in anger, never having been able to grow into a morning person. Roxie always reminded me of the Dr. Jekyll and Mr. Hyde book they made us read at school. She was typically the loveliest and funniest person in the world that made everyone smile and made friends everywhere because people were drawn to her sunny predisposition. However, if anyone tried to talk to her anytime before ten in the morning, they would be in for a serious surprise as they would encounter an overly grumpy and extremely rude creature that had to be avoided until the cheerful personality was ready to emerge from the sleepy alter ego. I was obviously used to it at this point and never approached any discussions on a deeper level ,when we woke up, saving them for later in the day when the "nice" Roxie escaped the clutches of the evil sleepy monster that lived inside of her.

This is the reason she was not a waitress at Fat Joe's diner, and always stayed in the kitchen working the grill and the deep fryer. He once made the mistake of putting Roxie on the floor when we first started, because he figured a pretty girl would attract more customers.

*Boy, was he wrong!*

Joe left her alone for five minutes as he went to accept the new shipment of motor oil at the back of the gas station, when he heard excruciating screams from the diner's side of his establishment. He rushed back inside, with his heavy frame knocking over an aisle of chip bags scattering them all over the floor and almost knocking me over as I ran over from the store counter to see what was going on. When we turned the corner into the diner, we saw one of the breakfast regulars with the remnants of coffee streaks streaming down his stained bald head. Roxie was standing beside him scowling with a heavy grip on the empty coffee pot in her hand.

Fat Joe was able to assess the situation rather quickly and shouted at Roxie, with every ounce of his body turning bright red from frustration, using an abundance of expletives that made my ears curl up.

Roxie calmly looked in Joe's direction deaf to his spewing screams and responded.

"I offered him pancakes and he mistakenly thought that I meant my ass and put his dirty paws on me. He was lucky that all I had in my hand was a coffee pot, and that it wasn't hot enough to burn his scalp off."

I held my laughter but beamed with pride, pleased that my formidable sister could take such good care of herself. There was not a grain of hesitation in my head that Roxie was getting fired on the spot, which Fat Joe considered, but luckily the local bible club stopped by for breakfast that morning as well and saw what happened so they stood up for the rebel in the form of my sister, saying they would never come back to this place if this type of misbehaviour was condoned. Fat Joe was a fearless man, but he had great respect for Father John who was the head of the bible club, so he hastily apologized for his immediate reaction and asked Roxie to pour everyone a cup of coffee on the house. Then Joe grabbed the offensive customers by the arm and led him out of the door saying that he was banned from Fat Joe's for life.

Roxie shrugged it off and continued working her shift, while everyone reverted their attention back to their breakfasts and forgot all about the earlier commotion. Only in the afternoon did my sister come over to the store side to see me.

"How could I do that? I could have seriously hurt him. So, what if he grabbed me, it's not the first time a trucker tried to grope me." She said in shock of her own reaction.

That was the "nice" Roxie finally coming out for a chat. I shook my head and laughed telling her that she was absolutely brilliant, and that the creep deserved to have a pot of coffee poured all over him. Since that day, Fat Joe never put Roxie out on the floor to interact with the customers and she was beyond happy with that decision.

"Did you figure out what to tell mom yet?"

Roxie brought me back to reality from the endless daydreaming, later in the afternoon, as she stopped by for a chat since the diner was not busy at the time.

"I think so. I wrote it all out here, so I just have to memorize it and stick to it when I talk to Alison."

"Let me read it, N."

She grabbed the piece of paper from my hand and read aloud.

*"Alison,*

*You have been a great role model over the years to us with your free spirit and determination to not let circumstances around you get the worst of any of us. You have taught us to fend for ourselves in this world and knowing that we have each other makes us so much stronger.*

*When I lost my parents, you worked so hard to get the guardianship, to make sure that I did not end up in foster care. I remember your continuous fights with the social workers when they tried telling you that you could not support the two of us, but you always got your way. I know it must have been difficult to take on a second child unexpectedly, but I am eternally grateful that you did. Without your guidance and care, I would probably be on the streets alone, but now I have you and my Rox.*

*This now brings me to my next point; you know this town does not offer a lot of opportunities for us. The prospect of working at Fat Joe's for the rest of our lives is terrifying. We are capable of so much more, especially because Roxie and I have each other. So, after careful consideration, we have decided to move to New York to pursue a career in the fashion industry. Ray has some connections, so he would help us around where he can. Once we get settled, we will let you know our new address so you can come live with us, or we can send you money if you do not want to leave your home.*

*We love you and will miss you very much.*
*Noelle and Roxie"*

"What do you think?" I looked curiously at Roxie.

"This is beautiful. I don't think you've ever told her how you felt about her taking you in."

"That's because she never let me feel like I was taken in, I always felt like a part of the family."

"Then, why did you never call her mom?" Roxie asked me.

"I couldn't because I still remember my real mother. I thought it would be unfair to her memory."

This was a sore subject for me, which I always tried to avoid since I hated for people to see me cry. It had been thirteen years since they passed away and the thought of my parents still made my voice tremble and my eyes water. The truth was, I really did love Alison and saw her as a mother figure, but I just could not address her as that because any thoughts of my actual mother were still very painful.

"I understand, I think my mom understands that too." Roxie said reassuringly, reaching for my hand.

I grabbed her hand and smiled; she always knew how to make me feel better. Roxie was the one person I was not afraid to cry in front of, and she knew it. At that moment, the glass front door of the store opened, and Ray briskly walked in wearing a sleeveless t-shirt with his toned arms on display. I jerked my hand back from Roxie and ran over to him wrapping my arms around his frame and pulling him in for a passionate kiss, he grabbed me by my waist and pulled me in for a tighter grip.

"Hey Ray." I heard Roxie mumble behind me.

Ray hesitantly pulled back and looked over in her direction

"Hi Roxie. I came to give you and Noelle a ride… and I also have a surprise for both of you."

"We still have ten minutes until the shift is over and I still need to wipe the tables." Roxie responded in defiance, unable to mask her distaste of seeing Ray.

"What's the surprise?" I anxiously asked, ignoring Roxie's statement.

Ray smiled back at me and mouthed "Patience" to me, raising his eyebrows conspicuously to create a sense of mystery.

"I'm sure Fat Joe will have no problem with you guys taking off early. Is he even here?"

Ray looked around the floor and glanced over in the direction of the diner.

"Yea, he is in the back. I'll go over to ask. Rox, can you watch the register? The lock on it broke earlier, so be careful and not to touch anything."

"I'll watch it. Let Roxie go and finish what she has to do in the kitchen." The chivalrous Ray jumped in offering to help, rushing us along.

*How could Rox not like this guy? He's amazing!*

I admired his eagerness to help me and my sister.

Fat Joe never let anyone who was not his vetted employee get behind the register, but then not all his rules made sense, so I hesitated for less than a second before nodding in agreement and headed towards the backroom to look for the boss.

When I came back to the front, Ray was sitting behind the counter mesmerized by the Playboy calendar on the wall.

"Admiring the art?" I walked over to him slightly jealous of his attention on the provocative photos.

Ray jumped in his seat, surprised by the sound of my voice, then turned around with his wide smile, revealing the pearly white teeth.

"Can we leave?" He inquired, while looking slightly flushed.

I sighed aloud from frustration and complained that Fat Joe insisted that we wait until the shift was over. Ray shrugged his muscular wide shoulders and said he would wait in the car because the stench of the grease and gas was starting to give him a throbbing headache. He gave me a quick peck on the cheek and walked out of the doors while I revered his tall, toned frame walk to the far side of the parking lot and get inside his red Dodge. Roxie and I busied ourselves for the remainder of our shift, cleaning up and mopping the floors.

Once we were done Fat Joe came from the back room to lock the doors behind us, so he could do some "real work". Roxie and I never knew what that meant, but never chose to ask. We said goodbye and told him not to overdo it with his "real work" and said that we would see him the next morning,

Then, we walked over toward Ray's sparkling clean car. I got into the passenger seat next to Ray, and Roxie settled in the backseat. His car still smelled like new leather seats, which was a much more welcoming scent for our troubled senses that were constantly poisoned by the smells that followed us from Fat Joe's. Ray started the car, pleased with the revving sound that came out of the engine, and drove out of the parking lot.

"So, what's the surprise?" I asked again, staring at him in anticipation.

"Right, then", Ray stalled with a dramatic pause to build up suspense and continued. "There has been a slight change of plans about New York."

The perfect picture of the imaginary life in the City started crumbling in front of my eyes, and I turned to him with regret to clarify what he meant.

"We are still going, but we need to go today. I'll drive you to your place, so you can pack up what you need but we need to leave within an hour."

Roxie jumped up in her seat and pulled herself forward so that her head was within inches of Ray.

"What do you mean an hour? We cannot just leave; my mother is not even home, and Noelle hasn't had a chance to talk to her. We can just take the bus later in the week maybe."

Ray reached for my hair, almost grazing Roxie's face with his hand, and started playing with my blonde strands twirling them in his long gentle fingers.

"I know it's not ideal, but something came up and I need to leave now. So, you can choose whether you come with me in this comfortable car free of charge, or you can wait to go on the putrid crowded bus with the last of your savings."

"Noelle?" Roxie shifted in her seat and moved close to the passenger seat to address her concerns. I hesitated to respond but knew that Roxie counted on me to be the encouraging and comforting voice of reason, so I countered.

"It's just a little blip, a hurdle on our way to success. We couldn't have expected everything to be easy, this is part of the adventure."

"But what about mom?" Roxie continued.

I thought about the conversation with Alison that I had been preparing for all day, and then reached into my pants pocket for the folded piece of paper that had my written speech.

"We can leave this for her on the kitchen table. You said that it was beautiful, and it would be almost as if we were saying it, because that's exactly how I prepared it. Only now, it's a goodbye letter."

Roxie leaned back in her seat and stayed quiet for the duration of the trip home, she was deep in thought undoubtedly assessing all the pros and cons of the situation. As we finally pulled into the driveway of our house and got out of the car, she finally spoke up and said:

"We need to make sure we pack our warmest clothes too; it can get cold in New York. Definitely those wool socks mom got us for Christmas last year, the ones that have reindeers on them."

"We'll take everything we can, Rox. It's going to be fine; everything will be great. We will call Alison when we get there. How does that sound?"

Roxie nodded in agreement and walked towards the house to unlock the door. We rushed upstairs, leaving Ray in the car as he drove off to run some last-minute errands and promised that he would be back in forty minutes, and we better be ready by then. It did not take us more than thirty minutes to collect all our belongings, we found it shocking how our whole lives could fit in just one duffle bag.

Our tiny closet was never filled with too many clothes, as we mostly shared all our outfits and spent the majority of our days outside of school in our work uniforms. As we pulled out our belongings, emptying out the drawers and shelves, our anticipation and giddiness of the immediate move grew with every minute. I reached under my bed and pulled out my two treasured items, a photo album filled with the happy moments captured prior to my parents passing away and my favourite book The Great Gatsby that I never returned to the local library; and put them in by backpack together with the other essentials. Roxie had her own photo album filled with pictures of us growing up, so she grabbed it from her nightstand and packed it away in her own matching backpack.

When we were finally packed and ready to go, we descended the stairs and stood in the middle of the living room admiring the small but cozy house that we have called home for so long. I pulled out the letter that I drafted for Alison from my pant pocket and strolled over to the kitchen table to place it on the counter. Roxie sauntered over to join me, picked up the letter and kissed it with her red stained lips leaving a print of a perfectly formed goodbye kiss. Then she shifted her gaze at me, and her sorrowful eyes were filled with pain and doubt. I grabbed her hand tightly for support and guided her towards the door.

Ray was already waiting for us outside leaning against the crimson surface of his car, he rushed over to grab our duffle bag and backpacks and put them in the trunk together with his own bag. Roxie and I dawdled over to the car, our fingers still interlaced in a tight clasp, then we stopped and glanced at the house one last time. Ray honked waking us from our entranced stupor, and without any further delays we turned around and climbed inside the vehicle as Ray had already started the engine.

"New York City, here we come!" I screamed as I got comfortable in my seat, turned my head back and looked at my sister. Roxie nodded smiling back at me, but there was a lonely tear running down her right cheek.

Chapter Four

*June 2006*
*Age 21*

    The room was cold, frigid cold, so cold that I could barely move my feet.
    I stared at my toes in a daze as my feet were settled on the arm rest of the couch where I was lying down, trying to recall the last time I painted my toenails. It could not have been recent since the nauseating red nail polish was chipping away and the pale nails below the audacious nail polish have already grown out. In fact, when I finally forced myself to move my gaze away from the toes and observed my surroundings, I could not even remember how I came to be in this concrete walled room.
    The greyness of the interior around me was hampered by a blurry haze and continued swirling in a constant motion so much that it was making me slightly queasy, resulting in a pulsating ache through my temples. I tilted my abnormally heavy head to the right and saw a filthy glass coffee table within my reach that was filled with cigarette buds, a half empty vodka bottle and powdered substance remnants next to a lone laser blade.
    This was not an unusual sight, as over the last three years there have been a lot of alcohol and drug infused meetings and parties that Ray took Roxie and I to in order to expand our reach. So, I was not surprised by the contents scattered about on the table, what alarmed me is how awful and numb I felt. It was also troubling that I could hardly remember anything that happened to me since I left our loft in Brooklyn this morning and came to a photo shoot in an abandoned looking building in the Bronx with one of Ray's new clients.
    "So, what is this photoshoot for today, babe?" I asked Ray, as I

stood in the kitchen making us a fresh pot of coffee in the morning before leaving the apartment. He was sitting on the couch rolling his usual morning joint and watching the sports highlights from the day before.

"It's a glamour shoot for a new internet website that is being launched next month. They are looking for someone who is adventurous, fearless and sexy as hell. You couldn't be more perfect!" He responded, while lighting up his morning fix.

"By glamour, do you mean nudity again?"

I asked cautiously, as I placed the coffee grains in the filter and turned on the machine.

Ray slowly got up from the couch and silently ambled into the open kitchen space, he hugged me from behind with one arm and offered a puff of his joint with the other. I reached for the rolled cigarette and inhaled deeply, waiting for the relaxing bliss to hit my body.

"You know that times are hard, and the competition is high. There is nothing wrong with nudity, you are so unbelievably sexy. You should not hide this rocking body and you must share it with the world."

He whispered in my ear, as his left hand travelled towards my bare breasts underneath my shirt.

I hesitated to continue but thought that if I approached the subject carefully, then he would understand.

"But I thought you said that it was the last time when Roxie and I did a shoot last week in the warehouse on the other side of Brooklyn, with that guy with greasy frost tip hair. I really do not want to do it anymore, babe. Rox and I can just find a job at a coffee shop or something. We can wait on tables, or work at an office, while we look for proper gigs."

Then I felt his body stiffen up against my back, his left hand jerked from underneath my loose top and grabbed my right shoulder tightly as he twisted my body around to face him. I closed my eyes, afraid to see his angry grimace that I have now come to see so often. His right hand that still clutched the lit-up joint flew to my chin and squeezed it hard and I shut my eyes closed, waiting for what was to come next.

"Look at me, you ungrateful bitch! Look at me when I'm talking to you." I did not dare to resist, because I knew the consequences. So, I reluctantly opened my eyes and met his frightening stare, as his eyes turned jet black and his face reddened in anger. "I do everything for you and your bloody sister. I spend days looking for jobs for you, so we can survive in this city. Do you think that you are so irresistible that every photographer and magazine on the planet wants to shoot you? Ha!" Ray laughed maniacally.

He then grabbed both of my shoulders and shuddered me violently with all his vigor, as if trying to shake some sense into me.

"You are nothing! If I tell you to go to a photoshoot and take your clothes off, then you do it. No questions asked. I put so much money and effort into supporting you two. It'll take you both your lifetimes combined to pay me off."

He then paused his screams as he saw tears collect in my eyes. This gave me hope for reprieve, that he still had some empathy and would stop with the forceful shaking. Instead, he seemed to smirk as if admiring my crying for a moment, then gripped my shoulders even harder and lifted me off the ground and flung me across the room.

"Stop it!"

I heard Roxie's voice as my head landed on something hard, that turned out to be the wooden TV stand. She instantly rushed over to me, to help me up.

"Do you want some of this too?"

Ray started towards her, then stopped catching himself from going any further.

"Ungrateful bitches! Clean yourself up, N. You have to be at the shoot in an hour."

Then he looked at Roxie and the black eye he gave her a few days earlier, when she came back later than he expected from the grocery store.

"We could have made double the cash today if you behaved, now I can't get you in front of a camera until next week."

He growled angrily at Roxie, then took a puff from the joint that he managed to maintain in his hand and climbed out of the window onto the fire escape, where he liked to sit and enjoy the view of the busy street.

Roxie cradled me in her arms as I continued crying, blaming myself for what happened, I knew better than to bring this up again. Ray has done a lot for us; he spent hours meeting new clients and introduced us to a multitude of industry people, so we grow our portfolio. So, what if we only managed to book nude shots up to that point, some of them were quite tasteful, while some were plain disturbing but those were the ones that paid the most amount of money. It was not like Ray was holding us hostage against our wills; we were free to leave. Unfortunately, there was nowhere we could go.

This was our home now; we were no longer welcome at Georgetown in the middle of nowhere away from this big and hostile City. When we first called Alison a month after we settled in New York, she yelled at us for five minutes straight and then cried for another ten minutes. From her sobbing and irate screaming, we understood that someone robbed Fat Joe the same day we left, and even thought he refused to believe that it was us, the police issued a warrant for our arrest. We were the only ones who had access to the money in the registrar that day, other than Fat Joe himself. This was a shocking revelation, and we tried to explain to Alison that we were innocent and that we did not take any money, but she said that because we left unannounced, it made us look guilty to the police and they were refusing to consider any other suspects. When we hung up the phone, Roxie and I gaped at each other in disbelief.

"Could it be Ray? Remember, we left him at the cash register for a minute when you went to speak to Fat Joe, and I went to clean up the kitchen?" Roxie wondered.

"Of course not! Ray is doing so much for us. He's borrowing money to make sure we succeed, he couldn't have." I responded with certainty.

From the conversation with Alison, we understood that there would be no way for us to ever return home, unless we wanted to be arrested. No one would care if we were innocent, no matter what we said, we had no evidence to contradict their assumptions. Our only option was to make a life for ourselves here in the City.

New York did not welcome us with open arms, and according to Ray he had to get in serious debt for us to be able to afford the life there, as we had to rent an apartment in Brooklyn and pay the expensive photographers for our modeling portfolios. He told us that the people in the fashion industry are ridiculously greedy, and everything costs so much, that we would have to work for years to be able to pay off all the debts that he had incurred.

Ray was hardly ever at home in the evening, leaving Roxie and I alone to watch television or read books, always locking us in the apartment for our own safety due to the many robberies in the area. He was always out late at night at restaurants and clubs making connections with the photographers to get us the new gigs, he bought bespoke suits to look good in front of the prospective clients at the many meetings that he had to attend, and then there were the drugs. Seemed like no deal ever happened without the drugs, no photoshoot ever took place without the photographer making you take something to take the edge off in front of the cameras.

At first, it all started with some laughs and rolled joints, then stronger narcotics were being offered to us, where we graciously refused, but Ray did not appreciate our disobedience of the requests. That was when I first noticed the change, where he started converting from the friendly and adoring boyfriend to a controlling manager. He told us that if we wanted to make it big, then we had to listen and obey everything that was being asked of us. I tried to object and resist, saying that we did not have to accept that kind treatment, but that was the first time he punched me in the ribs, and then looked at Roxie and asked if she had any objections to his simple request. Thankfully, Roxie is a quick learner and did not say anything, instead she helped me up to my feet and sat me down on the couch.

Almost three years later, here I was laying down on the strange sofa with a throbbing headache and chills all over my body. I lifted myself up to sit, wincing from the pain of an earlier head wound resulting from my head landing on the TV stand, realizing that all I had on was a silk robe with nothing underneath. Comprehending that I must have blacked out after another alcohol and cocaine infused photoshoot, I quivered and got up in search of something warmer to wear.

Spotting my green wrap dress on the chair in the corner of the room, I sluggishly walked over to it trying to stay steady on my feet and got dressed. My underwear was nowhere in sight, while I peered around the drab frigid room. I sighed in disappointment as it was my favourite pair from Victoria Secret that I bought myself for Christmas last year when Ray gave me and Roxie fifty dollars each to spend on anything we wanted. Noticing my brown leather purse and polka dot flats under the chair, I grabbed them and walked out of the room through a dark hallway towards the lit-up Exit sign.

As I opened the exit metal door, I was instantly hit with the wafts of the New York summer and warm air that comforted my chilled body. I stepped out onto the road, my bare feet hitting the hot pavement, prompting me to put on my shoes that I still had in my hand. I looked around the street to get my bearings and noticed the subway sign in the distance, I wavered contemplating whether I should enjoy the brisk walk for a few blocks since the weather was incredibly comforting. But then I realized that Ray must be waiting at the apartment and would not want me to be late, so I headed west towards the entrance into the underground and got on the train heading home.

As I got off the long subway ride from the other side of town, I decided to do myself a small favour and walk slowly for the two blocks to the apartment to enjoy the sun rays on my face and observe the happy faces of the people around me. While New Yorkers are generally very busy people running from one corner of the city to another with their endless errands, Brooklyn seemed more relaxed, filled with the younger and more free-thinking crowd. Joyous people of all ages were strolling in the park with their friends and cups of java in their hands, some folks got comfortable on the park benches captivated by their borrowed library books, others played on the lawn with their dogs making them chase a ball or a frisbee.

*If Ray goes off for a meeting today, maybe Roxie and I can sit on the fire escape and enjoy the weather.* I thought, admiring the joy of a summer day and being a bit envious of the people in the park, who seemed to have no care in the world.

As I sorrowfully turned the corner, I found myself at the entrance to the block of our apartments. While taking out the keys out of my purse and opening the building front door, I was lost in thought of going out for a nice long walk with Roxie, something we have not yet been able to do without Ray by our side. She loved being outside in the summer, she often recalled all the summer picnics and hikes we used to take back home. When we were carefree and oblivious of our futures, we hardly spent any time at the house in the warmer months, between working at Fat Joe's and the endless summer nights we always kept ourselves busy.

Thinking of those happy days, I walked up two flights of stairs and opened the door to our apartment. It was dead quiet inside, so I thought that maybe Ray was in a better mood now and he could have taken Roxie out for the day, knowing how much she loved the warm weather. Smiling and thinking that Ray was a nice guy after all, I started towards the bedroom to lay down and relax for a bit, reflecting on how great and thoughtful Ray really was and forgetting all about the earlier violent outburst. I walked past the kitchen towards the bedroom to get changed into something more comfortable and maybe take a quick nap before they got back.

As I opened the heavy bedroom door, I was at first confused at the troubling sight in front of me. There were two naked bodies intertwined on my bed, both painfully recognizable to me. One figure long and muscular and the other gentle and fragile, they were asleep in an embrace as if the larger framed body were protecting his prized possession. I stumbled backwards tripping over an empty syringe on the floor, that I did not notice on the way into the bedroom. The noise from my fumble seemed to stir Roxie in her sleep, but she did not wake up and remained in Ray's embrace.

Gasping for air and refusing to believe my own eyes, I remained motionless leaning against the door frame unable to move or look away from the painful image in front of me. The only two people that I relied on, my tiny and sometimes troubled family, the two loves of my life had betrayed me. As much as Ray was aggressive towards us, I still loved him deeply, he was everything to me. He supported us through the turmoil of surviving in New York, he guided us in pursuit of success in the modeling world, he was my first love. Now there he was sleeping with my own sister, I could not have imagined this even in my worst nightmare. Roxie always hated Ray, and she had never expressed any interest in him, and I trusted her wholly.

*That snake!*

I thought in anger, as I came out of my frozen stupor.

I clenched my jaw to contain my scream and forced my wobbly legs to exit the bedroom. The anger blinded me, and I could barely see anything in front of me as I hobbled towards the kitchen with my hand grazing the wall to keep me from falling. When I approached the safety of the kitchen island, I sat down on one of the metal highchairs and tried to clear my throbbing head. I sat perched up, lost in my feelings of abandonment and defenselessness, when the memories of me laying in the hospital bed so many years ago when I found out that my family had perished came rushing through my mind. That fateful day was the last time I felt equally alone. Alison was there to help me through the pain and comforted me, however this time there was no one to hold my hand, I was to survive this on my own. The slight haze from the earlier drug high was wearing off, but the adrenaline from the betrayal that was just witnessed started to pump through my veins.

*I can do this. I do not need any of this.* I reasoned with myself. *I do not need anyone.*

I swiftly got up from the kitchen stool and did a quick scan of the living room, then saw a duffle bag that Ray must have abandoned on the sofa when he came in earlier as he was lusting to rush and get into Roxie's pants.

I shook the disturbing image from my head to clear my mind, then walked over to the duffle bag to grab it. Knowing that I could not possibly go back into my own room, I concluded that I could find everything I needed in my sister's room. Then I walked over to Roxie's bedroom that was maintained so tidy compared to Ray and my room, we always made fun of her perfectionism when it came to her personal quarters. She always snapped back at us saying that she was finally glad to have her own room that she could keep just the way she wanted it, without me throwing my dirty clothes all over the floor.

The neatness and the organization of Roxie's closet helped me out this time, as I rummaged through her clothes and grabbed my favourite pieces then stuffed the duffle bag with the finds. I made sure to keep the noise level to the minimum, because the last thing I needed was to wake up the "love birds". I changed into a vintage Rolling Stones t-shirt that Roxie loved so much and put on a pair of her newly purchased VS panties, and then a pair of denim shorts that I was sure she borrowed from me and never returned. Then continued throwing in the rudimentary items into the depths of the duffle bag.

As the bag got full with Roxie's belongings, I lifted it to make sure I could carry it and then flung it over my shoulder. It was relatively heavy, but it was nothing compared to the boxes filled with motor oil, that I had to lift at Fat Joe's. Satisfied with my swift packing and determined to carry out my quick escape, I charged down the hallway towards the front door and left the apartment without giving it a second look. I was ready to leave this life behind, the life of resentment filled with anger and drugs.

With every step out of the apartment building, my fortitude grew more fierce. My head felt clearer because I finally believed that I knew what I wanted, my feet walked sturdier as the drug effects completely wore off, but the burning anger within me remained the lone driving force. All I knew at that point in time was that I had to distance myself away from that dreaded apartment and the people I have shared my life with up to this point.

There was no destination in mind, while I walked down the dirty pavement away from the building. The surroundings did not seem as carefree and fun-loving as they did only recently, when I was carelessly walking home from the photoshoot less than thirty minutes earlier. People were still out and about strolling in the park, families picnicking and throwing frisbees to each other enjoying their summer afternoon, but all the laughter and happiness seemed to stab me painfully in my thumping broken heart.

To get away from the jovial mood of the Brooklyn community, that I habitually appreciated from atop the fire escape, I turned towards the darkened entrance into the subway and boarded the next train that pulled into the station. Without a clear direction or destination, there was no rush for me to go anywhere. So, I got comfortable in the stained train seat and hugged the duffle bag for safety to make sure no one snatched it from my grasp, and for comfort because it felt soothing to embrace something even if it was an inanimate object. Squandered in the whirlwind of my emotions and the exhaustion of the events of the day, I quickly surrendered to the drowsy slumber with my head resting comfortably against my bulging bag.

A sudden jerk movement woke me up from the deep oblivion, quickly realizing that someone was trying to pull my bag out of my grasp causing me to clutch onto it harder in reflex. I saw a dirty hand with pale yellow nails in front of my eyes on the bag handle pulling on it, to free it from my clutches, so I opened my mouth wide and bit into the flesh with all my might. Above my head I heard a loud scream undoubtedly caused by the pain I had just induced, and the dirty hand loosening its grip. I swiftly got up from my seat to face the unsuccessful thief, realizing that there was no one else on the train but me and the culprit. The attacker was a man about the same age as me, dressed in an emerald green Adidas tracksuit and a baseball hat covering most of his long hair. He manically looked at me with his dilated pupils, considering whether to avenge his incurred pain. Grasping my duffle bag, I slowly walked backwards towards the subway doors as the train started pulling into the next station. The lights of the station lit up the assailant's face and I focused on his eyes, recognizing the familiar redness on the whites of the eyes and the enlarged pupils. He was undeniably high on crack or cocaine. Over the last few years I have grown accustomed to being able to recognize the effects of certain drugs.

As the train braked to stop, the man struggled to maintain his balance on his feet and fell backwards. The subway doors opened wide and without a moment to think, I jumped out of the train and ran up the stairs to the safety of the nocturnal New York streets without looking back. After running for a few blocks through the darkness and quickly running out of breath, I slowed down and turned to see if anyone was chasing me.

I was relieved to not see anyone behind me and took a moment to gloat at my quick thinking. Reassured that I could make it on my own and could defend myself, I looked around the street to figure out where I was. Only seeing the brownstones and a few storefronts on both sides of the street, without any specific landmark in sight, I was lost. I continued to walk in the direction that I was previously running in, and after a few blocks ended up on the banks of the East River. Observing a few destitute homeless people settling for the night as I walked down the street and along the river, I realized that I would have to find a place to sleep as well, and it would most likely have to be on a park bench along the embankment.

After a while, as my feet got tired and the bag started to feel heavier, I found an empty bench in a beautiful park that I had never visited previously. The bench was hidden from plain view as it was cloaked with the luscious greenery of the park and facing an enclosed enclave surrounding a miniature fountain. Unable to fully understand my surroundings in the dark, and only having the moonlight lighting the path, I walked over to the bench and sat down.

*This would do nicely today*, I thought. I resisted any negative thoughts that tried to overflow my senses, there was no place for fear or loneliness anymore. If I were to survive on the streets, I had to be vigilant and not get lost in the thoughts of regret. As the adrenaline of the day started to wear off, I started to get the chills and reached for the bag to look for something warmer to wear. Unable to see in the dark, I stuck my hand down in the depths of the bag and felt around to locate the fleece lined hoodie that I threw in there earlier. As I blindly searched around the bag, my hand stumbled onto some solid brick-shaped cartons beneath the clothes. Puzzled by my find and knowing that I had not packed anything of that size, I pulled one of the containers out of the bag. It felt solid to the touch, as if vacuum sealed to protect the contents.

*Must be something Ray left behind.* I realized.

Then a happy thought rushed through my head.

*Could it be money?*

I hastily ripped up the carton, and my fingers felt the plastic underneath the wrapping. I punctured a hole through the plastic with my long pointy nail and stuck my finger inside hoping to feel the smoothness of the dollar bills. Instead, my finger sunk into the powdered substance, and I instantly knew what this was. I pulled out my finger and tasted the powder that collected on the tip of my nail.

*Cocaine*, I recognized the bitterness of the salt granules.

Then I put my hand back in the duffle bag to see how many of these parcels were hidden beneath all of Roxie's clothes and counted four solid packages. I sat stunned uncertain what to do next, the last thing I needed was to get caught by the police carrying drugs and get arrested. I seriously contemplated inhaling some of the salts, knowing that the rush would make me forget all my problems, at least for the night. It was so tempting to detach myself from reality, to welcome the comfort of the euphoria as it took over my body just as it has done so many times before.

The deliberation and reluctance seemed to stir in my head for hours, until I swiftly forced myself to get up on my feet, grabbed the packages from the depths of the duffle bag and ran over to the riverbank behind the park. Without any further hesitation, I threw the packages over the railing into the dark waters of the East River. Then I rushed to get back to my bench where I carelessly left all my belongings, which fortunately remained vacant, and sat back down proud of my difficult decision.

*New life, new me*, I thought to myself, smiling as I thought of Ray's torment from waking up and finding the precious drugs missing.

I still felt the frigid chill of the night, so I reached back into the bag to find the hoodie and sweatpants which I put on immediately to warm up. Then I lay on top of my duffle bag to soften the firmness of the wooden slats of the bench, and stared into the clear night skies, admiring the stars flickering above.

*No more fear, no more drugs, no more provocative pictures, no more abuse.*

I kept repeating my new mantra, as I slowly succumbed to the unwelcomed sleep on my first night of many in the warm summer obscurity on the streets of New York.

## Chapter Five

*December 2014*
*Age 29*

  The feeling of loneliness had engulfed me and had beseechingly pumped through my body with every breath, it had completely possessed me to the point that I was unable to access any other emotion. I walked through the murky darkness, unable to see in front of me, only aware of the surrounding desolation as I continued my empty search. The sense of despair started to overshadow the isolation, as I picked up the pace and started running further into the depths of the gloom. Whilst I was running, I felt a scream forming within me, slowly finding its way upwards from the pit of my stomach to my trembling lips. Just as I was about to release a shrilling scream, I woke up.

  I promptly opened my eyes, still in the grasps of the emotions that had just contained me in my deep sleep and looked at the alarm clock beside my bed. The digital clock illuminated 5:30am on its display, just as it did every morning when I tersely woke up in cold sweat. Waking up before the set alarm had become an everyday recurrence, every morning a reiteration of the last, awoken from the disturbing dream that had now been haunting me for years. Regardless, every night while I got ready for bed, I made sure that my clock was set for 6:30am wake up time, in hopes that one day I will be able to fall asleep and wake up blissfully to the sound of the alarm.

  After reading a variety of articles on how to achieve the best restful sleep, I have developed a practiced routine that effortlessly put me to sleep but I eventually found myself consistently waking up at dawn distressed from the disturbing nightmare. Every night I would make myself a hot cup of chamomile tea, which I delightfully sipped on while reading a newly borrowed library book for about an hour or until a first yawn. Then as I brushed my teeth and washed my face, I would think of all the positive encounters that happened to me over the course of the day. There were always several negative thoughts that I refused to dwell on late at night, and typically wrote them down in my battered notebook earlier in the evening in case I felt like revisiting them the next day. Then as I lay in bed getting comfortable for another night's sleep, instead of counting sheep, I tallied up the positive thoughts of the day until I finally fell asleep.

Recounting the most impactful gratitude list of my life was also a helpful method for me every morning, when I struggled to regain my composure after waking up from the feeling of despair, which remained with me for the early part of the morning until I was able to shift my focus to reality. This morning was no different, as I sat up and propped two pillows behind my back against the wall to get comfortable in a seated position. Trying to calm my breathing which was still rapid, I shifted my focus to my surroundings and started welcoming the positive thoughts to start tallying my favourite facets of my current existence.

*My apartment.*

I started to count as I raised my index finger and looked around the four walls around me. Most would think that this apartment was farcical, with its miniature size where you could almost reach every wall without getting up from the bed and a minuscule nook by the entrance that served as a kitchen and dining area.

To me, this was my own little paradise, I loved everything about this space. The exposed brick on the walls gave it a rustic and concurrently a modern feel, and I had set up a few picture frames and bookshelves against the brick when I first moved in to make it feel more like home. The small but functional kitchen was perfect for cooking for one with its built-in electric cooktop with two burners and an over-the-counter microwave, I also invested in a toaster oven that I found on Craigslist a few years earlier but had to store in the back of the closet since there was not enough counter space. The main highlight of the apartment was that it had its own proper shower with its own stall, not just a shower head over a toilet that I had encountered a few times during my apartment search.

After months of rummaging around New York looking for my own place, I had almost given up on the notion of living on my own and started to consider a dark two-bedroom basement apartment that I had to share with three other ladies, who I suspected were street walkers. It was an absolute shock that I could afford this apartment all by myself, and I was so thankful that Enid gave me the lead on it when she told me that one of her friends was looking for a clean and reliable tenant to move in immediately and above all the available unit was within my budget. This apartment was an absolute dream, that I had conjured in my head when I slept on the streets almost nine years ago. As the memory of those cold and dark nights started creeping into my consciousness, I had to pause and expel the negative memory, so I could continue with my positive morning notions.

*Enid.*

I counted my second blessing and raised another finger. Even though my first memory of Enid had some negative connotations because it reminded me of the darker days, the unfortunate events of the day when I met her was what led me to become who I was today.

I recalled the faintly warm Fall day when I was sitting on what I had at that point started to feel was my own park bench, the same bench that I had found on the fateful day when I first became homeless. Every day I would roam around the city looking for food and a job, most times without any success, and then would wander back to the small but picturesque park by the East River and settle in the treed enclave on the bench hidden from sight of the passing by strangers on their late afternoon strolls.

The day Enid came into my life, I recalled it being an especially rewarding day because I managed to get my hands on a full meal. When I was walking along the path towards the bench, I spotted a couple of teenagers perched on a pew overlooking the river with a greasy take-out bag between them. Just as I was about to pass them, I heard them arguing loudly and then the scrawny looking girl stormed away followed by her equally angry boyfriend. In their anger, they left the grease-stained paper bag behind untouched, so I snatched the coveted treasure before anyone else got their hands on it and ran to my bench with my duffle bag rocking behind my back while I picked up the pace.

When I finally reached the safety of my shelter, I looked behind me to make sure that no one else had their sights on my find and lustfully opened the bag to reveal the sizzling smells of the freshly grilled meat and steamy fried potatoes. Without further hesitation, I reached for one of the burgers, ripped off the foil cover and bit into the hot juicy concoction.

Entranced in the deliciousness of my meal as I savoured every little bite of my burger, I noticed an elderly lady approach a bench positioned on the other side of the out of order fountain in the treed enclave. She sat down and reached into her vintage leather purse to retrieve a timeworn book with white crinkles on its creased spine. When she held it in her frail veined hands, I noticed the title The Great Gatsby written on the cover. I had not read a lot of books in my lifetime up to that point, but I read The Great Gatsby at least ten times and that eternally borrowed library book was one of the few items that I took from home when we were rashly packing to leave Georgetown but regretfully left behind in the dreaded loft apartment in Brooklyn when I was fleeing in a haste, along with my cherished photo album.

The elderly lady looked up at me through her black framed glasses sensing an incessant stare from my direction and saw my captivated glare at her book, then genuinely smiled and asked:

"Have you read this book, dear?"

I nodded while continuing to chew on another bite, unable to speak as my mouth was filled with the delicious mixture of charred meat, sesame bun and tangy garlic mayonnaise. I gestured to my mouth with my right hand, hoping she understood that I wanted to elaborate but needed a moment to process my food. The elderly lady acknowledged my predicament by nodding back and grinned revealing a lovely kind smile adorned by the two dimples and a series of crow's feet wrinkles etched in the corners of her eyes.

I laughed back shyly, swallowing my food, and finally responded.

"So, we beat on, boats against the current, borne back ceaselessly into the past". I recited one of my favourite quotes from Scott. F. Fitzgerald novel.

The elderly lady looked at me with delicate surprise and nodded her white bouffant styled head.

"The last line of the book."

"Indeed" I replied quickly.

"Do you know what that reference means?" She was eager to continue the dialogue.

"I never actually thought about it." I replied between bites feeling my hunger finally satisfied.

"Is it about having to row harder if you want to move forward?"

"That is one way of seeing it, but I think you will get the other meaning of it with time. Age brings wrinkles and wisdom, usually more of the first than the latter."

The elderly stranger laughed at her own joke.

"Now let me guess, the beautiful Daisy is your favourite character?"

She looked curiously at me. I shook my head in defiant

disagreement and responded.

"No way, she is a spoiled immature brat who doesn't know what she wants and is not willing to do anything to improve her life. I prefer Myrtle, she understands that she is trapped in her marriage, but she at least tries her hardest to flee the poverty around her. She is determined and she refuses to accept her circumstances, she is just unlucky that's all."

The elderly lady gazed at me with an analyzing look in her eyes as if finally realizing that she had been speaking to a destitute vagabond. From my rugged appearance and dirty hair, that I have only been able to wash in the public washrooms sink last week, it was easy to guess that I was not a casual park goer. She looked at the duffle bag beside me, one of my hands securely looped through the handles preventing anyone from snatching it from me.

"Pardon my directness, child, but is this where you sleep?" The elderly woman inquired, her hand gesturing to my abode.

I silently nodded, expecting her to get up with disgust and walk away just like any other New Yorker whom I have encountered over the last few months. Instead, the kind stranger got up from her seat and rather than head out of the enclave, she ambled slowly towards me and lowered her feeble frame next to me. With her face only an arms length away from, I observed her tender facial features in detail, her pale blue eyes beneath the spectacles projected kindness and eased my high alert self-preservation mode. The pale white skin lacked any visible pigmentation but showed obvious signs of her elderly age with a multitude of crease lines on her vibrant face that evidenced her inclination for prolonged laughing or smiling.

"You can't sleep on the bench much longer; it is only going to get colder."

She continued the conversation, resounding my biggest fear that I had yet to resolve. I tried to find a warmer place to sleep for a month up to that point, but all the heated or covered spaces had long been occupied by the other destitute wanderers who were unwilling to share their quarters. The homeless shelters in the City were at their capacity and if you wanted to secure a spot, you needed to line up before sunrise, but you could be subject to a violent fight that often broke out among the people who were desperate to get into a warm bed. Fully aware that I would never win in a fight with the more experienced drifters, I succumbed to the attempt to survive the cold nights on my treasured bench.

The inquisitive lady immediately spotted the anguish in my eyes, and without any further reluctance continued.

"Why don't you come with me, I know a perfect place that could use someone like you and there would be a warm place for you to sleep."

Noticing my anxiety changing to fear, as I had previously heard of many horror stories of what happened to young girls on the streets of New York, she laughed with sincere and exuberant undertones.

"Don't be afraid, you can walk beside me and if you feel at all uncomfortable then you can come back here to your bench. I'm Enid by the way." She stretched out her small, fragile hand to me.

I reluctantly extended my hand in response and shook hers, noting the frailty of her palm.

"Noelle."

I responded still considering her proposition and then after some hesitation, I figured that I could always run away or knock her over if she tried anything with me.

Following my new mature friend through the streets of Manhattan's East Side was the best decision I could have made, as Enid had with time become my guardian angel and a cherished mentor over the years.

Thinking back to that momentous day, was a great positive boost to my mood stabilizing morning routine. I returned to my gratification count and raised a third finger for the next blessing.

*My job.*

Doing what you love can hardly be considered a job, but if you get paid for it then so be it.

Meeting Enid so long ago when I had no prospects and no place to live, I remembered how I first ended up at the Green Light Women's shelter. As I followed Enid along the bustling streets of the Upper East Side, she briefly explained that about twenty years prior after the unfortunate passing of her husband, she had started a refuge for women with children fleeing an abusive household. Through the years, she was able to welcome hundreds of women with their children and provide them with the support that they needed to be able to enter the world without fear and aid them to develop a clear path for their futures. Enid was troubled by one concern, as she was getting older it was getting harder for her to find the funding to continue her commitment and the aging property needed a lot of maintenance, so she needed someone to support her in her endeavour. We walked for eight blocks away from the park towards a nondescript brownstone that resembled every other house on that block.

Enid asked me to stay at the bottom of the stairs, as she walked up to the door and pulled out a heavy set of keys that she used to open a multitude of locks, then let herself inside. I stood outside for about a quarter of an hour, scrutinizing the house before me that required some maintenance on the chipped stairs and the aging roof, unlike the other upkept neighboring homes of the street. The shelter's exterior was in a much lesser state of grandiose than the adjacent dwellings, not from the size as it was comparable to all the other homes but from the hostile appearance. There were no flowers by the entrance in the sills or flowerpots, all the windows seemed to be covered by blackout blinds restricting anyone from looking in through the glass, there seemed to be countless locks on the front door. This strange home sent chills down my spine, as all my inner senses were telling me to run for safety, away from this peculiar and unfriendly-looking building.

Then just as I was about to start walking away, I saw the door half open and a little girl of no more than two years old looking through the gap. She stared right at me and then playfully stuck her tongue out, to which I reasonably retaliated with the same gesture. The little girl laughed aloud and then I saw Enid appear behind her and lift her up into her embrace, then she waved me over. The fear of the unknown seemed to seep away at the sight of the happy grimacing child and Enid's kind-hearted smile, so I walked up the porch steps and through the entrance door. As I walked into the lit-up hallway, I got a whiff of freshly baked cookies and then heard several children's voices from the back of the house.

"Welcome to Green Light, Noelle." Enid said, as she put down the little girl in her arms back on her feet. "I forgot to lock the door, and this little one almost escaped. My memory is just not as it used to be, which is why I need the help."

Enid walked further into the house down the dark hardwood floor lined hallway, and as I followed her, I observed the interior carefully with an ounce of suspicion still lurking within. We walked past a spacious living room where I spotted three women watching television, while two of them were cradling newborn babies in their embrace. Then two young boys bumped into us as they hastily ran past playing tag in the hallways, they quickly apologized but did not stop as they were too caught up in their game. Enid led me into a large sunny kitchen which was much brighter than the rest of the house, with its blinds not closed shut and open to the view of the neatly landscaped private yard adorned with green plants and various flowers. In the kitchen there were two ladies preparing food, they were busy chatting away and laughing as Enid and I walked in interrupting their jovial conversation.

"Ladies, this is Noelle. She will be staying here with us and help me run things around at this juncture."

The women at first looked concerned by the appearance of a raggedly dressed stranger in their sanctuary, but quickly realized that Enid would not let any harm inside the home and walked over to hug me to welcome me. Aware of the pungent smell that my body was producing from a month of unhygienic life on the streets, I quickly apologized and stepped backwards. The ladies took no offense and beamed in understanding.

"Oh, where are my manners!" Enid exclaimed. "Let me show you where you would be staying. You can take a shower and get yourself all cleaned up."

She walked me out of the kitchen and down the stairs into the basement, past a series of closed doors until she stopped at the end of the corridor and opened the last door to a dim room.

"We don't use this as a room for the women and children as it's a bit too tight and can only barely fit one person. I mainly use it for storage, but there is a nice comfortable fold out couch in there that you can sleep on, if you are alright with that."

She turned on the light switch and I saw a heap of packed boxes stacked up on top of each other.

"We can ask one of the ladies to come and help you move the boxes, if you like."

Then possibly becoming more aware of the street aroma protruding from my body in the contained space, she gestured down the corridor and motioned in the direction of the washroom. Reaching inside one of the stacked boxes, she pulled out a clean bath towel and handed it to me. I thanked her for her kindness, barely able to contain my tears as this was the first time in a very long while since someone showed me any compassion. I excused myself and walked in the direction of the washroom, where I undressed and stepped into a meticulously cleaned shower stall. As the hot water washed the dirt and grease off my exhausted body, I finally let the tears run free. I felt the tightness around my muscles release as the defenses that I have erected to protect myself on the street started to lift.

After an extensively long shower, I dried myself off and noticed a folded bathrobe on the shelf that Enid must have left for me, when I was lost in the bliss of the running hot water. Dressed in the bathrobe, I exited the washroom and saw the boxes that had previously been stored in the room, placed outside in the corridor by the two women that I met upstairs. I rushed over to help them, but they had already managed to empty out the entire room while Enid was pulling out the clean sheets and bedding from one of the boxes and set them on top of the sofa that had been converted into a bed for me.

Once I was left alone in the room to get settled, I scarcely laid out the sheets without much effort of tucking in the corners and fell asleep immediately, wallowing in the comfort of the springs and cushion under my tormented body.

Since that day, I had not left the Green Light for longer than I had to and only did so to meet with the governing bodies to request funding support, to seek out new donors or volunteers to help us upkeep and fix the ageing house and establish connections with other shelters in the City. But mostly, I was inside the home greeting the new guests and acting as their initial emotional support until they were ready to meet with the qualified therapists, unscrambling years' worth of crumbled invoices and bills to establish a more concise journal to balance the books and organizing the donated toys and clothes in a structured pattern instead of just haphazardly stacking up boxes in the basement rooms. Over time, Enid and I were able to free up four more rooms from the clutter in the basement to accommodate the new arrivals.

Nine years later, and I was still looking forward to going to work every day. It was a hard decision to move out on my own, as I liked living at the sanctuary, but we needed to repurpose the basement room where I was staying to a much-needed office space. Also at Enid's insistence, she convinced me that I needed to distance myself from Green Light even for a few hours, seeing how my twenty-four-hour commitment of living and working within the same space limited my independence. I reluctantly agreed, not ready to part with the comfort of my reality but understood that I could not hide from the outside world forever.

The thoughts of my rewarding job, my guardian angel Enid and my beautiful apartment brightened up the morning, as I had finished recounting my short by cherished gratitude list. My mood finally lifted, and my thoughts were firmly planted to have another successful day, so I reached for my notebook that I had placed on the night table the night before with my carefully drafted To Do list for the day. I perused it, working on a plan of action and the busy schedule for the day. I had to visit a few of the sponsors to finalize the plans for the annual Christmas party that we had been organizing at the sanctuary and this year seemed to have attracted more donors than usual, so I had to make a few visits around the city.

Christmas at the shelter was always a special time that made all our guests forget about their torments and troubles. While the women gathered in the evening to wrap up the donated presents hiding from the curious children's eyes, Enid and I kept the little ones preoccupied reading the traditional Christmas stories, making our own decorations and singing everyone's favourite carols. It was always such joy decorating the house with the children, their tiny faces lit up at the sight of the colourful ornaments that they carefully placed on the beautiful tall evergreen tree that was donated by one of our former guests.

Determined to make this Christmas party another success, I finally made myself get up and get ready with a clear schedule forming in my mind. I would start the morning by making the first stop at Green Light to pick up some paperwork, and then proceed on my way to visit the charitable donors.

Less than twenty minutes later, I was ready for the day and admired my reflection in the full-size mirror that was left behind by a prior tenant. All the running around the city doing errands and working on the house has kept me in shape, without a need for an overpriced gym membership. My only grey wool pants suit fit me like a glove, Enid gave it to me for my birthday six years prior saying she needed me to wear more appropriate clothes to meetings with corporations, if we stood any chance of getting financial support in the future. She was right as per usual, because once I started wearing the business suit instead of my jeans and hoodie to meetings, the response rate has tripled and so have the contributions. After slicking down my hair that stuck out of the pinned bun, I quickly grabbed the keys and headed out of the door into the chilly morning.

That day was especially cold, and I remembered the extreme weather alert that was projected for the next couple of days, so as I exited the building I sunk in deeper into the winter parka with my face mostly covered by the faux fur collar and an oversized knitted hat, leaving just enough of a sliver to see in front of me. Unwilling to get frost bitten painstakingly waiting for a cab this early in the morning, I picked up the pace and trekked through the snow towards the women's shelter that was a mere six blocks away. As I trudged through the snowbanks that have not yet been ploughed, I admired the light snowflakes floating around me as if in a rehearsed waltz, twirling, rising, falling and revolving. Winter was my favourite time of the year, as I basked in the beauty of the stark white snow, the uniqueness of each snowflake, the crisp sweetness of the air.

The Upper East Side in the winter early mornings appeared uninhabited, almost deserted until the heavy snow ploughs made its way through the streets preparing the city for its usual heavy traffic. I enjoyed the early morning time, being on my own, lost in my own thoughts, reflecting about my life, and allowing only then to wallow in the heavy burden still buried deep inside. Other times I was too preoccupied with work, not allowing myself even a minute to think about the past and whom I left behind.

The snowfall suddenly started to accelerate and transitioned into a blizzard, with snowflakes whirling in a blinding pattern barring me from seeing much around me as I finally approached the Green Light home. Typically, there was no one outside waiting to get in because we were not a well-known shelter and only accepted new guests through references of the state-wide charities. However, this morning I spotted a lone dark figure pacing in one spot trying to stay warm while protectively holding her arms around her waist. The blizzard kept me from seeing whether this was one of the guests, but I was able to discern that the stranger was an expectant mother based on her shape and protective cradling of the barely noticeable bump. I also saw that she was not appropriately dressed for the season with a light trench coat and only a hood covering her head. Knowing that Enid would not have heard the strangers' knocking this early in the morning to let them in, I approached the figure and was relieved to see that they at least had a scarf covering their face from the freezing cold. Snow flaked her long eyelashes and the trench coat seemed to appear damp, I yelled out to the figure through the boisterous wind lashing our bodies.

"Give me a minute, let me open the door and we will get you right in."

I started slogging through the snowed-in steps in the direction of the entrance. I reached into the coat pocket pulling out the set of keys, it was a challenge unlocking the many locks with the bulky gloves on, so I briskly took them off and as I proceeded to unlock the door, I felt my fingers turn numb from the below zero temperature outside. Once I succeeded in opening the door, I turned around and waved the woman standing at the bottom of the steps over to follow me inside the house.

"Please be careful and watch your step, just place your feet in my footprints and hold on to the railing."

I said loud, hoping that she would be able to hear me. The shivering woman responded immediately and hustled up the stairs promptly to escape the clutches of the nippy weather and into the relief of the warmth of the house. As she timidly entered the home, I was rubbing my hands together to regain the feelings back in my fingertips so I could finally take the layers of clothing that have been wrapped around me. The female then reached to lower her hood to reveal beautiful jet-black curls wildly streaming down her shoulders, I loudly gasped recognizing the luscious locks. She took off her scarf revealing the all-familiar delicate features that have remained etched in my not-too-distant memories.

"Rox?"

I whispered, unable to move not only from the weight of all my clothes but also from the shock that has stunned every muscle in my body. Roxie furrowed her eyebrows in her typical adorable way which signified that she was seriously contemplating the circumstance that she had been facing, as she observed my heavily layered misshapen frame from top to bottom refusing to believe the logical reasoning in her head. But then without any further scrutiny, she quickly extended her right arm and yanked off the oversized colourful knit hat that Enid handcrafted for me a few winters ago, and dropped it on the floor as it revealed my flabbergasted face, then she stumbled backwards leaning against the front door.

"Noelle!" She cried.

Her wide honey brown eyes filled with burning tears, as her long black eyelashes tried to bat them away, but the salty droplets started rolling down her hollow cheeks. Roxie's body began convulsing in uncontrollable sobs, and I no longer saw the grown-up woman in front of me whom I have missed immensely, but a defenseless little girl unable to contain her emotions from the unfairness of the world around her. I snapped out of my rigidness and lunged over to comfort her snivelling, just as I did when we were in first grade and one of the older kids pushed her over in the hallway and she fell and bruised her knee, or when we were ten years old and a boy, she liked in our grade told her he thought her curly black hair was too nappy. Her uncontrollable crying brought back all the childhood memories that I have been trying to suppress for so many years. All the times I rushed to defend Roxie from the offenders, when I chased the older boys and kicked them in their shins after they pushed my sister down and when I spilled my tomato juice box all over her crush's head when he told her that he did not like her luscious locks. No one was allowed to hurt my sister, not then and no one was allowed to hurt her still.

As if the last nine years of separation never happened, I swept Roxie in a tight embrace, feeling her delicate body trembling from the sobbing. Unable to contain my own emotions, I felt stinging tears streaming down my face, the first tears since that fateful day so many years ago. It was like a trigger has been released, allowing my emotions to be set free, inhibited for almost a decade in the pit of my stomach waiting for the eventual extrication. There we stood leaning against the wooden door in the hallway of my sanctuary that brought me peace, when I was at my most vulnerable state, and now it reunited me with my Roxie.

The anger of the betrayal that I had for her dissipated many years prior, and I longed to see her. I remembered my helplessness when I staked out our old apartment to get a glimpse of Roxie and hid behind a lamppost to avoid Ray from seeing me, only to be told by one of the former neighbours that they moved out soon after I left. I had been searching for her for years through the variety of social media outlets, phone books, and seeking out her face through the crowds of the busy streets of the City. My regular calls with Alison steered away from the topic of Roxie, as she had not been in touch with her mother for years. Unwilling to cause any heartache and feeling responsible for losing Roxie, I attempted to keep the conversations casual and upbeat, but the calls always ended with Alison saying, "I miss you, both of you", and me responding "Me too".

But here she was, in my arms, I hugged her tighter to make sure that she was real.

"Noelle, everything alright?" I heard Enid's voice behind me.

Unable to fully separate from the embrace and still crying, I turned my head to see Enid's concerned face lit up by the hallway lights standing at the end of the wide corridor still dressed in her long nightgown. I nodded in response to indicate that I was fine and then said aloud, still unable to believe my own words.

"This is Roxie, I found Roxie."

Enid raised her blue veined hands to her face as her mouth gaped open in disbelief, she had known all about Roxie and Ray and every other bit of information about my life. She was the one person I trusted and confided everything to since the first day we met. Enid encouraged me to talk about my emotions and never be afraid to show them, "otherwise they'll eat you alive" she always liked to say. While I had no problem talking to her about my life, I resisted showing how I felt, and she had never seen me shed a single tear. Enid understood the significance of the moment, she knew how much this meant to me, even though I had never told her how much I missed Roxie in my life. I never even admitted it to myself, but Enid always saw through people around her, which was one of her many great qualities.

"Oh dear! Why don't both of you come in and get away from that drafty door. Come in! I'll make us all a nice pot of coffee."

Enid looked on, admiring our tight embrace and shuffled towards the kitchen, where I heard her open cupboards and take out the mugs.

I finally separated from the hug, slowed down the sobbing and stepped back to examine Roxie, while I took off my parka and other warm layers of clothing. Roxie's face and graceful frame remained unchanged, but there was a big bump protruding through her coat that I first noticed when I walked on the street towards Green Light. Roxie saw my surprise as I stared at her pregnant belly and chuckled through her tears.

"Yes, dear sister, you are going to be an aunt."

She was finally able to speak, while cradling her big belly in her arms. I helped her out of her drenched trench coat and felt her shivering from the cold, so I took off the extra cardigan that I had on top of my wool suit and put it over her shoulders.

"Let's get you warmed up, hun. Enid makes a mean cup of coffee." Then I paused, reminding myself that Roxie was expecting. "Or maybe just a chamomile tea for you?"

"That would be nice, very nice."

Roxie smiled and nodded as we walked hand in hand in the direction of the kitchen where Enid was already prepared to greet us. She walked over to Roxie and gave her a hug, a tight and motherly hug that only Enid knew how to give.

"Welcome to Green Light, Roxie." Enid said as she separated from the embrace and went over to pour three cups of coffee.

"Just two coffees and one chamomile tea." I jumped to help Enid with the preparations. Enid continuously refused the help with minor day to day activities, but as she was getting older it was getting harder for her to move around the kitchen. Enid sighed ready to object to me meddling in her pouring the coffee, but I continued.

"Roxie is pregnant, look."

"Indeed, she is, I felt that when I hugged her." Enid exclaimed . "How far along are you, dear?"

"About six months, I believe." Roxie beamed in response, unable to take her eyes off me, still in shock.

Enid grabbed the cup of coffee I poured for her and wisely understood that we needed to be alone to catch up for all the missed years, so she excused herself blaming her departure on a non-existent headache and retreated into her bedroom on the ground floor. I silently thanked her as I threw her my sly smile when she exited the room, then I grabbed the remaining steamy mugs from the countertop and walked towards the large kitchen table by the window. Roxie followed me and sat behind the table with her hands wrapped around the hot mug filled with comforting herbal tea to warm up. I sat next to her at the head of the table so I could look at her and be able to touch her, still staring at my sister in disbelief.

"I can't believe it's you…I don't even know where to start." I fumbled to start the conversation. "I've been looking everywhere for you."

"It has not been easy. I'm so sorry, N, you can't imagine how sorry I am for what happened."

Roxie grabbed my hand and squeezed it tight, I squeezed it back recalling the jolt of heart pain that I experienced so many years ago but have since long forgotten.

"It doesn't matter now." I tried to respond, but she shook her head in defiance.

"It does and I need to explain myself now, before you disappear from my life again. I have been thinking of what I would say to you when I finally saw you again, so you have to let me speak."

For the next two hours Roxie talked about her life and I listened intently, oblivious to the house guests coming and going from the kitchen as they understood to not idle and give us privacy. I was unable to control my tears as she walked me through what had happened in the last nine years, since I had left her and Ray in the apartment in Brooklyn.

When Roxie woke up from her deep sleep that day, she was dazed and confused, unable to comprehend why she was naked in bed in the middle of the day and then realized that Ray was in bed with her with just a sheet covering his stark nudity. She sat up in bed trying to recall the events of the earlier morning and was only able to remember Ray coming home after dropping me off at a photoshoot. Then she noticed an empty syringe discarded by the bedroom door and painfully remembered Ray forcing her to inject herself with heroin at knife point and then injecting himself, followed by everything around her starting to spin out of control and then finding herself waking up many hours later naked in bed with my boyfriend in our bed. Rushing to get up, refusing to believe that anything had happened between them, she ran into her bedroom and noticed all her clothes scattered around the floor and most of them missing. Still confused and her head throbbing from the effects of the drugs, she got dressed in what was left of her clothes and walked over to the living room in a haze to sit on the couch to wait for me to come back so she could tell me right away what had occurred. Roxie waited for hours motionless until it got dark, with the foggy haze finally wearing off, she started to realize that I had probably come home earlier and saw her in bed with Ray and then stormed off. Refusing to believe that I left for good, and that I would be back any minute, my sister remained on the couch waiting all night.

The next morning, Ray finally woke up to find Roxie sleeping on the couch and shook her shoulder to wake her up. He asked her where I was, but since my sister did not know she just shook her head in response, which provoked Ray to get viciously mad and slap her across her face. She ended up falling off the couch, but that only seemed to provoke him further because he walked over and started to fervently kick her on the floor, demanding to tell him where I was. Exhausting himself with his incessant kicks, he finally stormed out of the apartment screaming that he would find me and drag me back by my hair and then there would be hell to pay. He locked the door behind him, threatening that if she left the apartment, he would find her and kill her. Roxie was unable to move as her whole body was seized in agony from the abuse that she had endured, she was barely able to raise herself to crawl up on the couch and waited there in fear of Ray's return. He came back angrier than ever before later in the day, yelling and screaming, punching the walls and throwing everything that was loose around the apartment. Then he ran over to Roxie to undoubtedly throw a few more punches but noticed the blood on her face from the split lip and a black bruise under her left eye, so he spit on her and kicked the couch instead, then ran in the bedroom and slammed the door shut behind him. Roxie remained on the couch suffering the consequences of the painful blows, unable to get up to drink or eat.

Thus started a series of abuse, as Ray grew angrier and more aggressive every day. He moved them out to Harlem to a much smaller apartment where he could lock Roxie up and not release her for days. The photoshoots that Roxie and I were booked for before transitioned to explicit video pornography, where Roxie was forced to have sex with strangers filmed in rank basement studios. Her younger appearance was in demand and the loathsome directors liked to dress her up in school and cheerleader uniforms, as the film partners forced their way with her, while Ray ensured that she had enough drugs to subdue her defiance. Blaming me for all his financial debt, Ray forced Roxie to have sex or money and he took her to strangers' apartments throughout New York boroughs. She first tried to seek help from one of the clients, but all he did was complain to Ray and that resulted in a few cracked ribs later in the day, when the enraged Ray taught her the lesson of necessary discretion with his fists.

Sometimes Ray disappeared for weeks, locking Roxie in the apartment with barely enough food to survive but the weeks of solitude were a blessing compared to all the other days of abuse. It was during one of those weeks when she realized that she was pregnant, so she decided to keep it a secret from Ray for as long as she could. He could not possibly hurt the baby when he or she would be born, and maybe this would change him because this was undoubtedly his child. Ray made sure she used protection with all the other clients by supplying her with a variety of condoms, but when he periodically forced himself on her he never used any prophylactics.

It took a while for Ray to realize the extent of Roxie's condition, because she only started showing a larger bump in her sixth month of pregnancy, prior to that he was telling her to eat less because she was starting to look heavy. He did not take the news well and punched her in the face before storming out of the apartment. As Roxie recovered from the shock of a punch and rejection of the baby, she realized that she did not hear the click of the lock when Ray left so she walked up to the door and turned the knob enabling her to open it.

Terrified of missing out on the opportunity of escaping and in full survival mode, Roxie grabbed the first coat she spotted and ran out of the apartment. She ran for hours distancing herself further away from Harlem until she saw a Salvation Army sign outside a busy building and ran inside for safety. The experienced staff at the shelter were able to see through Roxie's distress and asked the visiting doctor to assess her immediately, who said that she and the baby appeared to show signs of good health but that she needed further tests and ultrasounds. Unfortunately, the Salvation Army were able to accommodate her for only one night but referred her to the Green Light Women and Children's Sanctuary that they knew had some availability. So, the next morning she woke up when it was still dark in her narrow bunk bed, unable to sleep as she relived the events of the previous day and hastily left the crowded residence in the direction of the Green Light shelter.

Roxie's traumatizing story crushed me as I felt completely at fault abandoning her in the grasps of the monster whom I regretfully brought into our lives. The jabbing pain of guilt for all that had happened to my sister was overwhelming, I knew that it would take me several lifetimes to make up for what I had done. Roxie refused to accept my self-blame, indicating that I could not have foreseen what was going to happen and instead condemned herself for driving me away. That was Roxie, always thinking of others, even in the darkest of moments.

We spent hours apologizing to each other and retelling our stories, crying and laughing, making up for years of separation and contained emotions. Then in the mid-afternoon, Enid approached us in the kitchen to ask if Roxie wanted to follow her to see the available room, but I quickly refused the proposal, insisting that Roxie would be staying with me in the apartment and that my bed was big enough for the two of us. Enid reluctantly agreed but asserted that Roxie must come to the sanctuary during the day with me so she could meet with the therapist and spend time with the other women in the sanctuary. After years of working at Green Light, I understood the benefits of abused women living in the sanctuary for all the help and support that was provided to them to aid them in their recovery, so I agreed with Enid's logic and affirmed that Roxie would come with me every morning. Excited at the fact that my sister would be living with me like when we were children, I declared the day as my official day off, and called to reschedule my appointments. Then holding on to my sister's hand, we slowly walked back to my apartment through the brightly lit streets, once the blizzard subsided.

After a full day of catching up and surprising the stunned Alison with Roxie's voice on the phone, we were both exhausted getting into my bed to sleep. Roxie fell asleep immediately, while I stared at her in disbelief realizing that I now had four blessings in my life and my life felt complete.

## Chapter Six

*Christmas Day 2014 – a week later*
*Age 30*

  The escalating beeping sound from the alarm kept increasing in volume until I finally emerged from a bright vivid dream. I reached for the off button on the alarm, reluctant to open my eyes relishing in the bliss of waking up restful unlike the many nights in prior years where I woke up abruptly in cold sweat before dawn. For the last six nights I have been able to sleep through the night without a hint of a nightmare, no longer running aimlessly, chasing the unattainable in the oblivion that consequently consistently ceased in a silent scream before an abrupt end of the night and a startling beginning of every morning. The sound of the alarm was a welcomed break, which I have come to cherish as a sign of another gratifying day full of life and complete with people I appreciated the most.
  "Happy Birthday, N."
  I heard a sluggish mumble from the right side of the bed, as Roxie woke up from her sleep. It was still a shock beyond comprehension to me every morning that my sister was here with me, just within my reach, not a ghostly figure in my nightmares or a face that I saw everywhere but nowhere in the sea of strangers on the busy streets of New York. She was right there, safe with me. The feeling of undeniable guilt would forever reside within me, for all the years that I had abandoned her in the worst possible circumstances. When I took Roxie home a week earlier, I vowed that for as long as we were alive, she would forever be safe with me by my side.
  "Happy Birthday, Rox!"
  I exclaimed being more awake and alert at that point than her. Then I quickly jumped out of the bed and walked over to the vintage dresser,

slid open the lower shelf and reached deep inside until my fingers touched the rustling smooth surface of a box that I had wrapped the day before.

"I know we said no gifts this year, but I just had to get this for you. Just don't get mad and trust me that all the necessary precautions were considered to get this gift and no laws had been broken."

Roxie looked alarmed at the festively decorated package that I handed to her, while I struggled to hide my giddy excitement. She ripped the wrapping to reveal a yellowing hardcover of her own most prized possession that had aged significantly over time and gone through a lot of tribulations.

"My photo album! But how did you get this? I left it at the apartment in Harlem. You didn't go back there, did you?"

Her sleepy face turned instantly to unbridled anxiety and her breathing became more rapid.

I had anticipated her reaction, having seen her through her many panic attacks in the recent days due to any thoughts or memories of Ray. The visiting therapist at the sanctuary had been coaching Roxie on how to overcome her panicked state and being a diligent patient, she has been following every instruction, so she learned how to collect herself and take a deep breath to relax. Noticing her instinctive response, I quickly reached for her and enveloped her in a tight embrace, feeling her body beginning to tremble.

"Shhh, don't worry, honey." I cradled and rocked her svelte upper body in my arms. "The police officers who we talked to when we filed the report against Ray, took me to the apartment. They let me take all your personal belongings. They still can't locate Ray anywhere, but they are working very hard on finding him and said that they would be able to trace him through his phone or his credit cards."

Roxie's subtle body tremors subsided, as she followed the therapists' direction and was able to breath through her anxiety. She pulled back from the tight embrace, and grabbed her cherished photo album, opening the cover and leafing through every page.

"Thank you, Rox. This is wonderful, all my memories, our memories right here."

She paused for a second, furrowing her eyebrows and her fingers searching for something in her album.

"I never told you, but when you left and Ray completely lost it, he ran into your room and started ripping up your clothes with his bare hands and everything you left behind. I knew what I had to do then, so I grabbed your photo album from the living room console where you kept it. I knew how much you loved looking through all the pictures of when you were a little girl with your parents, so I pulled out most of the pictures from the album just in time before Ray ransacked the living room collecting all your belongings. He then stormed outside towards the garbage bins and threw everything you owned in there."

At that point, her face smoothed out just as her concentrated look had alleviated, because her fingers finally found what they had been searching through the album and I noticed that a few of the photograph slots seemed thicker than the others. Then she pulled out the pictures hidden beneath the front facing photos and passed them to me.

"I hid these in my album, he wouldn't have ever found them in here. I knew I'd find you one day, and you would want these back."

My right hand as if on its own lifted to take the pictures from Roxie, my body rigid in anticipation of viewing the photographs. When I grabbed them and pulled them into my view, I gasped at the almost forgotten images of the happier times with my parents. I did not think that I had forgotten what they looked like but certain facial expressions had started to fade from memory, like how my mother wrinkled her nose when she laughed or how my dad always looked awkward when he was caught off guard in pictures. The way the two of them looked happily at each other as I sat atop my father's shoulders beaming from the thrill of the earlier teacup ride in the park. Time stood still as I flipped through the pictures, the cheerful memories from my happy childhood days flooded me.

"I'm sorry I didn't get you anything, N." I heard Roxie say and looked up at her while she leafed through her own pictures.

"This is the best present you could have gotten me. Thank you so much!"

Then my eyes shifted to the alarm clock on the bedside table, and I jumped to my feet.

"No time to waste, Rox. We have to be at Green Light in forty minutes to start preparing for the Christmas party. What a crazy day we have today, good thing we stayed there until late last night hanging up the decorations. Dibs on the shower first."

I ran in the direction of the bathroom, as Roxie remained on the bed silently flipping through the pages of her photo album, lost in the vortex of euphoric memories.

When I came out of the shower, Roxie was already dressed and ready to go reminding me that she showered the day before knowing that we would most likely be running late in the morning. Praising her logical reasoning and deduction methods, I quickly got dressed in a pair of jeans and a festive Christmas sweater.

"Do you have another Christmas sweater in your closet I could borrow?" My sister asked shyly, as she observed her reflection in the mirror dissatisfied with the appropriateness of her favourite Rolling Stones t-shirt that she reclaimed from my closet a week ago.

"Sure do!" I pulled out two bulky pullovers from my dresser.

"Would you like this vintage Rudolph inspired cardigan or this piece adorned with every colour imaginable hand crafted by the talented Enid?" I laughed displaying the available options.

"Well, as much as I love vintage and being a loyal Rudolph fan for many years, I would still have to choose the one-of-a-kind Enid couture."

She snatched the colourful bundle from my hands and pulled the bright knitwear over her head. Then she twirled around in front of the mirror, satisfied with the result and turned to me showcasing her outfit for approval.

I happily nodded endorsing her choice, then rushed her to put on the snow boots and the duffle coat. We swiftly put on the extra winter layers to keep us warm during our walk and headed out of the door. During our twenty-minute walk to Green Light, we talked excitedly about the Christmas party and all the surprises we had planned for the children. All the sponsors pulled through and we had an excess of donated gifts, so Rox and I spent the last couple of days delivering gifts to the other shelters in the area that accommodated children. It was such a rewarding experience to spread the joy beyond the walls of our own sanctuary. We felt like Santa's elves when we entered the other homes with bags full of wrapped toys to put under the trees. The children at other homes hid behind their mothers or caretakers backs as we strolled in proclaiming that Santa asked us to drop some presents off for "some children who have been very good this year", but they had to wait until Christmas morning before they could open them. The excited whispering followed by uncontained screams of excitement flooded the homes, as we came and went propagating the Christmas spirit.

After spreading the joy in other locations throughout the week, we were finally ready to prepare for the festivities at our own sanctuary. While we knew how thrilled the children would be, we were just as excited organizing and preparing the house for the celebrations. The day before, we spent hours making slightly burnt gingerbread cookies and decorating the gingerbread houses with the children in preparation for the competition for the best crafted house to be hosted the next day. Then we worked late in the night with the mothers as the children went to sleep, to wrap up all the remaining gifts and stuff the many stockings hanging by the inoperable but beautiful fireplace in the sitting room.

Undoubtedly the children had already been awake as we rushed to get to Green Light, so we would have missed their surprised faces at all the additional decorations Roxie, and I put up around the house. We would also unfortunately miss them opening all the gifts, but we knew that when we decided to sleep in after a busy night, that Christmas after all was a family affair so as long as their mothers were with them, the children did not need us in the very least. We continued walking past all the beautifully decorated streets adorned with the lit-up garlands, each home illuminated by the festive lights from within the homes, a wreath hung on almost every door in our path.

When we eventually approached Green Light, we were disheartened by the exterior appearance of the home because the shelter rules did not allow for exterior decorations, so as not to attract attention and remain discreet to the public eye. Every year I pleaded with Enid to be able to put some lights on the outside, but she remained stern in her position. The house will only remain a haven for those fleeing abuse, if no one knew of the home. Any attention drawn to the house was absolutely forbidden, but I could do whatever I wanted within the walls of the shelter.

This year Roxie approached Enid on the same subject, even though I had already advised her of the stringent guidelines, but when my sister returned from her conversation, she was gleefully grinning and announced.

"We are allowed to put up a wreath on the door!"

I gawked at Roxie in disbelief. "How did you manage that?"

"Well, after hearing Enid's very reasonable arguments, I just said that not having any Christmas decorations outside makes the house stand out even more and we would not want that."

So, when we observed the house from the outside on our approach, we were slightly disappointed that it was not more festive to reflect our spirits, however we rejoiced at the sight of the small pine wreath ornamented with a red ribbon and gold sprayed pinecones that we made with the children the week prior. We walked up the steps and I unlocked the door with my own set of keys, not wanting to disturb anyone inside from their hectic morning. When we entered the hallway, we were immediately struck with the sound of carols blaring through the television in the living room and excited yelps from the kids as they exclaimed at every opened gift.

"A fire truck! Just like the one we saw on the street the other day, mommy"

"A furby, I've wanted this all year! How did Santa know??"

We walked towards the loud shrilling voices to view the happy commotion in the room. The room was a complete mess with scattered wrapping paper everywhere, children playing with their new toys on every inch of the floor. The kids' laughter was intertwined with the Lalaloopsy dolls singing and adorable Furbies dancing to their tunes, as the older boys vroomed past with their toy trucks and miniature Lamborghinis zooming around the rooms in every direction.

"Merry Christmas, everyone!"

Roxie and I alerted the joyful residents of our presence. The children did not seem to take notice, being too entranced in their games, unaware of their surroundings. The mothers relaxing on the sofas interrupted their blithe chattering to get up and hug us to wish us a happy Christmas. Some of them had their new shawls wrapped around their shoulders, while others sported the new fuzzy slippers that were donated by a local retailer who was an annual supporter of our Christmas events. We all congratulated each other on the festive day, and they thanked us for the beautiful presents, they hadn't expected to receive anything as Roxie, and I kept this in secret and wrapped up the gifts for adults when everyone went to sleep the night before.

I looked around the room and noticed that Enid was not there.

"Where is Enid?"

"She was just here, maybe she went to lie down for a minute." Answered one of the ladies. "These kids can get a little tiring and she was the first one up this morning making some last-minute preparations."

Worried about Enid and her health, I quickly turned around to walk towards her room to check in on her and I saw her genial face right behind me.

"Don't you worry about me, I just needed to get something from my room." She defiantly responded as she noticed my concerned look. Then she glanced at Roxie and grinned in appreciation, as she noticed the sweater that my sister was wearing.

"That's some of my finest work right there. It fits you beautifully, dear."

Enid then pulled out two loosely wrapped packages from behind her back and handed each of them to me and Roxie.

"These are for you, girls. They should fit you both nicely!"

Having collected a vast assortment of Enid's ingenious crafts over the years, I ripped open my gift to find a pair of mismatched wool socks with one sock adorned with festive decorations along the sides and the other sock with an image of a birthday cake on the front and a candle in a shape of number 30 on the cuff of the sock.

"Very original, Enid. You've never made me mismatched socks before." I applauded her for her efforts.

"They're not mismatched, dearest. Roxie, why don't you open your gift?" She turned to my sister.

Roxie carefully unwrapped her gift to find the same Christmas and Birthday themed socks.

"They're matched, as long as you wear them together, you see." Answered Enid in her soft spoken voice. Roxie and I both threw ourselves to hug Enid, thanking her for such a lovely and considerate present vowing to wear them every Christmas/Birthday for years to come.

Separating from the embrace, I walked towards the kitchen to make myself my usual cup of coffee but noticed that the coffee machine was taken apart and laying in pieces on the kitchen counter. I walked back into the hallway, where Roxie and Enid were chatting away and laughing as they looked at the children playing with their toys.

"What happened with the coffee machine?" I awkwardly interrupted their enthralling conversation.

"Ah yes, it broke this morning after I made coffee for everyone. The good news is that one of the donated gifts is a brand-new coffee maker that I cannot wait for us to use. The bad news, my dear, is that it is one of those machines that may take some time to set up. The box is over there in the corner if you want to give it a go."

Enid gestured at the state-of-the-art coffee machine that was waiting for its debut in our kitchen.

"The conundrum is that I need coffee to think straight and be able to read any of those instructions. Not to worry, I will just run down to the coffee shop down the street and grab myself a large cup to wake me up. Rox, want to come with me?" I concluded.

"If you don't mind, I'd like to stay here and start cleaning up the room from all the wrapping paper. I assume the kettle still works, so I can make myself some tea."

She looked me directly in the eyes reassuringly, aware how I was hesitant at leaving her side since she came back in my life. Knowing that she would be safe at Green Light with a house full of people, I started getting ready asking if anyone wanted anything from the coffee shop. Since everyone already got their morning coffee fix, there were no takers, so I headed outside towards a coffee shop that was a few blocks away.

While I walked in the direction of the coffee shop, my mind shifted from the thoughts of Christmas to the fact that it was inevitably, also my thirtieth birthday. The thought of hitting a new stage in my life was slightly alarming, as I was no longer considered a lighthearted twenty something year old and have entered a brand-new unfamiliar territory of being a respectable age of thirty. With this new age come new responsibilities of starting to think like an adult, and I would have to one of these days start charting out my life for the future and stop living in my comfortable bubble of immaturity. The comforting thought of turning thirty was that I could finally close the disastrous chapter of my twenties with all of its disappointment, betrayal and abscond. Today was the beginning of a new decade that I was determined to turn into an absolute success, and there was no doubt in my mind that I had all the tools to make this happen. There was nothing holding me back, I had the support and love that I needed in my life, and I was no longer pulled back into the past in search of what was lost.

Unbeknownst of how long I walked captivated by my own internal dialogue, I found myself outside the local coffee shop. What I always loved about New York was that everything you need was always available within a couple of blocks. Regardless of holidays or weather conditions you would certainly be able to get your favourite cup of coffee or find a Chinese takeout place at any time of the day.

Glancing around the coffee shop I found it to be scarcely busy, with a few customers sitting at their laptops behind the tables, one couple enjoying their hot chocolates warming up from the cold and a tall man in a dark wool coat in front of me placing an order. While I stood in line to make an order, I was thinking of what the first steps in my new amazing life should be, whether it would be going to college or finding a job that allowed me enough time to volunteer at Green Light.

The young barista behind the counter interrupted my thoughts, as the man ahead of me finished placing his order and shifted to the end of the counter to wait for his beverage. I quickly made an order for a hazel macchiato as a special treat for the momentous occasion, instead of my usual black coffee. Then I reached into my coat pocket to rummage for the change to pay and felt a smooth rustle of a cash note that I was positive was not there earlier in the morning, then pulled out the surprising find to reveal a twenty-dollar bill. *Enid*, I realized the source of this find and handed the note to the cashier, then collected the change before dumping it back in the coat pocket.

*Maybe my first step in my new life should be a wallet.*

I thought to myself, remembering how Enid always scolded me for being so careless with money. This would also prevent me from alerting everyone when I walked, as the change loudly jiggled in my pocket with every step until I got home to dispose of it in the jar. Deep in thought of what type of wallet I should look for and figuring out when Roxie and I should go to Goodwill in search of this integral purchase, I heard my name being called by the barista and a paper cup placed on top of the counter.

Slightly surprised at how fast that took, seeing that my order was a bit more complicated than just the usual black coffee, I extended my grasp to take the cup. Just as I was reaching to grab it, I saw another hand zoom in front of my eyes to beat me to it. Confused but unable to stop my continuous motion, I automatically put my hand on top of the much larger hand that was already holding my coffee and felt a jolt of a static shock pierce my hand. I immediately jerked my hand back as the interloper hand also jolted from the shock and knocked over the cup.

"Well, this is an interesting development."

I heard a deep voice behind me and turned around furiously to face the hand owner who deprived me of my morning treat. Expecting a typical New Yorker arrogance and prepared for a shouting match, my eyes instead met a smiling face of a tall handsome stranger. His expressions portrayed no aggressive notions about the spilled coffee or the fact that I "shocked' him from the winter charge stored in my body, he was almost laughing at the situation in front of him. Unable to transition my anger to any other emotion on the spot, I stood in front of him enthralled by his blue eyes that matched my own. At last, I awkwardly smiled, and inspected my clothes to ensure that there was no harm from the spilled coffee and felt grateful for not spotting any stains on the outfit.

"I'm sorry that I shocked you, but you grabbed my coffee, and my brain is still half asleep to be able to control my extremities." I kept my gaze directly on his piercing eyes.

"Your coffee? I think you are deeply mistaken, miss. The nice lady behind the counter called my name."

He picked up the cup from the floor, as I stared at his neatly cut dark hair sway with his graceful motion, then he grinned even wider and turned the cup towards me.

"See it's even written on the sleeve of the cup.".

"Noel" I read aloud and returned my eyes fixated on the blue gaze. "Your name is Noel?"

"Would you like to see my ID?" He started to laugh, finding the situation more and more comical and as if to keep up the charade he immediately pulled out his driver's license from his pants pocket.

"See, Noel Fitzgerald, the one and only."

To humour him, I grabbed his ID from his hand as if to inspect it further and read the other details, one of the details startled me and I handed back the card to Noel.

"It's your birthday today!" I exclaimed, shocked by the double coincidence of our names and birthdates matching.

"I know, Christmas and Birthday all on the same day. A travesty when I was growing up because I never had a proper birthday party and always received one gift. I don't mind it so much these days, people are too fixated on celebrating Christmas that they forget it is my birthday and I can quietly escape the celebrations and spend the day alone at a coffee shop with a coffee and a book." He mused along easing my rigidness and wiping away my shyness. "That was my plan for today too, but some wildly attractive stranger decided to steal my coffee and as if to solidify her wickedness also sent an electric jolt through me."

The barista behind the counter placed another cup on the counter and said "Noelle", with a heavier emphasis on the last letters to clarify that this was my cup, then exasperated left her station to grab a mop to wipe the floor from the spilled mess. Realizing that the whole incident was my fault, I hurriedly grabbed my cup ready for the quick escape.

"I'm so sorry for the confusion, here is $5 so you could buy yourself another coffee. Completely my fault."

I handed the crinkled bill to "Blue Eyes", as I had already named him in my head.

"Your name is Noelle? That is quite a coincidence. Your birthday wouldn't by chance be one of these days?" He continued the conversation, ignoring the bill in my hand.

I nodded in response. "As a matter of fact, yes, today."

The barista returned with the mop and a bucket and asked us to shift somewhere else, so she could clean up the mess. As she dipped the mop in the murky water in the bucket, I was about to turn around and make my exit, but Blue Eyes walked to a table by the window and pulled the chair out, holding it, waiting for me to sit down. I hesitated for a moment knowing that I had to return to Green Light, but then reasoned that five minutes of conversation with a stranger in a public place would not hurt. Enid always said that I needed to make more friends and socialize with new people, that a pretty girl like me should not spend her days and nights hiding at work or at home.

*This is a new decade for me after all*, I thought, shrugging my shoulders yielding to Noel's proposal as I walked over and sat in the chair that he had then gently jostled from behind. He then walked to the other side of the table, took off his wool coat and hung it on the back on the chair before settling in his seat, which gave me an opportunity to admire his broad shoulders protruding through the navy jersey and the trim body frame that could imply that he could be athletic.

"I owe you a coffee." I quickly said, as soon as he sat down.

"Nonsense, I'll order one as soon as the lady is done with tidying up."

He glanced at the irritated barista, as she swiveled the mop back and forth.

"I'm very sorry for what happened. I was sure that I heard Noelle when she called your name. I mean they sound almost identical." I rambled on.

Noel laughed, shaking his head.

"Did you know that I have known you for a total of maybe five minutes and you have already managed to apologize at least three times? Are you always this remorseful or are you trying something new today?".

"Well, as a matter of fact, I am trying something new. Since I am entering a new decade in my life, I have decided to change things up." I responded enthusiastically, and then continued

"But the need for constant apologies seems to be the baggage I have carried over from the prior decade."

"A new decade? So, you must be turning thirty today? I would not have guessed it."

His blue eyes focused on my face, taking in every crevice of my features. Then as if mumbling to himself he quoted

"Thirty - the promise of a decade of loneliness, a thinning list of single men to know..."

"A thinning brief-case of enthusiasm, thinning hair." I instinctively continued the quote from the Great Gatsby, surprised that Noel was able to quote my favourite author.

His ocean blue eyes widened in astonishment, and he leaned back against his chair, taking me in from a different perspective. At that moment, a cup of coffee was placed on the table by the barista, who apologized for seeming a bit irritated earlier, all because her boss made her work on Christmas day, but she overheard that it was our birthdays today and this coffee was on the house. Noel charmed her by saying that she did not seem irritated at all and that he completely understood that working over Christmas was an unjust move on her boss's behalf, but she was doing an amazing job and he would commend her amazing skills on Yelp. There was not a single sign of irritation when the barista left our table, as she smiled widely feeling understood and appreciated.

"You really have a way with people." I praised him for his people skills, while I sipped on my hazelnut macchiato.

This was one field of improvement that I had to include in my list for the new decade. While I considered myself as a people person earlier in life, I have almost turned into a hermit hiding at Green Light and only leaving it to go to meetings or to go back to my apartment.

"Comes with the job. I am a lawyer and must work with a wide variety of people, and I'd say I spend the majority of my time being a therapist to my clients. What do you do? Actually, no, let me guess."

He straightened up in his seat and scanned me with his intense eyes trained at reading people at court. I giggled as he pondered in silence, while I continued to savour every sip of my delicious hot beverage.

"You're not from the corporate world, that's for sure. You are too real, no falseness about you. You're not in the media or the fashion world, although you could be if you wanted to, but you don't seem to be a fan of make-up or fake eyelashes.... or designer clothes."

Noel paused to raise his eyebrow at my festive Christmas sweater, before he continued.

"I would have initially thought that you're an artist or a museum worker because there is a certain calmness about you, but you don't have that wondering look in your eyes that I usually spot in people from the art world. You're definitely not a stay-at-home mother, because you are sane, and you haven't mentioned a child or shown me pictures of the kids like any other obsessed mother would." He paused for a minute, still trying to assess me looking intrigued. "You are a mystery, an enigma."

"I could be a serial killer." I chuckled in response.

"That was another possibility, but a serial killer would never offer that as an option in a conversation themselves, so there goes that."

His loud sincere laughter took me by surprise but infected me as I erupted in my high-pitched laugh. At that point I realized that I have not laughed like that for a while with another person, completely relaxed and genuine mirth. It felt so good to laugh, my body convulsing from the jolts of happiness, my head clear from any thoughts that usually haunted me. As the laughter subsided, all the heaviness of the responsibilities weighing me down seemed to assuage and I reluctantly glanced at the clock hanging up on the wall.

"This was great, Noel, but I'd have to stay an enigma as I return to my mystery world. It was so nice to meet you." I slowly got up from my chair, ready to leave to face the real world.

"You can't leave me just like that, Noelle. Why don't you give me your number?" He grabbed his phone prepared to punch in the digits.

I shook my head in rejection.

"I know it's hard to believe, but I actually don't have a cell phone. Only a work phone, but I'm not allowed personal calls there".

This was completely true, as I never had a need for a cell phone before, there was always a phone at Green Light if I needed to contact the sponsors or contact any government agencies.

"You know, I actually believe you, it brings more colour to the Noelle riddle. How about you meet me here tomorrow morning, same time, and I can learn more about you? Maybe I'll solve your mystery before tomorrow morning and will surprise you when we meet?"

He stared me deep in the eyes, with a pleading look which was hard to resist.

"Alright, tomorrow. Same time!" I gave in to his joyous response as he raised his arms in victory. "I will see you tomorrow morning, Noel."

"Can't wait to learn more about you, Noelle. And happy birthday, by the way."

He cheered me with his raised cup of coffee. I responded by tapping his cup with my half-full macchiato and wished him a happy birthday as I rushed out of the coffee shop.

While I strode back to Green Light, picking up the pace to make it in time before Santa surprised the kids, I was battling the thoughts of Noel and the rest of the Christmas party. I tried to focus on the party and what I still had to do, but thoughts of Noel whizzed through my mind interrupting my train of thought. His piercing blue eyes floating in my thoughts and the loud laughter echoing in my mind.

*I may be in trouble*, I thought to myself as I could not recall the last time I felt this way.

Once I got back to Green Light, I pulled myself together and immersed myself into the Christmas mayhem of cleaning up and judging the gingerbread house competition. Roxie threw a couple of puzzled looks my way, sensing a change in my behaviour, but without a spare minute to talk and too occupied with the children she decided to wait until later in the day to interrogate me. Noticing the delay in Santa's arrival, we kept the children entertained with singing carols and playing games to keep them alert for when the costumed man appeared at the door. This year we convinced our post man to dress up as Santa and surprise the kids, he was only too happy to oblige after getting to know us over the years. When the doorbell finally rang, we were relieved at the distraction from the endless games, and I ran to answer the door.

"Who is it?" I yelled as I approached the door.

"Ho Ho Ho." I heard Scotty the postman's voice on the other side and looked through the peephole to confirm my assumption. I swiftly unlocked all the locks and opened the door wide. Scotty, noticing that it was just me, promptly apologized for being late blaming his in-laws' for the delay. Before I had a chance to tell him that everything was fine, I heard loud footsteps running towards the door behind me.

"Santa, Santa is here!" they started screaming happily, as I rushed to close the door behind Scotty.

"Ho Ho Ho, children! Merry Christmas!"

He immediately got into character as the children tugged on his red robe and wide pants. The children led him to the sitting room, as their chatter got louder in the excitement of seeing their Christmas idol. They thanked the jolly old man for the gifts that they received earlier in the morning and bombarded him with countless questions about his reindeers. Scotty, being a creative fellow, was able to respond to each question in the most plausible manner, telling the kids that he left the reindeers in Central Park while he came to visit the children who have behaved the best all year.

Once the interrogation was over, I led the children to the centre of the room to play out the T'was the Night Before Christmas that they have been preparing for almost a week. They were so disciplined and anxious to please the guest of honour, that they kept to their scripts, and no one forgot any words. We all clapped enthusiastically once they took their bows, just like Roxie taught them earlier, Scotty praised them and applauded loudly for the great acting skills.

Afterwards, the ecstatic children had milk and cookies together with Santa while Scotty told the kids all about the North Pole. I was pleasantly surprised at Scotty's creativity and ability to describe Santa's village, fully aware that he never even left the boundary of the five boroughs. Then Santa asked everyone to be summoned in one room and said that he had a surprise for everyone and reached inside the enormous crimson jacket that he was wearing. It was indeed a surprise for me because all I asked Scotty to do was to dress up and play with the kids a bit. Rummaging through his inside pocket, Santa pulled out a thick envelope and handed it to me with a flicker in his eyes.

"Let's let Noelle read what's in the envelope!" Scotty declared loudly, as all eyes turned to me to reveal the contents of the envelope.

To match the dramatic performance that Scotty excelled in, I exaggerated my every move with ripping the package open and pulling out the thick cardboard texture rectangles.

"Well, Santa, these appear to be tickets."

I continued in my overacting manner, and then focused to see what was written on the vouchers. Once I saw what they said, I turned to Scotty in disbelief while he nodded for me to continue.

"These are tickets to the skating rink at the Rockefeller Square for today for the children and the mothers! Santa must have gone through a lot of trouble to get these."

"Anything for my favourite children and their brave loving mothers" Scotty chimed in.

Everyone in the room exclaimed in surprise, the children delirious at the idea of skating and the mothers excited to get out of the house and go to the most coveted skating rink in the city. I approached Scotty while everyone was chattering away, handing the tickets out to each other enough for each of the guests.

"How did you manage this, Scotty? These aren't even for sale on Christmas day, they're sold months in advance." I whispered to him.

"I've got connections, Noelle. Being a born and bred New Yorker has its perks. You're doing some amazing things here; a lot of people out there appreciate it." He responded, muttering back.

Then he turned to the rest of the people in the room and announced that they had ten minutes to get ready if they were going to make it in time. Without a minute to waste, the room cleared out quickly as everyone rushed to get changed with just Enid, Roxie and I staying with Scotty.

"I'm sorry that I couldn't get more tickets for you ladies, too. But I'll see what I can do for next time."

He guiltily apologized to us, while Enid came over to hug him and thank him for all his efforts and kind heart.

"I'm not much of a skater these days anyways." She chuckled. "And these two should get out of here anyways and go celebrate their birthday, away from all of us." Then she turned to us.

"This is your official day off, go hit the town and live it up."

"We'll clean up first, once everyone leaves and then we promise that we'll be out of your hair"

I responded to Enid, resisting her objections that she could tidy up herself.

Once everyone followed Scotty out of the house towards the subway station to get to the $47^{th}$-$50^{th}$ street, the house grew unusually silent. Roxie and I started collecting the scattered toys from all corners of the house, and then we heard Enid in the kitchen turning on the tap to do the dishes. I rushed over to take over the dish duty, urging Enid to go to her room and rest up. Enid tried to object fervently but then admitted that she did feel "slightly tired" and shuffled away in the direction of her bedroom. My eyes stayed on her frail figure as she slowly dallied away, my thoughts turned grim as I understood that managing this household was becoming harder for her every day.

Enid would never admit it, but I have noticed her hold on to walls when she felt faint, her pace getting slower as she walked. When she decided to move out of her master bedroom upstairs, she argued that she did not need the bigger room and we could easily accommodate four people in that space while she would be happy living in the small den at the back of the house on the ground floor. At the time her reasoning made sense and we did not see anything wrong with it, but I started to realize over the last month that the real reason she decided to move downstairs was that it has become harder for her to walk up and down the stairs.

*How could I possibly leave Enid and work somewhere else?*

I thought to myself as I put on the rubber gloves and squeezed the last of the dish detergent on the sponge. My new decade plan had to be revisited and I needed to conjure up a new strategy that would allow me to be able to support Roxie and the baby, while still helping out Enid on a full-time basis. Enid has been paying me a very decent salary since I started working for her almost a decade ago, which allowed me to pay for all my expenses.

Prior to moving out, I had been able to save some money which I subsequently spent on furnishing the apartment and sending Alison some money when she told me she needed money to pay for some medical expenses. If it weren't for Enid's connections, I would not have been able to afford the rent either, but when factoring in the accommodation costs and other expenses I did not have much money left over for anything else. Roxie had stubbornly insisted that she would find a job as soon as the baby is born, but I asserted that she needed to stay with the baby for at least a few months while she was finishing up the therapy sessions. My thoughts were then interrupted by a knock on the front door and with my hands still in gloves drenched in soapy water I yelled for Roxie.

"Rox, could you answer the door, please? Just make sure you ask who it is? And don't forget to look in the peephole."

"Yes, boss!"

Roxie chuckled in response as she ran over to the door, as another series of hollow bangs rapped the front door.

"Who is it?"

I heard her ask, her voice slightly muffled as I continued scrubbing the plates from the decoration glitter. The response followed, but I could not make out the voice as the running water subdued the other sounds.

"It's Scotty! He must have forgotten something."

Roxie yelled over, as she started opening the door, unlatching every lock. I faintly heard some commotion at the door, which I imagined was Scottie walking in, but I was slightly puzzled as I did not hear any dialogue between Roxie and him. I turned off the water trying to focus on what was going on by the front door, but only heard silence.

"Scottie, what did you forget?"

I raised my voice in question as I took off the rubber gloves. Further stirring sounds emerged from the hallway but no vocal response, elevating my awareness as I reached for a knife.

*It's probably another Christmas surprise*, I thought, accusing myself of being a complete neurotic unable to outgrow my phobias of the outside world. With only momentary hesitation, my self-preservation senses silenced any other thoughts as I grabbed the knife and proceeded with caution out of the kitchen into the dim hallway.

As I turned the corner, I saw two figures huddled by the front door in an awkwardly positioned embrace. Roxie was facing me, as the figure behind her dressed as Santa Clause hugged her from behind. The long hallway and the dim lighting prevented me from seeing Roxie's face, but I immediately sensed her fear.

"Scottie? Everything alright?"

I slowly approached the cowered couple, with the knife securely grasped tightly behind my back,

The tension and malevolence seemed to expand in the enclosed space with every step that I took. My eyes fixated on the figure behind Roxie, trying to analyze the situation and assess the person behind her. With every step it became clearer that this could not be Scottie, as the figure behind Roxie was much taller. Even though the Santa costume hid the real dimensions of the body, it was still visible that this person was at least half the width of Scottie. As I finally approached Roxie and the intruder at a closer but still presumably safe distance, I spotted a gun in the stranger's hand resting against my sister's temple. Her face distorted in horror and silent tears running down her pale ashen skin, her lips moving as if to say something but no sound materializing from her mouth.

"What do you want?"

I turned to the assailant calmly, remembering all the books that I had read over the years on self defence and articles on home intrusions.

"We do not have money in this house, but I could give you some food?"

I figured it was one of the homeless people on the street looking for easy money just to survive, he had probably robbed someone dressed in a Santa suit earlier in the day.

"I want everything you had stolen from me, you little whore."

I jolted at the sound of a familiar voice. Roxie winced in pain as the intruder grabbed her tighter with his left arm, his fingers digging deeper into her rib cage.

"Ray?"

I refused to believe my ears as the severity of the situation dawned on me.

"So sweet of you to remember me!"

Ray's wicked laugh escaped his lips that were still shielded by the fake beard.

"It took me a long time to find you, but I knew I would one day."

Then he scanned my body with his penetrating eyes, visibly dissatisfied by the bulkiness of my festive sweater and loose jeans.

"Take off your clothes, I want to see if you're still got that tight piece of ass that I've been craving for all these years."

I remained rigid, tightening my grip around the knife's handle, unwilling to follow his absurd demands.

"Why are you here, Ray?"

I remained calm while figuring out the best way out of this

situation. If I could only get the phone to dial 911, but I would have to walk further down the hallway and turn left, then walk through the living room. Any of these movements appeared to be completely impossible in the current situation, as Ray held my sister captive at gunpoint.

"Well, I was looking for my money-maker over here."

He squeezed Roxie tighter, prompting her to squeal in pain.

"I was so heartbroken when I came home and couldn't find my beloved Roxie" He frantically giggled in Roxie's ears as the fake beard hairs grazed her face.

"I couldn't let another one of my favourite girls, just take off and leave me. Especially when this one is expecting my child."

His hand clasped Roxie's bump, as her arms flung protectively over her stomach.

"Keep still! Or I will shoot your useless brains out."

His voice hissed at Roxie's response, then he continued.

"You see, when I returned to the apartment and she wasn't home, I was livid but then I noticed that all her precious belongings were left behind. I knew she had to come back, she had nowhere to go. My Roxie, is not like you, she knows her home is with me."

He glared at me with resentment.

"A week passed, and she did not come home, I almost gave up all hope... and then one day when I was coming home from a "meeting", who do I see by the building's entrance?"

He looked questionably at me.

"That's right! You, Noelle! Imagine my surprise. You brought some cops with you, that was not very nice of you. So, I got back in my car that I parked on the street, and waited for you so we could have a chat for old times sake. But you left with the cops, so I had to follow the cop car as they took you right here and dropped you off. I was going to follow you in right away, but then I noticed all the locks on the door and figured that there was no way you would let an "old friend" in. I left then, and since I could not go back to my apartment, I had to stay with an acquaintance of mine, trying to figure out how to make my way in and then it dawned on me...Christmas costumes. I would just dress up and you'd have to open the door for Santa, because I know how much you love Christmas."

He reveled in the flawlessness of his wicked plan.

"So here I am, knocking on the door unsure if this would work but then heard Roxie's voice asking who it was so I stayed in character and replied with my best *Ho Ho Ho*, then she unlocked the door and here we are. A happy family reunion!"

Ray mused waiting for a reaction from me, to commend him on his successful execution.

*I brought Ray here*, I realized in horror, *I am the reason for all our misfortunes.*

Attempting to catch Roxie's eyes to silently apologize to her for all the pain I have caused her, I tried to prolong the conversation as I formulated the escape plan. Then I heard a slight clunk at the back of the house, almost inaudible but it was enough for me to understand that Enid opened her bedroom door to see what was going on.

"What do you want, Ray?"

I tried to calm my nerves and elevated my voice to drown out any other sounds that would alert Ray, while the emotions in my body whirled around rapidly. The inside of my stomach felt like a thousand knots had been tied to oppress me, as my heart rate pounded uncontrollably in my chest and boomed loudly in my ears.

"So many things, Noelle! I want my two favourite girls back with me, I have so many clients asking me everyday about you, Rox. And Noelle, you can jump right in and help our girl out while she is out commission with this huge stomach. And then, when she has the baby, she will come back on board, and you can work together. There's huge demand for two girls of mixed race in the industry. We'd be rich."

Ray spoke enthusiastically about a plan that he had undoubtedly been developing since he found out about me. You could almost see the dollar signs in his eyes, as he counted the prospective earnings from all his dirty deals. While he was talking, I heard some rustling in the backroom, hoping that Enid was calling the police and this nightmare would soon be over.

"Don't forget, Noelle, you owe me huge. If you only knew how much trouble you got me in, when you left with the "coke bricks". Gee, so much trouble!"

"Good thing, our girl Roxie here, is such a hard worker. She is very popular with all my clients, you know. They have missed her dearly, so I am sure they are going to pay double when she's ready and back in shape to entertain them. Speaking of shape, I believe I asked you to take off your clothes. I need to know what I am going to be working with, I can't offer my clients subpar products. Hope you've been keeping up with your sit-ups and you're still as limber as you were."

Ray clicked his tongue lusting over the years when we were together and could blissfully spend hours in bed.

"I'm not going to ask again, Noelle."

He pressed the gun harder against Roxie's head. Hoping that Enid had managed to dial the phone and the police were on their way, I decided to obey Ray's orders as slowly as possible without provoking his anger. With my arm still held behind me away from his view, I tucked the knife at the back securing it under the band of my underwear. Then I unhurriedly pulled the wool sweater off my body, blinding me for a second as I pulled it over my head while taking it off. As I took it off, I saw Ray's shameless gaze admiring the shape of my breasts underneath the white spaghetti strap top that I had on. Since we were in such a rush this morning to leave the apartment, I regretfully forgot to put on a bra and settled for a light top under the sweater.

"Don't stop there, Noelle. I want to see it all."

He urged me to continue, as his dark eyes grew hungrier for more flesh. I unclasped the clunky leather belt that held my oversized jeans in place and pulled it out of the pant loops, which made the pants quickly recede to my hips. Then I slid the jeans down from my rounded hips along the length of my legs dropping them to the bottom of my feet, then I stepped out of the pant legs towards Roxie and within Ray's reach.

With nothing more on than the white tank top barely hiding my full breasts and the matching cotton panties, I tilted my head and welcomed Ray to touch me. His wide palm separated from Roxie's rib cage, releasing his tight grip on her and extended towards my upper body. His fingers caressed my shivering skin from the nape of my neck, along the spaghetti straps as he lowered them from my shoulders and pulled the rest of the fabric down to my waist.

Then I could sense his breathing escalating, as his free hand cupped my exposed breast, his thumb playing with my nipple arousing it from its slumber. I kept my gaze fixed on his eyes scrutinizing my body as his hand continued to explore my flesh, noticing his discomfort of not being able to grope me with his other hand. Unable to contain his lust, he dropped his other hand from Roxie's temple and brought it towards my other breast with his index finger still on the trigger and the barrel aimed at my head.

*This is my chance.*

I gently pulled my right arm behind me and wrapped my hand tightly around the knife handle. Then to avoid any sudden movement, I slowly brought my arm to the side of my body as Ray's yearning kept him temporarily oblivious to the surroundings. My eyes met Roxie's panicked eyes, as she noticed the knife in my hand, and I tried to calm her with a sly fleeting smirk hoping to ease her panic. Then without any further thought, I quickly raised the sharp blade in my hand and thrust it in Ray's stomach with all my strength.

Ray's shrilling yelp almost deafened me, as I was able to escape his clutches once he dropped his arms to his lacerated abdomen. I lunged for Roxie and grabbed her hand, pulling her away from Ray to run deeper into the safety of the house. She was frozen in her stupor, and I had to pull hard on her arm to get her to snap out. Once she started moving, she quickly stepped over Ray's crouching figure and clasped my hand with vigour. As I pulled her to follow me, I felt her tugging back so I sharply turned around to speed her along noticing that Ray grabbed her foot, and she was trying to shake it off. I immediately lunged over and stomped my right foot on top of his left arm hearing a crack of his radius. He let go of Roxie and we continued to run down the hallway towards the back of the house, as Ray started to shoot in our direction.

I heard a couple of bullets hitting the walls with a loud thud and one shot bolted by my ear barely missing my head. Then just as we were about to turn into the kitchen, I felt an iron fist punch strike my left side, which destabilized my body and I stumbled. Roxie noticed that something was wrong and put her right arm around me and pulled me with her as we ran down the stairs into the dark basement. She dragged my straggling body to my old bedroom, which had been turned into the office, at the far end of the floor and locked the door behind us.

"Noelle, are you alright? Let me look at you."

She set me down on the cold floor and inspected my body.

"You look fine, let me turn you around".

She raised my right side and lifted me, which sent painful jolts up and down my body. I heard her gulp for air at the sight of the blood on my back, and she quickly got up in search of towels to gauge the gushing wound.

"You'll be fine, N. It's just a graze, I'll just find something to stop the bleeding."

Roxie continued to rummage around the room, only being able to find my old hoodie that I kept on the chair for when I got cold working in the office. She grabbed it and bunched it up before placing it against the wound, rolling my body back to lay flat.

"How bad is..." I started to question Roxie on the state of the injury, but a gush of hot liquid gurgled my voice. The panic in my sister's eyes was undeniable and she could not hide it, not from me, I knew what

Roxie was always thinking. I knew when she lied to me when we were kids, and I knew that she lied to me when she said her next words.

"Nothing to worry about, N. Like I said, it is just a graze."

At that moment we heard loud banging above us, as if someone was breaking in the front door, followed by a boisterous thud pursued by numerous rapid footsteps and voices.

"Noelle, the police are here! You're going to be ok; we are going to take you to the hospital."

She said excitedly as her eyes filled with tears looking at my shivering body. I felt very cold, and I tried to tell her that but the flowing liquid that left an iron taste in my mouth, did not let me speak.

"Cold." I mouthed to Roxie, and she instantly lay down on the floor with me, hugging me tightly in her warm embrace. I turned my neck to face her, shuddering at the pain, and met her agonizing stare full of heartache and despair. As the commotion upstairs continued and the loud voices shouted back and forth, we silently stared at each other in a tight embrace, just as we did when we were kids huddling in my bed during a thunderstorm.

The weight of my eyelids grew heavier while the fatigue overflowed my thoughts, I peacefully closed my eyes giving in to the lassitude as it spread from the tip of my head to the bottom of my feet. All the worries and misfortunes fluttered away into obscurity, the burden of guilt lifted while the piercing pain subsided, and I no longer felt the unsettling cold. My last recollection before embarking into the oblivion, was an uncontrollable grievous wailing that slowly faded away as my life turned to darkness.

## Chapter Seven

*Lifetime II*
*December 25, 1984*
*Rebirth*

My unburdened mind was free from thoughts as I felt my body drifting, fully submerged in a warm placating solace. Peace and serenity were the only sentiments that I was able to comprehend, while at the time unaware of the significance of time, place or self. Over the duration of my lifetimes, I understood that this serene nirvana was the only constant that remained unchanged and therefore could only be considered as the genuine state of being. Time is only a momentary flash in our eternal consciousness, it is not a linear concept that we all dread it to be as the humankind have infinitely feared the impermanence of their being. Our entire existence is not short-lived, whereas a brief lifetime in a series of infinite possibilities is what is actually transitory. Albeit the fleetingness of these moments, they each leave a lasting scar in your consciousness that you inherently encumber as you are reborn into another journey.

With my first rebirth, I was yet unaware of the invincibility of the human consciousness and entered the new lifetime weighed down by confusion and fear. The terror, from realizing that the permanence of my nirvana was temporary, emerged when I felt the surrounding darkness contracting around me. The flowing substance that comforted me in my oblivion had abruptly receded, leaving me constricted in the confinement of a silk- lined enclosure. The violent vibrations around me intensified and an invisible force started to push me along the dark tunnel towards a shimmering bright light that had suddenly materialized in the distance. While my body felt the violent jolts squeezing it further along the smoothness of the tunnel walls, the fear of the eventuality once I reached that light intensified. The light grew brighter with every thrust, and I started hearing muffled sounds alerting me of the presence of others beyond the brightness. There was a long pause just within the reach of the gleam ahead, as the jolts seized, leaving me in hopes that I may be able to retreat into the comfort of the darkness. However, a few moments later I felt my body shoved vehemently forward forcing my body to squeeze out of the tunnel and into a brightly lit space.

The fear from deep within and the distress from the blinding light emerged in a loud shrilling scream escaping my lips as I felt my body lifted by a pair of strong hands. The unrecognizable sound of my own scream alarmed me only causing more ear-piercing tumult, when I heard a deep male voice.

""We've got her! It's a girl, a healthy-looking girl."

I struggled to see the possessor of the voice, as everything was blurry around me.

Then another pair of hands tenderly picked me up and carried me away from the male voice, subsequently my body was rested on a table while the gentle touches continued to inspect my body. I felt some intrusive prodding and coldness of metal grazing against my skin, while the blurry shape resembling a person observed every inch of my body until they were satisfied with their assessment. Once the intrusiveness of the inspection was completed, I felt my body lifted again and carried across the bright space towards a cluster of distorted figures.

Reveling in the conclusion of the invasiveness but confused of the continual relay, I was finally passed to a hazy image of a female that lovingly took me into a careful warm embrace cradling my body against her bare chest. Her soft fingertips tenderly caressing my skin, prompting me to recall the memories of the uniquely similar touch from long ago. My screaming subsided as I savored every stroke of the fingers, trying hard to focus on the face that was lowered so close to me. Then my body grew still as I heard a voice from the past pierce the blurry reality around me.

"Jack, she's absolutely beautiful."

It was undoubtedly the voice of my mother, a voice that I thought I long forgot but was able to recognize immediately. I tried to reach out my hand to touch the mirage in front of me, but my limbs seemed to disobey my instructions. Unwilling to believe my ears and unable to see clearly, I resisted to accept the notion that my shrunken body was cradled in a soft embrace of my deceased mother.

"She is absolutely perfect."

I heard an all-familiar male voice respond from a near distance, but out of my purview.

*Dad?*

I wondered in my confused state, trying to comprehend the surrounding situation. I tried to crane my neck in the direction of the voice, but my insubordinate muscles refused to cooperate once again. My whole body felt unusually light and foreign to me, as I tried to wiggle my toes and lift my arms. While some movement in my limbs did occur, it was mostly sporadic and predominantly outside of my control. Notwithstanding my inability to control my body's functions and unable to see beyond the blurriness of the opaque veil over my eyes, my other senses were heightened. My skin quivered with every stroke from the smoothness of the fingertips on my body and I was able to hear every hushed tone and slight movement in the room.

I sensed some movement behind me with a sound of footsteps and ruffling of clothes, as the female figure in front of me shifted to allow space for another being to slide into my view while I felt my body slide into an enfold of a stronger grip. The newly appeared face stared directly at me with his eyes hidden behind a pair of thick framed glasses, my eyes unable to focus on the details in front but my mind gradually filling in the missing pixels forming a clear image in my head. He lowered his head to kiss me on my head, and I felt the prickliness of his cheeks and smelled an earthy scent of wood mixed with burnt toast. It was my father, my awkward loving father, who I have missed so much over the years. Unable to contain my excitement at the sight of both of my parents, I tried to call for them but was only able to produce a shrilling yelp followed by a long yawn.

A person dressed in white came over and picked me up, while I tried to unsuccessfully direct my limbs to resist, unwilling to leave the comfort of my family's embrace afraid that the delusion would dissipate, and I would lose them forever again. As the lady in white carried me away from them, the outline of my parents began to vanish into the blurriness of the background with every step, until I was unable to see them at all. This unnerved me and more shrilling cries escaped my lips demanding their return, while I was placed in a comfortable crib where I surprisingly fell asleep almost immediately from an unexpected wave of exhaustion.

When I awoke from my brief dreamless sleep, I found myself to be in new surroundings, the space seemed less bright and appeared more confined than the vibrantly lit room before. The whiteness of the walls was easy to absorb, while I attempted to make sense of the other objects in the room. As my eyes caught a glimpse of two hovering blobs resting atop a bulky flat surface that I presumed was a bed, I heard a sound of an opening door followed by a skidding of rubber tires against the vinyl floor rolling by and stopping a few feet away from me. Then to my relief, I once again heard my mother's voice coming from the direction of the distant blobs I spotted earlier.

"Alison, congratulations!"

Her voice sent a flutter of butterflies in my stomach wild, as I grew ecstatic to realize that the delusion was more durable than I feared.

"Thank you, you too." I heard an assertive voice from the other side of the room, a much younger voice with certain recognizable intonations belonging to Alison.

My father's tall figure appeared in my line of sight, as he approached a rectangular shaped object and peered inside, sighing at the content inside the box.

"She's wonderful, Alison. Did you come up with a name, yet?" My dad's excited tones bounced off the walls

"I thought Roxie might be a good name, but I'm not sure if i..."

*Roxie!*

This could not possibly be. I pleaded with my body to turn, so I could see Roxie, but my head was only able to turn slightly to view an outline of a hazy object standing less than two feet away from me while my father introduced me to Alison.

A piercing thought penetrated my confused mind as I tried to make sense of the situation. *This is the day we were born.*

I remembered my parents telling me a story when I was little of how they met Alison and how I met Roxie for the first time, which was incomprehensible to my toddler brain because Roxie had always been in my life and there never seemed to be a beginning to our co-existence. Alison had subsequently retold her version of the story to us on every birthday, details changing with every year, but the core of the matter being that she met my parents on the most memorable day of her life.

*I must be dreaming and imagining all the details just as my parents and Alison described them.* I reasoned with myself, but everything seemed so real around me. My father's scent of his workshop mixed with the aroma of the slightly burnt breakfast, the pleasurable shivers from my mother's gentle touch, the firmness of my parents' embrace. These undeniable facts could not be my imagination as they felt incredibly authentic.

The thought of this being my new reality was staggering, I was given a new chance at life with my parents, who were alive and well. Unaware of the permanence of the new reality, I made the decision to absorb as much of it as possible with every living moment.

"Susan and Alison, I'm at your disposal for the foreseeable future. Would you like anything? Coke? Chips? Balloons? Ah balloons!"

My dad proclaimed as if he had an epiphany, storming out of the room before mom or Alison had a chance to respond. My mother giggled in her adorable childlike way that I was never able to replicate, as the door closed and looked at Alison silently apologizing for her husband's eccentricity.

"A coke would have been nice." I heard Alison announce boldly and then continued "But I guess the balloons are good too." She laughed to herself and looked in my mother's direction trying to read her reaction, but my mother recoiled at Alison's sarcasm with a loud rolling laugh. Laughter eased any leftover tension in the room from earlier in the day, as the new mothers were able to finally relax having been able to conquer the hurdles of labour and birth.

"Listen earlier today…I didn't mean to..." As the women's laughter subsided, Alison tried to explain herself to my mother. Uncharacteristic of Alison's confident nature to apologize to strangers, she knew that her roommate and her odd husband were kind-hearted people and did not mean to offend her.

"Nonsense! We crossed the line." My mother stopped Alison mid-sentence and then hesitantly continued. "You know, I haven't told Jack this, but I am absolutely terrified of being a mother. I do not know the first thing about raising a child, I'm probably going to be really bad at it. Let's hope I don't drop her the second they wheel me out of this hospital."

My mother's words surprised me, as being a mother seemed like second nature to her. She always knew what to say when I felt sad and hugged me tight when I needed it most. Her confidence in doing what was best to raise me never wavered and she spent hours coaching me how to stay within the lines when colouring or teaching me the alphabet so I could read all my favourite books. She was the best mother by all accounts, the best mother I could have had for the blissful fleeting five years of my life.

"I can't see that happening, it's just the little troubling voice at the back of your head that you need to start ignoring. I can see how you are with little Noelle, you'll never let anything happen to her." Alison stated having observed my mother in her new environment.

"I can say the same thing about you. Your little girl stole your heart the minute she was born. Did you know that you haven't been able to look anywhere but the crib for more than a second? You will be an amazing mother, Alison."

My mother returned the compliment with all her sincerity, sensing that her and Alison could be great friends. They chatted for the next little while getting to know each other, and by the time my father returned with a sea of colourful balloons, they felt like they were best friends.

"The store downstairs only had one pink balloon but then they had all these other colours, and I wasn't sure which one I should get so I got one of each."

He explained himself as he attempted to spread the balloons evenly across the room, to make sure that Alison felt that the balloons were not just for his wife. He still felt apologetic for his earlier blunder that offended Alison and wanted to make sure that there was no ill-will, trying to spread the figurative love with the overwhelming number of balloons. Alison appreciated the gesture and thanked my father for the efforts and said she did not like pink anyways and was much happier with the colours that he bought. I also enjoyed the view above me as the balloons hovered over my crib, because the colours were significantly easier to spot unlike the blurry faces.

My mother seemed to get tired after a while from the busy events of the day and fell asleep as my father kept his watchful eye over me and Roxie. Alison was unable to close her eyes even though my dad assured her that he would keep an eye on her daughter. Her adoring gaze was fixated on Roxie's crib, while her mind was lost in the world of deep thought. In this tranquil moment of silence, the door opened, and the doctor came in with the nurse to check with the newborns. After a few checks, they determined that everything was in order and asked my father to follow the doctor to fill out some of the paperwork while the nurse stayed behind to speak to Alison. Dad wavered unwilling to give up his post, but the doctor assured that this was going to be quick, and the nurse would stay behind to make sure everything was alright. Convinced that the girls were in safe hands, my father trailed behind the doctor out of the room.

I saw the nurse dressed in white approach my mother to confirm that she was fast asleep. Then my eyes followed the nurse from my mother's bedside to Alison who was wide awake and pulled up a chair to sit down next to her. Alison shuffled in her bed, and I heard the hydraulics in the bed working to raise it to a more comfortable position, then the nurse spoke.

"Alison, I brought all the paperwork now. All you have to do is sign at the bottom of each form that had been marked with a sticker." The nurse handed the stack of documents to Alison, as she silently flipped through the pages. I wondered in my crib what the documents were as I did not remember this detail in any of the stories that were shared with me.

"The Watsons are in the waiting room and can take the baby with them as soon as you sign these documents."

The nurse continued to speak as Alison remained silent. The words seemed to have difficulty registering in my brain, as I did not comprehend who the Watsons were or why they would take Roxie.

"They seem like very nice people, but you already know that. I heard you have met them a few times in your last trimester. The baby will be very happy with them, they'll love her dearly."

"She will be happy with me too. I already love her, more than I loved anyone else." Alison's voice trembled as she finally spoke, setting the papers aside.

"Her name is Roxie, and she has my heart. I don't want to give her up, not anymore. She is perfect, absolutely perfect. I'll take great care of her; she will be happy with me." Alison's voice grew stronger as she spoke to the nurse who was taken aback by the turn of events.

"But the Watsons?" The nurse objected. "They are very well off; the baby will be well taken care of."

"Her name is Roxie, and I can take the best damn care of my own baby. Tell them the baby has twenty-five toes, tell them she's sickly because her mom is a former drug addict. Or you can tell them the truth, which is that I changed my mind."

Alison grabbed the papers and forcefully handed them back to the nurse, who silently got up and moved the chair against the wall.

"I hope you know what you are doing." The nurse said as she left the room.

"So do I, so do I." Alison whispered, gazing adoringly back at the crib.

The shocking revelation stunned me. Alison never hinted at the fact that she was ready to give up Roxie for adoption at any point in time. She was a very headstrong woman who lacked the gentleness of a loving touch, but she loved Roxie with all her heart. They have argued constantly but always made up almost immediately because their love for each other was immense. When I entered their family after the tragic loss of my parents, I was not sure what I was going to encounter because Alison was so different from my own kind affectionate mother. However, Alison welcomed me into her home without any hesitation knowing the struggles with the courts and child services that she had to endure taking on an adopted child. While she lacked tenderness, she exceeded in other forms of love represented in encouragement and support that she provided to us while we were growing up.

I remembered how much it pained Roxie when we left Georgetown for New York, unable to say a proper goodbye to her mother, but she knew that if she saw her mother in person, she would simply be unable to leave her behind. They had a special bond that united them through all the hard times and through the long separation when Roxie was lost in New York. Alison never cried to me on the phone when I called her from Green Light and always maintained her composure, but I knew the real Alison and sensed the pained anguish behind her words as her only thoughts were of Roxie.

One of the rare times Alison cried was when Roxie and I surprised her with our call, when my sister re-emerged in my life on that snowy December morning. Alison struggled with her emotions on the phone, as years of agony lead to the much-awaited relief, while Roxie joined her mother in the sorrowful wail that was contained in silence over the years. There was never any doubt, Alison had always loved Roxie, and Roxie loved her back unconditionally.

My father returned to the room noticing that the nurse was gone and seemed irritated at the broken promise of her being in the room while he was gone.

"Can't trust anyone, no one at all. She is a medical professional, for god's sake. I was gone for less than ten minutes."

My father exasperated aloud, turning to Alison for support in his frustration. His new acquaintance did not seem to stir at his vexed tone, but she was sitting up and contemplating a clearly heavy weighing decision with her eyes transfixed on the tiny bundle in the crib by her bedside. Jack hesitated for a moment, looking over at his wife's bed for guidance on the social situation etiquette, but she was still sound asleep, so he cautiously decided to approach Alison.

"Everything ok, Alison?" He walked closer to her.

"I think so." She said with uncertainty, which surprised my father as in the short time he had known Alison, she did not seem uncertain about anything. "You know, I don't even have a baby seat to take Roxie home with me. I was not prepared for this. I have not bought her any clothes, or diapers or whatever else you need to get for a baby. How am I going to do this?"

She asked the question aiming it at herself, but my father always had trouble hearing the difference between an actual question and a rhetorical one, so he responded quickly.

"I was wondering the exact same thing just a few hours ago when I first saw Noelle. She looks so small, so defenseless, so fragile. I was afraid to hold her tiny body because I thought I would hurt her with my massive bulky hands, but then I looked at her and knew that I would do absolutely anything to make my little girl happy."

My father's comforting words warmed my heart, as I eavesdropped on his private conversation with Alison.

"You are going to take this beautiful baby home, raise her with love and care. You are her mother, and you will know exactly what needs to be done. I don't know the first thing about being a father, a thought that had terrified me for months, but I can tell you that I'll give it my absolute best shot." My father reinforced his message confidently.

*You were the best father.* I wanted to scream but was only able to produce a croaking sound.

"See, Noelle, is terrified of me being her father too." My dad laughed off my attempts at speaking. Alison sat in silence while my father spoke of his greatest fear, and then she snapped out of her daze.

"Jack, could you bring Roxie to me? I want to hold her in my arms."

"Of course."

My dad went over to Roxie's crib, where she had been sleeping almost the entire time since she was rolled into the room. He picked her up awkwardly, trying not to disrupt her deep slumber and carried her over to her mother. Alison outstretched her arms gently taking her daughter into her embrace, as my father stood back admiring the loving duo.

"Oh Alison, don't tell my wife that I was terrified to be a father. She'd probably kill me."

He jumped in, remembering that he feared his wife's disappointment in him more than anything else.

"Not to worry, Jack. Your secret is safe with me."

Alison responded slyly, fully aware that Susan would completely understand his concerns.

My father walked over to his wife's side and paced back and forth for a while, while I observed the different shapes and colours of the balloons hovering above my head. His swinging arms and shuffling feet disturbed the balloons from their dreary stillness causing a colourful motion of shapes to flash before my eyes. Then the balloons idled to their lifeless form, as my father's pace stopped.

"Say, Alison, I have to leave for a bit. I don't want to wake Susan up, but are you ok with me leaving you girls for an hour at most?", his voice sounded concerned at the thought of leaving.

"Don't worry. We have the nurse call button; in case we need help." Alison rashly responded appeasing my father's worries.

Without any further apprehensions, he left the room slowly closing the door behind him. While he was gone the room was completely silent, as my mother continued to sleep, and Alison held Roxie in her arms mulling over her next moves. My uneasiness about the incongruity around me had slowly dissipated and I fully gave in to the idea that I was given a new chance at my troublesome life. I could avoid all the irresponsible mistakes I made before which caused the disastrous havoc in Roxie's and my lives. This time, everything would be different, I was determined to avoid all the predicaments that led me astray.

*I could save my parents*, I realized abruptly.

I could do everything in my power to prevent the tragic car accident and make sure that my parents live past that fateful February day. For the next hour I was occupied at plotting the plan when I heard the door open and some banging and clunking emerging from the hallway followed by my father exhausted breathing. The noise woke my mother up from her sleep, as she saw my father holding a variety of bulging shopping bags and a baby seat in his arms.

"Jack...?" She raised her voice in her sleepy state.

"Susan, Alison mentioned that she didn't have anything for the baby, so I went home and grabbed the extra baby car seat our neighbours gave us and stuffed some bags with the clothes you bought recently at the dollar a bag sale. You don't mind, do you?" He timidly asked his wife, still breathing hard from the rushed trip home.

My mother must have shaken her head in response, because he rushed over to Alison's side and dumped all the bags in the corner of her side of the room.

"This will hold you over for the next little while, Alison. And you can always call us at any time."

"Thank you, Jack. Thank you, both."

Alison responded quietly, her confidence slowly growing in her portentous decision. She knew she could take care of Roxie, and contrary to her independent nature she knew that some help from strangers would not hurt. My attention from Alison shifted back to my plans on my future, the countdown was on, and I only had five years and two months to prepare for my parents' evasion of death.

## Chapter Eight

*February 14, 1990*
*Age 5*

    The plan was flawless, it was one of about a million other plans that I conceived in my busy scheming mind over the last five years. As the time went by, I appreciated every minute that I got to spend with my parents, through their clumsiness of caring for me in my infancy to sternly disciplining me in my toddler years. Recreating the impregnable ties was natural, enabling the bond between us to strengthen every year.

    My parents were wonderful people, and I knew that I could not let anything happen to them again, even though my physical capabilities in the five-year-old body were significantly limited. The balance between my factual age since the rebirth versus my mentality that was inadvertently inherited from the previous lifetime had been a struggle for me and unknowingly for my parents. It was incomprehensible for my parents to understand the reasons for why I refused to play with other children and preferred to stay home with them to watch The Wheel of Fortune or read books all cooped up in my small bedroom. Initially my father self-declared himself the "Savant Guru", when he falsely realized that I learned how to decipher words by his dedicated hours of reading to me everyday, but then regretted his "wise teachings" because I chose to read instead of spending time outside with the other children. I preferred not to argue his proclamations but decided to be more careful in any further careless reveals to my complicated situation that could frighten them.

    The only person who I tried to confide in was Roxie, when she came with her mother for our previous traditional Birthday/Christmas celebration. I realized a while ago that Roxie had no recollections of her prior existence, when she finally learned how to speak and we were able to communicate, but I still attempted to prompt some memories on occasion.

"Rox, do you remember Green Light?"

I cautiously approached the subject when our parents were distracted by their loud argument over whether the almanac should have been taken at a later time instead of 1955 in the latest Back to the Future movie they recently saw.

Roxie tilted her head sideways and looked at me with her childhood curiosity mimicking her mother's furrowing eyebrows, which for a second led me to think that she was trying to remember the familiar concept. However, a moment later she reached for a green block secured in the middle of a tower we had just constructed and pulled it out, prompting an inevitable collapse of the tall structure resulting in thrilled high-pitched giggles.

"This is green, N, but there is no light. Is there another block that lights up?"

Roxie asked, handing me a moss shade building block, while looking around for the missing piece.

Shaking my head regretfully, I took the block from her and started constructing another tall structure. While I took no pleasure in playing with other children in the playground with their senseless horseplay, I enjoyed spending time with Roxie in our quiet time in the safety of our home. My parents were content that I was not a complete sociopath and tried to invite Roxie over as often as Alison could bring her, and Alison was glad to drop off her daughter for play dates at least once a week. I have heard on multiple occasions my mother raising her concerns about me to Alison when they were chatting over coffee, but thankfully Alison always shrugged it off and typically responded with the same phrase.

"Eccentricity is an inherent aptitude for genius. Conformity is a taught skill that results in nothing more than being ordinary."

My mother would typically nod in agreement, with full understanding that I almost certainly acquired that trait from my father, which worried her slightly knowing how my dad depended on her in most social situations. Noticing my mother's worries, I tried to change my visible peculiarities and resorted to reading the adult books at night while switching to the brightly decorated senseless storybooks when around her and intentionally staying outside the lines of the colouring books which seemed to appease Susan.

While my parents were worried about me, I was equally worried about them. Their impending doom was constantly hovering over my troubled mind, as I continued to plot their survival. During the last year of preparation, I started sneaking out of my bedroom late in the evening and sit on the top of the staircase. It was the perfect spot to eavesdrop on my parents talking downstairs and remain unnoticed, while understanding more about their plans and their lives because they never talked about serious subjects that troubled them in front of me. This is how I learned that they recently took out a personal loan and remortgaged the house because my father decided to go back to college and finish his degree, while my mother struggled to find a job so decided to open her own travel agency. This finally explained as to where the money went from my parents' estate when they passed away. I never raised the subject with Alison because financial management was never my strong suit when I was growing up, but I had wondered about it in my final years when I had been reminiscing about my youth in Georgetown while in the comfort of my bed in the cozy New York apartment.

Discovering more details about my parents' lives was sensational to me, as I knew that I completely missed out on that important part of my life previously.

I learned that my father had previously held an academic scholarship at Stanford University where he was enrolled in the Computer Science program and he was fully immersed in his studies, missing out on the typical drink-filled college parties. He was originally from Milwaukee and did not know anyone in the area, so he focused on his education and enjoyed the silence of the evenings when the dorm cleared out as all the other students went out drinking.

One day, after his last exam in his third year, my father's roommate Simon convinced him to come and stay with him for a week at his hometown in Delaware and my father hesitantly agreed only because there was no more studying until the next term after the summer break. His scant bag was already packed with his meager possessions to go home for the three months, which he regretted because he was not looking forward to returning to the trailer park where he had been raised by his single mother. My father never got along with his mother, partly because she always bullied him about his incessant reading and inability to play sports with the other kids in the trailer community and, he despised her drinking habits that consequently drew her to become more violent towards him. Having grown accustomed to the spaciousness of his shared room and the proximity of the library where he could spend hours discovering new books, he deplored the thought of spending three months on his top bunk in the dark trailer while his mother entertained one of her new "gentlemen callers". My father would have been happy to stay in Stanford for the summer, but the scholarship only allowed him to stay at the university accommodation for the duration of his studies and he missed the deadline to enrol in the summer courses.

My father agreed to join Simon for a week by the ocean to forget his sorrows of returning to his loathed home and to celebrate the conclusion of yet another successful year. His roommate owned a well-maintained Ford, so they decided to drive through the picturesque countryside across the country to the East coast, where my father had never been in the past.

It was an exhilarating experience he talked about frequently with my mother, a few days on the road without any stress occupying his thoughts, marvelling at the wide plains extending as far as the eye could see, and eating the most satisfying gigantic plates of food at truck stop diners. When they finally made it to the tiny coastal town in southern Delaware, my father felt slightly dejected at the conclusion of their adventurous road trip but when he exited the car in the driveway of the red brick bungalow, he inhaled the balmy clean air that lingered in his lungs. The unfamiliar scents of the alluring sweetness intermingled with the tangy saltiness awoke his curiosity, as his inquisitive mind looked around in search of the source of the aroma. While there was no visual evidence of the origin, his ears perked up at the sounds of the crushing waves in the proximity of his location.

*The ocean*, my quick-thinking father identified the cause of the captivating smell and the rolling sounds. At that point, the front door of the bungalow opened, and a couple of middle-aged people ran out to embrace his friend loudly cheering at his arrival, *the parents*, my father concluded. He uneasily observed the unfamiliar interaction that had not been customary in his own household, trying to unsuccessfully recall the last time his mother put her scrawny arms around him.

There were many unwarranted slaps and unprovoked smacks on the back of his head over the years, but there were never any affectionate interfaces that was a conventional family habit which he ascertained through watching the television shows. To boost the awkwardness level, the strangers disengaged their affectionate embracing of their son and ran over to lock their arms around my father. Inexperienced in the appropriate response, he stood rigidly in his spot with his arms loosely dangling by his sides, waiting to be released from the gauche encounter. Thus commenced his week in Delaware, where every morning he was greeted with a friendly reception from Simon's parents and a casual chat over the family meals throughout the stay.

The next day after they arrived at the coastal town, following a full eight-hour sleep, my dad was awoken by Simon rushing him to get dressed to go to the beach and meet his friends. This was my father's first time at the beach, and he did not know what to expect, so he packed his backpack with three types of sun lotions, mosquito repellant and a variety of t-shirts.

It was an unusually warm May afternoon and as they left the house stuffed from eating the nutritious breakfast prepared by the matron of the household, they rushed down the street towards the sizzling white sands. My father was weighed down by the heaviness of his backpack and sweltering under the hot sun in his jeans and t-shirt but his yearning to see the ocean impelled him forward. He was relieved to have finally reached the sandy strip and followed his friend to a boisterous group settled in the sand, where my dad was introduced to everyone and cordially welcomed to sit down with them. He took off his backpack and rested it on the ground, while everyone around him quickly took off their shirts and remained in their swimming trunks. That was when my father astonishingly realized that he failed to pack the one item that was vital on the beach, and that was a pair of his ragged but still functional banana print trunks. Simon noticed my father's bewildered look and asked him why he was not changing, to which my father responded explaining his blunder.

"Oh Jack…Just go over to the stores on the strip along the shore. They have everything in those tourist shops." His friend responded, not at all surprised by my father's revelation having spent enough time with him over the course of their friendship.

My dad shrugged off the suggestion and remained in his seated position on the sand, trying to immerse himself in watching other people, while his new friends disappeared from his near-sighted view when they entered the chilly ocean water. He watched the families build elaborate sandcastles and unruly children chase each other around the open space of the endless sand banks, then he noticed a group of teenage girls to his left engrossed in an active game of beach volleyball. Unaware of the rules of the sport and uninterested in the game, he found himself mesmerised by the sight, more specifically one particular player. She appeared to be levitating in the air when she jumped high to spike the ball, while her long blonde hair defied gravity and floated in a beautiful, undulated pattern. Her moves resembled the graciousness of a gazelle that he remembered from watching the Wild Kingdom shows when he was a child, her lean muscles curved with her every lunge. Unable to take his eyes off the beautiful vision in front of him, he failed to move when one of the other players spiked the ball in his direction and hit him directly on the forehead with a loud thud. The shock of the unexpected blow did not hinder his instincts, as he grabbed the ball before it had the chance to roll away.

"Are you ok? Did that hurt?" The gorgeous blonde "gazelle" rushed over to him with a friend.

"I think so."

He responded shyly handing over the ball to the concerned beauty in front of him, delighted that he could have a closer look. Her wide blue eyes were filled with sincere worry for the poor fellow, who got hit because she was unable to defend her position. She asked her less alarmed friend to grab a bottle of water from their cooler, while she tried to assess whether my father was harmed by the blow running her delicate hand over his forehead.

"I'm Jack."

The words escaped my father's lips surprising himself, as it was unlike him to introduce himself to strangers.

The magnificent blonde revealed a riveting affable smile that could only belong to someone who was genuinely kind-hearted and extended her arm in introduction.

"Hi Jack, very nice to meet you. I'm Susan."

She held his gaze and felt his timid hand grab hers in response. Susan's friend returned with an ice-cold bottle of water, which she handed to him quickly before asking if Susan was coming back to continue with the game.

"You know, I'll sit this out and hang out with my new friend Jack for a bit."

Susan let go of Jack's hand and gestured to her friends to continue playing, which they proceeded to do without a second thought. Susan placed the cold surface of the bottle against my father's forehead to prevent a bruise, making my father wince from the chill on his bare skin.

Jack and Susan remained seated on the sand for hours, talking about their lives. Susan was not bored by my father's detailed account of his studies and Jack adored my mother's description of her childhood in Delaware and laughed with her as she described her exciting plans for the high school graduation in a month. They were both enthralled by their conversation, ignoring the pleas of their friends to go home as it got darker until they finally looked around realizing that the beach had emptied out and the sun was about to set. That was when they agreed to see each other every day until it was time for my father to leave, and they kept to that promise, spending hours walking along the endless stretch of the beach caught up in each other's presence.

"Can I write to you from Milwaukee during the summer, Susan?", he cautiously asked his new friend on the last day of his weeklong stay.

Susan nodded eagerly "I'd like that very much." She pulled out a clean napkin and a pen out of her daisy-print knapsack and scribbled her address. "Here, make sure you write to me as soon as you get there.".

That is exactly what my father did, he wrote to Susan as soon as he arrived at his old trailer after a few uncomfortable minutes of catching up with his mother, who seemed to forget that he was coming back for the summer and therefore almost seemed disappointed to see him.

When he mailed the meticulously written letter the next day, his only thoughts were fixated on whether Susan would write back, and his anticipation grew everyday while he checked the mailbox every hour. He was ecstatic to have finally received a letter only three days later and reread her letter several times, transfixed by the final sentence which ended in a bolded XOXO.

That was a start to their pen-relationship, as they wrote back and forth to each other and continued to do so throughout the summer and even when my father returned for his final year at Stanford. When the Thanksgiving holidays approached, my father was invited to join Simon's family for the week in Delaware noting that his parents enjoyed his company while he was around, and the feeling was mutual. While my father loathed every minute of staying with his mother, he blissfully reminisced not only the moments spent with Susan but also all the kind gestures towards him from the strangers whom he promptly grew to be fond of even over the short period of time. Eagerly accepting the invitation to stay in Delaware for a week, my father counted the minutes until it was time to leave. Unfortunately, Simon's car had broken down a week earlier and they had to take a long bus trip to the Eastern coast, but the discomfort of the trip did not hinder my father's excitement.

The first person he saw when he stepped off the inter-state bus was Susan, who leaped into his arms and hugged him tightly. Jack was relieved to finally see his pen-pal, whom he advised in his previous letter of his looming arrival, he held her tightly in his arms, for the first time not feeling awkward at the human touch. Hyped on the moment, he finally mustered all his courage and leaned in to kiss the stunning blonde, which she was only happy to reciprocate. This was when he knew that he would not be able to separate from her again, that exchanging letters was not sufficient for him and he needed to be with Susan at all times. He assessed his options throughout the week, while savouring the delicious meals prepared by Simon's mother and spending every possible minute with his kindred spirit. The thought of being apart from his Susan was deplorable, so as his short week in Delaware was coming to an end, he called his professor and advised that he needed to take some time off his studies due to certain extenuating circumstances. The professor implored him to change his mind, but my father remained stoic in his position and followed his heart to stay with Susan.

After a short thrilling month of courtship, my parents confidently made the decision to get married. My mother's parents were livid with their defiant daughter for marrying incredibly young and giving up on her future with a college dropout, so they refused to accept my father into their family and rebuffed the invitation to attend the wedding. Unable to change their opinion and determined to marry each other no matter the circumstances, my parents had a small civil ceremony attended by Simon's parents, Susan's closest friends and her grandmother.

My late great grandmother was the only person who accepted my father in my mother's family, because she saw the true happiness in my mother's eyes and my father's unconditional love for his new bride, so she was happy to welcome the newlyweds to stay at her house. Grandmother Lily lived alone for almost twenty years, ever since her late husband died of a heart attack, and she proclaimed in her wedding toast that her last wish was to be surrounded by love in her final years and would welcome the newly married couple light her house with their kindled affection. My credulous parents did not hesitate to agree, as the subject of the matrimonial home was one that burdened them heavily and moved in shortly after the wedding.

They loved living with my great grandmother in her comfortable two-storey home, however my father understood that he had to start earning an income because they could not leech from Grandmother Lily for the rest of their lives. With limited job opportunities in the area, Jack was only able to find a position in the computer repair store, but he assured himself and his wife that this was only temporary. He was confident that he would resume his studies to graduate as soon as they had enough money to pay the bills, but the longevity of the break lasted for years.

enjoyed our stay to the fullest, so he would be happy to rebook us to any other weekend. We'd just have to call back when we are ready."

Unable to hide my resounding relief, I jumped up excitedly from the sofa and hugged my mother snugly. My father broodingly looked at our cozy embrace and playfully mumbled in fake complaint.

"I see, you are ganging up against me, are you?" He gave us a quizzical look over the thick frame of his glasses.

"Never!" I exclaimed, as my mother and I ran over to him and tackled his body to the floor and rolled around intertwined trying to pin him down while our loud laughs filled the house.

*They are not going anywhere.* The happy thought rolled around in my mind as I play fought with my father supported by my cheerful partner.

On the formerly feared February Saturday early morning before my parents woke up, I quietly tiptoed downstairs shivering from the coldness of the hardwood floors over to the dark kitchen to grab a plastic foot stool that my mother kept under the table. Trying to remain quiet, I grabbed the stool and carried it towards the front door of the house. Once I placed it down, I raised my head locating the car keys secured on the hook by the door and climbed up on the step raising my body high on my toes with my fingers barely able to nudge the key out of their spot. They slipped off their resting place, and I instinctively caught them before they came crashing down on the floor. I stayed still for a moment to make sure there were no stirring sounds upstairs from my parents being alerted by the slight jingle of the metal when I clasped the keys in my hand. Assured by the still silence that my parents were still sound asleep, I slid the keys in my pyjama pocket and carried the foot stool back in the kitchen. I quietly paced upstairs back in the bedroom, satisfied with the completion of the final touches of my impeccable plan. While I was confident that my parents were not going anywhere that day, I still wanted to make sure that they did not try to leave the house.

The silence of the house comforted me while I lay in bed imagining the new reality as we were embarking on a different path in the fork in the road, steering clear of the dreadful dead-end turn. The images of my foreseeable future flashed before my eyes, my parents' delighted faces leering at me as I go up the podium to accept my high school diploma, my mother crying as they drop me off at college, my father proudly walking me down the aisle. Our new lives were going to be wonderful, filled with novel family events and attainable dreams.

The sound of my mother cooking in the kitchen and smell of the grilled pancakes stirred me from my daydreaming, so I quickly rose from my warm bed and walked downstairs. The funky eighties music blared through the radio as I entered the kitchen and saw my father twirling my mother around the room in his best attempt at dancing. I hid behind the door, watching them in their natural carefree element, forgetting about their financial woes and just enjoying each other's company in a light-hearted clumsy dance. When my father got winded from dancing, he pulled my mother towards him and kissed her firmly on the lips and she put her arms around his shoulders in a loving embrace. These were the moments that I cherished and appreciated, as none of these memories of them being a happily married couple stayed with me when they passed in the prior lifetime. The frigidness of the floor made me shuffle in my spot and alerted my parents of my presence as they separated from their loving grasp.

"I think we should eat these pancakes before Noelle comes down." I heard my mother's voice teasing.

"You know, you're right. Blueberry pancakes are her favourite, so we better finish them fast." My father joined her on the prank.

"Not if I finish them first!"

I jumped out of my hiding and ran over to the kitchen table to take my seat, while my mother brought over a steaming plate of my favourite breakfast dish placing it in front of me, as my father poured two cups of coffee and a glass of orange juice.

"Black coffee, your usual, Noelle?" My father jokingly placed a cup of aromatic java next to me, tempting me to grab the drink and take a sip.

*Boy, do I miss coffee*, I thought to myself and remembered how upset my mother was when I tried to drink some of her coffee once. Instead, I laughed at my father's traditional morning joke and reached for the orange juice then focused on eating the delicious hot pancakes drenched in the sticky maple syrup. During breakfast, my father announced that he will be making Valentines' dinner for us and to expect a meal worthy of a Michelin star. There were no objections from us, my mother was happy not to spend her day cooking a big meal and I typically liked my father's messy but great tasting dishes. What he missed out on the presentation skills, he made up in experimenting with great flavours.

Once breakfast was over, my mother said that she was going to prepare a hot bubbly bath for me and walked upstairs, where I heard her turn on the tap. While she was gone my father and I played "I Spy", guessing all the kitchen contents in sight. When it was my father's final

Grandmother Lily passed away in her sleep shortly before I was born, leaving the house to her granddaughter ensuring that the small but growing family always had a roof over their heads. Losing her beloved grandmother was a travesty for my mother and my father comforted her to the best of his abilities while realizing that he had to work even longer hours to support his expanding family and pay the house bills.

My subdued father remained at his job for five long years, fixing mundane computer problems, until he sat my mother down one evening and said that they could take out a personal loan and mortgage the house while he finished his last needed credits required for him to get his degree. This also meant that my father would only work an occasional evening or weekend at the computer repair shop for the time being, but once he graduated, he would have endless job opportunities. My mother keenly agreed with his stance and asked if they could use some of the loan to open a travel agency that she had been dreaming about, to which my father consented confident that once he graduated, he would be able to find a well-paying job which would allow him to pay off the loan swiftly.

My parents had a lot of dreams to fulfill, and they discussed their many grandiose plans in the evenings as they cuddled watching late night television, while I continued to eavesdrop sitting on top of the staircase night after night. As the fateful day approached, Jack had reached out to Delaware University to see whether he could finish his degree there, while discussing with his employer the possibility of scaling back his hours at work. Susan continued to stay home with me while formulating her business plan of opening the small agency where she would sell tour packages to all the elusive destinations that she had dreamed to visit herself.

Being a curious individual, my mother had always had a craving for travel but never had the chance to leave the boundary of the East coast. When we were home alone, she would typically tell me stories that she made up on the spot about a family of travelling mice who sneaked into planes, trains and cruise ships while exploring the world. The Mouser family got to see Paris from atop the sky-high Eiffel Tower, they sneaked in to discover the ancient underground tunnels of the Coliseum and see the wide plains of endless sands in the Sahara Desert. She knew all the curious facts about every country as she loved reading her grandmother's outdated travel guides and flipped through the pages of the many travel magazines Grandmother Lily collected over the years.

I tightly embraced my cuddly stuffed pig Winkie, and listened intently to my mother's wild imagination as she told me all about the wonders of the world visited by the family of mice, picturing us in their place.

*We'll go to see the world together*, I thought, determined to carry out my well-thought-out plan of making sure my parents survive the fateful Valentine's Day.

The first order of business on my agenda was to make sure that my parents did not make plans to go away for the weekend, so when they first brought up the idea of me going to spend two days at Roxie and Alison's house, I vigorously objected. This shocked them slightly as they thought that I would be excited to go to my first sleepover at my best friend's house. Then my mother tried to reason with me, trying to convince me to no avail of all the excited things Roxie and I would be doing that day and that Alison had great plans for us and would even take us to the movies. Her futile efforts did not make me budge from my firm position, so my parents gave up on their initial plan and started considering taking me with them. I was fully prepared for this turn of events, so switched my position to counter their attempts of going away together.

"It's cold all weekend, and the lady on the TV said that there is a chance of an ice storm. Remember the last ice storm? You could not even go outside to buy groceries. Why go somewhere far and not leave the hotel, if we can do the same here?" I tried to be the voice of reason trapped in a five-year old's body.

"Our baby girl is not wrong, Jack." My mother's position started to falter. "I saw the weather forecast too and it doesn't sound promising."

"But the hotel is already paid for, and we already made plans."

Jack maintained his view, unwilling to give up the deposit that he made earlier for the sea view room.

"If we call the hotel and explain the situation, maybe they'll agree to rebook us for a different weekend?"

My mother leveraged her travel guide knowledge to think of a way out of my father's predicament.

"Only if they agree to rebook us, then we'll stay."

My father conceded as his wife walked over to the phone, flipped through the address book on the coffee table and dialed the number. After a short exchange of pleasantries and a quick conversation, Susan hung up the phone and turned to face us.

"Looks like we're staying in this weekend. The hotel manager completely understood our position and said that he would rather we turn he said:

"I spy with my little eyes…something beginning with P."

"A pot?" I tried to guess, and he shook his head.

"Pancakes!" I responded confident of the answer, but he disagreed.

"A plate?" I tried a third and final guess, not spotting any pineapples or peppers in sight. My father shook his head again and opened his mouth to give his answer, when we heard my mother's voice summoning me to join her upstairs because the bathtub was filled. Impatient to jump in the scorching bubbly water, I slid off my chair and ran towards the staircase then remembered that we had not finished the game.

"What was it then, dad?"

"A princess." He responded winking at me, as I giggled at his response suppressing the need to tell him that a princess is a who and not a what. Then I continued on my way and joined my mother in the bathroom. She gestured to the foamy surface of the teeming tub for me to get in, I hastily undressed and enthusiastically submerged into the steamy bathwater. My mother stayed by my side in a chair, she did not like leaving me behind in the potentially dangerous depths of the bath, so instead she read a book while I preoccupied myself with floating in the tub and forming bubble figures from the foam. A knock on the bathroom door followed by my father's voice interrupting her reading, as she got up and stepped out of the bathroom cautioning me to be careful. Their quick exchange lasted less than a minute, as my mother would not leave me unattended for longer than that. When she re-entered the room, I was still busy engineering structures out of the foam around me, so she settled back down and continued reading.

After a while, when I noticed my fingertips pruning and the water started to cool down, I turned to my mother startling her with my voice. My mother raised her eyes from her book to look at her wristwatch and was shocked to see that an hour had passed since I first got in the tub. She briskly pulled me out of the tub and rubbed me down with the fluffy white towel, then helped me change into a fresh pair of pyjamas. When I came out of the bathroom, I felt very invigorated to start the day and spend the afternoon with mom and dad.

"Dad!" I yelled for him from the top of the stairs. "What do you want to do next?"

There was dead silence from downstairs, so I ran to my parent's bedroom to see if he was reading his textbooks there, but the room was vacant. Then I figured that he must have stepped outside to salt the stairs and clean the driveway to prevent the ice from building up, so I walked over to the large window in my parents' master bedroom and looked out onto the street but could not spot my father. Suddenly, I felt a jolt of panic piece my body when my eyes spotted the fresh tire tracks leading out of our driveway. My body froze in fear, while my bottom lip trembled from the frightful thought that I was afraid to acknowledge.

"Mom!" The terrified scream escaped me. "Where is daddy?"

My mother ran into the bedroom alarmed by my loud yelling, thinking that I got hurt but then exhaled with relief realizing that I was unharmed.

"Oh, don't worry, honey. He just needed a few ingredients from the supermarket for his extravagant dinner." Then she glanced at her watch looking slightly puzzled. "He should have been back by now, but he probably went to Frank's across town instead of the corner store. Frank's has everything. I told him specifically to avoid the icy highway today."

The worry inside me rose exponentially, flooding my body with fierce emotions, because I knew that to get to Frank's quicker you had to get on the highway. The single hope that resided in my mind was that my father chose to take a longer route and drove through the town to get to the store.

"Honey, you haven't seen the car keys, have you?" My mother asked me, busing herself with folding the laundry. "Your father must have lost them again, good thing we made a few spares just in case."

*Spares!* How did I not think that they would have had spare keys when they noticed the other keys being gone. My father lost keys with consistent regularity, so it would make sense for my mother to be prepared for the situation, but I did not think to look for the spares. I clenched my fists in anger of my own stupidity, every muscle in body tightening with tension, my eyes fixated on the driveway willing for my father to pull in any second.

"Why don't you go watch some TV, sweetie?" I heard my mother's voice faintly through the deafening buzzing in my head. "Ok, you rather stay and wait for your father to come back here? I guess I can read my book while we wait."

She settled on the right side of their double bed and started reading her book. Time passed slowly, and my hope dimmed with every passing car. After almost an hour, mom set down her book and joined me by the window. I felt her arms wrap around my tiny shoulders, so I looked up at her with my bloodshot eyes and noticed her eyes fill with concern, as she nervously peered out of the window.

"Your daddy probably stopped at Alison's to help her clear her driveway." She tried to camouflage her worried voice with fake calmness. "Let's go downstairs, so I could call her, and you can keep watch from the living room window."

I hesitantly nodded but followed her downstairs, where I perched myself up on the window seat and stayed focused on the driveway while my mother dialed the number.

"Hi Alison." My mother's voice lacked its usual perkiness. "Jack hadn't come over to your place today, has he?" She continued with a glimmer of hope then allowed for a pause for Alison to respond. Unable to hear the voice on the other end of the line, I listened intently for my mother's reaction.

"Oh. He just said he'd go to the store, but he'd been gone for almost two hours." Her voice was drained of emotion, once her friend confirmed that she had not seen Jack.

"Yes, I'm sure you're right. I am probably overthinking it. Will call you later, ok?" The call concluded, as my mother hung up the phone and stealthily took a seat on the couch.

Remaining unhinged by my father's long absence and further unnerved by the call, she turned on the television set to distract us from our mutual daunting thoughts. The unwelcomed sounds of raucous laughter and cheery dialogue interrupted the still silence but failed to deflect our escalating anxiety, as our individual worries continued to infect each other with uncontrollable force. I remained still in my position by the window, while my mother nervously wrung her index finger around her long golden hair lock in an endless circular motion. The quietness in the house grew denser until it completely obscured everything in the vicinity. The concept of time was lost to us as every minute seemed like an endless cycle filled with agony, while the only evidence of the passing hours were the changing shapes of the dark shadows inside the living room. When the daylight transitioned to darkness, it became harder to make out the passing cars on the streets as they changed to the characterless flickering lights fleeting by.

Suddenly a sound of the trilling ringing of the phone next to my mother pierced the overbearing silence, and she quickly leapt up to her feet and snatched the receiver from its cradle.

"Hello?" She almost screamed into the handset, then her voice changed to an audible tremble as she heard her friend on the other line. "No, Alison, he is still not back. It has been hours; we are both worried sick. Where could he possibly be?"

My eyes were still fixated on the darkness outside the window, while I listened to my mom on the phone as she poured out all her sensible worries to Alison unable to further contain her emotions. Then through the blackness of the late evening emerged two bright lights pulling into our driveway illuminating its path. The brightness hurt my eyes, so I covered them and turned to my mother immediately.

"Mommy, someone is here. Someone just pulled in!" I yelled, while running for the front door.

"Alison, he's back. Someone just pulled in, let me just put the phone down for a minute and I'll be right back." My mother rested the receiver next to the telephone and rushed over to the front door to join me as a determined knocking sound permeated the hallway. She swiftly unlocked the door and swung it open with a relieved smile fixed on her face, until she saw two unfamiliar dark figures expounded by the headlights from the car behind them. Her joyful glow changed instantly when she recognized the police uniforms on the two strangers, and I instantly knew that my worst fears came true, prompting me to leap at my mother and squeeze her legs tight, afraid to hear what the police officers had to say. My sudden movement made my mother stagger to the left, but she leaned against the wall for balance, and silently waited for the visitors to say something.

"Mrs. Anderson?" One of the men approached us closer, to which my mother responded with a regretful nod. The police officer dithered in his spot, looking at me with genuine sorrow as I mutely begged him not to continue. The second officer asked my mother if she could take me to a different room while they talked to her, but I vigorously fought off any of their attempts and stayed glued to my mother's legs.

"I regret to inform you that there was an accident on the freeway with multiple casualties." The officer took a deep breath and then verbalized our worst fears.

"Unfortunately your husband Jack Peterson did not survive the crash and was pronounced deceased on scene."

The inhumane wail escaped my mother's body bouncing off the walls of the house that suddenly seemed huge and infinitely empty. The terrified scream echoed in my ears, and I felt scorching excruciating tears run down my face while I felt my mother's knees weakening and leaning further into the wall. The police officers briskly walked into the house and one of them helped my mother up, and walked her over to lay down on the sofa as the other officer picked me up and carried me into the room. While the police officer was attending to my mother, the other office who was holding me in his arms noticed that the phone on the side table was off the cradle and picked it up to listen.

"Is everyone ok? Hello?" He heard Alison's terrified screams on the other end.

"Hello, this is Officer Johnson. Are you a friend of the family?" The police officer asked, while still holding me tight in his arms.

"What is going on? Yes, I am a friend." Alison continued to scream into the phone.

"Are you able to come to the Anderson household imminently? I believe Mrs. Anderson and her little girl may need someone here."

"On my way!" Alison knew not to raise any more questions and hung up before Officer Johnson had a chance to ask anything else.

The kind police officer held me tightly while my tiny trembling body shook with every grieving cry. He rocked me in his arms back and forth, just like my father used to do when I could not fall asleep, which only made me cry harder at the devastating loss. I grieved my father for the second time, this time being significantly harder because I grew to understand my father and fall in love with him as a person and not as a blurry figure from a childhood memory. He was a brilliant man who deserved to live his life and fulfill all his wonderful plans, but his short life ended once again on the same day as before. His undeniable love for my mother was unique in so many ways, something that I had not encountered in the past or present. The way he admired her with unquestionable devotion, was all I could hope to experience at least once in my life.

The police officers stayed in the house with us until the unlocked front door flew open and Alison stormed into the room with sleepy Roxie in tow. Quickly assessing the situation, she commandeered Officer Johnson to take me and Roxie into my room upstairs which he obliged and carried me in his arms with Roxie pacing ahead of him to lead the way. He set me down in my bed and I reluctantly unwrapped my arms, staring at him through the tears.

"You are a strong girl. You know your momma needs you more than anything right now, so you need to stay strong for her. Can you promise me that?" He asked and waited for me to nod before leaving the room and closed the door behind him.

Roxie waited for Officer Johnson to leave, then she climbed in my bed and covered us with the comforter to get warm. My body continued to shiver from the silent crying, until I felt Roxie's spindly arms hug me tight while her tiny body spooned me for comfort. She had her mother's innate sense of when words were unnecessary, thus she knew what I needed most was a consolable enfold of a comforting cuddle. We stayed tightly laced with my back pressed against her chest and I felt my breathing eventually stabilize to match her calm breaths. My tears eventually subsided, and I started to drift off to sleep thinking about my final happy moment with my father when he winked at me and called me a princess.

Chapter Nine

*September 2003*
*Age 18*

"It's unbelievable here, Rox!"

I exclaimed into the phone, while stretched out on the hard mattress of the single bed that I have grown accustomed to over the last week. The first week at UCLA was indeed unbelievable, and I had not been able to spend more than seven hours each night in the room that was assigned to me when I first arrived a week earlier. A maelstrom of university sponsored events, uncountable introductions to different people and the wild unsanctioned parties consumed my life and the concerns I previously had about being homesick were swept away in an instant.

When I told my mother that I was choosing to go to UCLA instead of the much closer colleges in the Eastern states, she was devastated. We celebrated every admission letter I received over the summer with the scholarship offers of different varieties, and she was confident that I would decide to attend a university within driving distance of our home. My final choice was a surprise to me too, as I had not planned to even apply to any colleges in California, but Mrs. Wallace the guidance counsellor at the school called me into her office one day towards the end of tenth grade for an informal chat.

"Noelle, what do you plan to do with your life?" She asked the question that I had myself been pondering for years. I was certain that I wanted to stay in Georgetown with my mother and help her at the travel agency that she opened with Alison ten years prior. Without having a fully formulated response for Mrs. Wallace, I simply shrugged my shoulders.

"Your grades are phenomenal, and your teachers all praise you for being a student who learns incredibly fast. Over the years, we have given you a few offers at skipping over a grade to match your academic level, but you have declined every time."

I remembered the arguments I had with my mother when she tried to convince me to accept the school's recommendations, but I was in no rush to graduate earlier than I needed to, and this also allowed me to stay in the same class as my one friend in the entire world.

"The only person you are friends with is Roxie. I know you get along with all the other students, but you should really make an effort and be friends with other people. You know colleges do not base their admissions strictly on your perfect grades, but also your social involvement and extracurricular activities. You have just over two years until your graduation, so there is plenty of time to improve on this."

Mrs. Wallace repeated my mother's words, which made me wonder whether my mom made a school visit and asked the guidance counselor to have a chat with me.

"You know, I was a bit like you in high school. My problem was that I did not know my purpose until I met a guidance counselor at my school and realized that I wanted to help kids just like me. So, you know what I did? I chose a college as far from home as possible to challenge myself. I wanted to completely take me out of my safety zone and be someone else for a while to understand who I really was and to affirm my goals in life."

She gazed at me waiting for a reaction, so I thanked her for the suggestion and assured her that I would give her suggestions a lot of consideration.

*What is my purpose?* I spent the next several months thinking about where I belonged and what value I could bring to the world.

If I stayed home in Delaware, I would not have a chance to discover myself being limited by the constraints of the local easy-going mentality. Throughout the years, I had convinced myself that I would stay by my mother's side making sure that she was safe, but my mother resisted the untraditional balance of parent being cared for by the child. When I first told her that I did not think I wanted to leave and go off to college, she vehemently disagreed, proclaiming that the only two things that would make her happy is if I furthered my education and gave her some space. Then her concluding point to the discussion was that my father would have undoubtedly wanted me to get a college degree, something that he was unable to attain in his short life. Eventually after months of analysing my life prospects I gave in to the proposed suggestions and on my first day in senior year I enlisted in the Debate Club, the Creative Writing Club and joined the staff of our school newspaper the *Telegram Journal*.

What my mother did not consider was that I would take her suggestion a step further and out of pure curiosity look for schools outside of her envisioned radius. I was still convinced that I would enrol in Delaware University so I could be closer to home, but I wanted to explore my options and see what else was out there. Then through my online searching at the school library, I stumbled onto a school I had only heard about on the many teen dramedies, the elusive and illustrious UCLA. All I knew about California overall at the time was what I had seen on TV, the tanned predominantly blonde girls dating extremely muscular good-looking guys in surroundings that only seemed to exist in postcards. Dating was not on my radar, but I did not mind being surrounded by handsome men instead of the alternative. Browsing through the college's list of Majors, I immediately knew that I wanted to enrol in the English program where I could continue to spend hours reading the classic masterpieces and meet like minded people who read for pleasure instead of being forced to do so by their teachers.

Once the submissions for college enrollment were opened, I sent in the completed applications supported by several recommendation letters to the four universities that my mother and I had discussed and then discreetly submitted a separate application to UCLA, along with an application for a full scholarship based on academic merit. The only person who was aware of the application for me to go to college in California was Roxie, who supported that alternative wholeheartedly.

"It's California, N! That is a dream. Look around, see all that grey muck on the ground."

Roxie gestured dismayed with her arm in a half circle motion to the grimy puddles as we walked home from school. "There would be none of that in LA. Plus you'll get to see all the movie starts, maybe even get to hang out with Brad Pitt." She continued dreamily.

"You know you can't tell my mom or your mom. I can't even imagine how mad my mom will be if I actually get in." I quickly reminded her of California being our own secret. "As a matter of fact, I'm slightly alarmed that you wouldn't care if I moved away. I know I will miss you, to Delaware and back, when I'm gone."

"No, you won't. You'll be too busy smooching Brad on the Red Carpet." Roxie joked, then stopped walking and turned to face me. "Of course, I will miss you, N! I do not remember a single day without you, but I don't want you to rot away in this dullness. There is a whole world out there! Also, I was thinking I might join you one day anyways."

"Without a doubt. I'm glad you're planning to stay here for a bit to help Alison and mom with the travel agency."

I responded, genuinely happy that Roxie would be safe staying with our mothers and away from the dangers of the big cities.

"Honestly, I'm just glad you're not going to New York, you know how that place gives me the creeps" She shivered, then raised her arm and rolled up her sleeve to reveal the raised hairs and multitude of goosebumps.

"It's just the cold."

I tried to convince her of the bodily reaction, but this was not the first time I had noticed that Roxie had an inherent aversion to New York without possessing any memories of ever being there. When we were children, she categorically refused to watch Home Alone 2 or Miracle on 34th street at Christmas time, unable to explain her discontent to Alison when her mother tried to keep her in front of the screen. In the senior year when the Drama Club that Roxie was a part of went to New York for three days, she made an excuse of prior family commitments to avoid going. Aware of Roxie's predisposition to disliking any mention of NYC and my own personal memories that I was unable to erase, I typically avoided the subject of New York in general.

As months went on, and the admission letters started arriving in the mailbox I finally spotted an envelope with a coveted UCLA logo, which I ripped open immediately to reveal the exhilarating news of being accepted. I was shocked at the acceptance but was already downright convinced that I would choose to go to Los Angeles over any other schools. After a predictable but extensive argument with my mother, I was finally able to persuade her, based on the fact that the admission also included a full scholarship for the duration of my studies as long as my grades were kept above an average of eighty percent. While the other schools also presented their attractive scholarship offers, neither included an equivalent offer which guaranteed that my mother would not have to spend her life savings on my education. My mother's and Alison's travel agency was doing reasonably well, and they could live a comfortable life from the earnings, but the university education was not cheap and I would have preferred if my mother spent it on the much-needed house renovations or the long awaited trips that she had been talking about for years.

Once my mother conceded to my arguments and understood that

she could not influence me otherwise, she made me promise that I would call her at least once a day or she was going to come to Los Angeles and drag me home. Accepting the seemingly reasonable condition, I hugged my resigned mother in exhilaration and called Roxie to come over and bring Alison so we could celebrate. While we waited for them to arrive, my mother busied herself in the kitchen baking a cake and I immersed myself in the many freshmen brochures that accompanied the UCLA admission letter. The perfect white-teeth smiles of impeccably groomed young people tickled my curiosity on whether I would start looking just as carefree after a while. I pictured myself wearing a UCLA hoodie, sitting on the sandy beach of Santa Monica reading a hefty tome while scribbling my thoughts on the notepad in preparation for an assignment due at the end of the week. Delighted by the thought, I heard a knock on the door and walked over to open it only to be immediately enveloped in a tight hug by a squealing Roxie.

"Congratulations, Noelle. Just make sure you stay away from those forest fires and wear lots of sunscreen." Alison said with her frame being blocked from my view by Roxie's wild hair covering my eyes. "And don't trust any of those handsome men, they are all trouble."

"Got it, Aunt Alison." I mumbled to Roxie's delight.

Then as we separated from the tight embrace, we started jumping around the living room in a boisterous celebration screaming the lyrics of Californication on top of our lungs. Alison and mom watched us in awe from the kitchen, amazed at our lung capacity and endless energy levels. That was one of the moments that I may have missed slightly when I woke up in the sunny mornings in my cozy dorm room, but I managed to quickly suppress the melancholy thoughts and rushed to meet new friends to explore the bustling metropolis that was my new home.

"Everyone is really nice here; I've met so many people. Some of us are going to Venice Beach later today in the evening. One of the orientation coordinators I met on the first day invited me to join him and his friends." I carried on my phone call with Roxie in my dorm room, thinking of all the exciting events that I have been up to over the last week.

"It's a he?" Roxie asked inquisitively with a scathing tone.

"Yes, his name is Jared, and he is a senior. He is really nice; you would like him. He is studying Finance and is already an intern at this big firm in the city. They've already promised him a job when he graduates."

I described my new friend, who had introduced me to so many

people and was so aware of his future while I still struggled to understand mine.

"So, he's just being nice to you for no reason and you're just friends?" She continued to press the subject trying to extract more information.

"Well, yes, but honestly I wouldn't mind if this evolved into something more amorous. He is so handsome and smart; I have never heard anyone speak so eloquently about life in general. He has been all over the world and I'm sure he finds me dull seeing how I've never been anywhere outside of Delaware before I came to California."

"You're so far from dull, N. You were the smartest kid in school for twelve years straight, you were a Chief Editor at the Telegram Journal, you have read every book in the school library…twice."

Roxie maintained her cheerleader role in my life and never failed to remind me of my accomplishments, even if they were slightly exaggerated.

"I was a Chief Editor only for the last semester and I could hardly read all the books in the library, although I did read some of the books twice." I retaliated submissively.

"Doesn't matter, the point is you are the most interesting and prettiest girl I know. This Jared should be so lucky as to even be in your presence."

"You are right." Then I paused and reluctantly continued. "He actually kissed me last night when he walked me home after a party and he was a proper gentleman. I did not want him to stop."

There was silence on the end of the line, as Roxie processed the information.

"See, it's impossible not to like you. Every guy in high school wanted to be with you, you just never gave anyone a chance." She laughed remembering all the awkwardly written Valentines' notes that I received and the declined prom proposals in our final year. "But, N, just be careful, ok? Don't jump into anything too quickly."

"You are spending too much time with your mother these days; you are starting to sound just like her." I tried to joke in response. "But I promise, I will be on high alert. Anyways, why don't you tell me the latest Georgetown gossip?"

Changing the subject seemed like the best approach, as I could not handle a lecture from my best friend today and was anxiously awaiting Jared to come by and pick me up in the evening.

"Georgetown is still standing, although it seems like it lost half of its IQ when you left. There is nobody to talk to in this little godforsaken town these days!"

Roxie complained about Georgetown even when I was there, so I could not take her latest woes seriously. "I did not tell you before because I wanted to know for sure, but before you left, I auditioned for the local theatre group to keep me busy when I'm not at the travel agency, and they just told me that they'd love for me to join. So that's kind of exciting! We are performing My Fair Lady in a couple of months and I'm playing the housekeeper role. Did not even know that there was a housekeeper in the musical, but obviously they could not give me any bigger parts since I just started."

"That's great news! I know how much you loved acting in high school. Maybe I'll make it home for Christmas/Birthday celebrations and get to see you in action."

I had not thought about the plans for the end of the year yet, but I assumed that everyone went home for the holidays.

"Also, I have some juicy gossip for you! Remember that weird creep we met at the party in August? What was his name…."

Roxie paused trying to recall the name that had been haunting my worst nightmares and occasionally caused me to wake up in cold sweat.

"Ray" I sat upright in my bed, my face immediately draining of any colour and heaviness setting at the bottom of my stomach, as I remembered the day when the vile monster from my most gruesome memories materialized in Georgetown less than a month ago.

There were no disillusions in my mind, and I fully comprehended that I would one day encounter Ray when he came to town that summer, seeing that I had no control over his actions and could not prevent his eventual ingress into our lives. My only determined hope was that the dreaded rendezvous would be fleeting, barely leaving a mark on our new lives. So as years went on, I grudgingly waited for the summer after graduation when Ray was expected to infiltrate our lives.

The summer started off on a high note when I placed the finished final exam paper in my Math teacher's hands. After two grueling hours but fully satisfied with my answers, I walked out of the classroom glorified with finally being done with high school. School was generally a breeze for me, considering that I had already gone through all the same classes and the identical exams previously with clear details of those days preserved in my enduring memory. While I was barely an average student in the prior lifetime, I was able to utilize the preserved knowledge to enhance my learning ability and propel me to the top of the class into a valedictorian upon graduation. Sure, I knew that I had an unfair advantage, but when the universe takes pity on you and smashes a pinata filled with propitious favours over your head, you grab as many as you can and stuff them in all the crevasses of your life hoping for a better outcome.

When I walked out into the schoolyard after handing in the exam paper, I saw Roxie sitting on a low wooden bench under the vast shade of an oak tree gleefully chatting with her friend Annie from the Theatre Club, so I ran over to join them interrupting their discussion.

"That was the last of it, no more high school! Adult life here we come."

I proclaimed on my approach, as Roxie jumped up from her seat.

"I'm not ready for adult life just yet, but I am definitely done with high school."

She mirrored my excitement, grabbing my arms and starting to whirl us around the yard as her friend laughed watching us from the bench. Then Roxie leaned in for a hug and whispered in my ear. "Thanks for the tips on that exam, it really helped me out.".

Nodding in response, I glanced over Roxie's shoulder to make sure that her friend did not suspect anything. Over the years I have looked after my best friend in every possible way, I have helped Roxie with her schooling in manifold trying to improve her chances at graduating with me and prevented her broken arm and stitched head accidents that she was not as fortunate in avoiding in her prior childhood. So, Roxie sensed that I had some celestial abilities but never drilled me on the source of my clairvoyance.

Once we were done with the celebratory dance, Roxie announced that Annie invited us to join her at a barbecue party that some of her friends were throwing at their house and we could not possibly decline because it was bad luck to miss the first party of the summer. Unable to resist Roxie's enthusiasm and inclined to spend some time in the sun, I eagerly agreed. The inner joy of the summer season and the final school days supported by the fact that Ray was only going to be in town in August, I still had a few months of the stress-free summer parties ahead of me. Thus, commenced my final summer in Georgetown, before taking the plunge into the blonde- tanned world of sunny California.

The summertime days were spent researching UCLA campus life through the online forums and the mailed brochures, shopping with my mother for the perfect outfits to blend into to the relaxed but trendy West-coast lifestyle and the pool parties that seemed to be hosted almost every day. I savored the joyful carefree canicular days with every passing moment, unjustly comparing it to the same summer period when Roxie and I worked at Fat Joe's and worked two shifts to support ourselves and Alison. We slaved away everyday working on our feet serving the never-ending flow of customers, despising the odours and the sticky oil that seemed to seep into our skin, but we were just as happy when we were able to leave work and go to a late evening party until early hours in the day only to wake up a few hours later to go back to the greasy joint.

Roxie and I lived a much more comfortable lifestyle now with our loving mothers and the luxurious ability to sleep in, but sometimes I would get a flicker of nostalgia over the moments when Roxie would perch up on the counter as I sat behind it on my stool gossiping about the rude customers while chomping down the giant greasy burgers. A need for a job was less trivial this time with my mother owning a profitable business, but anytime I suggested that I find a part-time job my mom refused profusely and insisted that I focus on my classes and all the extracurricular activities that I had signed up for, following the suggestions of Mrs. Wallace.

The summer months flew by virtually imperceptible while I kept myself busy in preparation for college and saying goodbye to my many school friends in town as they hastily left Georgetown towards their own chosen colleges. One sunny day turned into another filled with outdoor activities that mostly kept me out of the house.

One morning I walked down for breakfast, after my mother had already left for work, sat down at the kitchen counter with a bowl of cereal and turned on the TV, which I have been missing out on almost all summer. After flipping through some of the channels, I temporarily settled on the foursome of beautiful hosts arguing over the latest contentious fashion trend adorned by the barely famous personalities. The morning show mused about the celebrities' styles and then switched to the makeover segment, which revealed some less than impressive results. Unimpressed with the quality of the morning television and unwilling to watch the news, I reached for the remote to switch off the TV set when I heard the male news anchor's voice.

"Good morning, everyone, it is now 11am on August 6 and today on the news…"

I dropped the remote when I realized that in all the summer excitement, I had lost track of the days and we were already in August. Ray's arrival was imminent, and I had to be more aware of where Roxie and I go, so we could be more prepared when we inevitably would bump into him.

My troubling thoughts were disrupted by a car honk out on the driveway and I peeked out the window, noticing Roxie in the passenger seat with a bunch of our friends coming to pick me up to go to the beach. I waved to them and gestured with my hands that I just needed an additional minute, then ran upstairs into my bedroom and changed into my favourite plaid bikini and pulled a free-flowing summer dress on top. My beach bag remained packed every day, as the contents remained unchanged except for the alternating books that I brought to the beach with me.

Without further delay, I grabbed the voluminous straw bag from the floor and stuffed inside a book from my bedside table, then skipped down the stairs and ran out of the door, shutting the door behind me. The car was already at over-capacity with six people, but I managed to shove my slender figure into the back seat with half of my body resting on one of my friends. Crammed tightly in the tin car, resembling a can of densely packed sardines, we took off on a short drive to the beach where we joined more of our friends from school who arrived a bit earlier.

This was not unlike any other days on the beach with our friends that I embarked on that summer, but it was the first outing where I felt tense with lingering fear at the pit of my stomach. Unable to fully relax, I spent the day observing the perimeter in apprehension of the inevitable, dreading the uncertainty of when my murderer would reappear in my life. The day dragged on and my friends enjoyed another day in the sun, while I sank deep into the beach chair with a book in my hands but unable to focus on the plot because my eyes continuously scanned the surroundings.

To my relief, the group decided to pack up and return home relatively early because there was another party to attend later in the evening and they wanted to get home earlier to change out of their wet swimwear. We quickly packed into the car and headed back to town; my friends, exhilarated after a day out in the sun, were singing along the blasting music from the radio while I stayed quiet looking out of the back window deplorably sensing a cloud of anxiety soaring over me. On the drive back everyone was determined to go to the party, but I excused myself thankfully remembering that I had dinner plans with my mother. Roxie insisted that I join them after dinner, but I did not want to make any promises or inform her of my anxieties so assured her that I would do my absolute best to make an appearance.

Once I was dropped off at the house, I promised my friends that I would see them the next day for whatever impromptu plans they made up that day and waved them goodbye as they sped out of the driveway and into the street. I knew that I could not hide at home for the remainder of the summer and had to face my fears but felt that I needed an evening with my mother when I did not have to think about facing Ray just yet. When I walked into the house, I checked the hallway for my mother's shoes, but they were not there which meant that she was still out of the house, so I ran up to my bedroom and changed into a pair of track shorts and a t-shirt then settled comfortably in my bed with the book that I was too distracted to read on the beach.

Roxie was not entirely wrong, my love for reading had driven me to the school library more times than any other student and I thoroughly enjoyed the contrasts of coming-of-age British classics against the sorrowful ill-fated characters in the lengthy Russian tomes. Engrossing myself in the vast variety of genres gave me perspective of characters' lives through the centuries in the most divergent parts of the world. Every book shaped my sheltered viewpoint of the meaning of life and the world around us, the philosophy behind Brothers Karamazov astonished me with its teaching about morality and faith while the provocative humour of Laurence Sterne enlightened me that many people struggle to understand their own fate.

There was no book that I would not attempt to read, even if I struggled through the elaborate texts, but I knew that if I persevered to the end of the book there would always be some sort of lesson that I would take away. However, after reading an array of captivating books, I always returned to reread The Great Gatsby about once a year, it was the one book that could simply describe the true meaning of hope and how fast one can lose oneself when they lose all hope and no longer have a purpose in life.

As per usual, the book I was reading while waiting for my mother fully consumed me and I only realized that it was later in the evening because I was straining my eyes to read the letters in the swarming darkness. I got up to turn on the light but before I had the chance to reach for the light, I heard the car drive into the driveway and doors open. Assuming it was Alison dropping off my mother, as my mother never learned how to drive the car and always relied on Alison or public transportation to get places.

After my father's tragic accident, mom developed a severe aversion to cars but eventually conceded to accepting Alison's offers to drive her when she absolutely needed it, but she was utterly against me driving. It was a subject of our many fights, as all my friends including Roxie were proud owners of their drivers' permits that elevated them to a certain level of independence while I remained constrained by my mothers' fears.

Without turning on the lights I walked over to the window and looked out to see my mother on the driveway next to an unfamiliar vehicle, and a tall stocky man standing next to her. The man did not seem familiar to me as I examined his face illuminated by the streetlight, his wide nose twitched as he talked, and grimaced with a toothy smile, when he was listening intently to mom's every word. My mother looked different today, instead of the usual neatly pinned hair bun, she had her beautiful long blonde locks freely flowing around her shoulders. I looked closer and noticed a hint of lipstick on her lips as her lips curled in a sly smile at the stranger. This was odd since I had not seen her wear any makeup in years. Then I clearly heard my mother's rolling laugh which had become rare since my father's passing and her hilarity waned, I saw the stocky figure lean in for a too-tight hug and kiss her gently on the cheek. This display of affection startled me and pushed any of my earlier anxieties about Ray to the background. I had never seen my mother with any man other than my father so many years ago. The thought of her with someone else never crossed my mind, I had always assumed that she was happy with me, Alison and Roxie and she did not need anyone else. Alison brought up the subject of my mother needing to date a few times in front of me, which sent chills down my spine of the thought of a strange man in our happy lives, and my mother, aware of my reaction, fervently rejected the suggestions.

Alarmed by the sight of the stranger planting a sloppy kiss on my mother, I ran over to the light switch and immediately turned it on revealing my presence to the outside. Then I walked over to the window again and saw my mother looking up at me as I glared down at her in disapproval, while the man tried to convince her of something and her shaking her head. The man looked up in my direction with despair and then turned around looking defeated and walked towards the driver's side of his car before getting in and then drove off into the darkness, while my mother walked towards the front door and out of my view.

The sound of the lock turning and the door opening downstairs was clearly heard through the calmness in the house, as I maintained my position by the window crossing my arms in anticipation of an argument. My mother's footsteps shuffled up the stairs and to my bedroom door, when I finally heard her knocking before entering the room. Her face showed no signs of remorse, but instead she almost looked relieved.

"Good evening, honey."

She said walking over and sitting on the bed.

"Hi, mom." I responded stressing the sarcastic tone in my voice.

"How was your day? Were you at the beach today?"

She casually continued, noticing my bikini and beach dress sprawled around on the floor.

"Don't pretend like nothing happened, mom. Who was that?"

I started to fume at her nonchalant composure.

My mother got up from the bed and started picking up my discarded clothes from the floor.

"That was Steve." She casually responded, while folding my dress neatly on my bed. "I know you may have some questions, so please feel free to ask them."

"Are you seeing him? Is this serious?" The anger in my voice was undeniable.

"Yes, we have been seeing each other for about a month now. I did not want to introduce you to him until I was sure that it was going to become serious. Steve has wanted to meet you for a while. But I know how you feel about me dating, honey. I didn't want to stress you out especially with you leaving for college soon."

"So, you were never going to tell me. You were going to see me off to California and date this guy without ever letting me know? Was that the plan, mom?"

"Not at all, I would have told you eventually. Steve has been very nice to me; he has been nothing but a gentleman since we met. He has been sending me flowers to the office and telling me all about his wonderful life. Alison really likes him."

My mother caught herself as she inadvertently confessed introducing him to her best friend.

"Alison met him? So, she knows about him, but your own daughter doesn't? You know what, mom? You can have your wonderful life when I'm gone, and I'll make sure I stay out of your way while I'm here for the next few weeks."

The anger level skyrocketed, and I quickly walked out of the room slamming my bedroom door behind me.

The rage within me propelled me down the stairs and out of the house, as I needed to distance myself from my mother. I never questioned her devotion to my father because we continued to celebrate his birthday every year and I sometimes caught her falling asleep with his picture clenched in her hand. She was a beautiful woman who received a lot of admiring looks from men when we were out shopping and I was certain that my English teacher had a serious crush on her, but she never reciprocated the attention and seemed oblivious to the lingering stares. Steve's arrival into our lives was unprecedented and I was uncertain at how to process this development, so desperately needed some time away from the house.

The warm evening was soothing as I angrily seethed strolling around the streets without a clear destination in mind. Walking had been my respite through all the hard times in my life, or lives, as I remembered walking through the streets in New York escaping my troubles in the night. Strolling through Georgetown was immensely different than walking through the busy streets of New York where danger could consume you at every corner. The dormant survival instinct within me stayed unleashed in the calmness of my hometown where nothing remarkable ever happened. While a part of me prospered in the routine life of living in a small town, a certain element of my consciousness missed the bustle of the busy streets and the ability to be lost in a city of millions.

While I continued wandering through the dark streets wallowing in my disappointment in my mother and hindered by her atypical conduct of keeping secrets from me, a car sped by me and braked hard a few feet away.

"Hey Noelle!"

I heard my name called from the car, so I turned around to see my friend Adam leaning out of the driver's window. It was hard to see the other people in the car through the darkness, but I heard a few people yell my name through the open windows and the blaring music.

"Do you need a ride to the party?" Adam asked, glancing at the back of the car to see if they could fit one more person.

"You can squeeze in at the back. Come on, get in!" He yelled, followed by a few other voices urging me to join them in the car.

Figuring that going to the party to hang out with all my friends would be a better use of my time than drowning in my own sorrow while walking the lonely streets, I nodded in agreement and walked over to the car. The passengers all screamed in a loud welcome as the back door opened and I saw four more of my friends from school sitting in the back.

"Not sure if I'd fit in. Can I split the seat in the front?" I offered an alternative solution, to which Adam agreed and asked me to go to the front passenger seat.

I opened the door to the right of Adam and crammed my body next to the other person occupying the seat swiftly without a second look. Once I sat down and closed the door, I turned to see who I was sitting next to and felt my body freeze on the spot.

"Hi, I'm Ray."

The manifested beast cavalierly introduced himself, his face only a few inches from my own. My eyes were transfixed at him with horror as his dark eyes looked back at me and his broad smile that had once upon a time put me under his spell, spread widely on his face.

"Do you want to sit on my lap, it may be more comfortable."

"That's Noelle." I heard Adam introduce me and he started to drive. "She is way too smart for you, so don't even think about it, Ray."

The people in the back seat burst in unified laughter at Adam's introduction but all enthusiastically supported his statement.

"Noelle is going off to California on a full scholarship, so she can see right through your tricks." I heard Adam's younger sister Amy jump into the conversation from the back seat, sounding slightly flirtatious in an attempt to get Ray's attention. She was only fifteen but always managed to convince Adam to take her to the parties around town with him.

"What tricks?" Ray responded, still smiling at me unfazed by everyone's comments and then I felt his right arm extend around my waist, which caused me to jump up in my seat. The touch that had at one point sent delectable shivers down my body and caused my body temperature rise with anticipated burning desire, had now resembled sandpaper roughness against my delicate skin. The unforeseen adverse response to his usual charms took Ray by surprise, confident in his amorous abilities through years of being on the prowl, he was unaccustomed to being rejected.

"She doesn't seem to speak much for a smart girl and seems a bit jumpy."

He tried to hide his disappointment by joking at my expense, which only infuriated me even more and I squeezed further away from him, confined by the narrowness of the seat.

Sensing my discomfort, Adam told Ray to lay off and to leave me alone then apologized to me on Ray's behalf.

"I haven't even laid one finger on her." Ray responded aloud while his arm was still wrapped around me unseen by the people in the car, then turned to me and whispered deviously in my ear, "...yet.".

His hot breath on my ear when he leaned in felt like burning candle wax poured on my flesh, so I leaned my face further away from him with the built-up emotions erupting from their confinement.

"No!" I screamed and grasped one of the fingers that he was clenching around my waist, twisting it back hard, causing him to shriek with pain and raise his left arm in a fist ready to pounce me. Adam immediately noticed Ray's raised arm and grabbed it with his right arm, while his left arm was still on the steering wheel. The sudden movement made the car swerve to the side barely missing the curb and sending the people in the back to topple over each other.

"What the hell, Ray?" Adam yelled at Ray, stopping the car and instinctively looked back to check on his sister.

"All good, no harm done." Ray responded, as Adam looked over at me to see if I was alright. "Just a simple misunderstanding."

"I'll just get out here, if you don't mind, Adam. I can see the party from here, so I'll walk the rest of the way."

I opened the passenger door and hastily jumped out of the car.

"Are you sure you're, ok?" Adam asked through the open window.

"Yes, I'll see you at the party." I nodded and smiled back, avoiding any possibility of any additional eye contact with Ray.

The car drove forward towards the congested dead end, where the other cars were parked, while I contemplated my next steps. The temptation of walking away was unnerving but I felt the vengeance within me trump all weaknesses unwilling to let him go so easily. The phantom pains started to pulsate on the left side of my back from where the bullet hit me when Ray took shots at us while Roxie and I were running away at the Green Light Sanctuary. The throbbing intensified while I stood on the street deciding on whether to join my friends or walk away, the aching pounding against my spine felt like a shove from an invisible source pushing me towards my fear. My feet started moving in the direction of the house, while my mind was still unable to formulate the strategy of my revenge. Without a doubt I wanted Ray to pay for what he did to me and the years of torture that Roxie endured, but the Ray in the current timeframe is not yet the same person who embodied all the evil in the world.

As I approached the house, I heard the loud laughter of the young people I have grown to see as my friends and the atrocious music that I have gotten accustomed to over the years trying to fit in with the younger generation. Sometimes I forgot that I was a thirty-year-old woman trapped in a teenager's body, because I appreciated the carefree lifestyle that allowed me to not worry about the long-lasting consequences. I have grown to love the feeling of belongingness in a social setting, instead of the lonely life of a recluse that consumed me in my prior lifetime. *My other lifetime,* I thought of the misery that followed me through my thirty years where I seldom saw happiness and tragedy was my constant companion. In my mind Ray had embodied all the negative aspects of the missed opportunities and the wrong decisions that led my life to spiral downwards.

When I walked into the house, I saw a few of my friends and a lot of people I have never seen mingling throughout the house. There was a tremendous amount of people that crowded a relatively small house that was foolishly entrusted in the hands of a teenager for one night. Almost everyone had either a red plastic cup or a beer bottle clenched in their hands as I walked through the party casually waving and nodding at the familiar faces, looking for Roxie and keeping an eye out for Ray.

"Noelle, what happened in the car?" Adam appeared in front of me with a half empty brew in his grasp. "I've never seen you this shook."

"Nothing happened, I just had a fight with my mom about her new boyfriend so that kind of put me in a sour mood." I responded indifferently, steering clear of the subject of Ray.

"Parents! Not a day goes by when I do not fight with my old man. You know he is forcing me to go to the police academy in the fall? He says being in the police force is in our blood and I'd be the first idiot who would want to do anything different. He gives me the whole family tree lecture on all the law enforcement relatives we have, but I keep telling him there is more to life than patrolling the streets."

I continued to listen to Adam's woes, but kept my eyes out for Roxie or Ray.

"What do you want to do, Adam?" I switched my attention back to our conversation.

"Honestly, I don't even know because I'm not even allowed to think about any other jobs. I guess being a police officer is not all that bad, it has its perks. Besides not much drama happens in Georgetown so it would be a breeze."

"Excuse me, I'll go grab a drink. Have you seen Roxie?" I asked Adam and he motioned in the direction of the glass doors that led out into the patio, then jumped into a conversation with a bunch of guys from our school that stood behind me.

I started to make my way towards the patio but was inadvertently blocked several times by a few of my friends for a chat. When I finally approached the glass doors to look outside, Adam's sister Amy came in through the patio doorway.

"Hey Noelle." She said as I was about to pass her, but then she paused in the entryway and asked me. "You know that guy Ray in the car, isn't he super cute? Adam met him last week at some party and they've been hanging out a bit, so I've gotten to see him a few times. I totally saw him checking me out a bunch of times, especially when I wear my white bikini. Don't think Adam noticed, otherwise he probably would have beat the life out of that hunk."

Amy had always seemed to be in a rush to grow up, which was possibly caused by hanging out with her brother's older friends, but Adam wanted to keep an eye on his flirtatious teen sister, so he tried to bring her everywhere with him.

"Nah, Amy. He seems like a bit of a jerk if you ask me. I'd stay away from him, if I were you." I tried to caution the inexperienced adolescent, understanding how easy it could be to fall victim to Ray's charms.

"Well, I don't know. Roxie seems to be getting along with him just fine."

Amy moved out of the way to reveal the expansive backyard where clusters of people gathered in different areas of the space.

My eyes shot back and forth trying to locate Roxie and Ray, and then Amy pointed to the far corner of the yard where Ray was leaning against the wooden fence with both of his arms entrapping my beautiful sister friend in the opening between his limbs. Roxie did not seem disturbed but her defensive stand with arms crossed in front of her chest signified that she was not as open to this encounter. Just as I was about to walk over to them to interrupt and steer Roxie away from the monster that she failed to remember from the past, I saw my sister push one of Ray's muscular arms out of her way and walk away from him visibly unnerved. I took a step forward towards her when she finally noticed me and ran over in my direction, then grabbed my hand and directed me away from the yard and into the kitchen inside the house.

"Rox, what's up?" I was afraid of what she had to say.

"Must be something wrong with me, Noelle." She opened the fridge and pulled out an unopened beer bottle. "This handsome guy from New York just approached me in the yard and started telling me how beautiful I was and that he could see a great future for me in the modeling world in the City. Apparently, he has connections and could introduce me to all the right people. Isn't that incredible?" She asked as she used the bottle opener to lift the cap and I opened my mouth prepared to discourage her of any possibility of going to NYC with Ray.

"But get this, I was not at all phased by his speech. He gave me the total creeps before he even mentioned New York. All I could hear were alarm bells going off in my head... and look at my arm!" She lifted her right limb up to my eyes, which was coated in a series of goosebumps in horripilation.

"Yes, I saw that guy earlier in Adam's car. He gave me the creeps too. Glad you feel the same way."

I was thankful to the universe that Roxie's intrinsic sixth sense was able to navigate her away from trouble and give her a better shot at this lifetime. She did not need me protecting her all the time, because her experiences while long forgotten have formed an underlying foundation in prudent decision making. The enormous weight lifted off my shoulders, knowing that Ray would not affect me or my sister in this lifetime, and we were going to live a long happy life away from his clutches undaunted by the past. Retribution did not seem to be a priority anymore, as the feeling of safety over our futures blanketed my troubling thoughts.

Roxie grabbed another beer bottle and popped it open before handing it to me and clinked it in a toast, as if aware of my relieving thoughts.

"To our futures, N! You are going to have an amazing life in Los Angeles, and I will join you soon enough so we can conquer the city and become the real California girls."

"No fake boobs though." I laughed, taking a sip from the bottle.

"Not for you, because you have been blessed by mother nature. However, for little old me, I'd like some reinforcement in that department."

She joked back when a bunch of our friends joined us in the kitchen, and we all continued to fantasize about our not-too-distant futures. Seeing Ray in the background did not seem to bother me as much, as I made the decision that focusing on the future was more productive than wallowing in the past.

Resting in my dorm room in Los Angeles and chatting jauntily with Roxie while waiting for the handsome Jared to knock on my door, I felt like I was finally living out the future filled with new prospects and freed by the chain of the past. I propelled my thoughts back to the present conversation and focused on Roxie's Georgetown gossip.

"So yes, about Ray, I met up with Adam before he took off for the police academy yesterday and he told me about that creep. Apparently, someone called in an anonymous tip about Ray having drugs in his car, so he was pulled over by the police. And get this, they found all sorts of pills and weed on him. No wonder he gave me the creeps!"

I listened intensely to Roxie's account of the events.

"Anyways, so he got arrested on the spot and taken to jail where Adam's dad was put in charge of the case. So, he also got a warrant to look at Ray's phone, and he found naked pictures of Amy! Can you imagine? This creep Ray had been asking Amy to send him naked pictures of herself and convinced her to move to New York with him but got arrested before they had the chance to leave. Anyways so now there are child pornography charged laid on him too and since Amy and Adam's dad is in the police force, I don't think this guy is going to walk out anytime soon. Isn't that wild?"

"Unreal! Poor Amy." I responded.

"Oh, the creep never got a chance to lay a finger on her because you know how Adam keeps a close eye on Amy's whereabouts."

She giggled, while I felt the last of the burden from the tragedies of the past unclasp their hold on me.

"I'm glad they caught that monster before anything else happened." The words escaped my cunning smile. "Rox, I have to go, Jared is going to be here soon, and I have to get ready."

"Aww Jared. OK we will talk in a few days! Ciao!"

I hung up the phone, my hand sore from holding up the receiver for so long and walked towards the closet to pick out an appropriate outfit that would leave an impression on Jared. While I perused the selection looking for the perfect outfit for the date, my thoughts flashed back to a few weeks earlier in Delaware when I was at the beach and walked away from my group of friends to buy a soda at the store. While paying for the drink, I asked the clerk to use their phone and dialed a number that I had previously written down on a piece of paper and hid in the cup of my bikini top.

"Hi, I'd like to file a complaint about Ray Ferguson who drives a red Dodge with a New York license plate BCDE2467. In his car you will find a variety of illegal drugs, which he supplies to minors in the Georgetown community."

I hung up the phone when the inquisitive lady on the other line asked for my name, then ripped up the piece of paper with the phone number written on it and threw the fragments in the trash. As I briskly walked back to my friends who were casually playing beach volleyball on yet another sunny summer day in Delaware, all I could think of was that Ray would not be able to hurt anyone else for a while once my plan worked. The same thoughts resonated as I recapped Roxie's story in my head after Jared picked me up from my room and held my hand all the way to his car, where he opened the passenger door welcoming me to get in. There was no more devious monster lingering in my life, my hastily devised plot was a success, nobody could drag me backwards just the flickering bright lights of the future pulled me forward towards my new life.

## Chapter Ten

*August 2006*
*Age 21*

    Layers of white tulle and intricate lace draped my quivering body as I stood in front of the mirror entranced by the reality of the day. After almost a year of fastidious planning every single aspect in preparation for the momentous day, it had finally arrived. The built-up anticipation whirled deeply in my stomach and my exhalation was slightly more rapid, so I tried to breath slower to calm my nerves.

    "You are a vision, honey."

    My mother was standing behind me, looking over my shoulder into the mirror to admire my reflection. She was clutching a box of tissues in her hand, which was a practical decision seeing how she had gone through almost an entire box earlier wiping her tears and it had only been ten in the morning. Her loose locks had not been tidied up yet because the beauty experts had been working wonders on me first, giving my mother adequate time to uncontrollably weep about how fast time flies and that only yesterday I was a toddler and today I was already getting married.

    "Mom, the photographer is going to be here in an hour. You need to pull yourself together, so that Marko and Andi can start working on your hair and make-up. Take a deep breath!"

    I faced my mother and grabbed both of her hands, before loudly inhaling through my powdered nose to fill my lungs and exhaling through the crimson-stained lips. Understanding the immediate need to get ready, my mother obeyed and took a few long breaths while Marko sat her down in a chair in front of the vanity table and started to brush out her long blonde hair.

    *Where is Roxie?*

I wondered as I went back to look at my flawless reflection. Marko transformed my dull hair to look like golden silk cascading down to my cleavage in runway-ready vintage waves, while Andi's gifted talent managed to narrow my nose and enlarge my eyes whilst hiding any hints of the stress blemishes that I was certain would ruin the day. The artists' masterwork was impeccable, but it was the dress that I could not take my eyes from in my reflection.

Roxie moved to California and stayed with me a year earlier, so we spent days looking for the perfect dress within the budget that my mother allowed me to spend on the dress, having to rely on my mother and Jared's family to pay for all the wedding expenses I received firm instructions to stay on budget. We perused every bridal store in the California area where we saw the most beautiful dresses in a wide variety of styles, but none of the gowns felt right.

One Saturday afternoon, in an attempt to distract ourselves from all the wedding related plans, Roxie and I decided to take a stroll around the neighbourhood in Venice Beach where Jared and I were moving to right after the wedding. A few weeks prior at our engagement party, my future in-laws surprised us by presenting Jared and I with house keys to one of their rental properties located along the canals in Venice, only a short stroll from the hustle and bustle of the boardwalk. They said that they have signed over the deed in Jared's name, so we could move in whenever we were ready into our new home. I was ecstatic at the thought of moving into a house of our own, because while I have been sharing a tiny one-bedroom apartment with Roxie in Sawtelle to be closer to campus, Jared had been living in his own bachelor apartment overlooking the Santa Monica pier. We would finally be able to spend all our time together instead of the occasional sleep over at Jared's place, since he blatantly refused to stay over in my Sawtelle apartment saying he felt crammed in the confined space. So, Roxie and I decided to explore the newfangled neighbourhood and check out the new abode, while Jared had to leave on an urgent business trip for the weekend. We had a great time strolling through the lively streets visiting the tiny boutique shops and creative art galleries adorning the bohemian neighbourhood, when Roxie spotted a vintage store hidden in an inconspicuous alleyway.

"Echoes of Glory." She read the sign aloud to me. "Can we go in? I have an audition next week for this part in a TV show based in the "roaring twenties", maybe I can find something to wear so I feel inspired."

Fervently nodding and following her into the dim store, I once again tried to express my undying support of her career, but her endless unsuccessful auditions were extinguishing any hope in me of her becoming an actress. I envied Roxie's determination and enthusiasm every time she left the apartment to go and read for a part but knew that I would be comforting her in a few days, when she found out that she did not get the coveted role. So far, she had been in a few background scenes in a handful of crime dramas and was even given a line in a sitcom, but her part was edited out without having ever made it on the screen. The rejection would have driven me away from the cutthroat career in Hollywood, but not Roxie. Her vibrant spirit remained unhindered by the rejection, and every time she found out about an open audition she put on her best outfit, teased her wild curls and went on her way, determined to achieve her seemingly unattainable goal.

While we were flipping through the neatly organized racks of clothes in the circumscribed yet elegant vintage store, an elderly lady who instantly reminded me of Enid came over and asked if she could help. She matched the vibe of the store perfectly, dressed in an emerald green dress with a turn down neckline and a flared mid-calf length skirt cinched with a beige belt at her tiny waist. Her undyed grey hair was tightly secured in a complicated chignon at the nape of the back of her neck, and as she walked over to us, I could barely take my eyes off her vintage inspired look.

"No, thank you, just looking for some *je ne sais quoi*."

Roxie used a phrase she recently learned for an audition to play the role of a spoiled socialite.

The lady smiled in understanding and told us not to hesitate to ask if we needed any assistance, then just as she was turning around to retreat to the back of the store, the plump engagement ring on my finger caught her impertinent eye.

"What a beautiful ring!" She exclaimed, coming closer to me to get a better look.

"Thank you, I love it too."

I beamed in response, having been used to the many compliments from people admiring the unique creation consisting of a pear-shaped diamond atop a jewel encrusted band that Jared vowed he had specifically designed for me.

"When is the wedding?" The lady asked, spotting that there was no wedding band secured against the hefty engagement ring.

"In a few months, if we ever find the wedding dress."

I expressed my most dawning thought, knowing that I did not have much more time to waste if I wanted the wedding to happen.

The elderly lady stepped back and contemplatively scrutinized me from top to bottom assessing a deep thought that she failed to share with me, then walked away with a slight limp slowly towards the back of the store. Leaving me bewildered at the reaction and her swift departure. I was just about to walk over to Roxie and drag her out of the strange store, when I saw the saleswoman return with a plastic covered floor length bundle secured on a wooden hanger, which she hung by the fitting room to the right of where I was standing.

"How about you try this on while your friend is looking for her *je ne sais quoi*."

She motioned towards the fitting room and the mysterious plastic wrapped outfit. I glanced around to find my friend, but Roxie was hidden by the many racks of clothes but could hear her humming while she examined the garments, assessing the perfect outfit to fit the upcoming audition.

"*Pourquoi pas!*"

I responded shrugging my shoulders, having studied French at university. Understanding that we were probably going to be at the offbeat store for a while, until Roxie had a chance to look at every single item on the racks, I walked over into the fitting room to undress. The sales lady took the plastic film off the garment outside the fitting room while I stripped off my clothes and remained in my underwear feeling a bit chilly in the confined space.

"I will come in now and you will have to step into the dress, ok?"

I heard from behind the red velvet curtain and replied in agreement. The heavy drape lifted, and the lady entered the enclosure with the bundle of off-white material in her hands, then laid it by my feet allowing me to step into the opening. Then she masterfully helped to pull up the top of the dress up to my chest and suggested to take off the brassier so that I could get the full effect of the dress, which caused me to momentary hesitate but then I quickly unclasped the undergarment and slipped it off before securing the garment straps on my slender shoulders. When I was about to leave the fitting room to locate a mirror, the elderly lady raised her hand to signal for me to wait and stepped out for a quick minute to return with a pair of high heels, which she asked me to put on. Once the nude pumps were on my feet, she walked me out of the confinement of the room towards a full-length mirror hung on the opposite side of the wall.

The delectable image in front of me took my breath away as I saw my slim figure hugged by a fitted bodice decorated with delicate lace flowing into a skirt with seemingly endless layers of weightless tulle. The sheer lace straps held the dress in place perfectly, making it feel light and airy on my body without any constraints of a corset. The neckline provided a perfect balance between the provocative outline of my decolletage and the conservative coverage by the lace.

"I had a feeling this would fit you perfectly." Said the saleslady while giddily observing my fascination with the dress. "I've been saving this piece for the perfect customer. I didn't want it to go to one of those hipsters that were going to cut it up and turn it into some abomination."

"It is absolutely stunning!" I finally responded in a light whisper, still in awe of the beautiful gown. "Rox, can you come over?"

The sound of the wooden hangers clicking against the metal rack seized and Roxie's humming approached from behind the series of clothes racks. She emerged from the depths of the store with a pile of clothes bunched in her arms and looked at me in genuine astonishment.

"You look like a movie star, N. Like Lauren Bacall."

Roxie gasped at the sight and approached me closer, while the saleslady took the crumpled clothes from her grasp and hung them up neatly by the neighbouring fitting room.

Aware of Roxie's fascination with the movie actresses from Hollywood's Golden Era, I knew not to object because the stunning dress conjured up my own confidence in my striking appearance. While I always thought I wanted a stark-white princess gown for a wedding dress, I realized that this ivory vintage masterpiece was *the dress*. At that moment I knew that I no longer needed to spend endless hours at bridal stores, and that I finally found the perfect bridal gown. Then a concerning thought crossed my mind and I turned to the poised saleslady.

"I love this dress, but could you tell me how much it is?" My voice trembled at the idea of not being able to afford the dress, that I could so easily imagine wearing while walking down the aisle towards the gleeful Jared.

"$500 for you. I want this dress to be back in its glory and be worn by someone who appreciates the uniqueness of it."

The elderly lady admired my silhouette hugged by the ingenious masterpiece.

"N, that's within your budget! You can even buy those Manolos we saw on Rodeo, to go with it." Roxie exclaimed, completely forgetting her own mandatory guidelines of bargaining at a vintage store.

"I will take it and I promise that this dress will be the highlight of the wedding." I proclaimed, while Roxie adjusted the tulle skirt on the flowing gown.

Looking at my reflection back in my room, with my makeup and hair done, I was still mesmerized by the dress and thankful for stumbling on to the vintage store in my new neighbourhood that I was going to move into right after the wedding. Roxie and I have already given our landlord one month's notice that would allow enough time for me to move out and for Roxie to find her own place.

*Where is Roxie?*

The thought crossed my mind again as I glanced at the clock hanging on the wall. Slight panic started to set in when I remembered that I have not seen Roxie since the night before after we had our biggest fight to date, when she stormed out of the apartment in defiant fury. In my sleepless night, while I was running through the tight schedule of the day ahead, I was confident that I heard Roxie come home late at night and then leave the apartment in the early hours in the morning before I had the chance to see her.

The indelible events of last night's argument with my best friend replayed before my eyes, as I took a seat on the couch and blankly stared at Marko and Andi adroitly effectuating my mother's makeover. The night prior, I was sitting on the same couch trying to distract my racing mind from the wedding with some casual television. Flipping through the channels I felt my nervous tension intensifying without a proper outlet to release the escalating anxiety, so I started fuming at the fact that Roxie was still out even though she had promised to come home earlier so we could spend our last evening together. She vowed that we would have a perfect quiet stress-free night in our cozy apartment indulging in some Chinese take out food and casual chatting that would steer away any thoughts of the wedding. It was after eight in the evening, and she was still not home, I felt my stomach grumbling with harrowing hunger, so I walked over to the kitchen to make myself a sandwich. While I grabbed the necessary ingredients from the fridge and placed them on the counter, I was indubitably livid with Roxie's absence when I finally heard the front door open.

"Hi N! I just had the most wonderful audition; I definitely think that I got the part this time." She strolled in exhilarated, oblivious to my glaring cold fury.

"You said you'd be home early so we could order in and spend our last evening together, Rox." I said under my breath, struggling to keep the fuming temper from bursting out of me.

"I know, I know. I am sorry but I found out about this reading for a movie from a girl I met at an earlier audition, so we had to go from one studio to another. She's pretty cool though, she's in this theatre group that travels all over the States and…" Roxie stopped talking, noticing that I was avoiding looking at her as I busied myself with the sandwich preparation. "I'm here now, N. It was such a great part of me."

Her last words prompted a trigger of emotions within me, I felt the lid on the parabolic sealed box containing all my preoccupying thoughts and increasing anxieties snap and unleash the dreary feelings in an anger-filled speech targeted at the flabbergasted Roxie.

"I just wanted one quiet night with you, like you promised. A night about me for once, and not your constant talks about the endless auditions. I cannot possibly spend another night faking my undying support for your acting career. Rox, grow up! It has been almost two years and all you have done is pretty much nothing but go all around LA meeting people and reading for parts that you never get. I have been paying for this apartment and all our expenses with the teaching assistant's salary and the tutoring gigs that barely cover all the costs. You need to face the reality for once and get a real job."

The hurt in Roxie's eyes sobered me from my anger, and I quickly collected myself again prepared to apologize but before I had the chance to speak up, Roxie retaliated in her defense.

"Did not realize you felt that way, N. I did not realize that it had been hard on you to pay for the place all by yourself, but you could have said something earlier and I could have found a part-time job to help us out. You never said that you were paying for it out of your salary, I thought your new "pockets full of dough" family was helping you out. Jared seems to splurge on everything in sight, dinners, jewellery, clothes, including buying your own independence."

"What does that even mean?" I retaliated, taken aback by her comment.

"You are different now, N. You used to be the most self-sufficient distinctive individual I knew, who had big dreams with the big wide world at her feet. When you were moving to LA you were determined to find your purpose. What is your purpose now, N? Attend fancy parties and wear designer clothes?" Roxie raised her eyebrows at me, waiting for a response.

"Just because I love Jared and he loves me does not mean that he owns me. The reason he buys me clothes is because he wants me to blend in with his friends and colleagues when we meet them for dinners."

My answer made sense to me but seemed to anger Roxie even more.

"You are twenty-one years old, and you are already getting married. I think in Jared's mind he wanted to get married because that would mean that he would officially own you."

Her comment seemed ridiculous. Jared proposed to me in my third year of college after I confided that I was planning to spend my final year in an exchange program in London. When he heard about my plans, he seemed upset and left my dorm room, only to return with the beautiful diamond ring the next day and professed his love for me vowing that he would die if I left him for longer than a day and that he had been planning to propose to me for months. Without giving me time to snap out of my stunned silence, he placed the pear-shaped diamond on my finger then called his parents to announce that we were engaged.

"You are not like those other preppy schmucks; you are a disoriented soul who seems to be lost in the sea of luxury. I appreciate all the *fake* support you have been giving me over the years or possibly my entire life but know that I have been equally pretending to be excited about your marriage. That's how good of an actress I really am." Roxie announced before turning around and raced out of the door without giving me a chance to respond or stop her.

The unexpected fight threw me off balance, Roxie and I rarely ever fought, we seemed to agree about everything. Thinking back over the years, there were only two fights of the similar magnitude where one of us stormed off. The first occasion was when we were nine years old, and I refused to let Roxie get on a trampoline at a birthday party we were both attending because I remembered from the prior lifetime, that she was going to break her arm from a nasty fall when the badly constructed contraption was going to topple over and spend the summer with a heavy cast preventing her from swimming and playing with all her friends. She refused to listen to my reasoning while observing the other kids having fun bouncing around. She tried to push me out her way and I stood my ground, so Roxie yelled at me and called me a "control freak" then walked away and joined another group of girls who were busy bedazzling some t-shirts. She chose to ignore me for the rest of the day until she heard loud screams from the direction of the capsized trampoline and ran over to find a boy around our age crying hysterically holding on to his oddly loose hanging arm, while all the adults hovered over him in panic. The ghastly image of a dislocated shoulder triggered her to walk over to me and awkwardly apologize for her earlier behaviour, then she grabbed my hand and led me to the bedazzling table.

Our second big fight was shortly before I left for California when I came over to her house while Alison was at work, incredibly frustrated with my mother who I saw again hanging out with Steve at a coffee shop in town. Annoyed with the situation I laid on Roxie's bed rambling on about how ignorant my mother was to my feelings about her dating, the short-lived commitment to the memory of my father and the fact that she was acting like a child. Roxie listened intensely and quietly to the long digressive monologue about my mother, while sitting in her desk chair looking at my stretched-out frame on her bed. Once I was done, she paused in visible reluctance to respond, but then powered through her wariness and spoke up.

"N, can I be honest with you?" She asked hypothetically without expecting a response. "I have never seen your mother happier, anytime I see her in town or at the office she is always smiling these days. I mean your mom is an amazing lady and she is always happy to see me and obviously when she is with you, but have you ever seen her when she thought you were not looking? Sometimes, when I walked past the travel agency and saw Susan through the window sitting at her desk when no one else was in the office, she seemed so downcast, almost mournful. I do not remember your father, but I know how much your mother loves him because she talks about him all the time. But you and her cannot live in the past forever. You are moving to California towards a bright new future, but you expect your mother to remain in eternal grief?"

Roxie's logical reasoning failed to sink into my selfish narrow mind at the time, so I blamed her for being absurd, then jumped off the bed racing out of her room, enraged at my best friend's inability to understand my feelings. I spent hours walking around town frustrated with my mother and Roxie, feeling completely misunderstood and lonely in my misery. When I neared my home, it was already later in the evening and the neighbourhood had been veiled by the darkness, our house interior was illuminated by the lit-up bare windows unshielded from the neighbours.

On my approach I saw my mother busy in the kitchen through the window, preparing dinner for us unaware of me looking at her. Her slim body seemed to float around the kitchen in swaying carefree motions and her lips were rapidly shifting, as if she was talking to herself, until I realized that my mother was blissfully dancing and singing while cooking. This took me by surprise, I could not remember my mother twirling since I caught her and my father whirling around the kitchen just before he passed away. She looked so happy in her blithe moment while I watched her through the window, I could not take my eyes off her. She looked stunning, still youthful and full of life. Afraid to spook her from her rapture if I opened the door, I remained outside until she was done cooking dinner and floated out of the kitchen. I reached for my cell phone and dialed Roxie's number, she picked up the call on the first ring, as if expecting my call.

"I'm sorry for storming off like that, Rox. You are absolutely right; I have been completely selfish, and my mother deserves to be happy. It's about time we both moved on." I started the conversation without giving her the chance to speak first.

"I shouldn't have laid it on you this heavy though. But I am so glad that you agree. Love you, N."

Just like that our short-lived fight was over and there were no hard feelings. Considering the precedence of our past arguments, the disagreement before the wedding could not have possibly made her decide to stand me up on the day when I needed her the most. We have fantasized about each other's wedding since we were little girls and there was never any doubt that we would be each other's maid of honour, no matter where we were in life or how far apart. Our weddings would always unite us. There was no back-up plan, Roxie was the only person I pictured next to me holding my bouquet and calming me down from the wedding jitters.

*Where is Roxie?*

My selfish concerns faded away and I started to worry about my friend, putting the imminent wedding temporarily at the back of my mind. My cell phone was secured in my hand, and I have been checking for text messages from her every minute. I must have sent her a total of a hundred apologies for what I had said, but she had not responded to a single one.

*Could she be hurt? Was I too hard on her?*

"Is Roxie running late, honey?" My mother asked, as Marko was putting the last touches in her elegant updo.

"I hope so. She must be here soon." I responded, while still trying to preserve some level of confidence, even though the certainty seemed to abate with every passing minute.

The anxiety level within started to bubble up about to burst, nudging me to run out into Los Angeles streets dressed in my full wedding attire and look for Roxie, when I heard the keys outside jingle and saw the door open wide.

"Good morning, everyone!" Roxie appeared in the living room looking healthy and very much alive contrary to my worst fears.

She was dressed in her favourite Rolling Stones vintage t-shirt and a floor length boho-chic skirt, which combined meant that she had been at an ultra-important meeting as she had only worn her lucky outfit for the select "life-altering" events. Her radiant smile and lively appearance showed no signs of resentment about our earlier disagreement, as she hurried into the room and gave me a hug and my mother a peck on the cheek. Marko and Andi directed her into the chair in front of them, when my mother reluctantly vacated it, having been transfixed by her glamorous appearance in the vanity mirror.

"Rox, can I have a chat with you before you sit down?" I asked getting up from the sofa and walked over to the kitchen, while she followed me behind.

"Noelle, you look like you stepped out of the forties' movie screen. I absolutely love it! Jared is one lucky guy." Her happiness appeared genuine, as she paused to admire my transformation.

"I was worried about you, Rox. Is everything ok? Where were you?" My concerns erupted in multiple questions, that Roxie seemed to shake off.

"All good. I am so sorry I am late; I just had to handle a couple of things and I promise to tell you more after the wedding. Also, N, I am sorry about last night. You know I love you and people say the most stupid things to the ones they love the most."

She enveloped me in a tight embrace and then quickly pushed back realizing that she may crease my wedding gown.

"That must mean that I love you the most, because I was incredibly insensitive yesterday. I love you too, Rox."

I grabbed her hands and gave them a tight squeeze, as I felt my eyes welled with tears.

"Now enough with this gushing of emotions, we'll have plenty of time for that at the wedding. You must focus on keeping your make-up intact for at least the next couple of hours. This is your day, my beautiful sister friend, and I am fully at your disposal!"

She squeezed my hand and led me back in the living room when she sat me down back on the sofa and walked over to the beauty station to join Marko and Andi.

"If you two magicians could make me half as beautiful as Noelle and Susan, then you deserve a Nobel prize for wizardry!" She said to the giggling duo as she settled in the chair and succumbed to their expert hands.

There was hardly any work required to be done on Roxie because she was naturally beautiful with her long full eyelashes that never needed any mascara tinting and the perfectly unblemished skin, so her facetious comments about her looks were nothing more than a humorous farce.

There was a loud knock on the door and my mother rushed to open it to find the photographer and his assistant who were slightly behind schedule and visibly out of breath blaming the lack of elevator in the building on their delay. She escorted them to the living room, and they quickly set up their equipment around the preferred areas of focus that would allow for the best lighting and appear less crammed by the lack of space of our tiny Los Angeles apartment. I refused Jared's generous offer at splurging for a hotel suite at the Ritz Carlton for the photographs to be taken of me getting ready for the wedding. While I knew the pictures at the Ritz would turn out glamorous enough to be in a magazine, I felt that I needed to have the pictures in my tiny apartment as a sentiment of a final farewell to my old life. He reluctantly agreed to my reasoning but insisted that we stay at the Ritz suite for our wedding night to avoid the mess of his bachelor apartment and lavishly indulge in our wedding night on the luxurious sheets of the opulent hotel. Unable to resist the thought of our first night as husband and wife in the comfort of the oversized king bed and then waking up the next morning to an abundant breakfast delivered to the room, I hastily agreed.

The wedding photographer whom Jared found through the many recommendations from his circle of friends was a stocky middle-aged man who went by the name of Rubio. While directing me to pose in seemingly a million different poses, he was complaining about the constraints of the space relentlessly and yelled at his assistant with a multitude of instructions. Roxie remained in the chair while her hair and make-up were being finalized, whereas my mother and I were subjected to the countless commands from Rubio to look natural and to stop slouching. When there was a momentary break in the carousel of poses, I glanced at Roxie, and she grimaced at me in the vanity mirror to show her amusement at Rubio's dictatorship tactics.

"Just you wait." I mouthed back at her, terrified that Rubio may hear me.

After a few more photographs, Andi and Marko announced that they were done with their latest masterpiece and prompted Roxie to get up from the chair. While she still had her boho lucky outfit on, she managed to stun everyone in the room by her ravishing look with the tamed curls that glistened in the light and the vintage inspired make-up matching the forties glamour theme.

"Encantadora!"

Rubio announced while directing his camera at her and snapping a few shots before she rushed into the bedroom to change into the maid of honour outfit. When Roxie returned in the pale green off-the-shoulder gown that we also found at the "Echoes of Glory" vintage store where I bought my wedding dress, Rubio rushed her to join my mother and I in the incessant posing. Our next hour was filled with directives to pose, giving me the opportunity to see Roxie in front of the camera for the first time. Rubio praised her for being photogenic. She seemed to have an innate sense of how to look best on camera while my mother and I tried to mimic her moves in the most awkward way. At that moment, I knew that Roxie was meant to be a movie star and that I was completely wrong to question her. She seemed so unrestrained and rampant when following Rubio's directions, a born natural who deserved to be in front of the lens and not questioned by her ignorant selfish best friend.

"Rox, I..." I tried to catch her attention to tell her how I felt when Rubio's instructions ceased and he handed his camera to his assistant to signify that the shoot was over, but then her phone rang, and she rushed to pick it up.

"The limo is downstairs!" Roxie announced, after she hung up the phone and rushed everyone to pack up and leave the apartment. Andi and Marko packed their array of brushes and products in their respective beauty cases, while Rubio's assistant crammed all the equipment back in their hefty bags. My mother raced around the living room looking for her purse, and Roxie headed to the bedroom to pull out the bag that she prepared to take with her that contained everything I would need during the wedding.

"Everyone ready?" Roxie asked facing the group, as my mother finally managed to find her purse under the sofa. "Alright, let's do this."

The group of people gradually doddered out of the door and walked out of the apartment with Roxie leading the way. She guided everyone down the stairs and out of the building towards the black stretch limousine that was double parked on the street waiting for us. We quickly shuffled inside leaving Rubio and his assistant behind because they had their own vehicle parked down the street, having assured us that they were going to follow us directly to the venue. The smartly dressed driver ensured that we were all seated in the stretched vehicle and finally drove off towards the golf club where Jared's parents were able to secure us the outdoor space for the ceremony and the reception.

When Jared first took me to the exclusive private club, I was not entirely convinced that it was ideal for a small ceremony that I had in mind. However, Jared said that since his parents were paying for most of the wedding, and they knew half the city, so we had to expand our horizons and account for more guests that was initially planned. After walking around the venue with the in-house wedding planner, while she explained the placement of the tent and the decoration of the chapel, I was eventually convinced to accept my future in-law's proposal of the privileged space that was the most in-demand wedding location in Bel-Air.

While we were in the limousine rushing through Los Angeles traffic, Marko and Andi were sharing their hilarious experiences with the multitude of bridezillas over the years, which was a welcomed distraction from the jitters that I struggled to breath through. As I stared impassively at the chattering duo, I felt my mother's soft hand slip into my hand and her fingers clasping my own for a strong hold, she did not say anything but knew that I needed the solace. Once we exited the highway and drove through the winding roads of Bel-Air, Roxie was glued to the mansions outside her window while Andi told us about the famous residents in the area pointing out the celebrity homes. The sprawling estates represented the antithesis of our life in the tiny apartments and incomparable to the homes we grew up in in Georgetown.

I remembered the first time Jared drove me through the streets on the way to his parents' house in his new Porsche after a few months of dating, the anticipation of meeting his parents for the first time and the intimidation of the surroundings aggregated into a semi-panic attack. Noticing my growing anxiety, Jared pulled to the side of the road and assured me that there was nothing to worry about and that he was going to be by my side the entire time. This was the first time when he told me he loved me, which seemed to wipe out any earlier worries that consumed me.

The thoughts of that day and Jared's confidence in our future, eased my thoughts and my breathing stabilized as the limousine proceeded through the labyrinth of opulence. When the vehicle finally stopped and the driver came over to open the door, we exited the car to be greeted by the wedding planner standing at the entrance of the golf club.

"You're finally here. We are completely behind schedule; all the guests are here, and we only have ten minutes until the start of the ceremony. So please follow me, no time to waste." She rushed us into the building and down the hall into a bridal suite where she left us to do some last-minute preparations. Andi and Marko rushed over to me and made some adjustments to ensure that there were no fly-away hairs and that my make-up was "perfection", then checked on Roxie and my mother brushing off any skin glossiness.

"Honey, I'll go join Alison and Steve and I'll see you there shortly." My mother hugged me and left the room.

"Actually mom, I know we didn't practice this, but I want you to walk me down the aisle."

My request took her by surprise, but she eagerly nodded. When I was planning the wedding, I was constantly asked by the wedding planner, Jared and his parents as to who would be giving me away and I did not think that it was important to have someone by my side. However, on the limo drive while my mother's gentle touch held my hands to calm me, I knew that I needed my mother with me while she escorted me through the many curious gazes of the unfamiliar guests towards the safety of Jared's presence.

The wedding planner walked into the room followed by Rubio's assistant and asked Andi and Marko to take a seat in the chapel, which they obeyed and left the room before blowing me a kiss. I advised her of the last-minute change regarding my mother walking down the aisle with me, which she did not take lightly, clearly unhappy with any unconsented digression. Limited by time constraints and pressure to start, she escorted my mother, Roxie and I down the hallway to a set of patio doors that opened outside to a large stone patio with steps leading to an interlock stone walkway in the direction of the white chapel that was filled with the many guests most of whom I did not know. The music that Jared and I selected prior to the wedding as the perfect aisle walk song started playing from the live jazz band that was set up on the lawn, just to the side of the outdoor chapel.

"See you on the other side, N." Roxie whispered, while the wedding planner nudged her to start walking.

"This is it." My mother whispered, taking a strong hold of my hand, as Roxie started gliding down the walkway ahead of me to the rhythm of Moon River.

"I wish daddy was here." I whispered to my mother, as my mother's hold grew tighter.

"Me too, honey."

The wedding planner prodded us to start moving down the walkway towards the white linen draped entrance of the chapel. As we entered the space, I felt hundreds of eyes locked on me, but my mother's comforting grasp held me in control until I saw Jared standing at the end of the aisle waiting for me. He looked incredibly handsome in his tailored black suit with an ivory tie that matched the colour of my dress; his loving smile drew me closer with every step making me forget about the sea of strangers around me. He seemed oblivious to everything around him and only focused on me with his captive hazel eyes. The last steps seemed to be lighter as I floated towards him and our imminent future together. My mother stopped in front of the groom and gently pulled her hand out of my grasp, then gave me a tight hug before retreating to take a seat next to Alison and Steve.

"You look incredible, my bride." Jared whispered, as the minister asked us to hold hands, making me blush under the layers of makeup.

The minister started the ceremony with his well-practiced speech about devotion and love that makes the union impregnable to any hurdles in life. He seemed to speak endlessly about the importance of trust and credence in the sanctity of marriage, while I impatiently waited for him to ask the most essential question.

"Do you Noelle Anderson take Jared Wolfe to be your lawfully wedded husband to have and to hold, from this day forward, for better, for worse, for richer, for poorer, in sickness and in health, until death do you part?"

"I do." I spoke up confidently, as sure as I have ever been about anything in life.

"Do you Jared Wolfe take Noelle Anderson to be your lawfully wedded husband to have and to hold, from this day forward, for better, for worse, for richer, for poorer, in sickness and in health, until death do you part?"

"I do" Jared responded eagerly.

"In that case, I declare you man and wife. You may kiss your bride, Jared." The minister proclaimed, just as Jared leaped over at me and passionately kissed me while all the guests clapped to celebrate our union. When we separated from our first kiss as husband and wife, I felt

Roxie leap into my arms from behind and congratulate me. Then my mother and Alison rushed over, both with smeared eye make up, and enveloped Jared and I tightly in their embraces. Jared's parents followed shortly behind them, and his mother put her arms around me welcoming me into their family while his father resorted to a congratulatory handshake for both of us.

Then to avoid further distractions and the many strangers who wished to speak to us, Jared grabbed my hand and hustled me out of the chapel away from the crowd, back into the main building at the golf club where the private bridal suite was reserved for the day. When he closed the door behind us, he made sure to lock it and embraced me tightly with his arms wrapped tightly around my waist while his lips locked on the red stained rim of my mouth. His eager tongue caressed my embouchure, while his arms seemed to fiddle with the buttons at the back of my dress.

"You have to wait until tonight, husband." I pushed back, knowing where his head was at that moment.

"Not sure if I can wait another moment, wife. I've already waited four years!" This had been true; I was not ready to commit to a sexual relationship having had vivid memories of the relationship that was only based on the physical attraction with Ray. In this lifetime, I had trouble connecting with any man and it took Jared a lot of dates to get me to trust him, but I had still denied him any attempts at making love to me professing that I was saving myself for marriage.

"So, I'm sure you could wait another couple of hours." I argued, trying to get his lust to subside and sat down on the couch in front of him.

"If it wasn't for the hundreds of people waiting for us back there right now, I would rip off that dress and do some unspeakable things to you right here on the couch." Jared jokingly threatened sitting down next to me. The passion in his eyes was undeniable, and I had to resist the urge of succumbing to his wish, but I longed for our first time together to be less rushed. Jared leaned in to kiss me softly on the neck, and the tulle fabric of my skirt rustled upwards as I felt his right-hand glide along the smoothness of my leg to my inner thigh. Continuing to brush his lips against my neck, his hand momentarily paused as it reached the aimed target at the junction of my thighs feeling the lacy fabric of the La Perla lingerie.

"I see you are wearing my gift." He murmured in my ear regarding the delicate intimates that he presented to me a few days earlier, asking me to wear it on our wedding day. "I have been picturing you wearing it every waking moment, which made a couple of business meetings this past week extremely uncomfortable."

His fingers caressed the refined lace of the crevice in a gentle graze making any of my earlier anxiety flutter away and my only focus remaining was of my husband's soft touch teasing my senses. His gentle kisses ceased and to my visible discontent he moved his hand away from my inner thighs as he rose to his feet from the sofa and looked at me.

"See what you are doing to me, Noelle?"

His eyes were cast downward to the bulging outline of his arousal, then he swiftly dropped to his knees and declared. "I want to take a look at this lingerie closer, make sure it fits you in all the right places."

Jared placed his hands on my quivering knees and separated them widely allowing himself to position his head in between my legs hidden by the layers of the tulle from my sight. His expert hands traveled along the length of my legs and the warmth of his lips grazed my skin as my anticipation of his imminent approach to the core grew with every rapid breath. The culmination of his exploratory mission under the multiple layers of my skirts had reached its peak, when I felt his hot breath reach the delicate folds of my body obscured by the lace undergarment. He moved his hands away from my legs and reached for the curves of my buttocks cupping the cheeks in his grasp, then pulled my lower body forward to rest it closer to the edge of the sofa. The sudden movement made my throbbing inner lips shrouded by the lace fabric meet his hungry mouth as his tongue traced the arches concealed under the lingerie.

A deflecting knock on the door forced Jared to stop what he was doing to my utter regret as I longed for more.

"Mr. and Mrs. Wolfe, we need you for the pictures while the natural light is in position."

The voice belonging to Rubio's assistant behind the door announced, bringing my mindset to the unfortunate reality of our need to leave the confines of the suite and proceed with the tight schedule.

"Do we really have to?" Jared mumbled directing his question at me, still strategically placed between my thighs.

"Unfortunately."

I responded despondently while Jared separated himself from me and got up to his feet.

"We'll be out in a minute!"

My husband yelled in the direction of the door and then held out his arm to help me get up from the sofa.

"A few more hours, Mrs. Wolfe, and I will be able to take that lace panty off with my teeth. Just keep that in mind for the rest of the evening." Jared muttered looking at me while I adjusted my dress in the mirror and made sure that my make-up and hair remained impeccable.

"You are a tease, Mr. Wolfe." I responded playfully, turning around to face Jared and then burst out laughing at the sight of the erect appendage protruding through his perfectly tailored pants. "I think we need a couple of minutes for you to look less excited for the pictures and our guests."

"Why don't you go ahead first because all I can think of is our unfinished business, when you are standing there in your sexy gown, and that only makes it harder. Pun intended"

He ushered me towards the door and leaned in to kiss me tightly on the lips as I opened the door and slipped out of the room.

Behind the door, I stumbled onto Rubio's assistant who was awkwardly pacing back and forth waiting for us to exit the room to escort us to the locations set up by Rubio. I advised him that my husband just needed another five minutes, and we would join them outside shortly, making him leave his post and walk away from the door reluctantly, possibly because Rubio told him not to come back without us. As I watched the photographer's assistant walk down the hallway towards the patio doors, I noticed Roxie sitting by the entrance in the leather wing chair talking on the phone. She seemed remarkably animated with her arms flailing about and laughing loudly, which prompted me to walk down the long hallway and join her in the chair across to find out what was going on while she finished up her call. Roxie noticed me taking a seat next to her and winked at me, motioning that she was almost done.

"Understood, that sounds wonderful. I will be there first thing tomorrow morning. Thank you for the opportunity!" Roxie concluded her call and hung up before turning her attention to me.

"Well, Good Afternoon, Mrs. Wolfe." She greeted me in a mock curtsy.

"I haven't even decided if I'm changing my name yet, but I do like the sound of it" I snickered in response. "So, we have a few minutes before I'm whisked off for a long photography session and endless hours of entertaining people I never met before. What is going on with you? Anything I need to know?".

Roxie hesitated shuffling nervously in her seat while habitually furrowing her eyebrows to form a line at the juncture between the two brow ridges. After a moment, she collected herself and her eyes locked on me exuding determination and contentment with the news that she wanted to share with me.

"I was going to wait until after the reception but in this craziness, I might not even get the chance, so I guess I can tell you now. Remember I told you about my day yesterday?"

"Of course," I responded reluctantly recalling the mean assertions we exchanged the night before. "Did you get one of the parts from the two auditions?"

"I still don't know, but it doesn't matter. I told you that I met a girl who is a part of a traveling theatre group. Well, she messaged me last night when I was taking the stroll around the neighborhood and invited me to hang out with her troop at this artsy bar they go to when they are in LA. So, I joined them, and they were all so amazing, they are so creative and free-spirited. They are completely unrestricted by the meaning of home; they go where life takes them and they have each other." Roxie spoke excitedly about her new bohemian friends while I nodded my head to indicate my full attention.

"We spent hours at this bar, and I came home really late and crashed on the couch to let you get your beauty sleep before the wedding. Then I woke up ridiculously early from my phone vibrating continuously because someone kept calling me. Typically, I let it go to voicemail, but I decided to pick it up this time. It was the manager of the theatre group I had just met the night before, asking me if I wanted to join them on the next leg of their tour. At first, I declined, but then I thought I'd go in and get more information, so I went over to join them at their rehearsals downtown. They asked me to stand in for one of the actors and improvise while they acted out a scene, and I felt so natural on the stage with them. After spending hours at the theatre, I was convinced. You were completely right, N, I'm not getting anywhere with my auditions, but I want to act so this is a perfect opportunity for me." Roxie paused to gauge a response from me, while I tried to process her words.

"First of all, I was completely wrong, and everything takes time so I'm sure you will get an amazing part and become a movie star if you persevere. Secondly, when you say travel theatre group, does this mean you are leaving LA?" I stumbled to finish the sentence.

"Yes, actually we are hitting the road tomorrow and heading to Illinois. I know it's very last minute, but I feel like it is the right thing for me to do, N. I already told my mother and she seemed excited about me earning some money and traveling at the same time. I want this, N. Please be happy for me." She stopped talking and gazed into my eyes with a pleading look.

"Of course, I'm happy for you! I will miss you like crazy, so used to you being around. The two years when you were in Georgetown and I was here were almost unbearable, but I guess this is temporary too."

"Maybe, maybe not. A tour can last a while, but I am in no rush. I will miss you too, sister friend. More than you'll ever know."

Roxie walked over to my chair and sat on the arm rest, then put her arms around me and squeezed hard. My arms flung upwards to envelop her body in a tight embrace, resting my head against her chest willing myself not to cry.

"I'm just glad that I'm leaving you in good hands" Roxie announced aloud, as I heard footsteps nearing us.

"Everything ok, ladies?" Jared's voice protruded above our heads.

"Just wishing my beautiful sister friend all the happiness in the world in this new endeavour. Promise to take good care of her?"

Roxie raised her head to stare Jared directly in the eyes and kept her gaze until he readily nodded.

"She will be my top priority." Jared asserted. "Now, how about we get this show on the road and join the festivities?"

Roxie separated from our embrace and got up to her feet, while Jared helped me up from the low wing chair and I embedded my arm through the loop of his arm as we walked out of the building towards the many smiling faces rushing to congratulate us. The rest of the day flew by in a whirlwind of emotions and lengthy speeches from the sea of blurry faces that I was introduced to by Jared's parents, preventing me from spending a single minute with my maid of honour. As the evening drew to a close, and the guests started to leave, the wedding planner rushed Jared and I down the walkway to a parked limousine while the remaining guests waved us goodbye. Behind the crowd, I spotted Roxie with Alison and my mother with Steve as they blew me kisses and then Roxie mouthed, *I love you* just as Jared nudged me to get in the car without giving me a chance to respond. When I looked out of the window, I was not able to see the beloved faces of my most cherished people and as the car drove off, I kept staring in the direction of the guests searching for my family, but they remained concealed behind the nameless strangers.

## Chapter Eleven

*January 2014*
*Age 29*

"You only have an hour to pack your things and I will need to inspect what you put in your bag, Mrs. Wolfe."

The stern looking woman dressed in an oversized brown pantsuit stood in front of me while I tried to catch my breath on the velvet chaise chair, her words failed to penetrate my understanding and instead my thoughts focused on her frumpy fashion choices. In the meantime, our beautiful house was swarmed with police enforcement officers marching throughout the expanse of the two-storey home rummaging through the personal belongings. My eyes shifted from the plastic taupe buttons on the woman's well-worn blazer to the uniformed officers by the fireplace who struggled to unhinge a painting I impulsively purchased from an art gallery on Melrose a couple of years ago.

That day I was grabbing a coffee in the newly opened boutique coffee shop with Bianca, a wife of one of Jared's colleagues who I have become good friends with over the years, and when I was walking to my car after a few hours of catching up on the latest LA gossip I saw the art piece hanging on a far wall of small but elegant art gallery. The oversized canvas displayed an image of a wide wooden planked boardwalk overlooking the grass-spotted dunes above the shore with two sets of children's footprints permeated in the virgin sand. The image prompted fond memories of my years in Delaware and brought back flashbacks of spending the summers on the beach with Roxie, exploring the dunes and building the sandcastles while our mothers relaxed seated on the picnic blanket.

"Do you understand what I'm saying?" The Brown Pantsuit lady interrupted the happy memories associated with the painting that the officers managed to finally unhinge from the wall.

"Could they be careful with that piece? It's extremely special to me." I directed my attention back to her formidable stare.

"As I was saying, we are arresting all of your valuables and seizing the assets belonging to you and your husband for the duration of the investigation until we are clear on how these assets were acquired."

"But i..." I started to object to indicate that I could tell them exactly how all the items were acquired, since I was the one who purchased all the furnishings and décor pieces over the years.

"You have less than an hour to pack your clothes and after that you will not be allowed entry into the house, so I suggest you get up and start packing."

The Brown Pantsuit lady cut me off and then turned to one of the officers and asked him to escort me to my room and monitor what I put in my bag. The uniformed officer did not seem too enthused to be a glorified babysitter for an hour but followed his orders and walked over to the chaise and stood over me until I finally stood up. My legs traitorously resisted to cooperate as I struggled to maintain my balance while I walked out of the living room and up the stairs to our master bedroom with the police officer closely behind me. While we passed the library, I heard a short exchange between a couple of policemen who were closely inspecting the room unaware of my presence in the hallway.

"There is no way she didn't know, if you ask me, she's just as guilty as her crook husband."

"Maybe, but wouldn't she have fled the country with him?"

*I didn't know anything!* I wanted to scream on top of my lungs for everyone to hear, knowing that it would be completely futile.

The last twenty-four hours spent in a freezing windowless room interrogated by the Brown Pantsuit lady and her colleague about my involvement in my husband's dealings taught me that no one was willing to believe me. Everyone's distrust in my statements made me doubt my own mental ability because I could not fathom how the privileged lifestyle blinded me to the real life.

Jared was a stable force in my life who I trusted unequivocally with every decision because he spoke with such confidence about all his work and the bright future before us. At the beginning of our marriage, I tried to offer my supportive suggestions and personal viewpoints on his work over dinner when he came home late after another client meeting, but he only smirked at my attempts thanking me for cooking dinner and proclaimed that he would deal with his own problems and all I had to worry about was how to pass my days. While I was eager to work at first, Jared argued that the last thing he needed was an exhausted wife greeting him at home and what would be best if I was like his friends' wives whose focus was the house and the extensive charity work. Initially this took me by surprise, and I refused to accept my fate as a stay-at-home laggard but then I met a few of the other wives and we hit it off, as they whisked me off to an array of charity afternoon teas and fundraising events.

Vivid memories of the Green Light Sanctuary's financial struggles convinced me to dedicate my time to the charity causes, so I quickly immersed myself in volunteering for a variety of charitable foundations. While I knew that we were contributing to worthy causes by raising a lot of money through the auctions and the hosted brunches, I still craved the hands-on work that enthralled me when I hustled around New York in search of sponsors and organized in-house events for the children and their mothers with our consistently limited funds. The amount of money that we raised in Los Angeles was substantial, but we never got to meet the families who benefited from these funds, since we only ever met the heads of the charitable foundations who were just as well groomed as the privileged volunteers.

Once a year around Christmas, I sent a donation that I thought would be significant enough for Green Light's needs and small enough not to raise concerns with Jared. My husband never questioned my spending habits but only sat me down once when I withdrew five thousand dollars to give to my mother, during one of her visits, to help her with the house renovation instead of writing her a cheque. He indicated that while I had the full freedom to spend reasonable amounts of money, he needed full transparency of the spending, so he asked that I only use bank transfers or keep clear track records of the cheques. Aware of my husband's financial pedantry I maintained an overt account of all my spending, which he could peruse at his own leisure.

I loved Jared for his dogmatism and devotion fully aware of how hard he worked to support our lifestyle with all the late evening and absent weekends, but I knew he loved me back because of his obvious concern for my well being as he would check up on my whereabouts a few times a day and the relentless passion when we made love after his lengthy business trips. I trusted him wholly with our lives, recklessly happy with my carefree existence, which is why the events of the last week seemed to shatter the stable earth below my unsteady feet.

Three days ago, it was just another sunny Tuesday morning when I woke up around nine and turned my head slowly to my right in hopes to find indentation marks on Jared's pillow that could indicate that he came home from his unusually long business trip and spent the night before heading out to work. The pillow remained perfectly fluffed and untouched ever since my husband left abruptly almost four days earlier while I was out at a Pilates class with a few of my friends.

While I lay in bed, I thought back to the day less than a week ago, when I came out of the strenuous Pilates class, I was pumped to check out a new popular brunch spot with the girls and did not bother to check my phone until later in the day on my drive home. When I finally looked at my cellphone, I noticed five missed calls from Jared, which was not unusual because I knew how he liked to check in on me. I was aware of the fact that he probably got worried about my whereabouts, which was almost certainly going to lead to another grim talk at dinner. After a few unsuccessful attempts at calling him back, my calls remained unanswered, which could mean that he was utterly livid with me for disappearing on him. To fully comprehend the extent of my husband's fury, I dialed my voicemail where three new messages were waiting to be heard, so I diffidently prompted them to play through the car speakers expecting his loud yell to deafen me.

"Noelle, where the hell are you? I need to talk to you right now! This is urgent." Jared's booming voice bounced off the walls in my Range Rover with resounding anger at not having reached me in a short but concise message.

"Noelle, I really need to speak to you. Something very unexpected came up and I must leave the country today. I am heading to the airport right now and unless you call me back in the next hour, I will be out of reach for a while. Please call me."

The second message had a completely different tone, almost pleading instead of commandeering a response. It was not unusual for Jared to leave on a business trip on a few hours notice, especially since he left the Private Fund company where he worked four years earlier and started out on his own. Jared never fully explained to me what his new venture entailed other than it was linked to the newly emerging enigmatic world of cryptocurrency, but his business was doing remarkably well while his client base grew exponentially over the years.

When I first indicated my concern with his growing number of days away from home, he indicated that due to a lot of his clients being from abroad, his job required extensive international travel to finalize the deals and ensure the smooth execution of the transactions. He assured me that he was doing it all for our future and the future of our unborn children. This typically, seemed to calm me down because he knew how fervently I wanted to start a family, but Jared always said that he had too many unfulfilled goals before he was ready to settle down with a brood of screaming children that needed his undivided attention, which he was unable to provide at this time. I was understanding, glad that Jared was able to see his purpose, but I felt that the endless fundraising events and parties could not be my ultimate reason for the second chance at life and was hoping that growing my family could fulfill that empty void.

"I'm sorry, Noelle. Sorry for everything. Goodbye."

The third vague message was filled with pain and remorse that I had never previously heard from my typically stoic husband. Uncertain if he was sorry for yelling in his earlier message or the fact that he was unexpectedly leaving the country, I continued driving home. Thinking nothing more of his messages being relieved that I was not going to be reprimanded for being unavailable to answer the phone and instead shifted my focus on how I could integrate the rustic wooden accents in my house that have become so popular in the LA homes recently.

Four days later when I woke up still alone in bed unable to reach my husband just as he had promised, I vowed that once he returned, I would have to have a more serious discussion with him on concisely defining our life targets and deadlines so I could have a clear understanding on when we could expand our family. Just as I was about to get up to get ready for my yoga class in a Santa Monica studio that I was invited to by one of my friends, I heard my phone vibrating on my bedside table. Seeing my mom's number on the screen surprised me because she had been traveling with Steve around Asia and we never seemed to sync on our time schedules to catch up.

"Hey mom! This is a surprise! How are you?" I picked up the phone anxious to hear all about her trip, that she had been carefully planning for almost a year.

"Honey, are you watching the news? Steve and I turned on CNN just now in the hotel room and saw Jared's name. Please turn on the news."

My mother sputtered into my ear, instantly changing my carefree mood to a morbid concern about my husband, as I immediately reached for the remote control and turned on the large flatscreen on the wall. I flipped through the channels to locate the news channel that I typically skipped over in my search for slightly more entertaining shows until I saw the red and white logo with my husband's name on the screen and a startling woman dressed in the Marc Jacobs dress that I have been eyeing for some time, interviewed by the well-known host whose name I could never remember.

*International search for Jared Wolfe; charges of fraud.*

I read the headline aloud forgetting that I was still on the line with my mother, while her concerned voice pattered through the speaker failing to reach my comprehension.

"Mom, I'll call you back." I hastily snapped back to her objecting voice and pressed the red button to hang up.

"…but how long have you been aware of Mr. Wolfe's plans?" The presenter addressed his question to the woman in front of him, as she kept her almond shaped eyes focused on her interviewer and swept a lock of her jet-black hair behind her ear adorned by an elegant pearl earring.

"Jared had only confided in me about his unfortunate plans about five days ago and I reached out to the police immediately but because they did not seem to be too interested, I felt that it was my duty to go public with the information so no one else falls prey to this scam artist." The female spoke about my husband with visible antipathy, emphasizing the last words in her statement. The way she raised her perfectly shaped eyebrow and the patronizing tone in her voice seemed familiar, but I had trouble placing where I may have encountered her in the past.

"Let's refrain from any labels at this time, until the investigation is completed, and we have a clear understanding of the charges against Jared Wolfe." The host hurried to prevent the situation from escalating on air.

"Call him what you want, but the way he took advantage of all the trusting citizens and had embezzled millions of dollars out of the country under false pretenses of investing in the crypto market, is appalling to me. He took advantage of people's illiteracy in the emerging markets and promised them unbelievable returns without any intentions to deliver against those promises. Jared possesses this unique quality of being able to sell the air we breathe to the gullible consumers, who buy into his confident pitch and readily hand over their life savings. The supercilious always prosper by squashing the trusting population with their confidence."

The woman seemed to be gleaming at the attention that she was gaining through her eloquent tirade aimed at my husband.

"At the start of the interview, you indicated that Jared Wolfe confided in you because of your close relationship. Could you define the nature of that relationship?"

The raised question interested me more than the unfounded allegations against my husband.

"Jared and I have been in a romantic relationship on and off since we were in college and when I left Los Angeles for New York, he continued to fly here on most weekends to visit me."

The defiance in her words struck me with full force, as I thought of all the business trips that Jared went on over the years and how I always had trouble reaching him on his cell phone when he was away.

"I apologize for diverting to the personal questions, but my records indicate that Mr. Wolfe has been married since 2004. Are you suggesting that you and Jared Wolfe were involved in an extramarital affair?"

The prying host seemed excited at the turn of events that seemed to crumble the world around me.

"For full transparency, I am admitting that Jared and I have been involved prior to and during the years of his marriage. As a matter of fact, I was invited to their wedding and attended it at Jared's insistence. That was the only time I met his wife, I never understood why he chose to get married because he never seemed to be the commitment type of person. He even approached me during the wedding, and we consummated our infidelity during the reception in their reserved suite at the venue while his new bride was busy with the guests, until we were caught by one of the guests. The reason I am sharing this personal information is because I want to be fully transparent and assure the public that I have nothing to hide."

Her every word seemed to slap me on the face with the brutal reality of the cruel world that I have failed to comprehend through the happiness filter that I evidently erected over the years. When the extravagant paramour mentioned that she had attended the wedding, I quickly remembered speaking to her briefly while I blissfully accepted everyone's well wishes on what appeared to be the happiest day of my life.

*Who saw them together? Why didn't anyone tell me?*

I wondered why it took me eight years to realize that the most devoted loving man in my life was a cheating crook who failed to keep his cock under lock all these years.

"Well, thank you for being honest with us and coming forward with your story. We will closely monitor any developments as we learn more details in the next coming days. In the meantime, if you believe that you have been a victim of the alleged fraud masterminded by Jared Wolfe, please contact your local police unit."

The host concluded the interview and the images on the screen changed to a series of colourful commercials.

My phone started vibrating vigorously on the bed, but I remained still, unwilling to speak to anyone at that moment. My mind raced through the decade of our blissful lives together, trying to make sense of everything.

*How could I be so blind?*

The anger at Jared projected back at my own failure to see the reality for what it was, blinded by the expensive gifts and the beautiful gestures. We have shared the bed in our beautiful Venice Beach home for eight years, we have traveled the world on the most elaborate luxurious vacations, we have been a unit since we met during frosh week when I was only eighteen years old terrified of everything unfamiliar around me.

*Have there been signs?*

The freedom that Jared granted me in my day to day, was reciprocated by my genuine disinterest in what he did at work, knowing that all his free time was dedicated to me. While I knew not to bother him while he was at work or away on business, we spent all our time together when he was at home. We did not have to spend hours talking but could just lounge in the living room immersed in our respective books or binge watch the latest shows that I always abstained from watching alone.

The phone continued to vibrate on my bed, and I reached for it to feel for the power button on the right side and held it down until the device felt placid in my grasp. The jumble of contentions in my throbbing head prevented me from being able to verbalize any coherent sentences to anyone who was trying to reach me. Somehow, I managed to entrap myself in yet another relationship that blinded me to the true character of my partner, Ray with his violent exploitive traits and Jared with his passive aggressive pretense at love.

*Could this be my purpose?*

To continuously be disappointed in the male partners in my life, endlessly searching to be taught otherwise but eventually ending up with shattered pieces of my life at my feet. The universe could not possibly be this cruel, but the latest developments seemed to distortedly mimic my failure to fully understand the people whom I chose to love. Trying to find the silver lining, I momentarily considered that I had only managed to hurt myself this time without dragging Roxie down with me, selfishly forgetting about the hundreds of people whom my husband had scammed out of their money. The severity of the financial fraud circumstances was still a mystery to me, and the implications remained unclear for the time being, while I continued to wallow in my personal tragedy.

The meretricious sound of the doorbell and a clamorous incessant knocking on the door forced me to get up from my bed and look out of the window to see who was outside. The sheer drapes allowed me to see two police cars parked in front of our house and a few of the officers looking up at the house, until one of them spotted my figure through the translucence of the drape and gestured for me to open the door. I separated myself from the window and draped a silk dressing gown around my matching pyjamas, then walked downstairs to open the door to find four uniformed officers standing on the porch. One of them introduced himself and showed me his badge, then asked if they could come in, to which I responded with a vaguely visible timid nod.

"Mrs. Wolfe, we need you to get ready and come with us to the police station for some questioning regarding your husband." The officer observed my disheveled, unsettled appearance and continued. "There is nothing to worry about, the detectives and the Financial Crimes unit have some questions for you."

"Do I need a lawyer?" I asked, recalling the proper response gained from watching multiple crime shows over the years.

"That's at your discretion. However, you are not under arrest, you are simply needed for questioning about your husband."

The officer repeated his intent and asked me to go upstairs to get ready, to which I obliged and walked upstairs to change. Unaware of what one wears to a police station, I chose a pair of black slacks and a white sweater as the most appropriate outfit to represent my professional and yet casual demeanor. After a few minutes of getting ready, opting to tie my hair up in a high ponytail, I stuffed my cell phone in my purse and walked downstairs to join the officers as they escorted me out of the house into one of their cars. As I was about to get in the car, I staggered remembering that I forgot to lock the front door but the officer behind me prevented me from turning around to head back to the house, indicating that two of the police officers will remain at the house until I return. Doubting the legality of their actions, but unaware of the correct procedures I settled in the back of the police cruise as it pulled away from my house.

This was a first, I had never been at the back of the police car in the past and was thankful for being lucky enough to avoid the unpleasant experience. It was tight and uncomfortable, confined by the lack of legroom and the bulky partition separating me from the officers in the front seats, restraining me from any potential sudden movements. The sole positive aspect of being driven in the police car was that traffic abated when the cruiser approached any congested areas on the highway and we were able to make it from Venice to Downtown LA in less than ten minutes, while it would typically take me at least thirty minutes to maneuver around the stalled vehicles to cover that distance.

When we arrived at the police station, the police officers opened the back door for me to exit the vehicle and firmly asked me to follow them into the police station, having no regard for my shocked state. The moment I stepped out of the car; I was immediately surrounded by a group of journalists with a multitude of video cameras pointed at my panic-stricken face as I struggled to move from the curb. The petulant police officers came to my rescue and pushed the loud reporters away from me, as the indignant newshounds continued to throw incensed questions that I left unanswered. Feeling like a convicted felon I kept my head down following the officer in charge into the solemn grey building tailed closely by two other officers in a morbid procession. Once inside the building I was escorted down the winding hallways and up the stairs into a crammed windowless room sheathed with dark grey cement walls and a lone ceiling light fixture casting light on the table positioned in the middle of the confinement with two sets of plastic chairs on opposite sides.

"Take a seat right there and the detectives will come to see you."

The grouchy police officer pointed in the direction of one of the chairs closest to the opposite side of the wall, which I silently obliged and walked over to take a seat. The heavy door closed with a click of a lock behind the officer, leaving me confined within the four walls of the grim room.

Without having any distractions within the space, feeling abandoned in the reticence around me, the thoughts about the daftness of my life consumed me. The pretense of a fairy tale lifestyle was just a made-up fictional existence, that I immersed myself in without ever trying to lift the rose-tinted glasses to observe the truth around me. In morbid reality, deep inside I remained an orphaned little girl trying to alter her unfortunate circumstances by choosing to fabricate a perfect life that existed in the fictional stories I grew up reading. My eyes filled with tears and my bottom lip started to quiver as I was consumed by the wallowing self-pity that I had despised so much in all the weak female characters that I had always criticized for being subservient to the assertive lead figures. Dismayed with my own weakness and refusing to succumb to my own inferiority, I wiped away the betraying tears and clenched my fists tightly. This was not the time or the place, now was the time for me to be strong and confident if I wanted this nightmare to be over.

The heavy door opened ajar, and two people walked in taking their seats across from me, one of them was a clean-shaven man dressed in a bespoke black suit that complimented his wide shoulders and an athletic frame and the other was an average height female with mousy hair tied back wearing a loose fitted brown pant suit with taupe round buttons. The man introduced himself as an FBI agent and the woman said she represented the Financial Crimes division; their names did not register in my head, so I decisively named them "Bespoke" and "Brown Pantsuit".

"Mrs. Wolfe, thank you for coming in to speak to us today." Bespoke started first, while I wondered if he thought that I actually had the choice when the officers escorted me out of the house.

"I understand that this may be a hard time for you, but we need to ask you some questions about your husband and his dealings. Can you tell us about your husband's whereabouts? Do you know where he went four days ago?" The man continued while the female kept her dour gaze at me.

"No, I do not know where he went. All I know is that he left me a voicemail message saying he was leaving the country, and at the time I assumed that it was yet another business trip. Could you tell me if what they reported on the news is true?"

"Too soon to say, Mrs. Wolfe. But there is an overwhelming amount of evidence against your husband and the FBI and Financial Crimes Unit are going to work hard for a while to follow all the leads. Back to the voicemail, do you still have it?" Bespoke seemed to be the lead of this questioning session, as the Brown Pantsuit remained silent.

"I do, I have all of his voicemail messages from the last couple of weeks." I was happy to have a definite answer to his question.

"We will need to obtain that from you as part of our investigation. Now, I need you to be honest with us, can you describe the extent of your involvement in your husband's business?" The FBI agent hit me with the hard question.

"None at all, he did not like to talk to me about work. Jared encouraged me to focus on the charity work that I am involved with and did not want to trouble me with his deals. All I know is that Jared used to work for a large investment firm for a number of years, but saw an opportunity in the blockchain market, so he decided to start his own business. Now, do not ask me what blockchain is, but that's one word he used a lot when he explained what he did when we were out at dinner with friends." I remained truthful with my responses, knowing that honesty is the best policy especially when dealing with the law enforcement.

"I have a hard time believing that in all the years you have been married, you failed to learn more about your husband's work. Did he never confide in you about his troubles at work or any difficult decisions?" The Brown Pantsuit jumped into the conversation, looking at me with unconcealed accusation.

The painful jolt of self-pity made another attempt at destabilizing my composure, as I felt a mist cloud my eyes with uninvited tears.

"He never did, he always insisted on keeping work and home as two separate facets of his life."

I responded, batting my eyelashes to sweep away any hint of despondence hoping that my weakness remained unnoticed.

Bespoke and Brown Pantsuit continued with their questioning for the next several hours on all the details about our lives from the moment we met in college to the last time I saw him before heading out to Pilates four days earlier. Their repeated questioning about Jared's business dealings transitioned to a more sensitive topic about the multiple extramarital affairs that they have learned about since the news expose, not limited to the "love interest" that was interviewed this morning. The details I learned about my husband's life were outrageous and hard to believe, but after hours of questioning my attitude grew more impassive with every new revelation, as the rollercoaster of emotions seemed to numb my feelings. Detecting my eventual change in demeanor, the interrogators left the room saying that they will be back in a couple of hours to continue with their questions. Tired from the emotional turmoil of the day, I folded my arms on the table resting my head atop the fold and closed my eyes thankful for the temporary reprieve. Instead of the grim grey room I imagined myself on the beach in Delaware with my parents engrossed in building a tall sand structure, while the jovial Alison and Roxie played in the warm summer tide in the distance. A feeling of warmth and pure happiness enveloped my body, as I succumbed to my exhaustion and fell asleep.

A clicking noise of the door lock startled me as I was awoken from my blissful slumber, temporarily making me forget about the predicament that I was in. Briefly confused by my surroundings when I opened my eyes, the memories of the day rushed back when I saw the grumpy police officer who escorted me into the room earlier walk in and place a glass of water and a sandwich in front of me.

"Thank you." I mumbled gratefully, realizing that I have not had a chance to eat all day.

"I have someone here to see you, I'll show them in." The officer walked out of the room and returned a minute later with a couple of familiar faces behind him.

"Ada, Joseph!" I was surprised to see Jared's parents in the room, it was unusual to see them surrounded by the grim concrete walls away from their opulent mansion and the luxurious golf club.

"Hello, dear." Said Jared's mother as they both sat down in the chairs across from me.

"It's good to see you. Are you here for questioning too?"

I was glad to not feel alone.

"Yes, we have been interviewed earlier and then we were asked to come here. Our lawyer is outside, where is your lawyer?" Jared's father questioned the obvious.

"I did not think that I needed one, I have nothing to hide. Jared never told me anything about any of this, and I absolutely had no clue about his work." I rushed to profess my innocence to his parents.

"You should always have a lawyer, that is just how things work." Joseph Wolfe argued dismayed at my foolishness.

"Did you know?" I directed my question at Jared's mother, trying to gauge her involvement in Jared's dealings.

"No, dear, we did not know about his business. Jared was always so secretive about these things. When he left the investment firm, he asked us for an initial capital investment for his new venture that he was so confident about, so we wrote him a cheque to help him out" She affirmed my guess of their initial involvement.

"What about his extramarital affairs?" I asked after a momentary hesitation, shifting my gaze from one to another trying to stare them straight in the eyes as they both looked at each other.

"No, but we had our suspicions. Jared had always been popular and had a myriad of girlfriends, so when he met you, we hoped that he was going to change. He seemed so enamoured with you. He seemed to be more focused on his career at the investment firm, and he stopped his constant drinking and partying. After he introduced you to us, we thought that you would be a perfect match for him who would support him in all his endeavours and steer him away from the spiraling out of control drinking habit and the revolving circle of girlfriends."

Ada stopped talking, looking at her husband for help as she was reluctant to continue.

"So, I told my son that he should marry you if he wanted to see any financial support from me. I told him to stop with all his bimbo girlfriends and the endless partying, and settle down with you, or he was not going to see a penny from me."

Jared's father blatantly stated the facts from years ago that I was oblivious to at the time, believing in the power of true love where a rich handsome boy could fall in love with a small-town girl without a penny to her name.

"I'm sorry, honey, but we hoped this would change him. We saw how much you loved him, and he seemed to be really taken by you. Over the years we affirmed our decision because he seemed to be such a good husband to you. In his own way, we are confident that he loved you very much. We only started to get suspicious of his returning habit because of his increased overnight business trips. Unfortunately, we were right. We are very sorry, Noelle." Ada reached for my hand and squeezed it.

"You forced him to marry me?" I struggled to believe the facts provided to me.

"We never forced him, we gave him a choice and he made the right one." Joseph responded defensively leaving me speechless as I leaned back in the chair pulling my hand away from Ada's grasp.

"I think you should leave. I don't want to regret what I may say next, as I have too much respect for you."

I got up from the uncomfortable chair and walked over to the door, knocking on it to notify the officers outside of the conclusion of the family reunion. The door quickly opened, and a new police officer appeared on the other side.

"Mr. and Mrs. Wolfe need to reconvene with their overpriced lawyer, could you help them with that?" I directed my question at the young officer, who agreed and waited for the elderly couple to get up.

"We only wanted the best for our son, Noelle." Ada said, looking at me for affirmation as she walked out of the room, while I diverted my gaze and walked back to my chair.

"You should really get a lawyer." I heard Joseph's deep voice as he provided his last piece of advice on his way out.

*What I need is a shower and a change of clothes, not another person to tell me what to say or do.*

I thought to myself, as I reached for the wrapped sandwich that remained untouched since it was placed in front of me. Taking off the plastic cellophane, I found a decent looking turkey and cheese wrap that I immediately sank my teeth in, thrilled to finally be able to eat. While the wrap lacked the gourmet quality, I grew accustomed to over the years, it satisfied my hunger and was able to awaken my brain from its calorie deprived stupor. When Bespoke returned with Brown Pantsuit, I was prepared to undergo hours of additional questioning until late in the evening leaving them content with my answers, that I indeed was another kept wife who was blissfully unaware of her husband's affairs.

"Mrs. Wolfe, we are done with our line of questioning for the day, and you are free to go but unfortunately you cannot go back to your house as it is currently secured for the forensics and financial crimes unit as part of the investigation, while they continue to search for evidence. Is there anywhere else we could take you?" The Brown Pantsuit announced just before midnight of the conclusion of the grueling interview.

"Can I use my phone, so I can call some people to see if I can stay at their homes?" I asked, reaching for my phone in my purse once the Brown Pantsuit nodded with permission, this was the longest time I have been away from my phone and was expecting to see a plethora of missed calls from all my girlfriends to check in with me.

Instead, there were twenty-five missed calls from my mother, five from Alison and fifty-one from an unknown number with an area code I was not familiar with. Having been assured that Jared left the country and was now being searched by Interpol, I knew that it could not have been my husband calling me from the unidentified number.

*Must be some journalist who found my number.*

I reasoned, not knowing who else could be calling me that many times. My circle of friends only involved people who lived as far as Pasadena, as I failed to maintain my ties with any of my Delaware high school friends. I have not even been able to see or even speak to Roxie for years, she was perpetually busy with her theater tour group and the endless rehearsals. When I tried calling her, she either could not pick up or would respond with a quick hello and then assure me that she was fine before rushing to the stage. When she made it to Los Angeles on one of her tour stops a few years ago, she reached out for us to meet and catch up, but I was overseeing a fundraising event and could not afford to miss a minute during the day. I thought to invite her to the house, but

Jared vehemently refused to have Roxie over, saying that she was a bad influence for my fragile mind, and I have been an improved person since she left. He insisted that if she was a true friend, then she would do her best to stay in touch with me, but she failed to maintain a conversation longer than three minutes when I did manage to catch her. Seeing a certain reason in his arguments, after some self-debating, I accepted the fact that Roxie and I grew apart, divided by the circumstances of our lives and we both lived out the paths that we chose for ourselves. So, I texted her to say that it was an exceptionally busy time for me, and we could not meet, to which she responded with a simple "Ok".

She tried calling me a few times over the years, but I resorted to texting her once a year on our birthday, to which she usually responded with a reciprocal message. Last month, was the first time my birthday message remained unrequited, so I called Alison to see if there was anything wrong with Roxie to which Alison assured me that everything was fine and that her daughter was on tour in Canada and had some new prospects lined up for the new year. Relieved that everything was fine, I continued with yet another day of shopping with my girlfriends forgetting about any of my earlier concerns about my former best friend.

Staring at my phone in the police headquarters I was surprised not to see any missed calls from any of my friends, so I tried calling a few of the girls from the charity group but every ring resonated with a pang of abandonment as the calls remained unanswered. I tried calling Bianca who I often met for brunch and who was married to one of Jared's old colleagues from the investment firm, but the call seemed to drop the four times that I tried calling her.

"It's probably just too late, they are all most likely asleep and have their phones off or on mute. I'll just stay at a hotel nearby, I guess." I tried to make excuses for my friends, even though I knew that each one of them tended to stay up watching television until at least two in the morning.

"I'm afraid all your credit cards have been blocked as of this morning, Mrs. Wolfe." Bespoke said nonchalantly depriving me of any choice of where to sleep for the night.

"How about you stay the night at the station? And tomorrow, we will take you to your house to collect your essential belongings and hopefully by then you will figure out where to stay for the duration of the investigation." I caught a glimpse of compassion in Brown Pantsuit's dark eyes, as she offered the only available option.

Stooping to the new low, I accepted the offer of free

accommodation at the police station, then left the confinement of the contcrete-walled room where I had been kept for over twelve hours and was escorted to a single cell in the depths of the vast building by Brown Pantsuit and another police officer. As the caged door slid closed behind me, Brown Pantsuit said that she will be waiting for me at the house first thing tomorrow morning and that one of the officers would take me there. Accepting my silence as agreement, they left me to settle in for the night in a hard single bed while the noises from the other occupants of the neighbouring cells clattered ceaselessly. Confident that the screaming and the banging will keep me up all night, I reluctantly laid down on a plastic mattress and covered myself with an itchy wool blanket and drifted off to sleep as soon as my head hit the flat pillow.

    The next morning, I woke up rested from a dreamless sleep to an officer opening the caged door and inviting me to follow him. Without a moment of hesitation, I sprung to my feet and raced out of the jailed confinement relieved for the unpleasant experience to be over. The officer escorted me down a series of endless hallways to the outside, where I was startlingly grateful to see the sun and breath in the fresh air having spent twenty-four hours in the dark depths of the police station.

Without slowing down, I swiftly got into the back of the police cruiser and ignored the discomfort of the drive because I was eager to get home. When we approached the house, I noticed an array of police cruisers and unmarked vehicles parked on the street while the neighbours and strangers I have never seen in the past congregated on the crowded sidewalk.

    Once I stepped out of the car when the car door was opened, I heard multiple people run over equipped with their cameras and microphones looking for an exclusive and badgering me with intrusive questions. Paparazzi was not a novelty on the streets of Los Angeles, and I had seen the swarm of cameras surround an occasional celebrity leaving a restaurant or a store on Rodeo drive, but I never thought that I would be dodging the cameras myself. A few police officers rushed over and helped me make my way to the house, while I covered my face with my hands until I entered the safety of my own home.

    The deceptive safety only hid me from the noisy journalists, but inside I encountered a throng of law enforcement officers uprooting and packing all the pieces that I had carefully collected over the years to make this Venice house a home. The Persian rugs that I purchased in Sacramento have been rolled up and set aside, the restored walnut dining table that I special ordered from Oklahoma was unceremoniously flipped upside down, a collection of boxes was stacked up by the entrance with neatly printed labels attached to the top and the side of the containers. While I observed the mess of my own home in stunned silence, the Brown Pantsuit approached me and asked me to take a seat on the chaise chair that remained in the middle of the room. This is when she explained to me in detail, that I no longer had access to any of my possessions and could only gather my most essential belongings of no significant value.

Once in my room, it was hard to decide what was considered as essential or of significant value since everything I owned had some significance whether it was monetary or personal. Figuring that Brown Pantsuit would not object to me taking my photo albums and favourite books, I placed them first in the medium sized luggage. Then I walked through my walk-in closet filled with the unique designer creations, I regretfully looked at my collection of red sole pumps and sophisticated stilettos and reached for the more practical flats and athletic shoes to take with me. Flipping through the racks of clothes, crammed with the stunning long evening gowns and designer logo outfits, I selected a couple of sweatshirts and a few pairs of jeans that I kept at the back of the closet. Knowing that taking any jewellery was out of the question, I skipped the secured drawers camouflaged underneath the underwear drawer. Instead, I grabbed two handfuls of the bras and panties and stuffed them in the suitcase.

"You only have ten more minutes." The officer announced standing by the door.

I hastily started rushing around the expanse of the room randomly throwing things into the suitcase without any serious thought of its significance, then abruptly stopped and realized that I may not have access to a shower for the foreseeable future and needed to immediate change out of the clothes that I had been wearing for over a day. So, I selected a pair of black skinny jeans, a white Gucci t-shirt and a Michael Kors oversized cardigan and laid them on my bed. Then, I walked into my spa worthy bathroom and turned on the water in the walk-in shower, before stripping out of my clothes that seemed to be infused with the stale smell of the police station. Relieved to be able to wash off the stench of the previous day, I stepped onto the mosaic shower floor and positioned myself under the toiling large rain showerhead which generated the relieving flow of steaming hot water as I closed my eyes and felt the shame and regret wash away. I had no idea where to go, I had no money, my friends were non-responsive, I was not allowed to live in my own house, my husband abandoned me to deal with everything by myself, but I was determined to enjoy the next five minutes in this scorching shower before I had to leave and face the cruel reality. For the next five minutes the world stopped spinning out of control underneath my feet, all my worries drained with every droplet into the intricate plumbing system flowing into the endless ocean. This was just a bump on the path that I chose for myself, I was going to overcome it and get myself back on track.

"Time to go!" I heard a loud knock on the door.

"Ok, let me just dry myself and get dressed." I screamed back, turning off the healing shower.

I stepped out of the glass enclosure and grabbed the soft Egyptian cotton towel wiping myself dry. Feeling significantly better from the shower, I wrapped the towel around my body and exited the room to find the officer standing outside. I asked him for some privacy to change, while he hesitated unsure if he should leave his post but then followed his instinct and left the room. Without a minute to waste, I hastily got dressed in the outfit that I had laid out on the bed and zipped up my suitcase before wheeling it out of the room.

The officer helped me bring the suitcase down, while I waited for further instructions from the Brown Pantsuit. She seemed preoccupied with some paperwork in front of me, so when she saw that I was packed and ready for her to inspect my belongings, she looked up at the police officer who monitored my packing and asked him if he had any concerns. The officer confirmed that I had only packed the bare minimum and he did not see any inappropriate actions that could impede the investigation.

"In that case, you are free to go, Mrs. Wolfe. Please keep your phone with you in case we need to reach you. I understand you have family in Delaware, is this where we may find you if we need to talk to you?"

"Yes, Delaware. I will be staying with my mother in Georgetown." I realized that coming home was the best solution and I could ask my mother to buy a plane ticket for me.

"For what it is worth, I am sorry this happened to you. I could sense that you had no awareness of the circumstances when I saw genuine pain in your eyes, that is something a guilty person can never recreate. Goodbye, Mrs. Wolfe." The Brown Pantsuit revealed a hint of a smile, as she reached out and shook my hand.

"Thank you. Goodbye." I responded with relief of finally being understood, then grabbed the handle of my suitcase and rolled it out of the house and down a steep set of steps. Once I stepped outside the front yard, I was immediately surrounded by the swarm of journalists and without the police officers to protect me, I felt defenseless from their incessant questioning and the buzzing from their bulky cameras that were mere inches away from my face. I remained stoic as I started to walk down the street with the suitcase's handle safely planted in my grasp, but the hungry hyenas starving for their coveted exclusives refused to give up and remained by my side.

Suddenly I felt a bulky jacket blanket my head from the view of the cameras and a comforting embrace of an extended arm cradle my side.

"No comment!"

A painfully familiar voice yelled at the reporters, as the firm arm guided me forward and into a car parked by the curb. I got into the passenger seat instantly, while my saviour grabbed my suitcase and shoved it in the back seat in one swift motion. I could still hear the journalists and the camera clicking outside the car window, so I kept the cover over my head even when the driver got in and started driving, while honking at the reporters to get out of the way.

"Ok, it's safe now. You can take that stupid jacket off your head." The voice announced once we drove out of the neighbourhood into the busy streets of LA.

Trusting the familiar female voice, I slowly removed the safety cover from my head and looked at the driver, tears forming in my eyes.

"Roxie."

I could not believe my eyes, as if a ghost from my past appeared in front of me. Without being able to say a single word, I finally felt a wave of emotions hit me and the tears that I had been battling so hard for the last twenty-four hours seemed to have found an outlet and unable to further contain my feelings I surrendered to the bitter overpowering tears.

"Oh, Noelle. It is all good. Everything is going to be alright. Crying is good, otherwise tears can drown you from the inside." Roxie comforted me while whizzing down the congested streets. "I've got you now, it was my turn to save you from a fall just like you did for me when we were kids. Only I was too late, and you got hurt, but it will all be alright."

"I'm so glad to see you, Rox. How did you know? Where did you come from?" I asked through the loud sobbing.

While she steered her car down the busy highway, Roxie revealed how she resurfaced in my life and came to my much-needed rescue. Alison woke her up early morning the day before when Roxie was in bed at her hotel room in Vancouver after an all-night wrap-up party of the Canadian tour and asked her to turn on the news, where she saw the exotic looking harlot boast about her love affair with Jared. She tried calling me from her Canadian number right away, but it just went to voicemail every time. Concerned about me, she immediately got into her car and drove for twenty hours straight to my Venice home. On her drive, she continuously tried to call me, but I never picked up the phone which raised even more fears in Roxie, and she broke all the possible speed regulations trying to get to California as fast as possible.

When she arrived at the house, she saw the police cruisers and other vehicles parked outside, while the reporters were pacing back and forth on the street interviewing the neighbours. Roxie got out of the car, ignoring the unsteady pace from the lengthy seating, she approached a lone journalist who seemed bored of waiting in the sidelines and inquired about my whereabouts to be told that I was not home yet but was expected to arrive from the police station before lunch. His sources turned out to be correct because after a few hours of waiting in the parked car, she saw another police cruiser drive up and stop in front of the house, then she saw me emerge from the back looking tired and terrified of the screaming reporters. Roxie could not get through to me then but knew that I would eventually leave the house, so she waited anxiously for me to come out.

My tears full of kept-up anger, regret and self-blame seized mid-way through her story, disrupted with overdue realization that true friends are those who are by your side not when you are on the top of the world but when you are about to crash land at the bottom of the darkness-consumed pit.

"I have to tell you something, N. This is all my fault." Roxie started to say, surprising me of how she could hold herself responsible for the recent events. "I was the one who walked in on Jared having sex with that floosy at the wedding reception, and I never said anything to you. You were so happy that day, I could not muster up the courage to shatter the perfect image of your life at that point, I just could not do it then and as time went on, I tried to distance myself because it was eating me up from the inside. When I finally decided that it was time for you to know the truth, I came to LA, but you justly refused to meet me."

I sat in silence listening to Roxie's long delayed confession, while she pulled to the side of the road in an unfamiliar neighbourhood.

"I have missed you so much over the years and thought about you every day, while I was away from you. I'm so sorry, N." She turned her head to look at me, and I saw tears streaming down her beautiful face.

"I probably would not have believed you if you told me at the wedding, Rox." I responded after some time. "I'm so glad you are back in my life. I have missed you to Delaware and back!"

"I've missed you even more, N!" Then she leaned her body forward and embraced me in a loving hug that I have craved for so many years.

*Reunited, yet again.*

I thought to myself, confident that I would not let anything else tear us apart and we would remain by each other's sides for years to come.

## Chapter Twelve

*December 25, 2014*
*Age 30*

    The sun had barely started to rise, and hints of the daylight glow protruded through the shut blinds of the small hopper window set at the joint of the ceiling and the wall, when I opened my eyes. It had been almost six months since Roxie, and I moved to New York when she got an offer to be in an Off-Broadway production for a play produced by one of her friends from the theatre group. Since the opening day in September, the play had done exceptionally well and had received raving reviews from the critics and audience alike praising the quality of the production and the stellar cast, singling out Roxie by naming her "The One to watch". I was still apprehensive of our move to the City, and reflected back on the day when we made the decision.

    "N, you would not believe what happened!"

    Roxie returned from her audition to the small studio apartment that we shared in North Los Angeles. We had been staying at the studio atop the garage that belonged to one of her eccentric theatre friends, who lived in the adjacent two-story home since the day when Roxie picked me up from the darkest day of my lifetime.

    "Do tell! Did you get the part?"

    I was determined to support my sister friend in anything she decided to do, resentful of how I discouraged her the day before my wedding.

    "Definitely not, the audition was kind of sketchy actually. It was in this apartment in Burbank and there were two sleezy looking creeps who after I read for the part told me that they thought I would be perfect for the role and then asked me if I would be agreeable to full nudity. Before I had the chance to say no, they said they needed me to strip off my clothes so they could assess my physical compatibility with the character. Can you believe that? Hollywood!"

"Gross!" I shivered in disgust. "So, what unbelievable thing happened then?"

"My friend Anton from the theatre group, who is absolutely fabulous by the way, asked me to come to New York and play a lead in a play that he is producing. Apparently, the script that he wrote himself, is getting a great buzz in the industry and they have found some very generous investors behind it."

Roxie could not contain her excitement as she jumped around the spacious studio, almost knocking over a table lamp that we recently salvaged from the nearby dumpster.

"New York!" I bellowed in horror, the thoughts of our prior calamities in the Big Apple hurtled before my eyes. "I thought you didn't like New York, you always said that it made your skin crawl."

"Very true and so weird, I've never been there but it has always given me the chills." Roxie concurred with my statement, as she stopped pacing around the room and sat next to me on the futon. "But, this is an amazing opportunity! I just have to suck it up and get over whatever my imaginary "spidey senses" tell me."

"Maybe they are not so imaginary?" I made a weak attempt at convincing her that she is correct to be frightened of NYC.

"My sixth sense was right about that creep we met the summer after graduation! Remember that? He turned out to be some drug addict who tried to coax young Amy?"

Just as she recalled the events of that summer, she noticed her tiny arm hairs rise and an eruption of minuscule goosebumps blanketed her bare arms. "See! Still gives me the creeps. I got the same reaction earlier when Anton asked me to move to New York, and trust me my first response was to decline but I really want this, N. A lead in a big production!"

"Guess your mind's made up." I knew not to push the subject, terrified to be the reason for my best friend to lose out on the amazing opportunity. "When are you leaving?"

"What do you mean by *You*? *We* are leaving together in June. There is no way in hell, I am going to New York by myself. After Anton told me about the offer, I clearly hesitated considering the move, my only caveat to the very generous offer was that you would have to move with me."

At this point Roxie stopped talking and turned her pleading gaze at me, silently begging me to agree to move to the one place I avoided all my life. While I was ecstatic for Roxie's remarkable chance to prove to the world that she was an incredible actress, my deep buried trauma of the prior lifetime still lingered in my occasional nightmares. On the other hand, like former president Roosevelt said, "The only thing we have to fear is fear itself", so maybe moving to New York would help me treat my mental wounds and cure Roxie's "spidey sense". After all, it was not New York that caused us both pain, it was Ray's ingress into our gullible lives, and we were both smart enough now not to let some manipulative imbecile control us.

"I guess *We* are moving to New York." I gave in to Roxie's pleas. "It would be good to get away from LA anyways, I've been locked up here avoiding the cameras and afraid of bumping into anyone I used to know on the streets. Last time I spoke to Brown Pantsuit, she said that they were concluding their investigation and did not need me for any further questioning. If they need me to testify, I could just fly back."

Roxie jumped up from the couch and grabbed my hand to pull me up, then started to twirl me around the large open space that we have been sharing through the hardest months of my current lifetime. As we swirled around the studio holding each other's hands, the elated feeling of a new chapter in our lives seemed to sweep away the earlier worries and the thrill of the next path chosen devoured our minds.

The joyful memory of that day was the first thought when I woke up early in the morning in our Brooklyn basement apartment on our thirtieth birthday. Roxie's offer as the female lead in the play included a lot of perks in addition to a seemingly substantial monthly salary, an amount that neither of us had earned in the past combined. To offset the expensive rental expenses of the high-priced city living, the offer also included a subsidized two-bedroom basement apartment in Greenpoint that was perfectly located a few steps away from the East River and a breathtaking view of the New York jagged skyline. When we moved into the apartment, we were overjoyed at finally having our own rooms since there was no privacy in our studio loft in LA. Overtime as we decorated our new pad, Roxie turned her larger sized bedroom into a bohemian shrine adorned with the unique art pieces on her walls and a preloved Native American rug which we scouted at the flea markets in Brooklyn, while I collected multiple driftwood pieces and integrated them into the bedroom décor to resemble the Delaware coastal theme. Six months later, our cozy apartment felt like home and any jitters that first made us feel unwelcomed in the big city quickly dissipated.

Roxie spent most of her days away from the apartment at the theatre and returned late in the evenings, exhilarated with adrenaline pumping through her entire body. I would wait up for her every evening knowing that she would want to share her emotions with me when she got back, otherwise, she would be unable to fall asleep. So, every time I heard her unlock the apartment door, I would set my book aside and stroll over to the kitchen to turn on the kettle to prepare some calming chamomile tea. Once Roxie entered the apartment, she never failed to bring an overbearing amount of energy with her that seemed to bounce off the walls and consume the entire space disturbing the silence that had occupied its vastness for the duration of the day.

Last night was only a slight deviation, when Roxie returned home just before eight in the evening, euphoric from the successful Christmas Eve matinee performance, it was the earliest she had been home in months. She extolled the amazing reception from the audience and how the play ended with a standing ovation from the packed auditorium.

"It was just magical, a perfect ending to my twenties! Thirty starts tomorrow and I can only imagine how much greater that would be. We should make a list of what we want to achieve in our thirties, N!"

Roxie grabbed an old water bill from the counter and flipped it over, scribbling our names on top and drawing a vertical line across the page to create two separate columns.

"I'll start! I want to win a Tony Award for the lead actress, obviously I want the play to win too but this is an egocentric list of things I want for myself." She wrote down her first goal, then moved on to the next bullet points. "I want to be a lead in an uber-popular Broadway production. Oh, and I would love to move to the West End in London for a year to perform on stage for the British audience. I heard that they are brutally honest but if they accept you, then you are a legend in the theatre world. That is three, what else?"

"How about a family?"

I treaded towards the forbidden territory because Roxie always avoided the subject of relationships and children in her future. This was always disconcerting to me, seeing how happy she was when she was pregnant with her unborn child at the exact same stage at the cusp of entering the new decade in the prior lifetime. Unfortunately, I never lived to see her give birth or bring up her baby, but I would have imagined her to be a wonderful doting mother. In my wishful fantasies about the life beyond my existence, Roxie and the baby moved back to Delaware to live with Alison who devoted her life to the grandchild, while Roxie met a loving supportive man whom she later married in a beachside wedding, and they lived out their life "happily ever after".

*Could something have happened after I died that caused her to defer any relationships and love prospects, or thoughts of having children?*

"That can probably wait until I am in my forties, my thirties are going to be all about me. *Livin La Vida Loca!*" She once again changed the subject of family and sang the popular line from the Ricky Martin song, mimicking his signature gyrating hips. "Speaking of *Loca*, I want to do something crazy, something I have never done before. Maybe skydiving or bungee jumping. So, cliché though! Oh, how about streaking naked on all seven continents while I still have the slender fit body of a thirty-year-old?"

"That might be hard in Antarctica." I contemplated in response.

"True that! Strike the naked bit, but I heard they run marathons in Antarctica. How about I run at least one marathon per continent in the next ten years?" Roxie wrote "run a marathon" atop the scratched off "streak naked".

"Did not know you liked to run, Rox?" I jokingly criticized her selection.

"No, I don't, but it looks like everyone in New York jogs, and I really think we should blend in and start jogging too. As a matter of fact, first thing tomorrow morning we are going for a run!" She defiantly declared before writing down the goal.

"I need to come up with a few more, but let's do yours now. What do you want to do before you turn forty?"

Roxie switched her attention to the column on the right with my name written on top.

"Well, I need to find a job finally. Can't mooch off you for the rest of my life. I'll need to get more creative with my job search, since surprisingly no one want to hire an English Lit graduate whose only recent experience is brunching and shopping."

My colossal frustration with the job market in New York was one of the many hurdles preventing me from enjoying our otherwise upbeat life in the city. After sending out hundreds of resumes, I had yet to receive a single call for an interview making me doubt my own competence in the professional world.

"For one, I don't care if you "mooch" off me because what's mine is yours." Roxie quickly shut down my morbid thoughts. "And secondly, you will find the perfect job for you soon. Why don't you have a chat with that homeless shelter lady that you have been helping in Uptown, you said that she had a tonne of connections so maybe she could introduce you to people?"

"Her name is Enid; you should stop calling her the homeless shelter lady. It's not a bad idea though, she does seem to know all of New York."

When we first moved to New York, I felt extremely lonely with Roxie being busy with the endless rehearsals and not knowing anyone else in the City. Frequently, I would take a ferry into Manhattan and walk the streets endlessly reminiscing about the days I spent running around the same avenues. I would often find myself in the Upper East Side passing by the sanctuary to glance at the front door above the concrete steps, resisting the urge to knock and allow myself to enter the doorway into the past. The dark memories of the past haunted me with a hint of a whisper, while I categorically avoided walking past the neighbourhood where Ray and I lived together with Roxie while foolishly believing in true love and our undeniable success in the fashion world. The proximity to Green Light, when I briskly walked by seemed to invoke a mixture of contrasting emotions filled with a warming comfort, sense of belongingness and self-fulfillment, while overshadowed by the paralyzing fear of the eventual plummet into oblivion. Although the evocative recollections dragged me backwards to distance myself from the elusive front door, I felt Green Light calling to me and every day I always found myself walking down the familiar tree-lined street east of Central Park towards the unmarked door which contained so many of my memories.

One day on one of my regular walks, I once again found myself walking up Park Ave and took a right turn into the less busy streets that were typically avoided by the crowds of curious tourists as they generally only ventured as far as the Metropolitan Museum of Art and the charm of the real Uptown streets eluded them. As I breathed in the smell of the freshly baked bagels pouring out into the streets from the local bakeries, I basked in the last days of the warm Fall days knowing that the treacherous winter storms were not too far ahead. The locals living in the opulent neighbourhood did not seem to share my enthusiasm for the balmy weather, as they briskly rushed past me towards the nearest subway station or competed for a cab that there always seemed to be a shortage of this early in the morning during the morning rush hour. The more prominent residents of the area took advantage of the black limo car service that patiently waited for them every morning, while their clients hurried out of the house glued to the screens of their phones in their hand without glancing up to admire the clear blue skies. Once again, I was baffled by the workings of the human mind, while I observed the visibly stressed strangers rush to the captivity of their stodgy offices for the rest of the day, without taking a second to savor the simple things that life had so generously bestowed on them.

While I silently strolled in the opposite direction vainly trying to catch the eye of an occasional stranger to give them an encouraging smile, I noticed a frail limping figure ahead of me heading on the same course as me and my heart skipped a beat. Her unmistakable grace that she was able to maintain throughout the years to her old age had barely been overshadowed by the visibly deteriorating health that caused her to slow her pace. It was Enid, I had covertly hoped to bump into her on the streets during my walks but was unsure of how I would be able to strike up a conversation without alarming her. While we maintained our annual anonymous correspondence, Enid always responded with a sweet letter when I sent the cheque to Green Light with a quick note wishing her a Merry Christmas. From knowing Enid far better than a lot of the other donors, I knew that she was genial with everyone who wished to donate to the cause, but she never truly opened up to any of them erecting an invisible shield protecting herself from the unknown. There was always a cloud of mystery to Enid that even I was never able to crack, but I knew that she was one of the very few people in the world who I could trust with my life. There had been a deep void during my second chance at life without having Enid's calming presence and guidance, so when I caught a glimpse of her in the distance on the street, I realized that I may have a chance to regain her trust in me.

With every step as the distance between us shortened with the quick spring in my feet and her shuffling slow pace, I failed to come up with the appropriate introduction that could disarm her and accept me into her sheltered life. Just as I was about to reach her, Enid suddenly stumbled and tripped over causing her to fall on her knees while the contents of her purse spilled all over the pavement. It appeared as if I was the only one who saw the elderly woman fall because the well-dressed ignorant strangers on the street continued their uninterrupted gaze on their phones without pausing to help. Shocked by people's ignorance, I darted to help Enid to her feet while she struggled to get back up. Her lightweight body felt like a feeble feather in my arms, as I pulled her up and leaned her against the nearby tree.

"Are you ok? Should I call a doctor?"

My concern for her well being was that of a granddaughter caring for her loving grandmother.

"Not to worry, I just felt a little lightheaded for some reason. Do not worry about me, dear."

Enid's kind smile sent me back a memory lane of all the late-night chats we had over tea when I was still living at Green Light.

"Are you sure? Let me just get all your stuff.."

I bent down and started gathering her belongings and put them back in her purse. While I was crouching, reaching for her handkerchief, I noticed Enid's lipstick that I tried to grab when a passerby kicked it away from my reach and continued walking unaware of his unenlightened malevolence.

"Human sympathy has its limits."

I murmured under my breath, boring a hole in the passerby's back with my penetrating stare while he briskly walked away. In frustration, I lunged to grab the elusive lipstick and jumped back to my feet handing Enid the purse while she looked at me with vivid curiosity.

"Thank you for helping me." She took the purse from me and asked. "Did you just quote F. Scott Fitzgerald? "

"Yes, I did. Sorry, it's a bit of a habit, I usually tend to have more control over it." I apologized remembering how Jared and all my friends in Los Angeles disliked my use to quotes, finding it unnecessarily pretentious and old fashioned.

"Don't you ever apologize for quoting great authors, especially Mr. Fitzgerald."

Enid scolded me for being less assertive, just like she had done so many times in the past.

"I will take your wise advice under consideration." I appeased her, knowing that I needed to learn how to be more confident and not succumb to other people's opinions.

"So, let me guess, your favourite character in the Great Gatsby must be Daisy."

My old mentor raised the same question she asked me when she first met me.

"You know, a lifetime ago I would disagree and say that I preferred Myrtle for her strong will to survive, but selfish acts at the cost of others and those who love me is a very morbid way to live. Daisy's carefree style and the way she captured Gatsby's love is obviously every girl's dream, but it is all a fairy tale. She is just as selfish and careless about others' feelings, while she lives in her own reality unwilling to see the world for what it is." I shared my latest thoughts about the colourful characters of my favourite book, having widened my outlook on life over the years.

"What an interesting perspective from a young lady. Are you in a rush? Would you like to take a walk with me?" Enid asked after assessing my thoughts. "My name is Enid, what's your name?"

"Noelle. It's a pleasure to meet you, Enid, and I would love to join you on your walk."

"What a beautiful name." Enid uttered, then started on her idle promenade along the streets of the prosperous community while I strived to maintain her slow pace.

We spent hours talking about our favourite authors and discussed controversial plots of some classics, while walking around the same block of streets too enthralled by our discussion. When Enid talked about the books, inadvertently her pace hastened, and her gestures became more dramatic while the sparkle in her eyes gleamed with excitement of a freshman college student. It felt like a reunion of two souls that had been separated by a myriad of years and infinite miles, to be reunited as if no time had passed at all and no distance had ever kept us apart, as our reverent discussions from the past carried over into the present without skipping a beat.

"This has been a surprisingly lovely day, my dear." Enid stopped outside the Green Light Sanctuary, looking slightly tired from the continuous walking and the passionate discussion. "There is something so familiar about you."

"I have enjoyed our walk too, Enid." I responded, while wishing that I could tell her all about the years we spent together, when she was the only person in the world who took a chance on me and welcomed me into her life with open arms.

"Would you mind coming back and visit me again? We haven't discussed the Russian classics yet, and I'd love to get your perspective on Anna Karenina."

Enid was the one who instilled the love for the Dostoyevsky and Tolstoy masterpieces in me, while I devoured all the tomes that she had lent me when I lived in the basement room at the sanctuary.

"I can come by tomorrow, if you wish."

"I'll be waiting, just come by and knock on this door. Until tomorrow, my dear." She gestured to the front door of the building I used to call home and then headed up the stairs, noticeably struggling with every step.

Ever since that morning my life had regained its cerebral luster with the intellectual discussions about the world of literature, I have come by every day to visit Enid for a couple of hours for our morning walks. When I first came to knock on the front door announcing that I was there to see Enid, a timid looking young girl in her early twenties opened the door after unlatching the myriad of locks. She was not someone I recognized from the past life, which was a bit surprising as I expected to see one of the guests that had been staying at the house when I used to work there. The girl looked terrified at the spans of the street behind the front door, visibly hesitant to speak to a stranger even though she had clearly been advised by Enid that I would be coming by. Then Enid's figure appeared in the doorframe, and she put her delicate hand on the girl's shoulder, which seemed to appease her as her strained face filled with fear relaxed slightly and a hint of a smile materialized on her lips.

"Thank you for opening the door, my dear. You know with my speed these days; we would have made Noelle wait for at least twenty minutes before I managed to walk here from the kitchen. Now, I will be gone for a couple of hours, so you are in charge, which I am sure you would be great at. Maybe you can read the kids that Treasure Island book I showed you yesterday?"

I recognized Enid's encouraging instructions which echoed her words when she first brought me to Green Light. The panic in the girl's eyes at losing Enid for a couple of hours, leaving her to run the household full of women and children mirrored my own fears when Enid left me in charge for half a day during my first week there to meet some potential sponsors.

"Will you have your phone with you?" The girl asked with hope in her voice.

"Oh no, dear, I'm afraid I forgot to charge it last night, so I will be completely out of reach. But don't you worry, I believe in you. The wounded soldier stands taller when he knows when to abandon his crutches."

Enid left the girl confused with her last proclamation as she closed the door behind us. I remembered when Enid said the same allegorical statement to me, when I started panicking about being put in charge of my first meeting alone with a new sponsor because Enid could not attend the meeting, but after a while I realized that she was right. If I continued to depend on her, then I would forever remain living in the past wallowing in my own wounds without seeing the opportunities around me. It dawned on me that the timid girl was just like me, a "wounded soldier" mistreated by the circumstances in her life, who Enid took patronage of to save her from the streets because she recognized the dire conditions.

Over the next couple of months, when I came to pick up Enid for a walk, I noticed visible changes in the girl's appearance whose name I learned to be Isabella. When she answered the door, she was more assertive in her greetings, and she directed her gaze directly at me instead of looking at the street or down at the floor. Her hesitation at being left alone at the house dissipated, and as time went by, it was her turn to tell Enid not to worry and take her time on her walk because she had everything under control. On our walks Enid never disclosed the details about Isabella's life, but she told me that she saw a lot of potential in the girl's future.

At first, Enid did not talk about Green Light until she found out about my best friend being a lead actress in the popular stage production and that being a reason for our move to New York. After some hesitation, she unveiled the details about the sanctuary that she opened in her own home when her husband Mark passed away from a sudden heart attack almost thirty years ago. She rarely talked to anyone about her private life, and it took me years in my first lifetime to learn about Mark when I accidentally walked in on her holding his picture in her hands, but Enid's inherent comfort with me seemed to release her most sacred feelings within a short few months period. The disclosure about the Green Light Sanctuary was a necessary prelude for Enid to diffidently ask if there was any possibility for the theatre production to donate a couple of tickets to the women staying at the house, while her and Isabella would babysit the children. Praising her for her commitment to the great cause, I assured her that I would ask Roxie if this was possible and get back to her on one of our walks.

When I spoke to Roxie about Enid and Green Light, I explained everything that Enid had accomplished over the years in her selfless determination to help the mistreated mothers with their children and what a treat it would be for the women to get out of the house for the day to watch the play.

"I thought I would never get to see this side of my sister friend again. I have missed that passion in your voice, N." Roxie looked at me with solace, wistful of the days when I showed as much enthusiasm about life. Determined to support me with my newly found purpose to help Enid's cause, Roxie went to the rehearsal the next day prepared to have the discussion with Anton about allocating a half a dozen free tickets to a charitable foundation. Unable to withstand Roxie's determination, Anton yielded to the pressure and was able to allocate the reserved tickets for the residents of Green Light.

When I told Enid on our next walk that there were tickets waiting at the Will Call window at the theatre for next week, she grabbed my hand with her feeble but eager grasp in gratitude. I also revealed that Roxie was able to get an extra ticket for Enid to go as well, while I could stay with Isabelle and babysit the children. Enid's initial reaction was to decline the offer, saying that it was already too much, and she knew the real price of those tickets, but I argued that this amazing play needed at least one audience member who appreciated the true value of art. Her thirst for the theatre was undeniable as her pale blue eyes glassed over thinking about the prospect of being in the auditorium and submerged herself in the dramatic performance by the actors for a few hours. Then she silently nodded in acceptance succumbing to her real feelings and once again squeezed my hand in her tremulous grasp.

Since then, I have tried to help the Green Light Sanctuary whenever Enid allowed me to volunteer my time. While our walks continued their regular daily occurrence, our conversations sometimes steered away from the rhetoric discussions into the necessary strategic planning about raising funds for Green Light.

My jumbled thoughts, while I remained in bed procrastinating until it was time to get up for my birthday, circled back from my reunion with Enid to Roxie and the incomplete list of Things to Accomplish in our Thirties.

"After the first bullet point of finding me a job that Enid may help me find, how about we include a second bullet for opening another Green Light location? I know it's a long shot, but I want that as a goal." I saw Roxie write down the second bullet point on my side of the list. Then without a pause or consulting with me I saw her scribble a third point that she hid from my view.

"What are you writing now? Don't I have a say in my own list?" I complained in jest.

"Just something you don't want to admit to yourself, but I know you will soon enough." She quickly folded up the list while I tried to grab it out of her hands. Being a much more limber person, she managed to slither out of my clutches and hide the piece of paper away from me.

As I lay awake staring at the wooden surface of the driftwood secured on my bedroom wall, I remembered that Roxie's bucket list included early morning jogging plans to prepare her for the marathons around the globe. Braced for the outcome of the ambitious commitment, I got up from my bed and walked out of my bedroom just as the light started to penetrate the window above the headboard. Without bothering to knock, as this was something neither of us typically did, I opened the door into Roxie's darkness-filled room as she preferred sleeping with the blackout blinds blocking any sunrays ascending into her obscure Bohemian chamber. As I approached her bed, I saw her sound asleep with her cover half hanging off the bed and her body pillow tightly gripped against her slim body.

I took a deep breath and released loud notes with my untrained voice.

"Happy Birthday to you! Happy Birthday to you!! Happy Birthday, dear Roxie. Happy Birthday to you!".

Roxie's eyes barely flickered but she stretched her arms away from her body towards the opposite side of the bed, and not a second later I felt a throw pillow tossed at my face.

"We were going to go jogging. Remember? Train for the marathons." I egged her on, while Noelle's eyes remained shut. "To travel the world and run all around the global attractions."

"As a birthday gift to me, leave me alone. And as a birthday gift to you, I promise not to kill you for trying to wake me up this early." Roxie's mumbling was barely audible, but I hardly expected her response to be different.

"In that case, your wish is granted, and I am off to Green Light to help them set up for the Christmas party. Love you and I'll see you around three for our Birthday lunch." I said walking towards the door, while I heard the rustling of her sheets behind me.

Quickly lunging out of the room and shutting the door behind me, I heard a thump of yet another throw pillow hitting the surface of the door missing its intended moving target.

I took my time getting ready, knowing I still had plenty of time until the occupants of Enid's sanctuary woke up. Once I stepped outside the low-level apartment building, I inhaled the sweet crispiness of the morning breeze, it was not an overwhelmingly cold day, so I felt that I was dressed appropriately in my goose down winter coat. Aware that the ferry service was not operating on Christmas Day, I walked towards the Subway station to board a string of virtually empty trains that took me into the Upper East Side.

The typically busy streets of the opulent neighbourhood were serene, undisturbed by the incessant foot traffic of its residents. Peaking into the festively decorated homes as I passed by, I admired the ornately decorated trees proudly showcased through the large bay windows where families started to gather at this morning hour to open the presents. It was a relief to see that the morning mercenaries, who overlooked the wonders of every morning being focused on their phones while racing to their desks, took at least one day a year to slow their pace and devote their dearth of time to their families.

Just as I was about to turn into the street where Enid's home was located, I remembered that I still needed to get breakfast and it was still too early for me to join the early morning festivities at Green Light. Even though I knew every child and woman staying at the house personally from the past and in my current reality I have spent a couple of days helping Isabelle babysit the children, I was still a stranger to them, and they probably would not want to spend this special morning with an outsider intruding on their special day. Enid recognized this as well when she graciously accepted my offer to help them with the Christmas party but asked that I come later in the morning once the celebratory ruckus of opening presents quieted down. Instead of turning towards the sanctuary, I continued onwards to the local coffee shop to grab a hazel macchiato and indulge on a blueberry muffin.

Once I entered the comfort of the warm coffee shop, I had an instant flashback of walking through the same doors a lifetime ago on my fateful birthday. As my thirtieth birthday approached, the grim memories of the day's eventual end flooded my realism while I strenuously forced them out of my head.

*Ray is out of your life; he cannot hurt you.* I reminded myself again, urging my thoughts to focus on the positive actuality and not wallow in the bygone iniquity.

Summoning the encouraging memories from the same day to drown out the desolation, as I stood in front of the counter while the grumpy barista was busy cleaning up the only empty table, I remembered the enchanting conversation that I had with a complete stranger.

*Noel.*

His broad shoulders and tall frame in a dark wool coat shimmered from my memory forming a phantom figure just as it had been etched in my mind. Strangely enough, the handsome transient who was barely a noticeable notch in my prior lifetime had flashed in periodic memories throughout my current existence in the most inappropriate times. His square jaw and blue piercing eyes were the features I conjured in my mind when I closed my eyes in my first kiss with Jared, I imagined his strong muscular arms envelop me when Jared embraced me after I accepted his proposal, and Noel's sly smile flashed before my eyes when I eagerly surrendered to the intimate pleasures of Jared's skilled touch as he delved inside me. Fully devoted to my husband during our marriage, I never considered an iota of a notion of cheating on him but outside of my control, the face of a person who I briefly met a lifetime ago intruded my most intimate moments.

"How can I help you?" The barista's voice roused me from my fantasies as the hazy phantom from the past shattered in a million translucent pieces.

"Oh yes, I would like a large hazelnut macchiato and a blueberry muffin for here, please."

I paid for my order and stood against the wall waiting for my name to be called. My scrutinizing eyes lingered over every figure at the occupied tables of the limited space of the cafe, the laid-back early risers were preoccupied with their conversations or enthralled by the screens of their laptops but none of them resembled the imprinted image of a tall dark-haired stranger from long ago.

"Noelle!" I heard the barista call my name while she placed a large disposable coffee cup with my name scribbled on it and a muffin on top of a white plate. "Sorry, we are running short on mugs today, I'm the only one here and haven't gotten around to load the dishwasher yet."

Remembering the struggles that I caused her before, when I spilled a freshly made coffee all over the floor and she had to clean up, I assured her that I preferred paper cups and grabbed my order before walking over to the only available table that had empty chairs on opposite sides. It was the same table where Noel and I sat down for our chat, so I chose the same seat where I sat before, facing away from the door and onto the back window which allowed me to admire the beautifully decorated street and people watch an occasional passerby.

Steering my thoughts towards the plans that I still had to fulfill today, with the Christmas party at Green Light and then the low-key Birthday lunch that Roxie and I agreed to have at home, I took off my warm coat and hung it on the back of the chair. I reached into the coat pocket to look for my phone and as my fingers brushed the cold metal surface of my cellphone ready to pull it out, the fingertips grazed the rustling smoothness of a folded piece of paper. Puzzled by what this could be, I pulled the mysterious object out of the pocket to reveal an old water bill.

*Why would I have this with me?* I stared at the paper blankly and unfolded it, then turned it over to reveal the unmistakable Roxie's scrawls of two columns and bullet points of goals that we never finalized from the day before. After Roxie slithered away refusing to show me what secret goal she included for me, she ultimately decided to sneak it into my coat pocket so I could read it the next day. I carefully read the short lists for each of us.

*Things to accomplish while we are in our thirties.*

| Roxie | Noelle |
|---|---|
| Tony Award for Lead Actress | Awesome job |
| Lead in a Broadway Production | Open another Green Light |
| Something crazy: ~~Run naked Marathon per continent?~~ | Find Mr. Right |

*Find Mr. Right?* That was the secret goal that Roxie included for me, no wonder she did not want to show it to me. After the fiasco marriage to Jared, whom I was still legally married to until the courts granted me the divorce in his absence, I was not ready to think about jumping into another relationship. My trust in the male species was significantly limited before the marriage and had dwindled to non-existential after the revealing truth about my sham marriage. There was no way that I was going to make this the focus of my thirties, I have learned one thing about myself over the two lifetimes and it was that I have an absolutely awful taste in men. In reality, it would probably take me a million lifetimes to weave out all the jerks on the planet before I managed to find Mr. Right. That was an incredibly dreadful thought, and the prospect of an infinity filled with failed relationships was not something I wanted to devote my time to today as I sipped on the delicious macchiato.

"Hi, excuse me, is this seat taken?" I heard a male voice behind me inquire about the empty chair in front of me. I quickly glanced around the coffee shop noticing that all the tables were still occupied, while the only empty chair was at my table.

"Sure." I was disappointed with the outsider interrupting my peaceful solace but I reluctantly agreed for him to join me.

"Thank you, I promise I will leave as soon as another table opens up." The stranger walked around me towards the empty seat, his dark wool coat grazing my arm.

A fleeting thought raced through my head, and I raised my head to meet the friendly gaze of the piercing blue eyes that I never failed to forget. The materialized phantom from my dreams placed his paper coffee cup next to mine and took off his wool coat then hung it on the back of his chair, before settling in his seat.

"Who knew this place would be so busy on Christmas Day. Don't people want to be with their families?" Noel tried to make small talk with me, while I foolishly smiled to indicate my agreement.

Feeling incredibly awkward about what to say, I reached for my coffee at the same time as Noel's hand grasped his own cup making the skin on the backs of our hands graze against each other. A jolt of static electricity that evidently shocked us both, caused me to topple over my cup of coffee while Noel managed to maintain his grasp on the cup.

"Oh my, I'm so sorry."

I grabbed a stack of napkins from the napkin holder on the table and tried to soak up the spilled coffee. Unable to douse up all the coffee, I rushed over to the barista to ask for more paper towels gesturing to the spilled coffee on the table. The barista rolled her eyes and said she would be over in a minute to clean it up, while I returned to the table where Noel was sitting upright with a look of undeniable shock on his face.

"Are you ok?" I asked him, concerned by his stunned appearance. "Did you get the hot coffee on you?"

He shook his head, raising his hand to his head and brushed his fingers through his shiny dark hair.

"Have you ever had a déjà vu?" Noel's voice expressed an array of emotions.

"I guess on occasion." I started to guess where he was heading with his question, the circumstances of our first meeting were identical.

"I just had the strangest feeling like all of that had happened to me before. Just like that. A jolt of static shock, spilled coffee, your apologies. I have never even met you before, how can I possibly have a distant memory of you apologizing to me? Am I wrong?"

His voice escalated as he tried to make sense of his feelings, just as the barista came over to clean up the mess. We both got up to our feet to allow her to mop up and the tabletop to be cleared from the dark coffee puddles.

"Can I get you a replacement coffee? I feel partially responsible for this debacle." Without waiting for a response, he picked up my empty cup that the barista left on the table to read the coffee order written on the sleeve and noticed my name scribbled on the coffee sleeve.

"Your name is Noelle? This is just getting weirder and weirder." Noel walked over to the counter and asked for a refill of the hazel macchiato.

"So now you know my name, what's yours?" I tried to act nonchalant to ease Noel's confusion over the paranormal, when he walked back to take a seat at the table.

"I'm Noel." He stretched out his hand waiting for me to shake it, to which I gladly obliged squeezing his strong callous grip. "It wouldn't by any chance be your birthday today, would it? Just a random shot in the dark."

"As a matter of fact, it actually is, why do you ask?" I carried on the conversation, aware of his response.

"Serendipity at its finest! It is my birthday too, which is why I am hiding out in this café avoiding the typical morning birthday calls. Why are you here on your birthday? Everyone seems to be locked up at home with their families today."

"My mother is traveling the world with her boyfriend and my best friend refused to get out of bed this early in the morning, so I decided to treat myself to some alone time with a macchiato and a muffin." I spilled my personal details to a complete stranger who felt like a close friend.

"Same with me, my parents are spending the holidays in the Bahamas. To be fair, I cannot even remember the time when they were around for my birthday in New York. And I always refuse to leave New York for Christmas, this is my favourite time when I can take some time off work and catch up on all the reading I missed out on during the year."

Our conversation flowed so freely as if we had known each other for years. He shared details about his childhood growing up in the Upper East Side, while I told him about the simple life of living in the coastal Delaware. We did not talk about his work or the fact that I was unemployed, sensing that this was a subject neither of us wanted to bring up, but we talked about everything and nothing blissfully unaware of any awkwardness between us. By the time I finally looked at my phone to check the time, I was surprised to see that I had spent over two hours with Noel and was running late to help Enid and Isabella.

"My apologies, but I do have to run to join the Christmas festivities that you clearly try to avoid." I joked with regret of having to leave.

"Can we meet here tomorrow? Same time?" The hope in his eyes matched my inner wishes for another conversation.

"Same time." I nodded in response. "Happy Birthday, Noel."

"Happy Birthday, Noelle. I will be here waiting for you with your macchiato." He tapped on the table with the top of his index finger.

As I left the coffee shop, I felt an inexplicable sense of lightness in my feet that carried me forward without any effort of my own while an image of the bluest azure eyes lingered in my thoughts. We have only ever touched each other twice, both times resulting in an instant winter prone static sending mild shockwaves through our bodies, but I pictured us walking down the street together, our fingers intertwined in a stronghold as if holding to the dearest asset in your life. Against any of my earlier convictions on avoiding men in the future, I indubitably was going to come back tomorrow and meet the man who had consumed all my current thoughts and had managed to awaken the numbed sensations in my gelid heart.

When I finally knocked on the door at the wreath adorned front door of the Green Light Sanctuary, I had to pull myself together and gravitate back to the Earth's pull so that I could be of some use in helping the jolly residents of the home. Isabella answered the door and after recognizing my voice, unlocked the door and let me inside into the well-lit hallway. She showed off her elf ears that the kids made her wear in the morning when she was helping them unwrap the toys. Her elevated happiness was contagious and soon my occupied mind was filled with the Christmas spirit that seemingly infiltrated my recently thawed heart.

The next hours glided by in a carousel of colourful emotions while the children presented us with their well-rehearsed play, building barely stable but visually appealing gingerbread houses and endlessly playing with the recently gifted toys. It felt like I was back in my old lifetime, surrounded by the same happy little faces and the content mothers who briefly forgot about any of their life troubles and appreciated the feeling of belongingness in this temporary home that Enid dedicated her life to with her kind open heart. While Enid did not actively participate in the games, she sat on the couch in the living room where she could observe everyone's joyous faces smiling at the product of her lifework, bringing peace to families that needed it the most.

Suddenly we heard a loud knock on the door, which immediately sent me back the morbid memory lane and my body grew frigid with fear. Isabella rushed to answer the door, while my vocal cords seemed to contract, preventing me from screaming for her to stay away because there was a murderous monster waiting to burst inside. Forcing myself to get up from my knees where I was helping the children set up their

Hot Wheels ramp, I sluggishly dragged my impervious legs towards the hallway, mentally preparing myself for my inevitable fate. Once I got to the hallway, Isabella had already unlocked the door and let in a man dressed in the Santa Clause costume, who she was whispering with inconspicuously by the door.

*How does she know Ray?*

Out of her peripheral vision, Isabella noticed me standing nearby looking unusually pale with my face drained of any emotion.

"Are you ok, Noelle? Kids got you tired? Don't worry, Scottie and I prepared a surprise for them so why don't you sit with Enid and take a break." Isabella's sincere concern for my ashen reflection sent warm waves of renewed safety to my numb limbs, as I realized that the person, she was talking to was not Ray.

*How could I forget Scottie?*

Our generous and always kind mailman who managed to get everyone tickets to the coveted skating rink. I retreated to the living room and settled on the couch next to Enid still feeling shaken up from the fright of reliving my death. Enid sensed my unease, as I felt her comforting hold on my still trembling hand, she did not say anything, but I knew that she understood that I had deeper inner demons that I still had to battle through. We both sat in silence, as the last of the fear shivers released my body from their captivity, while the children surrounded the bearded man inundating him with their youthful curiosity. Enid held my hand tightly until she felt that my composure had returned, and my breathing had stabilized, then her attention briefly shifted to the exclaiming children and women who found out about going to the Rockefeller square and thanked Scottie for his resourceful connections that managed to provide the valuable tickets. The room quickly emptied out as everyone ran to their rooms to get ready so they could follow Scottie to the venue, while Enid got up from the couch to speak to the mailman disguised as the old Santa Claus. I pulled myself together and raised my body from the couch to start helping Isabella clean up the messy room. By the time the group of the home residents headed out of the door warmly dressed for their exciting day of skating, we were mostly done with tidying up the space.

As Enid closed the door behind the rambling bunch, she turned to me and asked me to follow her to her room. We walked through the long hallway, past the vast sitting room and living room that still retained their luster of the intricate crown moulding and the solid oak doors. When we approached the small but cozy bedroom at the back of the house, that Enid had chosen over her substantial master bedroom upstairs, she walked towards a neatly organized vintage dressing table and picked up a modest sized package wrapped in festively decorated paper.

"This is for you, my dear." She handed me the unexpected present.

"Thank you, Enid. I feel so bad, because I don't have anything for you." I realized in regret that I forgot to get Enid a present.

"No worries, my dear. I'm just happy to have spent time with you over these last couple of months, I feel like a certain weight was lifted off my shoulders." She said stealthily leaving me confused by her statement.

"You mean by having someone to talk about your favourite books?" I clarified her statement.

"Yes, something like that. Open the gift, Noelle!"

She nudged me excitedly, as I carefully removed the tape securing the wrapping paper in place revealing a strikingly familiar wool hat that was identical to the one that she made me once upon a time. My eyes filled with tears as I held the handmade creation, the gift was a reminder of all the things that Enid had done for me then and now.

"Thank you, Enid. I absolutely love it." I hugged her frail body and felt her arms wrap around me.

"You are so very welcome. Happy Birthday and Merry Christmas, dear. Now run home to your friend Roxie, because I'm sure you have some celebrating to do today." She separated from the embrace and waved in the direction of the front door. "I'm just going to lay down and relax here for a while, I'm not as young as I used to be, and all this excitement has tired me out."

"Of course, I'll let you be. But I will see you tomorrow for our walk!" I said before closing the door behind me.

I walked through the length of the house, catching Isabella sweeping the floor in the living room and asked her if she needed any help with anything but she thanked me saying that she did not have much left to do. So, I put on my new wool hat, the warm coat I left hanging on one of the hooks by the door and the fur lined boots then left the house, as Isabella locked the myriad of locks behind me.

There were more people out on the street now, as families left the coziness of their fireplace warmed homes and enjoyed the crispiness of the winter air.

*Maybe Roxie would be convinced to go for a walk in the neighbourhood when I get home.*

I wondered about the plans for the rest of the day, as I descended into the subway station and boarded the train to go back to Greenpoint.

When I got out of the subway station by the house, I felt a colder breeze in the air and silently thanked Enid for my newly gifted birthday wool hat to keep me warm. *Happy Birthday and Merry Christmas*, Enid said to me when she gave it to me. Then a jolt shot though my system as realization of her words dawned on me.

*I never told Enid about my birthday; it just never came up.*

I was certain that I never told her about being born on Christmas, so how did she know.

*Could Roxie have told her when they met after the play?* It was the only logical explanation of her inexplicable knowledge of my birthdate because it was impossible to even consider any other alternatives.

Remembering that I promised to pick up lunch, I stopped at the tiny grocery store a block away from the apartment and picked up a large bag of cheese Doritos then walked across the street to my favorite burger joint that reminded me of Fat Joe's and ordered two large cheeseburgers and the complimentary orders of fries. Twenty minutes later, with the greasy bag in my hand and the Doritos bag under my other arm, I knocked on the door of the apartment waiting for Roxie to open it so we could indulge in our celebratory luncheon. The knock went unanswered, so I figured that she was in her bedroom playing loud music or napping. I placed the Doritos bag on the floor and fumbled for my keys in my coat pocket.

I unlocked the door and entered the sun-lit apartment, an immediate sense of threat started to crawl up my skin as I saw the wooden coat hanger toppled over in the hallway and heard loud screaming from the television. My sensory alarms screamed for me to get out and get help, but I stood frozen in my spot observing the scattered mess in front of me when I finally realized that the TV was turned off and the noises were actually coming from Roxie's bedroom. I could hear her desperate crying and begging, her pleas were one-sided and in response I heard a slightly hoarse rhythmic grunt, matching the loud thud of my heartbeat.

I looked around for something to use to defend myself and rescue Roxie, and immediately spotted a large knife on top of the chopping board which I grasped in a strong hold and walked towards the open door of the bedroom, where Roxie's wailing just got louder. As I walked through the open-door frame, I saw the intruder's large naked torso thrusting with ignorant viciousness, while confining my beautiful defenseless friend under his weight disabling her from being able to get away. The assailant jerked his head sideways as he heard my feet shuffle into the room, making me stumble in my approach as I immediately recognized the slight hook in the nose and the limp dark strands.

*Ray, he found us.*

The panic in my head drowned out any other thoughts and turned my self-preservation mode to its highest peak, as I ran towards the bed screaming with my loudest shrill yowl. Wielding the knife in both hands above my head, I sunk in the blade just below his muscular shoulder blades. The surprise attack made him jerk back, his entire body ready to attack me, but I mustered all my strength and pulled out the knife out of his flesh and continued to stab him until his body grew still. Leaving the knife in his tattered back, I stepped backwards and leaned against the wall, silently observing the staggering amount of crimson stains on the bed.

"Noelle" I heard Roxie's trembling voice, and felt a great wave of relief that she was safe from the monster. Unable to say anything from the pumping adrenaline that made my entire body twitch in overwhelming anxiety, I looked up at her terrified face staring at me in horror.

"Noelle, what did you do?"

Her voice quivered looking at me, as she remained still trapped under the weight of the lifeless body. Taken aback by her question, I craned my neck to the side trying to comprehend the source of the accusation in her terror filled voice. Roxie lifted the heavy frame from herself and slunk out of the bed, the starkness of her naked body seemed absurd in the presence of a bloodied corpse. She grabbed me by my shoulders and started shaking me, trying to bring me back to my senses so I could finally speak. Bitter tears started running down her cheeks, as her clamorous voice grew stronger and her blaring words that failed to register in my head finally penetrated my comprehension.

"You killed Anton! Why would you do that? Noelle, why would you do that?"

Her violent shaking of my body became more vigorous, until I finally snapped out of my hazy dwam and slowly pushed her to the side. Refusing to believe her words, determined at my successful attempt at destroying the monster, I sluggishly plodded around the bed frame to look at Ray's face to prove to Roxie that she was wrong. The corpse's head was turned sideways facing the window, his eyes were wide open while his gaping mouth retained the final scream that never escaped his lips. Ray's hooked nose and sly smile morphed into a face belonging to the narrow delicate features belonging to Roxie's boss. Confusion over the transfiguration left me thunderstruck. I tried to make sense of why Anton's body lay still on Roxie's bloody sheets, until the horror of my own actions dawned on me. I sprung away from my innocent victim, stumbling over his clothes that he rashly took off before making love to Roxie. A sorrowful wail of grim realization of my deceitful mind's tricks rushed out of my body.

"I thought it was ..." I violently shook my head trying to reset the image of the blood in front of me. "I thought it was..."

"Who?" Noelle screamed at me, dismayed at seeing her secret lover's corpse on her bed and her best friend turned into the bloodthirsty killer. "Why did you do this?"

"I can change it. I can change it all!"

A euphoric thought of epiphany jolted through my head like a lightning strike. Without a second thought, I rushed out of the bedroom and wiped my bloodied hands on the kitchen towel, as Roxie ran after me.

"Where are you going? We need to call the ambulance, maybe they can still help him."

Roxie kept yelling, as I handed her my phone and asked her to dial 911. Then I wrapped my arms around her tightly, as her naked body continued shaking from the exasperated crying.

"I'm so sorry for everything, Rox. I love you so much. I will fix everything, I promise." I separated from her and ran out of the apartment before she had the chance to stop me.

Oblivious to the curious stares of the onlookers on the street, I sped by in a haste, images of my life flashing before my eyes. Seeing my parents' happy faces when I first emerged into this cruel world, my father calling me his princess, moving to UCLA and meeting Jared during campus orientation, our elaborate wedding, Roxie saying goodbye to me as Jared and I left the reception venue, the news report of my husband's scams, the intrusive police interrogation, moving to New York, the calming walks with Enid, the brutal murder. Every glimpse into my life zoomed by with lightning speed in a persistent circular motion on a continuous loop.

I quickly descended into the subway station a few blocks away, it was unmanned by anyone on Christmas Day, so the blood stains on my clothes and face did not raise any questions. The platform was almost empty except for a couple giggling girls busy taking selfies on the opposite side of the station. I stood back waiting for the train. The memories of my life continued to fly by in front of my hazy eyes, making me feel slightly lightheaded, however my determination in fulfilling my hastily made plan grew stronger.

The rambling of the approaching train was faintly heard in the distance of the long dark tunnel, as the memory of the happy times with my parents in the kitchen of our old home in Delaware slowed down in front of my eyes and I paused to think that this was probably the happiest moment in my life. The next image was of my father reading me bedtime stories as I squeezed Mr. Winkie in my strong embrace, while my mother sat in the rocking chair in my bedroom watching us.

The roaring sound neared the station, as I saw the illuminating light bright the tunnel. I took a step forward and as the thundering sound entered the station, I leaped from the edge towards my fate. Just before my body hit the tracks, I heard a loud shrilling scream from the near distance which was drowned out by the deafening sound of the booming engine. I closed my eyes shut, blinded by the nearing brightness, and then instantly felt the excruciating pain sear my entire body as the massive weight of the ironclad machine decimated my body, dragging my fading consciousness along the tracks until there was complete silence and the agonizing pain dissipated into the dark void.

## Chapter Thirteen

*Lifetime III*
*December 25, 1984*
*Re-Birth*

The all-encompassing darkness around me felt unnervingly still as my consciousness floated aimlessly, there were no thoughts generated in my mindless existence, but a dreadful sense of unease lurked in the encompassing gloom. There was something different, something that lacked the previously comforting calmness that enveloped me in the preceding rebirth. The sensation of the endlessness of time in the boundless obscurity remained consistent, while my weightless awareness drifted through the ambiguous shadows towards the unknown.

*How long?* I cannot say.
*How far?* I cannot see.
*Why?* I do not know.

The obscurity surrounding me imploded just as suddenly as it consumed me in its infinite grasp, as I became acutely aware of the bright light unexpectedly emerging just above my head while an alien object intruded into the expanse of my confinement draining the fluid around me. Once the hollowness around me settled my body against the softness of a satin lined support wall, a pair of enormous hands emerged through the lighted gap and cradled my shoulders before tugging me out of the murky captivity.

"Congratulations, it's a beautiful baby girl." I heard a deep male voice announce to the unseen audience. "We just have to draw some of the fluids from her lungs, nothing to worry about, just a regular procedure for C-Section births."

The lurid brightness of the room was overwhelmingly luminous as I tried to comprehend the surrounding settings, a pair of hazy figures hovered over me while they guided an intrusive suctioning instrument inside my mouth. After some discomforting prodding, they pulled out the tube and I immediately let out a loud shriek to make them aware of my displeasure of their invasive tactics.

"Hear that, Susan? She sounds perfectly healthy. Got a great pair of lungs on her!"

I finally heard the familiar voice I was longing to hear. Shifting my limbs and trying to move my head in the direction of the voice while the female nurse continued to hold my tiny body, I was unable to get a glimpse of my father. All that mattered was that he was alive, which meant that my impromptu plan worked, and I was able to reset my life. A strong hold carried me to a table away from my father's voice and laid me on my stomach, while I felt the coldness of metal instruments against my back. The check-up seemed to last a lot longer than I remembered and instead of the playful cooing of the nurse as she inspected my body, there were two people exchanging medical terminology I was not familiar with in an inconspicuous voice.

"Meningocele, severe form, exactly what I was afraid of. We need to schedule an immediate surgery." The older male voice said with a note of worrying concern.

"I tend to agree but will also get an X-Ray done right away to confirm the diagnosis." A younger voice belonging to another doctor responded.

The complicated dialogue continued, while I felt pressure from their prodding around my torso until they were aligned on their next plan of action that required expedient urgency. The state of confusion was unnerving, as I strived to comprehend what was wrong with me. The younger doctor stayed by my side, continuing his assessment of my condition, while the older doctor stepped away.

"Now Mrs. and Mr. Anderson, congratulations on the birth of your baby girl. The C-Section went well, and we have stitched up the incision." A mature male voice, belonging to the foggy figure of the doctor who took a while to inspect me walked closer to my parents. "Like Dr. Hernandez and I had advised you before the surgery, your daughter has a severe form of spina bifida just as we suspected from the ultrasounds. We have to take your daughter to the neonatal intensive unit, where we will take great care of her, and we will schedule a surgery immediately to prevent any long-lasting effects."

*Surgery? Spina bifida?*

The doctor's incomprehensible words left me completely

dumbfounded, struggling to understand the cause for my unprecedented birth defect. I was born perfectly healthy in the former rebirth and the birth before that, every time immediately taken to my mother's soft embrace, but in the new reality I remained on the uncomfortable flat surface away from my parents' yearning reach. The panicked alarm consumed my newborn body materializing in a loud wail of emotions, when I heard a recognizable female crying in my vicinity. What I longed for the most, was my mother to hug me and tell me that everything was going to be alright. As if sensing my wish, I heard my mother ask through her whimpering cries.

"Could I hold her before you take her away?" She asked in a quavering voice, almost pleading with the doctor.

"I'm afraid, we can't let you do that. Your daughter has a growth at the base of her spine where the nerves developed outside her body, leaving her spine exposed and unprotected. Any accidental contact to the area may cause severe lasting damage. Our expert staff are well trained in dealing with babies with *spina bifida* growths and they will ensure that your baby is safe pre- and post- surgery to avoid any complications." The doctor's understanding tone did not seem to ease my mother's worries.

"Can we at least see her up close?" My father interrupted the exchange.

"Of course."

I felt a pair of hands lift me from the table and place me on a smooth surface of a rolling cradle flat on my stomach spreading my feet to make me more comfortable. Then the hospital crib was wheeled towards the crying sounds of my apprehensive mother and the heavy sighs of my father, allowing the rolling to stop directly in front of them granting me an opportunity to see the outline of their blurry bodies. My heart ached, while I observed the unmistakable dark messy hair figure belonging to my father who was perched on the edge of the surgery table, where my mother was resting laying flat after the operation.

"She is so beautiful, Jack. Our poor baby girl."

My mother's crying escalated again at the sight of the visible protrusion on my body.

"She is the most beautiful baby. It will be alright, just like the doctor said. They will perform an immediate surgery and then she will have great chances at a full recovery." My father assumed the uncharacteristic role of the consoler.

"Thank you, Helen. Please take baby Anderson to the intensive unit where they can look after the cleanup of the neural tube."

The nurse followed the doctor's instructions and rolled the crib away from my parents, sending me into a series of loud wails demanding to stay by their side as the distance between my mother's and my own cries grew vaster.

Over the next hours, I was taken to a host of merely identical medical rooms where my defenseless body was lifted, poked, prodded, pressed, squeezed while more unidentified voices continued to discuss my diagnosis. I felt like a stuffed toy being passed from one doctor to another, while they unceremoniously discussed the impending surgery, unaware of my seemingly undeveloped mind barely comprehending their unfamiliar lexicon. Sometimes I tried to interrupt their discussions with my whimpering cries, hoping that they recognized my need to see my parents, but they chose to ignore it being too preoccupied in their scrupulous medical planning. Instead of my mother's gentle touch that would comfort my increasing anxiety, I was surrounded by a variety of experts who were well versed in how to heal my body, but no one seemed to be concerned by the bewildered fear in my eyes while I longed for a consoling embrace.

After all the necessary checks through the long agonizing day, the doctors had been able to unitedly confirm the diagnosis that the older doctor suspected when he pulled me out of my mother's womb. Without any further delays, my wheeled crib was rushed into a brightly lit operating room elevating my already sky-rocketing level of unease. Once the ride halted by the centred table surrounded by countless buzzing machines and tall lights, my body was lifted from the cradle and laid down on a sizable table, fit for an adult making me feel like a Lilliputian resting on Gulliver's bed. Then I felt several barely noticeable pricks on my body while a plethora of tubes were attached to me. I was thankful for being on my stomach and only being able to catch glimpses of moving shadows instead of the potential horror of seeing the brightly lit operating room filled with the nurses and doctors. The sheer vastness of the space through my angled vision was enough for me to handle, hoping for the nightmare to be over at once. Then my vision became blocked by a figure standing just above me, shoving some elongated tubes through my nostrils causing mildly discomforting pain that I braved through.

"Apply anaesthesia." The instruction came from the familiar voice belonging to the younger doctor named Dr. Hernandez.

"Applying anaesthesia. All indicators are normal, heart rate is fine.

10, 9, 8..."

*7, 6 5...* I continued the count in my head. Just as I was about to continue to count further, I felt my body fill with familiar lightness resembling the intermittent moment between death and rebirth, as my consciousness distended from my defenseless body over the heads of the doctors and nurses who focused on repairing my damaged back.

While I hovered over the operating table observing the focused professionals, I suddenly felt a forceful pull of an unidentified source luring me away from the brightly lit space down a series of tangled corridors. Just as I was abruptly pulled from the operating room, I was just as suddenly pushed into a smaller room with two occupied beds and a male figure pacing back and forth to the visible annoyance of the patient with dark curly hair.

*Mom, Dad, Alison!* I wanted to scream, but I had no voice, so I observed them in silence. My mother seemed to be sleeping, her closed eyes were visibly puffy and the redness on her nose were clear evidence of her incessant crying. Unable to deal with his emotions, my anxious father was trying to calm himself by walking around the confined space but refused to leave my mother on her own. He lifted his hand to his face and wiped his eyes.

*Was he crying?* I wished that I could run up to him and hug him tightly to tell him that I was going to be fine, but will I be fine? This was all new, unfamiliar territory, the only day in my life that I expected to remain an invariable constant in my lifetimes, had turned into one of the scariest moments of my existence.

*Why?* I directed my silent anxious screams into the vast emptiness that held me afloat. In response, I felt a forceful tug pull me back vigorously making the questionable reality around me spin out of control, as my awareness hurtled backwards causing my surroundings to disappear. The lightning speed charging in reverse would have been terrifying, if I had longer than a moment to comprehend what had been happening but instead the zooming flight ended abruptly in a dim, large open space.

*Subway station?* I recognized the drab greyness of the underground stop near our Greenpoint apartment. There were barely any people at the platform, only a few of teenaged girls playing with their phones and making faces in their cameras. Then I heard a fast tapping of rapid footsteps racing down the stairs from above descending onto a platform, revealing a distraught female covered in sticky grime. Her hair a tangled mess in patchy colours of blonde and burgundy, while her face speckled with what resembled red paint, that seemed to transfer onto her light grey winter coat trimmed with fur. The wildness in her eyes belonged to a mad person on a mission, while she stood perfectly still focusing on the darkness of the tunnel. Her eyes widened with determination when she saw the lights appear through the murkiness of the underground and the sound of the speeding train emerged onto the platform. Once the thunderous boom entered the station, she took a step forward towards the edge and when the train made its eventual approach, she lunged from her spot down onto the tracks.

*No!* The terror in my silent scream mirrored the identical anguished yell from the direction of the platform belonging to another female who had only a moment ago appeared on the surface. Her accelerated breathing demonstrated her rush to get here, dressed in an oversized hoodie just covering her body to her thigh and a pair of running shoes.

*No!* She repeated her scream, running towards the edge of the platform, as her wild springily curls bounced freely swooshing from one side to the other. Looking at her discernible swooshing curls that typically made me laugh when we ran around chasing each other as kids or when we did our happy dance to celebrate our little victories in life. There was nothing cheerful about the bouncing curls at this moment. *Roxie, I'm here*, I wanted to scream to her.

When Roxie approached the edge of the platform and looked down, she found a splatter of red specks and a growing puddle of blood emerging from my crushed body jammed under the wheels of the train. A loud agonizing wail escaped her body, as she crashed to her knees, her bare skin touching the dirty surface bemired by the thousands of footprints passing through the station everyday. The teenagers on the platform stopped taking pictures of each other and turned their focus to the scene in front of them, where my amazing, beautiful friend who I have failed so many times continued her desperate cries.

*I'm sorry, Rox, I'm so sorry. But I needed to reset the life, so we could start again.*

The sudden jolt of realization shot through my body. I had already been dead at that point, but life continued with Roxie mourning my fatal decision to end my own life. Life did not reset for her, she kept on living out her lifetime. At that moment of instant epiphany, my consciousness was once again pulled forcefully away from the gruesome image.

The invisible force yanked my weightless awareness through time and halted a year later in the lifetime where I no longer existed. The setting of my new view from above was of a dark room, I had never seen before. There was a table littered with cigarettes and empty bottles of vodka next to a filthy couch, with a pile of blankets and coats hid a wheezing person deep in their sleep. As I inspected the room closer, I noticed a soiled old water bill with Roxie's handwriting on it resting beneath the vodka bottles, a list of aspiring goals that we crafted together determined to achieve in the decade ahead of us. The quietness of the room was unexpectedly interrupted by a loud ringing of the phone resting on the messy table, which seemed to rouse the dormant occupant of the sofa. An arm protruded from underneath the blankets and reached for the phone bringing it to their face to see the caller ID.

"Hi Mom." I heard Roxie's lethargic voice answer the phone.

"Hi, Roxie. Glad to hear your voice. I have been trying to reach you for days." Alison's voice blared through the speaker, making Roxie's face wince at the loudness of her tone.

"Yea, I've been busy. Very busy." Roxie was lying, I could always tell when she was lying. She always repeated herself twice when she tried to sound like she was telling the truth.

"Did you go to see that psychologist that I found for you in the City?" Alison's question seemed to disturb Roxie, as a look of exasperation crossed her face.

"I already told you that I was fine, mom. I don't need some shrink who costs a fortune to tell me that I need to be medicated." Roxie argued with her mother.

"You are not fine, honey. It has been a year since the incident, and you have been hiding from everyone since then. You have not come to Georgetown since the funeral, you would not let me visit you. You have moved and you would not even tell me where you are living now. Just come home, Roxie. Forget New York, come back to Georgetown." Alison's pleading voice begged Roxie to consider her invitation.

"I'm fine, mother. I have to run to an audition now, so I've got to go."

Roxie hastily hung up without letting her mother say anything in response. Then she put her phone back on the table and stared at the ceiling, making me wonder whether she could sense me looking at her. She has changed, her face had sunken from the unnecessarily shed weight and the darkness under her eyes signified restlessness. My friend was not herself; she had succumbed to the darkness that I tried to save her from while I was alive.

*Roxie, you need to fight this. Get help!*

I wished that she could hear my urging, but she continued to blankly stare into the empty space. After a while, she closed her eyes and fell into her deep sleep, disguised as the pretend sense of security.

*I did this to her? What can I do to change this? Will Roxie be, ok?* I appealed to the invisible force to nudge me in the right direction and give me a glimpse into the subsequent events. In response, I sensed the cogent shove and my consciousness propelled away from the gloomy room through time and space stopping in front of a solid door positioned on top of the steps leading up from the tree-lined street. Roxie was standing at the bottom of the steps, her skinnier frame in the loosely fitted clothing was shivering on a sunny warm summer day. Her eyes were fixated on the door while she contemplated whether to walk up the steps, then she clenched her fists in conviction and marched up the stairs. She confidently knocked on the door and waited for it to open.

"Who is it?" An elderly female voice on the other side answered the door after some time passed.

"I'm here to see Enid." Roxie announced herself. "My name is Roxie, I'm a friend of Noelle."

The sound of the myriad of locks being unlocked followed, then the door opened revealing the frail figure of an elderly lady leaning on her supporting cane. Enid has aged significantly since the last time I saw her. Her aged face has drooped on one side revealing a possible stroke that she had suffered in the last couple of years since my passing. She was still able to walk but required the cane to lean on while she struggled to walk the spans of the house.

"Hello, dear, I was waiting for you to come and see me. What took you so long?" Enid welcomed the surprised Roxie into the house.

"I honestly did not think that you remembered me from the play, and I had to search high and low to find the address for Green Light. All Noelle ever told me was that it was in the Upper East Side." The mention of my name, sent a painful memory through both of their minds.

"Thank you for coming to visit the old lady." Enid regretfully referred to her ailing self, while she struggled to secure the top lock on the door. "I'm in search of some full time help now with the sanctuary, because my helper Isabella was able to find an amazing job and had to leave. I do not blame her at all, she deserved that job, but I'm afraid I'm a bit helpless on my own."

Roxie walked behind Enid, as she slowly shuffled through the hallway towards the bright kitchen at the back of the house. She admired the ornately decorated home that she was seeing for the first time, but I immediately sensed that Roxie felt like she was at home.

"I'm sorry to barge in on you like this, but I just had this sense that I had to visit you. It has been over two years since Noelle's passing and I just felt like I wanted to connect with someone who she spent all her time with." Roxie explained her reason for coming to Green Light.

"No need to explain yourself, dear. Like I told you on the phone when you first called me to inform me of the sad news, you are welcome here anytime."

Enid turned on the kettle in the kitchen and opened the cabinet to grab two mugs but struggled to maintain her balance. Roxie quickly jumped to her rescue providing her shoulder for support, then picked up the two mugs from the open cabinet herself and placed them on the table.

"Why don't you settle in, and I'll take it from here." Roxie offered, as Enid settled in a chair and gave her visitor instructions on where to find teabags. They spent the next couple of hours chatting about the sanctuary, about my walks with Enid, about books that I liked to read and would talk about endlessly, while I observed them in peace sensing relief over their reconnection. At the end of their chat, when Roxie was getting ready to leave, she turned to Enid and asked.

"Would you mind if I came to visit you everyday?"

"Not at all, my dear. In fact, are you looking for a job by any chance? I really could use some help."

"I would gladly help out." Roxie responded without any hesitation and agreed to join Enid in her endeavour. When she left the sanctuary, I saw a smile on her face, it was not her usual wide toothy smile, but it was a step in the right direction.

*She will be alright.*

An abrupt pull dragged me away from Roxie, speeding away from her frail figure as she walked down the steps and stepped onto the street. The surroundings changed to the zooming incomprehensible images, as my consciousness was once again dragged in the unknown direction.

*What next?* I wondered about the next stop, but when the vigorous rush ceased, I found myself hovering above the operating table where the doctors were working on rebuilding my damaged spine.

*I did this to myself.*

I now understood the cause for my birth trauma. Every action has a consequence and running away from my responsibilities foolishly hoping that leaving my troubles behind would lead me to a happy life without any baggage was an incredibly reckless decision. A decision I would never consider in any of my future chances at life. After this realization, I felt my consciousness crush down from its hovering position back into my tiny body.

"Hi, Noelle." I heard my mother's voice, as I opened my eyes. I was in an enclosed glass container and saw my mother and father leaning their faces to get a closer look at me.

"Your daughter will be just fine." The doctor announced to my parents, and my mother sighed with relief in her wheelchair, while my father unexpectedly jumped to hug the doctor. "She will need some physiotherapy and osteopathy throughout her childhood, just to ensure that her growth spurts don't affect the healing process. But she will have a happy healthy life otherwise."

*Yes I will.* I tried to smile at my mother who maintained her doting gaze at me, while my father tried to lift the doctor from the ground in his tight embrace.

*I will make the best of this lifetime.*

## Chapter Fourteen

*June 14, 1990*
*Age 5*

"Slow down, Noelle, you will pull my arm off!"

My mother chastised my rushed pace, while I pulled her by the hand, dragging her with all my ineffectual strength forward, down a maze of paths in the direction of the blaring speakers. She was walking unnecessarily slow, as if completely oblivious to the significance of the occasion. Instead of hastening her leisurely walk, she slowed down to curiously examine the grandiose buildings looming over the perfectly manicured lawns. If we did not have to rush to take a seat, I would probably be just as enthralled by the ornate details of the tortuously designed buildings and the elegant arched entryways inviting the inquisitive minds to enter and explore their undoubtedly equally lustrous interiors.

The strident sounds of the triumphantly cacophonous melody became evidently formidable when we were finally able to find our way out of the complex meandering web of paths and emerge onto a large open space teeming with equally excited people. The women strolled around wearing bright coloured light-fabric dresses to be able to sustain the smouldering heat of the atypical June summer day in the San Francisco area, while the men smartly clad in their business attire tried to hide their visible discomfort from the sweltering temperature finding relief in the shade of an occasional tree. I led my mother towards a lined-up cluster of people waiting by the entrance of the open-air stadium where we positioned ourselves behind a rowdy family with three children, whose ages spread closely on either side of my own painfully young physical development.

While we stood waiting for our turn to walk into the stadium, the children belonging to the family ahead of us were entertaining themselves by running around in circles playing tag and their parents looked apparently exhausted to discipline them. I gawked at the happy disobedience of the childhood oblivion in dismay. *Weren't they too hot to run around?* They would be all sweaty and would have to sit in their moist clothes for the rest of the humid day.

"What a pretty little girl."

The mother of the boisterous children looked at me with a hint of envy, admiring the flowery dress I had picked out for the special occasion and my neatly braided hair that my mother fashioned herself earlier in the day. Then she glanced in the direction of her own children whose unkempt appearance from the endless running, became more obvious in comparison to my neatly polished image.

"Only child?" She asked my mother, trying to find a good enough reason to excuse herself from the many unsuccessful attempts at making her children look more presentable.

"Yes, just one."

A note of relief escaped my mother's collected composure while she observed the playing bunch. I looked up to watch her, to try and catch her slyly smiling in unified appreciation of how disciplined I was in comparison to the dirty disheveled children but instead I saw a grain of sorrow fleeting in her eyes. It had been apparent over the years that my mother blamed herself for me not being able to play with other children because of my limited ability to strenuously exercise due to the inborn spine defect. The doctors had assured her that this was not an inherent trait and was not a consequence of any of her wrongdoing, but her incessant researching of subject led her to believe that it was lack of folic acid in her body that led me to develop the spina bifida while she carried me in her womb. It was impossible for me to explain to her the underlying reason for the deformity.

*How do you tell your parent that the reason the tip of my spine and nerves developed outwards was because that was the exact spot where it was crushed by a subway train in my previous lifetime?*

My mother was already alarmed at my inability to socialize with other children, and I was certain that if I told her about the prodigious reality then she would sign me up for psychological evaluations in addition to all the regular physiotherapies I attended.

"So much easier when it's just one." The woman in front of us shrugged off any of the pressure she had felt to defend herself being a good mother.

"You are absolutely right. You have a beautiful family." My mother responded assuring the woman that she carried no judgement, prompting a smile on the woman's weary expression.

The line of people moved forward, and the woman hollered at her kids to get back, which they obliged and joined their protective mother and silently sweating father. After checking their tickets, the noisy family was allowed through the gate and we were asked to present our invitations. My mother handed the coveted pieces of papers that she had so carefully preserved over the last couple of weeks on top of her bedside table, afraid that she would lose them. The usher checked the validity of the invitations and then allowed us to enter through the gateway directly behind him. We walked into a majestic venerable oval-shaped ground surrounded by the skeletal stands crammed with proudly radiant attendees. A young sophomore usher standing at the edge of the field, directed us in the direction of the empty seats up a series of steps. We eagerly obliged and walked up the crowded stands to a pair of available seats, which provided us an unobstructed view of the field and the centred stage structure facing in our direction.

"If we did not get lost, we could have sat closer." I whined to my mother, while settling down in my seat.

"You wouldn't have been able to see that much better if you were closer, Noelle." My loving mother retorted in annoyance.

I sat perched up on my seat staring at the empty white chairs arranged in the perfectly straight rows directly on the green field, while the herds of other guests continued to flow into the stands rapidly filling up all the available seats. Exasperated from the increasing heat unconventional for the summer in San Francisco, my mother reached into her purse and pulled out a Chinese styled handheld paper fan and started waving it with vigour to produce a hindering sense of respite. The penetrating sun did not bother me much, since the blistering heat resembled the Los Angeles climate that I adored and reminisced in my current existence.

My mother was not a fan of the heat and she had yearned for the cool summer nights of Delaware that kept the house cool through the open windows. She had hesitated for months before agreeing with my father that moving to the West Coat made the most sense, so he could take a better paying job that could afford the growing medical bills that they endured due to my condition. Their savings dwindled out quickly after I was born and my father's job at the computer repair shop was barely able to afford them food and pay the house bills. Their hopeless state led to a growing tension at the house resulting in numerous arguments over money. My mother suggested that they sell the house and move into a smaller apartment. My father argued that this was a band-aid solution because the growing doctors' bills and lack of medical insurance would mean that any money that they made from the sale would soon dissipate.

One day, after another argument with my mother when she realized that I grew out of all my baby clothes and needed new outfits, my father finally decided to forego his pride and called his former professor from Stanford for much needed advice. His old mentor was shocked to hear my father's voice, having assumed that my father had abandoned his old life completely when he permanently moved to live in Delaware. My father's initial hesitation to revisit his neglected academic life swiftly transitioned to a lively nostalgic natter with an old confidant. They shared stories from the past and present, my father listened intently to the updates on the scholar's life and then reluctantly shared the woes that he had endured since he left the university. Respectful of my father's abilities and in recognition of the unaccomplished prospects, the professor had never forgotten his favourite student leaving his studies unexpectedly to pursue a married life in the East coast.

"How do you feel about moving back to San Francisco? One of my former students reached out to me looking for talented people to join their new but very promising company. The company's focus is on revolutionizing the tech world and bringing a computer to every household. They are doing exceptionally well right now and in order for them to get to the next level, they needed new talent."

"But I don't even have a degree." My father reminded his mentor.

"Not to worry, you can get reinstated at the university and attain the remaining credits on a part time basis. Should I put you in touch with Jim?" The offer lingered in the air with its inviting allure.

"I would appreciate that, Professor Bernstein."

My father thanked his mentor before hanging up the phone. My mother held me on her knee as we both sat quietly listening in on the entire conversation, afraid to miss a word through the resounding speaker. When my father placed the phone on its cradle, a glimmer of hope glowed in his eyes which reflected in my mother's gaze at him.

Meanwhile, a wave of excitement oscillated in my toddler body because I knew that if we moved away then it would be an answer to all my haunting thoughts and planning on changing my third attempt at a happy existence. If we moved away then we would be far away from the pile up on the highway in February of 1990, which took my parents' lives causing an escalating series of events. Moving away would be a complete restart of our lives, away from all the daunting memories allowing me to start our lives afresh without any reminders of the heavy baggage of the past.

Unfortunately, this would also mean that I would grow up without Roxie in my life, without seeing her at school or hanging out with her at Fat Joe's diner chomping down the humongous burgers. However, being out of Roxie's life was one of the considerations for a better life for both of us, that I contemplated when I spent a month in intensive care after my birth. If Roxie and I were not friends then she would have never been entrapped in sex slavery by Ray, seen her best friend murder her love interest or deter her from pursuing a career in Hollywood. Our codependent relationship was toxic for her, where she continuously suffered due to my error in judgement and subsequent madness that drove me to kill an innocent person.

It was seemingly easier to let go of Roxie this time around because she had not been in my current lifetime since birth. Due to the fact that my parents spent most of the time watching me in the neonatal ICU, they did not spend much time in their hospital room with their roommate Alison, which trampled the setting for the structure of their strong bond and lifelong friendship. But I always held out hope to run into her on the streets of Georgetown or eventually enroll in the same class at school where we would be able to reunite and build a relationship.

This was not to be, because after a few phone exchanges my father received an incredibly enticing offer to join the company in San Francisco which offered full medical insurance for his family and paid for the moving costs to help us migrate our life to the new location. Professor Bernstein was able to put in an astounding recommendation for my father to his former student, and he was quickly convinced by the astonishing compliments and my father's astute knowledge of the science behind the emerging information technology. We were only given a month to pack up our lives and sell the house, which put a lot of stress on my parents. However, they persevered and were able to receive a very reasonable offer for the family home within a week of putting it on the market.

When the house contents were all packed up in the back of the truck, the empty rooms that carried infinite memories of happiness and tragedy appeared larger than ever. I stood in the doorway looking into the unrecognizable space, that lost any of its memorable charm of being a home, while my parents' voices echoed through the bare rooms. Once my mother locked the house for the last time, she wiped the tears from her eyes that seemed to flow endlessly since she found out that the house had sold. Then without any further hesitation, she hastily walked down the driveway and climbed into the passenger seat of the truck where I had already been seated in the secured car seat in the middle space between the two seats. The packed truck was filled with all our furniture and belongings that would forever remind us of our old lives in Delaware, but we all knew that our lives would be completely different in California.

"Mom, look! They are all finally coming out onto the field."

I screamed at my mother, while she continued fanning herself switching her hands on occasion to wave the fan over me. The upbeat music started blaring even louder throughout the stadium while the organized procession of graduates walked onto the greenery and proceeded to their seats. They all looked identical, dressed in the floor length navy frocks and square shaped flat hats adorned on their heads, preventing anyone in the audience from distinctly recognizing their loved ones. I stood tall on my tip toes trying to see my father but was unable to distinguish him from any other frock dressed graduate.

"Honey, sit down before you hurt yourself." My mother gently put her arms on my shoulders and guided me backwards into my seat.

"But I want to see daddy." I exclaimed.

"Don't worry, your daddy isn't going anywhere. You'll see him soon."

*Yes, I will.*

My mother did not understand the magnitude of her own words, but she was trivially correct. The current reality included my father, as the fatal doom of the damning February day had passed months ago, and he continued to exist in this alternate lifetime.

The next couple of hours rolled on tediously long with congratulatory messages from the Stanford academic staff and a motivational speech from an elderly politician, that captured the audience with its notions of inspiration and wisdom. I conceded in my continuous search for my father's head in the crowd of other students and waited for his name to be announced when the ceremony had switched to the diploma granting segment. The strangers' names were announced while the happy men and women walked up on the stage, accepting their aspired ribbon tied rolls and shook hands with the

Stanford staff before descending the steps on the opposite side of the podium.

"Jack Anderson." I finally heard my father's name announced, making my mother and I jump to our feet simultaneously and scream on top of our lungs hoping that our screams traversed to my father's ears. His tiny figure in the distance ascended the steps as he strolled up on the stage and accepted the presented diploma before approaching his professors to shake their offered congratulatory hands. Just before walking down the steps to leave the podium, he looked up at the audience and held up his diploma proudly high above his head. He looked exhilarated, happy, gratified but most vital to me, he was alive.

Chapter Fifteen

*Through the years*

When there are no tragedies leaving a permanent imprint on your existence, time scurries by resembling a stallion galloping through the vast plane meadows; unhindered, steady, effortless, extricated. Your unfettered mind does not continuously gravitate to the fateful moment that relinquished you of your freewheeling choices, allowing you to continue your life in peace, without the colossal burdens fastened on your back weighing you down. Years, weeks, days, minutes lose their peril and turn into the mundane life of an average person, filled with only the thoughts of the present and the future. A boring reality for most of the population, but a thirsted dream for me.

Determined to thrive in my third attempt at a worthwhile life in search of my true purpose, I made the ultimate decision to detach myself from my prior experiences and dedicate my time to being my best self. Growing up in San Francisco away from the familiar places and people of Georgetown, it was easier to be immersed in the new environment. There was very little to remind me of my old life, over time even my mother's longing for Delaware had dissipated as she met new friends and dedicated her time to my upbringing. Her stories of the pristine sand dunes and the rolling fields of corn slowly started to dwindle out and turned to the discussions about her admiration of the quirkiness of the San Francisco residents, the convenience of the cable cars and the abundance of the street musicians.

While it took my mother almost a year to feel like she belonged in her new home city, my father quickly assimilated without skipping a beat. The day after we settled in our rental unit in a formerly grandiose family home that had been converted into four separate apartments, my father left for work early in the morning and did not return until very late in the evening. My mother and I initially started to get very worried, wondering if something had happened or if he got lost getting home through the unfamiliar streets of the new city.

When dad finally came home, he looked utterly excited and could not stop talking about the company that employed him. I looked at him in amazement, because I had never seen the same level of exhilaration in my father that seemed to ignite the fire within him that he unfortunately extinguished when he moved to Delaware. His alien babble of the operating systems, binary codes and other unrecognizable terminology left us in the dark, however the kindled spark in his eyes assured us that this is where my father belonged. After a few months of dedicated work, my father's former professor reached out to him and offered to reinstate him in his studies on a part-time basis at Stanford. Unfortunately, my father was no longer eligible for the previously granted scholarship program, but his employer eagerly agreed to pay for his tuition if he committed to staying with the company for at least ten years. Over time, my dad managed to graduate from Stanford and achieve amazing results at work, which resulted in a series of well-earned promotions.

My father was making an unexpectedly lavish income by the time I was about to graduate high school, allowing my parents to save enough money to pay off the mortgage for the modest size home in the prime neighbourhood that they purchased a year after we moved to the Bay area. They initially chose the neighbourhood based on the school rating to allow me the best education in the city, but then once they were made aware of my "gifted" abilities in junior school they transferred me to a different school that was more catered to the children inclined to excel on the same academic level as me.

The school was located further away from the house, but I much rather preferred attending the new classes where the teachers were open to the intellectual discussions about literature instead of shying away from it. The other students at school were just as focused on their education, whether pushed by their parents or naturally talented to reach their academic capabilities, which gave me a certain sense of belongingness. I no longer stood out like a "know it all" but was encouraged to speak my mind and share my ideas with the others in the classroom. I got along with everyone in the class and as years passed by, we attended each others' birthday parties and collaborated on various school projects, but I never got close to anyone.

It was a conscious decision that I made as a damaged adult trapped in the infant's body after my medicated delusion of the out of body experience.

*Do not let anyone close enough to get burnt by your own impaired judgement.*

While I had many classmates and acquaintances, I could not call anyone my friend, no one was ever invited to come to my house, and I found excuses to leave when someone tried to share their secrets with me. Secrets meant trust, trust meant dependency, which in turn meant a bond. I chose not to be bonded with anyone, building personal connections was out of the question, if not for my benefit then definitely for theirs. Although, sometimes in the evenings when I was finished with all my homework and glanced outside the window at the children playing on the street, I would feel a fleeting sense of loneliness tickle my senses. The only respite for that ailment for me was to grab one of the books from the immense collection that I managed to gather over the years and divert my attention to the characters in the books away from the gloomy thoughts. If I did not distract myself right away, I knew that the feeling of loneliness would bloom into deeper memories of Roxie, which was unacceptable, if I had any chance of pursuing a thriving life without any heaving burdens on my mind.

My dedication to education to avoid any personal relationships resulted in me being able to graduate from high school at the age of sixteen and an early admission to a variety of universities around the country. The prospects of going to any of the Ivy League colleges that invited me to join their programs was rewarding considering all the hours that I had spent studying to excel in subjects that I had been only moderately good at during my prior stints at high school. After a lot of debating with my parents, they insisted that at my young age it would not be wise to be too far away from home so the best option would be to go to Stanford, which was only a thirty-minute drive away. They categorically refused to allow me to live on campus, fearful for my impressionable mind to be surrounded by the partying and the luring fraternities.

At first, I was unhappy with their position but then realized that living on campus meant blending into the social aspect of the student life which would jeopardize my rule of not letting anyone close. My choice of the program had also surprised my parents, as they had expected me to enrol in English or Literature majors, but that was because they had no awareness of my prior life's education where I was already able to attain that degree and therefore wanted something different to challenge myself. The allure of the unfamiliar world outside of the United States drew me to elect International Relations, and after some consideration I also chose to pursue a minor in Human Rights.

The privileged reality that I inhabited in this alternate lifetime was at first hard to comprehend, but as time passed by, any flashback memories of the prior existence seemed like fading images from an old movie: less vivid and vibrant than the existing truth around me. The acceptance from the university did not include a scholarship offer but my pragmatic parents had set up a separate savings account for my studies, when my father started his job in the emerging tech world that slowly accumulated money overtime, which was enough to afford the over-priced tuition.

The long days at Stanford were intellectually challenging and taught me to see the world through a different lens, while the professors imparted their academic curriculum. They insisted that in-class education was only half the training and that practical on hand experiences were essential in gaining full knowledge of the subject. It became evident overtime that my limited view of the world impeded my studies, not from the academic standpoint where my achievements were excelling with higher-than-average marks, but from the utilitarian perspective.

*How do you make an impact on the world, when you have only seen a minimal fraction of its surface and only met people like yourself?*

Driven to find my eventual purpose, I knew that limiting my education to the general subject of the world stage would not allow me to be an active player in that field.

"Mom, Dad, I have some news."

I confronted my parents when we sat down at our favourite Italian restaurant to celebrate my eventual graduation from Stanford. They were still beaming with pride at my accomplishment and could not help themselves but tell all the waiters and other patrons seated at their tables about the occasion. After awkwardly accepting the many plaudits from the strangers, I finally decided to address my plans about the future.

"Us too!" Mom quickly interrupted me. "Jennifer from my book club said that their company is looking for an intern in their marketing department. She asked that you reach out to her right away. It is an unpaid internship, but you will be able to get your foot in the door."

"That's great, mom, but I don't think that I can do that." I took a deep breath and continued with my rehearsed speech. "After a lot of contemplating, I have decided to pursue a law degree at Harvard. I have not told you anything about it before because I did not want to raise your hopes, in case I did not manage to get in. But, I received the admission confirmation last week. They offer a great opportunity of studying for a term abroad, which would enable me to practice law in

Europe and the US." I paused to take another long breath.

"That's wonderful, honey." My mother spoke up, glancing at my father who started to look slightly worried. "But we have not saved up enough to pay for any more tuition, the education fund has been drained. We do not want you to get any student loans either, it is such an unnecessary stress on a person. You will spend the next fifteen years worried about paying it off."

"Harvard is an expensive school." Dad nodded in support.

"Yes, so about that. You know that since I was fourteen, I asked you to open an account for me and to send money there instead of giving me presents? Well, I managed to invest all that money in some great dividend paying stocks that have had tremendous gain over the years. I may have enough now to pay for the tuition for the next two years but may need your help in paying for my living expenses. Therefore, I will only need to get the student loan for the remaining eighteen months, which should be manageable." Having a certain level of awareness of the stock market from being married to Jared and listening to him talk about the surges in certain industries, I invested in the tech industry and some retail companies that all grew to be gigantic money makers.

"I have wondered about that account, but your mother and I reasoned that you used the money we gave you to spend on yourself."

"Spending it on my education is better than buying heaps of unnecessary clothes and purses. So, what do you say?" I asked, hoping that they agreed with my plan.

"You have always managed to astonish me, since you were a little girl. Ever since I walked in on you reading a book when you had not even turned three yet. I knew we were in for a lot of surprises in the future." My mother reached across the table and gently took my sweaty hand in her soft palms. "Let us worry about the remaining eighteen months, I am certain we can set some money aside when the time comes. You know how I feel about loans, Noelle, so anything to avoid that stress."

"But Harvard is in Boston, that is on the other side of the country." Dad found another argument that I was prepared to counter.

"You moved across the country once, and you don't regret it. Right?" I looked at my dad turn to gaze at my mother with a smile.

"You got me there. But you must promise to come back for Thanksgiving, Christmas and the entire summer." This seemed like a reasonable compromise that I eagerly agreed to, leading my father to raise a glass of wine in celebration of my graduation from Stanford and a new upcoming chapter at Harvard.

"One more thing I forgot to add, and this does not go against our agreement since I haven't left to go to Harvard yet, I signed up to go to Costa Rica for the summer to help build homes for low-income families. If I am ever going to be a functioning member of the society, I need to learn more about the other cultures and see as much as I can before I figure out my place in this world. And don't worry, I made them aware of my condition, so I will not be responsible for any heavy lifting or excessive strenuous tasks."

"I actually think that it is a great idea, Noelle. I completely support you, and so does your mother." I caught my dad putting his arm firmly on my mom's thigh, just as she was about to say something.

"Just take all your shots, honey." Was the last piece of advice my mother gave me before we carried on with our dinner.

Listening to my mother's wise suggestion, I took all the necessary precautions and felt fully prepared when I left San Francisco for Costa Rica. However, when I arrived at the camp that was set up by the organizers in the middle of the dense rainforest without any of the comforts that I was accustomed to in the States, I grasped the severity of the living conditions in this less fortunate part of the world. For the locals, having a secured roof over their head was a luxury that many could not afford, resorting to the salvaged scraps of metal loosely laid onto their makeshift shacks.

The thirty days that I had thought would be sufficient to help the cause, was a merely noticeable droplet in the endless ocean of boundless labour to achieve the ultimate goal of providing a home to all the families in need. The real shock that left a lasting effect on me was that the local families all came together to help build each other a home, there was a sense of camaraderie in unified goals. People were eager to help each other, the children were giddy observing the foreign volunteers sweating profusely in the heat, when the periodic tropical rain would suddenly plummet from the skies the locals rushed us into their unstable shacks for cover. While I was there, I hardly ever heard any complaints from the locals about their discomfort. They were all thrilled about getting a new home, but they never felt the need to gripe. All the incessant complaining about "nothing to wear" or "leaky faucets", that the privileged world occupied its time with, appeared awfully petty and unimportant.

When I returned to the States, my parents were waiting for me at the airport and exclaimed loudly when they saw my tanned slender figure approach them. My mother cried out in disapproval and insisted that I looked emaciated, but I argued that it was all muscle from working on my feet every day. On the drive home, my mother chose to sit by my side in the back holding on to my hand as if I were still a young child that may run away, while my father drove occasionally glancing in the rear-view mirror to catch my eye and wink back. It was great to be home with my parents, a simple family moment which was one of thousands, had once again convinced me that our reshaped reality was a step in the right direction.

After spending less than a month between my return from abroad and leaving for Boston to embark on another three years of schooling, I was finally ready to leave my parents. My trip to Costa Rica was not only fulfilling for my lacking worldly view but also allowed me to understand that I did not have to be with my parents constantly to make sure that they were safe and sound. They lived a blissful life in ignorance of their prior grim experiences, and I needed to let go and let my guard down regarding their wellbeing. Moving away was an appropriate step towards my own independence and their autonomy as a couple and not doting parents.

Following the many tearful goodbyes and explicit warnings to be careful, my parents finally released me from their tight embraces and let me walk away towards the Gate where my flight had already been boarding. Once I was let into the plane, I walked past the rows occupied by families with children and snobbish men dressed in business attire who looked displeased being seated in the audible proximity to the playful toddlers. My seat was located towards the back of the plane, the second to last row, which still allowed me to recline the seat if I decided to sleep through the long flight. Just as I got comfortable in my seat and put on a new pair of headphones my parents got me in the summer, before I managed to turn on the music on my iPod, I suddenly heard a voice that I instantly recognized.

"Can you stop complaining already, Kanani? You know all the business class was sold out and these were the only seats available." The male voice addressed his companion as they walked down the aisle.

"We could have waited for the next flight!" The female argued, lifting her Louis Vuitton purse up in the air, afraid that it would graze the dirty plane seats.

"No, we could not. This was the last flight out of San Francisco today and I must make this meeting first thing tomorrow morning in

Boston. You did not have to come with me, you could have gone home to New York, and I could have come after I was done with all the meetings."

The voices neared my row of seats, and I finally confirmed my instant guess. In front of me I saw Jared, just as handsome as ever, dressed in a light grey business suit that was tailored to fit his herculean body perfectly. Next to my former husband was the exotic seductress that broadcasted to the entire world about their affair and his financial schemes that were a shocking revelation to me in the preceding lifetime.

They walked towards the back row of seats, where Jared's companion had started whining incessantly about their allocated places.

"These do not even recline, Jared. This is exactly how I wanted to end our honeymoon!" She exclaimed in a sarcastic tone in her high-pitched voice that made everyone nearby turn around and look in the direction of the noise. I sat still in my seat, stunned by the news.

*They got married.* I tried to comprehend the oozing of emotion that this information aroused within me. It was not jealousy, it was not pain from betrayal, it was not a sad feeling at all. It was a sense of relief, this is how things were supposed to be, they deserved each other and if I were not in the picture before then they would have most likely been together. Maybe he would turn out to be a better person with her and would not scam innocent people out of their money, maybe they would live happily ever after together 'till old age, but a part of me secretly wished that they got what they both deserved.

"Just take a seat, Kanani. You're making everyone uncomfortable." Jared growled at her, frustrated by the whining.

"It's not me that is making them uncomfortable, it's these tight stained seats that are making them uncomfortable!" She declared loud purposely to ensure that everyone heard her, then she plopped her tiny figure in the chair and stayed quiet in protest.

I tried to listen in to hear what else they would say, but they both stayed silent while the flight attendants performed their last checks, and the plane was taxied out onto the runway. Smirking to myself at their mutual snobbery, I turned up the music on my player and quickly fell asleep. I only woke up, when the plane jerked as the landing gear grazed the surface of the Boston airport runway. The sun shone brightly welcoming the new arrivals into the warm Boston early Fall day, as all the passengers eagerly waited for our plane to approach the gate to disembark and disperse into the diverse directions.

Once the plane halted in its designated spot and the aisles filled with people ready to leave the plane, I also raised myself in my seat to stretch my legs. At that moment, I glanced behind me and saw Jared's new bride resting her perfectly groomed head on his broad shoulder while he had his arm around her. There was no animosity, they seemed happy together, caught in their quiet moment of contentment.

*Best of luck, Jared.* I wished to him in silence and joined the queued-up passengers as the line slowly trickled out of the packed plane. That was the last time I saw or even thought of Jared, it was an unexpectedly needed closure that the ruthless universe delivered to me to enable me to move forward into my new life.

Life ahead of me indeed moved hastily through the years at Harvard, the new legal principles and theoretical knowledge were at first difficult to conceptualize but eventually I joined the academic rhythm of the similarly struggling students and we pushed each other to excel. While I kept my promise to visit my parents for the holidays and the summer vacations, I spent most of the time at home revising the information that I had studied throughout the year to solidify the learnt material in my keen brain. Towards the second semester at college, I became a proficient student with a reputation for being a quick learner complimented by my innate heightened ability for logical reasoning. The professors gladly accepted me into their research projects and legal proceedings which enhanced the merely theoretical knowledge of the legal concepts and allowed me to utilize the learnt material in real life cases. At the end of my second year at law school, just as I had hoped, I was accepted into the Joint Program to study at one of the most prestigious universities in England.

When I called my parents to share the news of me moving to the United Kingdom, the line went silent as neither of them knew what to say. I hoped that they would be happy for me, but if having me in Boston was hard for them then the idea of me being on the other side of the world was incomprehensible.

"But why?" Was the first question I heard from my mother after a few moments of silence.

"Because I want to practice law that can have an impact on the world and doing that in the States would not allow me to do that. Think of the experience that I would gain, think of all the doors this would open up for me." My uncontained excitement was hard to miss.

"Couldn't you just go for a month, like when you went to build homes in Costa Rica?" My mother continued with her questioning.

"I could go and build homes in Africa or in the less fortunate countries in Europe. This is different, this is my education that would allow me to practice law in Europe."

"Your mother and I will support you in anything you decide to do, Noelle. In fact, we were planning to travel around Europe for some time now, so this would give us a perfect excuse to come and visit you." I could almost see my father holding my mom's hand trying to calm her nerves.

With my parents' support, both affirmational and financial, I left the United States and flew to Europe. This had been an unattainable dream coming true, to travel the world, which my mother had described in vivid detail in her made-up tales of the mouse family, but I never got the chance to fulfill that wish.

The architecture dissimilar to anything I grew up seeing exuded the centuries of history that I had only read about in books. I could walk around the streets for hours exploring the unfamiliar neighbourhoods. The locals were different too, at first, they seemed taken aback by my American accent but overtime I got used to the reactions and the people I talked to the most stopped making fun of how I spoke.

Studying abroad was different from what I had experienced in the past, while both Stanford and Harvard had high levels of expectations from their students, it seemed that Cambridge Law School had an even more elevated outlook on their students not just limited to their education but also their demeanour and outward conduct. Through some extensive research and consultations with the various professors while at Harvard prior to my departure, I eventually narrowed down the focus that I wanted to pursue in my education at Cambridge and subsequent career around the world.

I needed to do something that was rewarding enough to allow me to come home and feel like I had accomplished something great, almost immeasurable, while providing a meaningful impact to the world and the defenseless population whose voices remained unheard. I knew that being a divorce lawyer, while financially rewarding, would not fulfill my itch to do more and being a criminal lawyer would be equivalent to me selling my soul to the devil. So, I decided to pursue a career as a Human Rights lawyer with a particular emphasis on the victims of human trafficking, an unfortunate underground industry that had plagued the world.

While conducting my independent research in the field and attending the lectures, I also joined a free legal clinic where I volunteered on a part-time basis, which introduced me to a wide spectrum of a variety of people seeking help. Anytime when a frightened woman with fast pacing eyes came into the office seeking advice, I would instantly have a flashback of being back at the Green Light Sanctuary where we provided shelter for women and their children escaping their abusive partners. It was hard not to get personally invested in all the cases that reminded me of the disadvantaged women I met over the years in my first lifetime, but in order to help them I had to stay professional and distant so that they could take my advice seriously and remain convinced of their plans to pursue legal action against their abusers.

One Saturday a young anxious-looking girl in her late teens came into the clinic, her long dirty blonde hair was woven neatly in an intricate French braid, after the many failed attempts at getting attention, she sat down quietly in the reception area. Even though I was swamped with the paperwork and all the other legal advisors were equally busy, none of us had the time to see her that day, she sat silently in an uncomfortable plastic chair hoping to speak to someone. Her silent persistence paid off, because after hours of filling out endless applications on behalf of our clients, I looked up and she was still sitting in her spot. Heaving myself from my seat, feeling my whole body numb from sitting too long, I walked over to the relentless client.

"Can I help you make an appointment for another day? I'm afraid everyone is a bit busy today." I inquired.

"No, I need help today. You see me today?"

The young girl had a heavy eastern European accent, but her vocabulary seemed simple enough to understand.

"Like I said, it looks like everyone has their hands full today." I regretfully had to decline again.

"But I need help, my sister need help. Police no help, embassy no help. I no have my passport. What I do?"

She looked at me pleading for help, and something in her eyes reminded me of Roxie when she came seeking help at Green Light when she escaped Ray's clutches. There was a significant amount of fear projected back at me but her relentless determinism to seek help at whatever the cost warranted further attention.

"Is this about extending your visa?" I had to ask, but my inner senses have already given rise to the actual cause for her visit.

"No."

The girl shook her head vigorously, sending her elaborate braid to sway back and forth. "I run away from Ivan, but my sister no. He does bad, very bad things to us. Force have sex with men, keep us in dark room."

"Come with me."

My guess at identifying a victim of sex smuggling in front of me was confirmed, so I escorted the victim to an enclosed conference room that was typically reserved for larger meetings, but it provided enough privacy for us to be able to speak confidentially.

"What is your name?"

"Irina." She answered after some hesitation.

"You said you went to the police, what did they say?" I asked her once she sat down in a more comfortable chair, relieved to finally be heard.

"They no believe. They say I mad at boyfriend, and I lie to have him arrest. No true!"

She slammed her skeletal arm on the table in frustration. "Ivan have my sister. I lucky, climb in window and jump in tree." She raised her arm up so I could see the many scratches covering her exposed skin.

"I go shelter; they say go free legal clinic. I am here. You help me?"

The pain of being let down by the system and helplessness at the situation did not deter this confident young victim to pursue help from a stranger.

The need to help her outweighed any of my previously learnt protocols on how to act in the situation, and I hastily rushed her out of the office leaving all my scattered paperwork on the desk. I caught a taxi on the street and asked the driver to take us to the nearest police station immediately. My frightened companion's exterior became less timid but more confident as she finally felt that she was being supported by someone who believed her. As I talked to her in the cab, trying to get more information on where she came from and how long had she been held captive, she reminded me of Roxie so much that it started to hurt. There was nothing similar about their physical appearance or their speech, but the indistinguishable mannerism of an abused woman forced into the sex industry was evident. When we arrived at the police station, I forced the police officers to listen to Irina's story and demanded that they send the officers to the location that she was able to describe so vividly. The police officers were taken aback by my perseverance, while Irina stood back with her widely opened eyes amazed by my eagerness to help her.

After the incessant persuasion, the officers agreed to send a car to the apartment but did not allow us to follow them. So, we stayed at the police station to wait for the outcome, Irina paced back and forth along the corridor, her lips silently moving as if in a silent prayer for the safe return of her sister. I sat back on the wide wooden bench with my back resting against the wall, hoping that Ivan did not flee the apartment with Irina's sister, impatiently waiting for any news. After a while, a police officer approached us and asked us to come with him in his car, which triggered Irina to start crying and yelling something in Russian. I was not sure if she was afraid of being arrested or if she was afraid that the police came too late, and something had happened to her sister. So, I hugged her and gently led her into the car, assuring her that there was nothing to worry about and the police probably wanted her to confirm the location of where she was held captive.

When we approached the site that Irina had so perfectly described in her limited but colourful English, we saw a plethora of police cars outside parked along the street. There was a lot of commotion with police officers swarming the area, preventing the public from getting too close. The policeman who drove us to the scene, opened the back door asking us to follow him and to stay close. I started behind him and felt Irina's hand grasp onto mine, so I squeezed it back to let her know that I was going to be with her to the end. We followed the police officer through the crowd of curious neighbours into the three-story building and walked up two flights of stairs, into a dirty apartment that smelled like sweat and cured meats. Irina's grasp on my hand became stronger as she recognized her confinement immediately, while she looked around in fear or seeing her abusers.

"Ivan?" She asked in her trembling voice.

"He and a couple of his clients were taken to the station for questioning a few minutes ago. Could you come with me?"

A man dressed in civilian clothing, that I learned to mean that he was the detective in charge, overheard Irina's question about her captor. We walked behind him through the filthy living room where the sofa was overturned and pieces of clothing were scattered all over the floor, into a hallway that had four widely opened doors. I heard voices coming from each of those rooms, and Irina's ears perked up as she slowed down to focus to hear the one voice that mattered to her the most.

"Masha!" She yelled in hope to hear a response, but momentary silence followed.

"Ira!" Another voice finally screamed back from the furthest room in the hallway. Irina quickly released my hand and ran towards the voice, where she saw her sister safe and sound.

While the two girls cried loudly at the happy ending of their months' long captivity, I remained with the detective in the hallway, who informed me that there were three other girls in their teens all from Ukraine held against their will in the apartment. They had already called the embassy and the translators were on their way to take the statements from the victims, but there was no question that Ivan would not see a day of freedom for a very long time.

"Scumbag!" The detective swore at the mention of Ivan's name. "These girls are so defenseless, they are promised jobs, modeling careers, money, clothes and scumbags like him take advantage of their naivety. There are so many of them out there, but only a fraction ever gets caught."

He was right, and I knew that I had to do something about that. The experience with Irina and her sister Masha pushed me to study harder and research the subject of human trafficking further for the rest of my studies at Cambridge and then when I returned to the States for the final semester back at Harvard. Through that eye opening experience, I knew that researching the subject would not be sufficient, so I met the many survivors who shared their inspiring stories and told me about their fallen friends who were no longer around to share their own narratives.

Once I graduated from law school, I could not wait to act and save the world but first needed enough experience at professional law firms to allow me to be an accredited lawyer. A few law firms in Boston had extended their offers to me, and I gladly accepted the internship with the company that was known for their pro bono work and large-scale cases that had an impact on the underrepresented population of the country. Over the years of working with the firm, I met countless people who came to seek help, illegal immigrants fighting their deportation, asylum seekers separated from their families, and I eagerly helped them to win their individual cases, but I still thought back of Irina, Masha, Roxie and other girls like them that still needed my help.

When I was twenty-eight years old, after five years with the law firm, I was invited to speak at a seminar hosted by the small but effective group of volunteers who raised awareness about family abuse. The fact that the seminar was to be held in New York did not deter me from going, as I figured that I would fly into the city in the morning and would fly out in the evening without spending any unnecessary time there. This was not the first time I had to fly into New York for work, but I always planned the day to only stay for the required meetings and leave without spending the night in the city that had brought me so much pain.

My flight this time was delayed, and I arrived in New York later than I expected, which meant that I would be slightly late for the panel discussion and the introductory speeches. This did not worry me because I knew that my presence was mostly required towards the end of the day, when I was required to speak about legal options for the abuse victims in front of the women who were seeking the help and the support workers who wanted to learn. When the flight finally landed in La Guardia Airport, I caught a cab to take me into the city to the YMCA downtown and managed to get to the venue in record time considering the New York traffic jams along the route.

When I walked in, I followed the signs to the auditorium and opened the doors to enter the packed space without an open seat in sight. The stage was lit up and there were experts sitting up in their seats answering questions from the audience, which I tried to listen to while looking for a spot to sit. Finally, I noticed an empty chair closer to the podium and quietly made my way down the aisle making sure not to disturb the enlightening discussion. Once I finally shuffled through the row to sit down, I looked up at the experts to see if I recognized anyone from any of the prior conferences I attended. As my eyes shifted from one face to another, I sat back in shock at seeing the last person seated farthest away from me on the opposite side of the stage.

*Enid.* She looked exactly as I had remembered her, her kind face always slightly smiling, sending positive energy to the men and women who joined to discuss the important topic that she felt so passionately about and had consumed much of her life.

"Next question." I heard the moderator ask the audience when the woman from the panel dressed in a grey business suit concluded her informative answer to the question about the statistics of victims of abuse in the States versus other countries. "Yes, the lady in the third row"

It almost looked like they were pointed to me, but it was a woman about my age seated directly behind me who had raised her hand.

"Thank you. I have a question for the panel."

The audience member behind me mustered up the courage and spoke into the microphone louder than she had expected, which sent a round of chuckles around the room.

"Every choice I have made seemed to be the wrong one, and I tend to blame those around me for my own decisions. How do I change my mind frame and assume the responsibility for my own life and my own choices?"

The question seemed personal and took the panel of experts on the stage by surprise. They were eager to share numbers, statistics, chart and graphs but they were not equipped to answer the question that the troubled woman behind me had for them, until I saw Enid reach for the microphone.

"The first step is to own up to your own choices, dear, which you seem to have done. While it is exceptionally easy to blame others, who come across your path for where you ended up, the person making the decision needs to understand that in the end they are responsible for their own choices."

Enid looked in the direction of the lady asking the question, but I felt her gaze directly on me instead.

"Every choice creates a ripple effect that can overtime turn into a barely noticeable wave or an overpowering tsunami. It is up to you to stay afloat and not drown in the vortex of the repercussions. Swim hard, keep your head above water, kick with everything you have, because the strong-willed always survive to be given a chance at an infinite number of other choices in their lifetime. In my old age, this is what I have learned life to be, a finite path of multifarious decisions. There are a multitude of options that we are all faced with in life, but if you accept your decision then be ready to confront the consequences. There are no monsters out there but only the inner fear trapped inside of you that pulls you down with the current, face your fears, live through them, challenge yourself, embrace the force of the tsunami and you will survive it."

In my mind there was no dispute that most of that speech was addressed directly at me, I am the coward who chooses to steer clear of my fears and opted to live a life away from all the wrong or right decisions that I had made in the past. Running away from my past was a choice that I made at the inception of the life I was going to have if I had any chance of living to old age like Enid. It has been a great life thus far, my parents were both alive and healthy living a prosperous life in San Francisco. I managed to attend the best schools in the world and attain a previously unreachable law degree. I passed the bar exams that allowed me to practice law in the States. I was helping people who needed help the most. Every day when I came home after a long day at work, I felt tired but also content that I spent another day achieving something that had a greater impact on the world. However, there was also a sense of emptiness deep inside of me, a void that I kept filling with long hours of work and new challenging cases, but it still craved a missing ingredient that I failed to supply.

"Hi, my name is Noelle Anderson." I approached Enid at a coffee break between the sessions of the seminar, when I spotted her outside finishing up a conversation with the girl who had been sitting behind me. "I just wanted to say that what you said at the panel discussion is a great message to these women who came seeking motivation to act and inspiration to move forward."

"Hi, Noelle. I'm Enid." My old friend smiled back at me and raised her hand to shake mine. "I figured that being an old woman, I have some experience in living out my decisions to fruition and the outcome is not always what I had hoped it to be, but it is always a learning experience."

"But don't your decisions sometimes pull you back, preventing you from living your life to its fullest?"

"The past always draws your back. So, we beat on..." She quoted the book that had brought us back together again and again through different lives.

"Boats against the current." I continued the quote from where she left off.

"Borne back ceaselessly into the past." Enid finished the quote from the Great Gatsby and looked at me with intense curiosity. "What does this quote mean to you, Noelle?"

"That if you have any chance of moving forward, then you need to row harder, otherwise the past may consume you."

"What do you do, my dear?" Enid asked .

"I am here to provide some legal counsel for the women later in the day, just came in for the day from Boston." I answered with confidence, proud of my purpose for being at the seminar.

"So, you are a lawyer? That is very impressive." Enid kept her studying gaze at me, observing me with wonder. "A lifetime ago I met a wonderful young girl on a bench in a park who quoted Scott F. Fitzgerald back to me, just like you. You remind me of her, she had a lot of potential too but unfortunately she could not withstand the emblematic tsunami."

"A lifetime?" I stuttered in response.

*What could she mean by lifetime?*

"Ignore an old woman's babble, my dear." Enid laughed off the question. "Lifetime just means a long time ago, a very long time ago, so long that I can hardly remember when it happened."

A group of women approached us waiting for Enid to finish her conversation with me, so that they could ask her a question.

"Well, it was very nice to meet you, Enid." I reluctantly ended the conversation, yearning to speak to her longer.

"If by any chance you are going to be in New York tomorrow, I would like you to come by my place and meet someone." Enid stopped me from walking away.

"I was going to go back to Boston tonight." I reminded her of my short visit.

"I understand, dear, but I think that you could really help the young woman who is staying with me. In fact, I think you would be the perfect person to speak to her." Enid insisted, which was a bit surprising because she had never seemed to be the demanding type in the past.

"I'll see what I can do." I hesitantly responded and turned to walk away.

"Hope to see you tomorrow." She replied and handed me her card with the address, and as I walked away to prepare for my own session, I felt her soft inquisitive stare locked on me.

The rest of the afternoon did not provide me a free second to think about my reunion with Enid or her offer to visit her the next day, my undivided attention was fully devoted to the wonderful courageous women who came to the session to ask me their hard but important questions. Their enthusiasm and directness were boundlessly infectious, keeping my adrenaline high, while I answered every legal inquiry that was prepared for my professional counsel. The discussion rolled on well past the allocated time slot and I did not manage to leave the seminar until much later in the evening ,than I had been anticipating to be able to catch my flight home. In my mind I knew that there was still another flight late at night that I could take, but my heart ached begging me to spend the night.

The battle between my two inner forces was eventually won by the strong sense that I needed to remain in the City for one more day, where my mind conceded with the reasoning that since the following day was a Saturday there was no imperative need for me to come to the office early in the morning. Succumbing to my hastily made decision, I caught the next available cab and asked to be taken to the opulent hotel towering over the Central Park in the Upper East Side where I had previously attended multiple lunch meetings and met clients whenever I came to the city. To my relief, there was an available suite at check-in when I walked into the lavish lobby and inquired regarding the availability for a one-night stay. After grabbing the card key and following the careful instructions of the poshly dressed receptionist, I took the elevator to the fourth floor and walked down the hallway to open the door to my lovely room for the night. Without skipping a beat and feeling a wave of exhaustion hit me, I quickly stripped off my designer suit and lunged into the soft bed linen that hugged my body with its delicate smooth fabric. Just as I was about to close my eyes to succumb to the tiredness that weighed my eyelids down, I heard Enid's voice in my head.

*There are no monsters out there but only the inner fear trapped inside of you that pulls you down with the current.*

I did not think that I still carried the weight of the monster from my past, I lived a life that did not offer up any reminders of Ray and it was only when I came to New York that I would have a flashback of the prior horrors. I knew that I was consciously lying to myself when I refused to spend longer than a few hours in the city where I lived through the moments that I chose to forget, convincing myself that my workload in Boston could not wait and I had to return once the business meetings in Manhattan were concluded. However, as I was now jerked awake from remembering Enid's words of wisdom that she shared with the attendees today, I knew that the monster still lingered in my consciousness preserved as a trigger for the release of the deepest fear buried within the hungry void inside me. The previously looming sleep had been wiped out with the daunting thoughts, and I lay awake lost in the grim memories.

*Face your fears, live through them, challenge yourself, embrace the force of the tsunami and you will survive it.*

Enid was right, I could not live on with the same fears that kept pulling me back into the past. I drowned in the tsunami of my own guilt plagued by the memories of Ray in the past, I could not go on being haunted by the same thoughts. Diverting the memories and continuously suppressing them was not the solution, but just a temporary band-aid that I needed to rip off once and for all. I reached for my cell phone resting on the bedside table, and quickly started typing a text message on the screen to a detective who I have become friends with over the years having interacted over many intriguing cases in Boston.

"Hi Rick, need a small favour. Could you run a check on Ray Ferguson, born in New York City on March 28, 1978? No rush. Thx"

My finger hovered over the Send button as I reread the message over and over again, until my heart and my mind once again united in their decision and released me from my doubts. Once I sent the message, I put the phone down and settled back in the bed convinced that I would remain awake for the rest of the night lost on the dense jungle of my inner reflections. However, after a few minutes my busy mind surrendered to the much-needed slumber and remained in a deep dreamless sleep for the remainder of the night until I was awoken by the shrilling sounds of my pre-set alarm on the phone. The annoying ringing continued until I finally grabbed my phone and turned off the alarm. It was nine in the morning and time to get up if I wanted to accomplish half the things I planned for the day.

Staying in bed was never a luxury that I allowed myself through the years, there was so much to life than the four walls around you, so without hesitation I made myself rise and walk to the bathroom where I proceeded to take a long hot shower guaranteeing myself a great mood for the rest of the day. When I finally emerged from the shower, the entire bathroom was filled with thick heavy steam, so I wiped the mirror over the sink with a towel and started to brush my teeth with the complimentary disposable set courtesy of the hotel. While my energetic brain schemed out the day ahead of me, I heard a ding from my phone which meant that I received a text message, so I walked over to look at the lit-up screen and saw Rick's name. Still holding on to the toothbrush and vigorously giving my teeth a good cleaning, I rushed back to the sink and rinsed out the foam, then went back to sit on the bed and swiped the screen to reveal the message.

"Hi Noelle, Ray Ferguson was found dead in the Hudson ten years ago. Badly beaten, his skull crushed in. Based on his impressive rap sheet, mostly drug related, I'd say he crossed paths with a local gang. Body unclaimed, no leads, no suspects."

The informative text lacked any emotions, which is so characteristic for a veteran detective who was used to dealing with these types of situations. However, the content of his message left me stunned, unable to pinpoint the exact emotion that this provoked within me. I stayed seated on the bed. Ray was dead, that meant that there really were no monsters, he was just a figment, an illusion that I carried through the lifetimes with me. There was nothing to be afraid of, he got what he deserved, probably killed by one of his drug dealers or a family of another innocent girl that he lured away from home.

"Everything ok?" A second message lit up on the screen from Rick, as he probably wondered about the reason for my inquiry.

"All good, Rick. Thanks for the prompt response. I owe you lunch." I typed back swiftly .

Forcing myself to snap out of my frozen state, I walked over to my only outfit that I wore the day before and got dressed. One of my biggest pet peeves in this more privileged life was to wear the same outfit twice in a row, opting out to wear a fresh pair of clothes the next day, but there was no other choice. Glancing at the time on my wristwatch, I hastily left the room and checked out of the hotel having spent no longer than a total of ten hours in its exquisitely furnished suite. The hotel was conveniently located within a five-minute walk from Green Light, so I figured a quick visit to see Enid would allow me to get to the airport for an early afternoon flight that would still give me time to work through the paperwork that needed my attention at the office.

The crisp chill in the area of the late Fall was invigorating as I walked through the familiar streets of my old neighbourhood. Everything around me exuded positive vibes from the past. For the first time, New York did not dissuade me from my imposition but welcomed me into its perfectly groomed neighbourhoods like a gracious host greeting a long lost relative. There was no evil hiding to attack me from the dark alleys, the veil of wickedness that was only visible to me was finally lifted, allowing me to finally see the City in the positive light that had previously eluded me.

When my confident strides finally led me to the front door of my old home, my own private sanctuary, I loitered outside observing it like an old lost friend. Its grey nondescript exterior was not a deterrent, because I knew all the positive energy that flowed throughout the long hallways and spacious rooms of the household. I trekked up the stairs and knocked on the door, waiting patiently for someone to answer it.

"Who is it?" I finally heard Enid's voice on the other side.

"It's Noelle, the lawyer from yesterday's seminar."

This seemed to be the most fitting introduction, for someone who had only met me once and may have forgotten about her extended invitation.

The myriad of locks being opened behind the door meant that Enid remembered me, when the front door finally opened, I was greeted by her openly gleeful face genuinely happy to see me.

"So glad you decided to come. There was no doubt in my mind that you would." She confessed, welcoming me inside.

"The session last night went longer than expected so I missed my plane and had to reschedule it to the next available flight early this afternoon today. Unfortunately, I cannot stay long otherwise I'd be stuck in New York for much longer than I can, I have a lot of work to attend back to in Boston." I decided to make her aware of my immediate plans for the day, so there was no expectation for a longer visit.

Enid led me through the interior that I used to call home, that always ended up drawing me back in, no matter the different the circumstances of my lifetimes I always ended up inside Green Light. There was an inseparable bond between me and the house that kept me on its long by impervious leash, pulling me back when my soul needed to be incited from its hiding. When we reached the kitchen, my old mentor showed me to the kitchen table, while she went to grab a couple of mugs and turn on the coffee machine.

"Sasha is running a bit late; she always comes on Saturday mornings but had a last-minute appointment early today. She is the young lady I told you about that I was hoping you could speak to; I think you two would hit it off."

Enid expanded on the reason for her invitation, while pouring the fragrant coffee into the mugs and then walked over to join me at the table.

"I'd be happy to help, in any way that I can. If I do not get to meet her today, then I can leave my contact information at my office with you that you can pass to her." There were so many people that needed free legal advice and I tried to help each person, but my firm had strict policies regarding their clients and generally frowned upon unsanctioned meetings.

"She'll be here before you have to leave." Enid asserted.

"Well, while we wait, I just wanted to tell you once again how much I appreciated the message that you shared with the group yesterday. I saw how many women wanted to speak to you after the meeting, you have an amazing way with people who need advice." I wanted to switch our conversation back to Enid, which was the real reason I came. After seeing her the day before, I realized how much I have missed my chats over coffee when she guided me out of my misery when I lived on the streets and when we walked around the neighbourhood discussing the classic authors in the not-too-distant past.

"I don't have much to give, but I try to help in every way possible. My advice is generally well accepted by those who actually seek it." Enid was right, her guidance could only be heard by the people who needed it the most, whether they knew it or not. In my case, I initially chose not to confront the magnitude of the wave, afraid of its blow, and decided to ride it out at its peak, looking down at all the people in my life from afar. The safety of coasting by in my life was comforting, I got carried away in observing life around me instead of living it.

"Your words hit me pretty hard too." I admitted. "Last night I finally decided to face the looming tsunami, filled with fear based on something that no longer existed. Today I woke up alive and well, unscathed."

Enid's face lit up in a wide smile, as if she had heard the most wonderful news in a while. I was a stranger to her, and she still showed happiness for someone that was able to benefit from her words.

"I wish you knew how happy that makes me feel." She extended her hand and brushed away a loose strand of hair on my face in her motherly way.

My response of staying still and not flinching away from her touch took me by surprise, because I typically cringed every time someone tried to show any physical affection, my parents being the only exception to the rule.

"So glad I could help you. Unfortunately, I cannot help everyone, and I wish I could. Like Sasha for example. She is such a wonderful, spirited, kind person who is seeking the truth about her past, so she can finally move on with her life. I met her at a nearby park on a bench almost a decade ago, she had clearly been living on the street for months and she did not belong there. When I spoke to her, she was very educated and eloquent, but there was something troubling her. So, I took her here into my Sanctuary, which I created to help mothers and children escaping abuse. Sasha stayed here in one of the empty rooms in the basement and started helping me out at the house, helping our guests. Overtime, she started to come out of her shell and confided in me as to why she ended up on the streets.

Sasha grew up in an affluent home in Connecticut, not too far from New York. Her father was a very loving man who spoiled her with his attention and gifts, while her mother remained a reserved woman annoyed by her husband's parental tactics. In her younger years, Sasha never had a struggling moment, she went to a private school and took private piano and dance lessons. Then suddenly her father passed away from a heart attack, leaving sixteen-year-old Sasha and her mother alone in their sumptuous mansion. They never developed the strong connection that Sasha had with her father, so the previously happy household turned into an awkward abode that no longer felt like a home.

A day after Sasha's graduation from high school, a place which she had considered her escape from home, her mother summoned her into her father's private office located in the west wing of their home. The office remained untouched since its owner tragically died, and almost seemed like a shrine to the much-missed member of the family. That is where her mother broke the news that Sasha was adopted at birth at her father's insistence. Now that Sasha had graduated, the woman that she had known to be her mother, stated that she felt that she fulfilled her husband's wishes in raising her. Then she asked her to move out, assuring her that she will provide a monthly allowance that would allow her to live a good life.

The woman did not even try to be subtle with her own daughter, that she raised from birth. In any way, some people are not meant to be parents and should not be forced to bring up children. So, I partially hold the husband responsible too." Enid offered her opinion, and then continued.

"In a state of shock, Sasha ran to her room and packed her backpack with her belongings and ran out of the house before anyone could stop her. From that day and until fate brought us together, Sasha had been living on the streets. She was a great help for years while she lived here at the sanctuary, but then she finally found her purpose, so she got her own place, but she comes to visit every weekend." Enid concluded the vicarious story that left me feeling mad at the cruel adoptive mother and empathetic with the stranger I had yet to meet at the same time."

"This story is unbelievable! So, I am assuming that Sasha is looking for the financial compensation that she had surrendered when she left home, is that why she needs the legal advice?" I inquired.

"On the contrary, Sasha wants nothing to do with her adopted mother or the money. She wants to find her birth parents, to understand where she came from."

"I see, and there is no consent on file to release the identifying information that would be available for her to find." I finally understood the legal advice that was being asked of me. "This may be impossible, laws vary by state, but generally there needs to be consent by the birth parent to release that information. Do you know what state Sasha was born in?"

"Yes." There was a knock on the front door that made Enid rise from her chair and walk to open the door, while she continued to answer my question. "Delaware."

*My home state.* I thought while I remained alone in the kitchen. I heard Enid greet someone at the door and shuffle her feet to join me back at the table.

"That's Sasha. Told you she'd be here before you had to leave." Enid beamed, and I caught a glimpse of a sneaky smile momentarily appearing on her face.

"Did you say Delaware before you walked away?" I inquired to confirm if I heard the state correctly.

"Good morning, sorry I'm late!" I heard a voice behind me entering the brightly lit kitchen. I knew that voice, the voice that followed me through all the bad and good things in my past, a voice that only remained in my dreams, a voice that I thought I would never hear again.

"Roxie!" The name escaped my lips in a loud whisper. Just as the name escaped my lips, Enid exhaled loudly and started coughing as if the last of the air escaped her lungs. Roxie ran over to Enid to make sure that she was alright, until the old lady stopped coughing. While my best friend hovered over Enid, I inspected her materialized body form in front of me. Fighting the urge to poke her to check if she were real, I noticed that her hair was braided neatly and she was dressed in black slacks and a white t-shirt, something that my Roxie would never do. Nevertheless, it was unmistakably Roxie in front of me, and her slightly augmented appearance could not deceive me.

"Hi, I'm Sasha." The tidied-up version of Roxie sat in the empty chair next to me and extended her hand to shake mine.

"Noelle." I responded with an introduction, trying to read my friend's face for any signs of recognition.

"I told Noelle, all about you Sasha. And I also told Sasha about you Noelle, the successful lawyer from Boston who could maybe help. Why don't I let you two catch up and learn about each other, while I get out of your way?" Enid got up from her seat and slowly walked out of the room, leaving us alone in the kitchen.

Unable to fully formulate sentences in my dazed surprise, I asked Sasha to give me her version of the story that Enid had told me. Her story stayed true to the details that Enid gave me but provided slightly more colour to the description of her happy carefree childhood that she had when her father was alive. The sorrow of his loss was still perceptible, any mention of her father caused a glassy film to form over her eyes, and she paused slightly at her happy memories before moving on to the events that followed. When she was done with retelling her life story, I was finally able to speak, assured that it was in fact Roxie in front of me. It never dawned on me that Alison actually gave her daughter up for adoption and that she now had a different name. I have looked for Roxie's name on the wide network of social media and search engines ever since the internet surfaced into this reality, but all my sleuthing remained fruitless.

The unimaginable ripple effect of my immoral decision to end my life in the previous lifetime, managed to sweep Roxie under its forceful impact. If I had not jumped under the train and had my spine crushed, I would not have been born with a life-threatening deformation that kept me and my parents outside the hospital room where they had previously met and bonded with Alison, without my parents' encouragement and kindness Alison decided to give her baby up for adoption, and Roxie grew up in a home where love was limited and finite. There was no one to blame but myself, a series of choices made by a group of people created another tsunami wave that almost crushed Roxie's under its magnitude, if it was not for Enid who came to her rescue.

We stayed in the kitchen enthralled in our discussion, oblivious to the occupants of the household coming into the kitchen and curiously looking at us, it seemed like our conversation could be endless. Our loud raucous laughter could be heard throughout the house as we shared funny anecdotes about our lives, building a relationship that I thought was long lost. Sasha's passionate talk of her recent successes in the small screen roles left me amazed at her success, she was equally astonished at my dedication to eradicate human trafficking. The day went on and our dialogue continued to flow. I had missed my afternoon flight, but couldn't care less. I was elated to have my sister friend back in my life.

When I finally convinced myself that it was time to leave as it started to get dark outside, I promised to help Sasha locate her birth mother and that I would be willing to go to Delaware with her to meet her if she needed me to come. Sasha eagerly accepted my offer, and we exchanged our phone numbers to stay in touch. I walked to the door to leave, and Sasha went to get to Enid to say goodbye, when I finally put my coat on and buttoned it up, Enid approached me in the hallways. She walked up intimately close and embraced me in her gentle loving hug.

"Enid, you asked me yesterday what Scott. F. Fitzgerald's quote meant regarding the current bringing the boats back into the past. My response to you yesterday was not entirely accurate. I believe, we, the people, row hard against the current of life, trying to push forward, but no matter how hard we try we are inevitably brought back to face our past. But if we are ever to move forward, then we need to embrace our existence with all the remnants of the past, which may eventually lighten our load." I confided in my old friend.

"Remember how I told you that you remind me of a young girl I used to know? On a second glance, you are a much stronger confident woman than that young buck who struggled with her own monsters. You are different, you are your own tsunami, the evil in your path does not stand a chance."

"Enid, thank you...for everything." The words were limiting but the appreciation for the woman in front of me was boundless, her home and her gravitational force always managed to pull me in the right direction. I left Green Light with lightness in my feet and my mood elevated without a troubled thought in my mind, and as I made my way to the airport and boarded the next flight to Boston, I finally felt that the unfillable void that remained insatiably empty in the depth of my current existence was finally imbued.

Chapter Sixteen

*Today*
*Age 95*

    I have lived a long life, in my old age people tend to look back over the years and wonder what they could have done differently. If I told them that they would find out themselves eventually, they would laugh at me, so I stay quiet. People do not want to believe in the wonderous stories of reliving their lifetime, and rather trust that there is a glorious paradise awaiting them at the end of their journey. In their defence, the idea of a place where all your problems are magically erased and you have no responsibilities weighing you down, where you are reunited with the loved ones, it all sounds great. But if you ask me, the idea of having no challenges for eternity and floating around on the clouds sounds a bit daunting. It sounds like a wonderful temporary reprieve, like a vacation we all wait for all year and when it finally comes then we let go of all our problems for a short amount of time, but by the end of it we get tired of doing nothing.
    The reader, like yourself, may label my existence as eternal damnation, and I may agree. Being stuck in the same story in the book is eerily like the infinite limbo, but I choose to write my own story. I make my own decisions, choose my own path, and follow the different directions my new lifetime may take me. Life is boundless, you can do whatever you choose to do in life, and I am given the gift of exploring the unknown and pave my own road in the ceaseless diversity of opportunities.
    I am ready to move on to my next adventure, my paved path is coming to an end, and I am only slightly sad to reach the eventual finale. The rewarding career that I built over the years led me to defend cases in front of courts around the world. I felt that I achieved the unachievable

by implementing new regulations to exterminate the immoral human smugglers when I became the chairman of UN Commission on Human Rights, but there was still so much more to do. So, while I am sad to move on, I look forward to perfecting my attempts in my next life.

As I write this, I can hear my children and grandchildren gathered for dinner downstairs, an occasion that had not happened since they all moved away to pursue their own purpose in their diverse lifetimes. The doctor asked them all to come back home and stay with me in my last few days, as the tumour spread its tight grasp around my failing brain. I lost my ability to speak a month ago and can no longer walk, but I am thankful that my right hand still functions, and I can still write the remaining thoughts lingering in my failing mind.

There is so much more to be thankful for in my lifetime, my beautiful children being an important extension of me. Unfortunately, due to my inborn spine defect, I could not bear my own children and after a lot of contemplating my husband and I decided to adopt the children who needed a home. Over the years, we traveled to many countries and discovered our wonderful, beautiful children residing in different parts of the world, waiting for us to find them. My work kept me away from them a lot of the time, for which I am regretful, but they knew how much I loved them, and even if I was not around, I always called them before bed and told them the creative stories about the adventures of the traveling family of mice, that my mother used to tell me.

Their godmother, Sasha, and her mother Alison were always available to help too, residing together not too far from us in the Upper East Side neighbourhood, reunited and inseparable shortly after I helped my sister friend locate her birth mother. Sasha adored my children, just as much as she loved her own lively daughter, Roxanne. Her film career grew exponentially since we were first reunited at Green Light, gaining her multiple awards and worldwide recognition on the silver screen and theatre worlds. When she got older, she slowed down her pace, and settled back in her townhouse nearby and we would go on morning walks together where people would always recognize her. It was a sad day, when she passed away a couple of years ago before my health started failing, a day I do not want to remember but my unshakable memory refused to block out Sasha's funeral attended by a sea of her adoring fans and friends. What made that year more tragic, was that my husband of over fifty years had passed away in his sleep shortly after Sasha.

It is an unfortunate curse of old age, when you see your closest friends and family pass away. I was thankful for being able to spend more time than I ever had with my parents, and they got to see their grandchildren grow up, they lived a happy long-life until their last days. Enid passed away a long time ago, leaving the Green Light Sanctuary to the foundation that Sasha openly supported and was on the board of to continue Enid's legacy to provide shelter to the abused women and children. When Sasha's adopted mother passed away, she left Sasha the entire inheritance and a short note, which only said that she wished that she could do more and that it was her deepest regret that she did not know how to be a mother. While refusing to show emotion, when my friend called me to share the news, I could hear the pain in her voice, the pain of the little girl who never received the love that she deserved. So, after very little consideration, Sasha donated the entire inheritance to the foundation in hopes that the courageous mothers who fled abusive homes with their children received the support that they needed.

It has been a long life, but I always faced my fears and embraced any consequence of the choices that I made. My feet were always securely planted on the ground, ready to withstand any crushing wave to try to sweep me away. I knew that I could and had to survive any hurdles in my way. There were very few choices that mirrored any of the choices from my previous lifetimes, but there was one path I knew I had to retake an infinite number of times in the future. A path that would forever be the only paved road that I would choose to pursue again and again, the best decision that I chose to make on my thirtieth birthday.

I sat behind a small wooden table watching the Christmas decorations adorning the festive homes of the Upper East Side through the large window, waiting and hoping that the chosen path would lead me in the same direction. My hand clasped a hot paper cup tightly, as I savoured my sizzling birthday treat with every sip. The decision to come to the coffee shop was unavoidable, and I was determined to pave the rest of the path that remained unexplored.

"Hi, is this seat taken?" I heard the familiar husky tones directed at me. "Don't mean to intrude, but there are no other available seats here. Promise I won't bother you much."

"Of course." I nodded, allowing the handsome man with stark blue eyes take a seat across from me. "I'm Noelle." I extended my hand to introduce myself.

"I'm Noel." He set his cup down on the table, raising his eyebrow at my directness, and reached for my hand to shake it, as his palm touched my own, we both felt a jolt of static electricity bolt through our bodies.

"Nice to meet you, Noel." I laughed, once his elbow jerked back and knocked over both cups on the table causing him to burst out in a reciprocal boisterous laughter.

Sometimes we create our pathways, but never see them through to the end, unaware or what may lay ahead. I am grateful that I continued in the unexplored direction towards my fate, resulting in the two separate narrow paths merging into one solid wide road filled with a multitude of happy memories, as our beautiful family grew over the years spawning off other paths as our children left the home. Noel was my rock, and I missed him dearly, but instead of looking forward to meeting him in the mythical afterlife, I knew that I would meet him again and again through my endless existence.

*Until we meet again.*

Printed in Great Britain
by Amazon